JONATHAN'S VOWS

MARK LAGES

authorHOUSE®

AuthorHouse™
1663 Liberty Drive
Bloomington, IN 47403
www.authorhouse.com
Phone: 833-262-8899

Published by AuthorHouse 02/23/2021

ISBN: 978-1-6655-1798-0 (sc)
ISBN: 978-1-6655-1797-3 (e)

CHAPTER 1

THE CONCOCTION

I, Jonathan, choose you, Samantha, to be my wife. I am choosing you according to my own free will. I am of sound mind and sound body, and your father is not aiming a shotgun at my back. Out of four billion women in the world, you are the one I have chosen to live the rest of my life with, and now I take these vows.

Then come the vows I take. They're up to me. What the heck should I say?

I believe in the institution of marriage, and these vows are important to me. In fact, the promises I make in these vows are likely to be the most important promises I make in my life. I do not take them lightly, and it is because of this that I must make them sincerely. And because I am making them sincerely, I must make them thoughtfully. I don't want to just throw around some high-sounding words and clichés and then say, "I do." I want the words to count for something. I love you, Samantha, but I don't want to mislead you or make promises I will not keep, and I don't want to make promises that will not stand up against the test of time.

Love is a funny thing, isn't it? It seems simple and to the point, yet in reality, love can be as shapeless and nebulous as smoke. Will I love you for the rest of our lives, or will this smoke change shape, grow, move away, or dissipate? Will our love for each other be the same ten years from now as it is today? Or twenty years from now? Or thirty, forty, or fifty? What are we promising to each other? Are we promising today's love or tomorrow's love?

I believe we should be looking toward tomorrow. After all, isn't that what vows are all about? Making promises for tomorrow? What do you see in our future? Me?

I see two lovers moving toward the twilight of their union, moving closer each day toward that inevitable disappointment we call death.

1

We'll be approaching the end. Approaching the closing of the curtain, the dousing of the stage lights, on the doormat of the ominously still and icy void of nothingness. I will not be the same person as I near the end of this play. Father Time will have had his way with me. My hair will be gray and thin and maybe even balding. I might have age spots on my face, and there will be wrinkles where my taut and youthful skin once shone. My teeth might be false, and my hearing will not be what it used to be. And you? Let's just say that neither of us will be kids anymore, and it would not be accurate to say we're going to love each other the way we did when we were young. It simply won't be possible.

Decades from now, we'll each say, "I love you," but it won't be the same. That burning, desirous, unrelenting passion that once inspired our vows will have faded away—replaced with what? That is the question, isn't it?

But this new love is all that I can realistically shoot for in my vows. I mean, let's be honest: there's a big difference between the love two people have for each other after decades of living together and the love two people have when they have just recently discovered each other. Years pass, and bad habits are no longer cute. Disagreements are no longer interesting, and character flaws are no longer just charming idiosyncrasies.

It is with these thoughts in mind that I will write my wedding vows to you. I will write them out of love but also out of respect for reality. As they say, reality is where the rubber meets the road. I believe this is precisely what I should be aiming for as I write my vows and as I say, "I do." Ideals are great, but reality is where the wise and thoughtful person sets his sights.

Now comes the challenge. Knowing what I know now, I must figure out where this decision for us to get married will take us in the years to come. Is that even possible? I'm hardly a fortune-teller. I have no crystal ball, and I don't own a deck of tarot cards. I am only twenty-one years old, not exactly wealthy with life experiences. Yet I see what I see, and I have decent powers of observation.

Are we too young to be getting married? Some people think so, and they have told us as much. Our parents? They haven't really weighed in, have they? I think they all know it's more or less inevitable, and they don't want to rain on our parade. You and I have been boyfriend and girlfriend since we were juniors in high school, and now we're going to the same college. Why put it off any longer? That's more or less what we told each other when we decided to get engaged and set a date for the wedding. Some things are just meant to be. I don't think either of us has any doubt that this commitment is right for us in every way. But the vows? The vows are important.

Don't you think it's interesting how different we are yet how much we love each other? Is it true what they say—that opposites attract? We're not really opposites, but we are different. For example, I like all kinds of rock 'n' roll music, and you like Taylor Swift. She's the only artist you listen to. When you're cooking dinner for us, you say, "Alexa, play Taylor Swift." When you're on the elliptical, working out at your parents' house, you say, "Alexa, play Taylor Swift." When you're working on one of your school projects, you say, "Alexa, play Taylor Swift." It's funny, and I tease you about it. You just say defensively, "Listen, I know what I like, and I like Taylor Swift."

We've never taken any classes together since we started college. You're majoring in architecture, and I'm majoring in journalism. We never choose the same electives. We meet often for lunch and talk about each other's classes, and school is exciting, with so much to learn and so many different roads to take. It's nice to have your future up in the air, yet we will soon be nailing so much of it down, exchanging rings, standing in front of our friends and family, taking our vows, and making lifetime promises. These promises will affect so much of the rest of our living days.

I know a thing or two about making promises. When I was eight years old, I made a promise to my dad. He sat me down and had a serious talk with me. He wasn't making any promises, but he wanted to elicit a promise out of me. It was typical of a parent. It was a one-sided affair, but I was too young to know any better than to do anything but agree. He said, "When I was your age, my father and I had a conversation, the same conversation you and I are having right now. It was about the truth. Do you know what it means to respect the truth? All great men respect the truth. George Washington respected the truth. Abraham Lincoln respected the truth." He said this as if I would someday become the president of the United States. He then said, "I want you to grow up to be your own man, but there is something you will always owe me. Because I am your father and because you are my son. You, Jonathan, owe me the truth. And I'll expect it from you. No matter what. No matter how difficult it is to be honest, I will always expect nothing short of the truth from you. Here and now, you are going to make the same promise to me that I made to my own father. You will promise to always tell me the truth. Can I depend on you? Am I making sense to you?"

I nodded and said, "Yes, sir."

"No matter what?"

"Yes, no matter what," I said proudly. I hadn't even been put to the test, and already I was proud of myself.

Now let me tell you about a friend of mine named Alex Hardy. You might remember him from high school. Alex lived several houses down from us with his innocuous mother and strict father. Seriously, Alex's father used to scare me to death. Even when he was trying to be nice, he came off as mean as a grizzly bear with a cramp in his foot. It was interesting that a mischievous boy like Alex would have such an overbearing tyrant for a father. By *mischievous*, I mean Alex was always getting into trouble. You name it—if something annoyed adults or other children, Alex would do it. I don't know why he was like that. He just was. It was in his DNA, I suppose.

When we were in fifth grade, Alex got a hold of several packs of firecrackers. He bought them using cash he had stolen from his mother's purse. We knew Alex's dad would throw a fit if he found out about the firecrackers, so we decided to play with them down at the end of the street, away from his parents. It was great. We had such a good time, but the problem was this: a woman named Mrs. Bartlett lived at the end of the street, and she did not appreciate the joy we associated with lighting and throwing firecrackers. We were exploding them in front of her house, and the woman sort of freaked out. She called the police.

A patrol car showed up about ten minutes into our fun, and the cop parked along the curb. He opened his door and stepped out. Alex stuffed his firecrackers into his jeans pocket. We didn't make a run for it. Maybe if we had been older, we would've run away, but instead, we froze. The cop stepped up to us and said, "Hello, boys. How are we doing this afternoon?"

"Fine," Alex said.

I said nothing.

"We got a complaint from one of the neighbors about some boys playing with firecrackers," the cop said. "Do you boys have any idea who the culprits might be?"

"There were some older kids here a few minutes ago," Alex said. "But they left. Maybe it was them."

Again, I said nothing.

"Older kids, eh?"

"Yes, sir," Alex said.

"Do you know who they were?"

"No," Alex said. "Never seen them before."

"I see," the cop said. He was smiling.

I could tell from his smile that he knew Alex was lying. *He's a cop*, I thought. *You can't lie to a cop!*

Then the cop said to us, "How about you boys emptying your pockets?"

"Our pockets?" Alex said.

"Let's see what you've got in them," the cop said.

"Just junk," Alex said.

"I'd like to see," the cop said.

Alex pulled the firecrackers out of his pockets, and the cop was no longer smiling. He looked as if he wanted to smile, but he was acting serious. I think he was trying to make us nervous.

"I guess I lied," Alex said with his hands now full of firecrackers.

"I guess you did," the cop said.

"Are we in trouble?"

"You know that firecrackers are illegal?"

"Yes, sir," Alex said.

"You boys were scaring the nice lady who lives in this house." The cop looked at Mrs. Bartlett's house. "The lady just wants a little peace."

"We didn't mean to scare anyone," Alex said.

Then the cop looked at me. "You're awful quiet," he said to me.

"Yes, sir," I said.

"Do you have anything to say?"

"I'm sorry," I said.

Finally, the cop smiled again. I figured maybe he was going to let us off the hook. After all, we were just kids, and it was not as if we were shooting guns or lobbing hand grenades. We were just tossing around a few firecrackers.

"Where do you boys live?" the cop asked.

"Down the street," Alex said.

"How about I take you home? And I'll take the firecrackers. Hand them over."

"Yes, sir," Alex said. He handed the cop his firecrackers, and the cop then led us over to his patrol car. He opened the rear door and motioned for us to climb in. I'd never been in a cop car before, and it was kind of cool and terrifying at the same time. The cop told us to tell him which houses were ours, and he dropped Alex off first. He pulled into Alex's driveway and turned off his engine. Alex's dad was mowing the lawn, and he stopped to see what the cop wanted. You should've seen the look on his face when he saw Alex in the back of the car. Jesus, he looked like he was going to kill someone! The cop talked to him for a minute and then let Alex out of the car. Alex's dad grabbed Alex by the ear and pulled him into their house. Poor kid.

When the cop dropped me off at my house, no one was outside. He went to the front door with me and rang the doorbell. Mom answered, and the cop explained what had happened. My mom thanked him for bringing me home, and the cop got in his car and drove away. Did I get in trouble? No, not really. I told my mom and dad exactly what had happened, and my dad thanked me for telling the truth.

But for Alex, it was a different story. His dad was boiling mad. Enough was enough! His dad made him drop his pants and underwear, and then he proceeded to whip Alex's bare rear end with his leather belt. Alex said he didn't cry. Alex never wanted his dad to know how much the whippings hurt. He was stubborn that way. "My dad always thinks I'm going to cry," Alex told me. "But I never do. I won't give him the satisfaction."

In addition to the whipping, Alex was grounded for a week. He was furious. But he wasn't really angry with his dad. The old man was who he was. Alex was angry with Mrs. Bartlett for having called the police on us. "I'm going to get even with that ugly old prune if it's the last thing I do," he told me.

I figured Alex was just blowing hot air, until three weeks later. He told me exactly what he did, and I couldn't believe it. When Mrs. Bartlett's husband died, she became the beneficiary of a large life insurance policy, and what was one of the first things she did? She went out and bought herself a brand-new Mercedes-Benz. She kept it parked in the driveway. Anyway, Alex's scheme was simple. He created what he called a "concoction." This concoction was made up of raw eggs, rubber-cement glue, wood varnish, house paint, and a dash of Drano. He mixed the ingredients in a bucket, and late at night, while everyone in the neighborhood was asleep, he snuck over to Mrs. Bartlett's house. She never locked the doors of the Mercedes, which was a big mistake in hindsight. Alex opened the car door and poured his concoction all over the leather driver's seat.

The next day, Mrs. Bartlett climbed into her car. She didn't see the mess, and—*squish!*—she found herself sitting in Alex's concoction. It was now not only all over the seat but also all over the back of her dress. Well, needless to say, Mrs. Bartlett threw a fit. The first person she thought of was Alex, that rotten kid down the street. Who else would have done this?

Two days later, she went to Alex's house, complaining about her car seat to his dad. Of course, when his dad confronted him, Alex denied knowing anything about it. Alex's dad assured Mrs. Bartlett he would get to the bottom of the matter, and he called my parents to tell them what had happened. He asked my parents to ask me about the mess. He wanted to know if I knew anything. My dad sat me down on the family room sofa, and he asked me. He said, "I expect you to tell me the truth. You promised to always tell me the truth. This is a serious matter. Mrs. Bartlett's dress is ruined, and so is the front seat of her car. She's going to have to get it reupholstered. This is more than just a prank. It's vandalism. It's a crime, Jonathan. If Alex did this, we need to know."

Well, hell, what was I supposed to do? Yes, I had promised to always tell my dad the truth, but now? Would I be a rat and spill the beans, or would I protect my friend? After all, Alex had told me about the concoction in confidence. It was supposed to be a secret. If I told Dad about Alex, the poor kid would be in all kinds of trouble. Who knew what his dad would do to him? If, on the other hand, I lied to my dad, no harm would come Alex's way. And Dad wouldn't know the difference. So all things being carefully considered, I did what I had to do. I lied to my dad and told him I knew nothing about Alex and his destructive concoction. I broke my solemn promise to my father. I flat-out lied.

Samantha, I don't want to break my promises to you. Vows should be sacred, right? Vows should be realistic. Vows should be specific. As I said earlier, vows should operate where the rubber meets the road. So how do I do this? How do I write my vows? How do I temper my desire to see us being happy with the inevitable future realities of marriage? I've decided it boils down to this: I need to know.

Does this make any sense to you? You're probably wondering what I'm talking about. But it's simple, isn't it? I mean, it's simple if you think about it. I need to know what's going to happen to us. Of course, I can't know for certain, but I can take a stab at it. Human beings do this all the time. They examine the past, look at the present, and then try to guess at the future. It isn't ideal, but it's all we can do. So I will start at the beginning. The lights go down, and the audience is quiet. The curtain rises, and the play begins.

CHAPTER 2

SMALL TALK

The vows have been said. We kissed and ran through a shower of rice. We are now at the reception. Everyone is there. The music is loud, and the champagne is flowing. We are making the rounds, making small talk with all the guests.

I wind up talking to Burt Harper while you are talking to others. Burt is my dad's boss. He is a funny-looking man in his fifties, and his wife is not with him. It is just Burt and me. While Burt talks, I look at his double chin. He is not exactly fat, but he does have a double chin—maybe even a triple chin—which makes him look sort of like an alien from a *Star Trek* movie. I've never seen a slender man with such a pronounced double chin. It's as if his head has grown right out of his chest, and I wonder what other oddities I would discover if he took his shirt off. Three nipples? Another arm? Multiple navels?

Anyway, Burt tells me a joke. He says, "This husband and wife have lived together for forty years, and one day the wife has a heart attack and drops dead in their house. The husband calls the police, and they send out the coroner. They check the woman, and sure enough, she's as dead as a sack of potatoes. They load her body up on a gurney to remove it from the house. They go out the front door and down the porch steps to a path that leads to a front gate. At the gate, there is a large post off to the side, and carelessly, the men bump the gurney into the post.

"Suddenly, the woman sits up. It's a miracle! They check her pulse, and sure enough, she is alive. They remove her from the gurney, and she walks back into the house. She goes on to live ten more years with her husband, and nothing happens until the tenth year, when she drops dead again from a heart attack.

"Again, the husband calls the police, and they send out the coroner. They check the woman, and she indeed appears to be dead. They then load her up on a gurney and wheel her out of the house. When they approach the front gate, the man suddenly shouts, 'Whoa there, fellas! Look out for that post!'"

I laugh at Burt's joke.

Burt says it's one of his favorites. Then he changes the subject and says, "So your dad tells me you're a journalism major?"

"I am," I say.

"My wife was a journalism major. Have you met my wife?"

"I don't think I have," I say.

"She changed majors when she met me."

"Oh?" I say. "What does she do?"

"She spends my money."

I laugh and say, "She must do more than that."

"I wish," Burt says, smiling. "The kids kept her busy for a while. Barefoot and pregnant—isn't that what they say? Make sure you have kids. You'll be better off for it."

"Okay."

"What does Samantha plan to do?"

"With what?"

"With her future. Is she also interested in journalism?"

"She wants to be an architect."

"Ah, an architect. That's good. That'll keep her busy—you know, until you have kids."

"Where did you and your wife go to college?" I ask.

"We both went to UCLA. That's where we met. You're going to USC, right?"

"Yes, my wife too."

"Good school."

"It's okay," I say.

"You'll get out of it what you put into it."

"Yes, that's true."

"Have you heard the one about the college dean and the girls' dormitory?"

"I don't think so," I say.

"The dean of a college holds an orientation meeting with the freshman class of boys, and he says, 'We have two dormitory buildings on this campus. One is the boys' dormitory, and the other is the girls' dormitory. The girls' dormitory is off-limits for all boys. Any boy caught in the girls' dormitory will be fined twenty dollars. It that student is caught a second time, the fine will be fifty dollars. If he is caught a third time, the fine is one hundred dollars. Do you have any questions?'

"One boy raises his hand, and the dean calls on him. The boy asks, 'How much is it for a season pass?'"

I laugh politely at Burt's joke. He winks at me as if we have something in common. "That's good," I say.

"Your dad tells me you met your bride in high school."

"That's true," I say.

"Do her parents like you?"

"I think so."

"My wife's parents never liked me."

"Oh? What was their problem?"

"They thought I didn't take life seriously enough. Her dad is a medical doctor. A very serious man."

"I see," I say.

"I don't know how my mother-in-law can stand him."

"Oh?" I say.

"I don't think I've ever seen him smile."

"You're kidding," I say.

"Well, he tries to smile every now and again. But it's a forced smile. I can tell. It's like the look one gets while he's having a bowel movement. It's kind of gross."

"Maybe he has a lot on his mind."

"His wife smiles all the time. And she laughs a lot. She's his opposite. But I think she smiles and laughs more out of nervousness than joy. Do you know what I mean by that?"

"I guess," I say.

"Have you ever stopped to wonder what makes certain couples tick? What keeps them together?"

"Sometimes."

"They're all different, you know."

"I guess that's true."

"My father-in-law's seriousness makes his wife nervous. I think he likes that. It makes him feel important. He has people's lives in his hands, and he likes being the center of attention. And he likes it that his wife gets nervous around him because it makes him feel like he is the backbone of the family. He wants people to lean on him. It makes him feel strong."

"I can see that."

"It's why his daughter fell in love with me."

"Oh?"

"She'd had enough seriousness to last her a lifetime. I was her ticket out. I was fun."

"I guess that makes sense."

"Of course, that was then. Who knows what she thinks of me now? Things change in time. Oh, do they ever. Why did you marry Samantha?"

I think for a moment and then say, "Because I love her, and she loves me."

Burt laughs. "Of course, you're still just puppies."

"Does there have to be more to it than that?"

"There's always more to it," Burt says. "There are forces at play that none of us will ever even be aware of."

Suddenly, Burt's wife joins us. I learn that her name is Clara. She too is in her fifties, and she is well preserved for her age. I'm just guessing, but I figure she spends a lot of money to keep herself looking so good. She's fighting time, but so far, she's winning the battle.

"What are you two talking about?" she asks.

"Marriage," Burt says.

"It was a lovely wedding ceremony," Clara says to me.

"Thanks," I say.

"Who was your florist?"

"I don't know," I say. "Samantha handled all of that."

"I need to get their name. They did a wonderful job. It's so hard to find good florists these days."

"What the hell do you need a florist for?" Burt asks.

"I don't know," Clara says. "You never know. A good florist might come in handy."

"Do you want to know the key to having a successful marriage?" Burt asks me.

"Sure," I say.

"You've got to have a sense of humor."

"If that isn't ever the truth," Clara says.

"You see?" Burt says. "There *is* something we agree on."

I laugh at this. I guess I should tell you about Burt. I should tell you what he does for a living. He owns the medium-sized advertising agency where my dad is employed as a writer. Dad writes all the copy you read, composing it with the intention of making you get out your credit cards to buy products. They say advertising is the heart and soul of capitalism, which makes it sound a little loftier than it actually is. It's actually just the dirty work a business needs to do in order to convince people that they need to buy things. Yes, it's the dirty work. It isn't necessarily honest, helpful, or constructive. I've always wanted to be a writer like my dad but not like him. I mean, I want to be a writer, but I want to write about the truth. I want to enlighten readers and help them make good decisions.

So you see, in a way, I don't like Burt much. I don't dislike him. I just don't like him much. My dad has a flair for writing, but the way I see it, Burt takes advantage of my dad's talents. He is using him. He is corrupting him. I didn't catch on to any of this when I was younger, but I came to realize it in high school.

I have this in mind as Burt talks to me—as he tells me about the importance of having a sense of humor, as he tells me his jokes, as he spars playfully with his wife. If Burt didn't have a sense of humor, he'd be up a creek. I'm not just talking about his marriage. I'm talking about his life and what he's chosen to do for a living. Or maybe he didn't choose it. Maybe he just fell into it. Adults do a lot of falling.

"Burt tells me you were a journalism major in college," I say to Clara.

She smiles and says, "I was."

"And you changed majors?"

"No, I still majored in communications. But rather than focus on journalism, I focused on public relations and advertising. Three years after we graduated from UCLA, Burt and I started up the agency. Then, when we decided to have children, I left the agency to stay home and raise them."

"Interesting," I say.

"You want to be a journalist?" Clara asks me.

"I do," I say.

"It's a tough racket."

"Don't discourage the boy," Burt says.

"I'm not trying to discourage him. I'm just telling it like it is. It *is* a tough racket."

"How many kids do you guys have?" I ask.

"Two," Burt says. "Our son, Michael, is about your age. Our daughter, Julia, is five years older."

"Julia works at the agency," Clara says.

"Michael is at Chapman College," Burt says. "He wants to go into politics. He wants to be a famous campaign manager."

"Interesting," I say.

"He still hasn't decided if he's a Democrat or a Republican. I guess it will depend on who offers him a job first."

I laugh at this.

"How's your brother doing?" Burt asks me. "I saw him here at the reception, but I haven't had a chance to talk to him."

"He's doing good," I say.

I should tell you a little about my brother. He is still in high school. His name is Lewis, and he's four years younger than I am. Burt asks me if Lewis has plans to go to college, and I tell him that Lewis wants to go to a community college to become an EMT. "Lewis is not very cerebral," I say. "He likes action. He'll get lots of action in working out of an ambulance."

"That's for sure," Clara says.

"I don't know how those guys do it," Burt says. "All the awful things they see."

"Me either," Clara says.

"Have you heard the one about the EMT and the fat guy?" Burt asks.

"No one wants to hear another of your dumb jokes," Clara says.

"Jonathan might want to hear it."

"If he says so, he's only trying to be polite."

"The woman has no sense of humor," Burt says to me, shaking his head.

"I married *you*, didn't I?" Clara says.

"Very funny."

Just then, Amanda Brinkley joins our group. She is a friend of my mom's, the wife of an architect. She knows Burt and Clara from a Halloween party my mom threw last year. She is married to a man named Chad. "How nice to see you here," she says to Burt and Clara.

"It's nice to see you," Clara says.

"I barely recognized you without your costumes. Weren't you a cat?"

"Yes, and Chad was Scooby-Doo."

Everyone laughs.

"Didn't you love the wedding?" Amanda says.

"We did," Clara says.

"Samantha was beautiful," Amanda says to me.

"She was," I say.

"What's Chad doing?" Clara asks Amanda.

"Oh, he's having the time of his life."

"Where is he?"

"He's across the room. Do you see him? He's talking to Samantha. They're talking about architecture. Chad can talk about architecture for hours. He's probably talking the poor girl's ear off." Amanda rolls her eyes. To me, she says, "He's trying to impress your bride."

"How's his business doing?" Burt asks.

"He's busy. I've never seen him work so many hours. Day and night. You'd think he was Sir Christopher Wren."

"What's on his drawing boards these days?"

"Warehouses."

"More warehouses?"

"He got his foot in the door with a developer in Santa Ana who builds spec warehouses. They build them by the dozens, all over the country. It's hard to believe. There doesn't seem to be any end to it. I guess there's a lot of money to be made in building warehouses."

"Does he enjoy the work?"

"It's paying the bills."

"Does he still drag you to museums?"

"Every chance he gets."

"I went to an art museum last month," Burt says. "I asked the guard if it was okay to take pictures, and he said no, they had to stay on the walls."

Amanda and I laugh, but Clara just rolls her eyes.

"Honestly," Clara says.

"You're going to miss me when I'm gone," Burt says.

"Are you going somewhere?"

"I mean when I die."

"Don't be morbid."

Burt then looks over at me and says, "She says not to be morbid, but I bet she'll spend all my life insurance money two days after she gets it."

"In one day," Clara says, correcting her husband.

Everyone laughs.

CHAPTER 3

SOPHIA

For our honeymoon, we fly to Hawaii. We've reserved a suite at Mahamaha Maui. Some friends told us about this place, and they said we'd love it. Neither you nor I have ever been to Hawaii before, and we can't wait to get there. Our parents are footing the bill for the whole thing.

The plane trip is miserable. The air is stuffy; the lady next to us has a baby that cries almost the whole way to the islands; and the kid behind us keeps kicking my seat, even after I politely ask him twice to keep his feet still.

Finally, we land, and after standing in line for a rental car for an hour, we are on our way to the hotel. The air is balmy, and the sun is bright. We've rented a convertible, and we have the top down. There's nothing quite like the first day of a vacation, is there? We have a whole week ahead of us to eat, explore, swim, sunbathe, and make love.

What a surprise! The Mahamaha is better than we expected. It's classy, and we both like that. It's only a few years old, and it's right on the water. It has its own beach. It has a great big sparkling swimming pool, a water slide, a waterfall, and a swim-up bar. After we arrive at the room, we unpack our suitcases and get dressed for the pool. You spend a half hour in the bathroom, brushing your hair and working on your makeup. I am patient. I know you just want to look your best for me. While you are getting ready, I watch a dumb sitcom on the TV.

Finally, you are ready, and the two of us leave the room. We take the elevator down to the ground floor and walk out of the lobby to the swimming pool. It is warm outside, but there is a gentle breeze. We can hear children playing and splashing in the water over at the shallow end of the pool. There are flowers everywhere, and the place reeks of them. Flowers, sweat, and coconut oil. Sweet and warm. We walk around the pool until we find two vacant lounge chairs, and we set our things down. You go to get some towels, and we lay them on the chairs. We kick off our sandals and step to the water, where I am the first to jump in.

"It's warm," I say. "It's like bathwater."

"I'll take your word for it," you say, and you jump in. Your young face glistens with chlorinated pool water.

"What'd I tell you?" I say.

"It's perfect."

"Let's swim over to the bar," I say.

"Okay," you say.

We swim over to the bar and sit on the tiled underwater seats. There is a bartender, who asks us what we want, and we order a couple of frozen strawberry daiquiris, charging them to our room. The bartender makes the drinks and sets them before us in plastic cups with chunks of cut pineapple.

"To us," I say, raising my drink.

"To us," you say, and you raise yours. Then we drink. "I feel like we're a million miles from home," you say.

"Paradise," I say.

"On another planet."

"In another galaxy."

"And a whole week ahead of us."

"Yes," I say. "I don't think I could be any happier."

The bartender laughs, and we look at him. "Newlyweds?" he asks. We laugh and tell him yes.

It's great, isn't it? It's everything we've dreamed of. We finish off our drinks and order two more. The alcohol relaxes us, and we then swim back to our lounge chairs to lie in the sun. You've brought a novel, and you pick up where you left off on the airplane. I lie on my belly, and the sun beats upon my back. I can feel myself breathing. My skin begins to turn warm, and I can still hear the children playing in the shallow end of the pool.

My eyes are closed, and then I open them. The first thing I notice is a girl who is sitting on her own lounge chair approximately twenty feet away from us. Like you, she is reading a book. She is gorgeous. She is like no girl I've ever seen. She has a body like that of a *Playboy* Playmate, and she is wearing next to nothing. Her swimsuit barely contains her, and I can't help but stare. She must've been here for a week or so, because she has a deep tan from the island sun. Tan and perfect, like a dream. And her face! She has the face of an angel and a pair of large sunglasses that make her look like a movie star. I have never seen anything like it.

She seems to be alone. She stops reading for a moment to wipe the perspiration from her cheeks. Then she goes back to her book. She doesn't know I'm staring at her, but I decide to play it safe. I pretend to be sleeping, squinting my eyes so that it looks like they're closed, but they're open just enough so that I can see past my eyelashes.

"Jonathan?" you say. I turn my head toward you and open my eyes.

"What?" I say. There you are, skinny and pale. There is the face I fell in love with.

"What do you feel like eating tonight?"

"Eating?"

"For dinner. Where should we go?"

"Wherever you want. It's up to you."

"They have an Italian restaurant here at the hotel. Do you feel like Italian food?"

"That'd be fine," I say.

"Or there's a seafood restaurant across the street. It's supposed to be good."

"Whichever."

"I'm kind of in the mood for fish."

"Okay," I say.

"But some pasta would be good."

"Pasta sounds good."

"Of course, we could eat fish tonight and go to the Italian restaurant tomorrow."

"That's fine with me."

"Or we could eat in Lahaina."

"Just pick a place," I say. "I'll be okay with it."

I turn my head, and my heart sinks. The girl I was looking at is gone.

"I say we go to the seafood restaurant," you say. "Are you sure that's okay with you?"

"That's fine," I say.

Where did she go? Where is she from? Whom is she with? I know this is wrong, but I can't stop thinking about her. Will I see her again?

We go to the seafood restaurant, and you look great. You are wearing a yellow tank top and white cotton shorts, and your blonde hair is braided. You look good in yellow, and I love it when you braid your hair. Then in walks the girl from the pool. She is with an older man, and I wonder if he's her dad or her lover. It's hard to tell. Jesus, she is even prettier now than she was by the pool, and I pretend not to notice her, but I also can't keep from staring. *What the heck is wrong with me?* You are looking at your menu, and I pick up mine.

"The halibut looks good," you say.

"Yes," I say. I pretend to be reading the menu, but I'm looking over the top of it at the girl. She is now seated and facing me. She is no longer wearing sunglasses, and she has the comeliest eyes I've ever seen. She is talking to the man she's with, whose back is to me.

"Or the swordfish sounds good," you say.

"Yes," I say. "Swordfish is always good."

"What looks good to you?"

"I don't know."

"You like snapper, don't you?"

"Snapper is good."

You then set your menu down and say, "What are you looking at?"

"Looking at?" I ask.

"You keep looking over there, behind me."

"Oh, that."

"What is it?"

I have to think fast. "That man over there, seated by the kitchen door. He looks like one of my professors." I am making all this up, of course.

You turn your head, but you don't notice the girl. "The guy with the plaid shirt?"

"Yes," I said. "He looks just like Professor Booker. He teaches American literature."

"Is it him?"

"It looks like him, but I don't think it's him. But he looks just like him."

"Why don't you go ask him?"

"No, I don't think it's him."

"I'm going to have the swordfish."

"That sounds good," I say. "I'll have the same thing." Then I look at your face and say, "You got a lot of sun today."

"Am I tan?" you ask.

"You're red."

"I always get red. I never get tan."

"You'll get tan."

"I want to look like one of those girls at the pool."

"You will."

"Have you ever seen so many beautiful girls?"

"None of them hold a candle to you," I say.

"You're sweet."

"I love you."

"I love you too."

After we order our dinners, I spend the rest of the evening talking to you and eating, trying not to look at the girl at the other table. It is horrible. I'm glad she's there, yet I'm not glad at all. I feel sorry for you. You deserve better than this.

When we arrive at our hotel room, we undress and climb into bed. We then do what newlyweds do. All is well. It's going to be okay. Even though I am still thinking of the girl, I am making love to you.

The next morning, we have breakfast brought into the room. Then we go down to the pool to grab a couple of lounge chairs. The girl is nowhere in sight. I know because I make it a point to look for her.

Then, after an hour or so, she shows up. She is alone, and she takes a chair about forty feet away from us. I'm not exaggerating when I say she looks even better than the day before, and I lie on my belly, staring at her through my eyelashes again. The longing I feel for this girl is unreal. I notice she doesn't have a towel, and after setting down her book on the chair, she heads toward the towel desk. I stand up and tell you I have to use the restroom, and I walk, following the girl—not too closely but close enough to keep up with her. When she arrives at the towel counter, I stand behind her as though I am also there to pick up a towel for myself. She shows her room card key to the kid behind the counter, and he hands her a fresh towel. As she turns to leave, our eyes meet for a second. Then, as she's leaving, her card key falls from her hand and lands on the ground near my feet. She doesn't notice, and I bend over to pick up the card.

"Excuse me," I say. "You dropped your key." I hand the card to her, and she smiles. She smiles at me!

"Thank you," she says.

"You're welcome," I say. I smile, but I bet I look like an idiot. Why? Because I am an idiot!

Then I show my room key to the kid, and he gives me a towel. Meanwhile, the girl is gone. She is walking back to her chair, and now I have a towel I don't need. I place the towel on an empty chair and walk back to you.

"Can you put some of this on my back?" you ask. You are holding up a plastic bottle of sunscreen, and I take it from you. "I don't want to get burned. I burn so easy." You then lie on your belly and move your hair out of the way.

I squirt the sunscreen onto your back and go to work. I look over, and the girl is now reading her book. Suddenly, the older guy she was with at the restaurant shows up. He sits on the chair beside her. I pretend to look at your back, but I'm watching the man and girl through the corner of my eye.

"That's good," you say.

"Pardon me?" I ask.

"That's good. That's enough."

"Of course," I say, and I stop massaging the sunscreen on your back. I lie back down on my chair, on my belly, spying on the girl. She stands up and steps to the pool. Then she steps into the water, while the man remains seated in his chair. She dunks her head in the water and then slicks back her hair. The morning sun glistens on her wet skin. I've never seen such a beautiful girl in all my life. Then a cell phone rings. It is the girl's phone, and the man looks over at the girl.

"Sophia," the man says loudly. "Your phone is ringing. Do you want me to answer it?"

"I'll get it," she says. She climbs quickly out of the pool and steps to her chair, where she left the phone beside her book. She picks up the phone and answers it before it stops ringing. Pool water drips from her tan body. With one hand holding the phone to her ear, she grabs her towel with the other hand. She then dries herself and talks into the phone at the same time.

I can't hear what she's saying, but I have learned something: her name is Sophia. *Like Sophia Loren*, I think. The perfect first name for the perfect girl. *God!*

After an hour or so of lying in the sun, the man sits up and looks at his watch. He says to Sophia, "We should get going." Well, I think that's what he said. I am reading his lips. She doesn't say anything in response. She just closes her book and stands up. She puts the book in her bag and steps into her sandals. Then she leaves with the man.

Where are they going? I don't know. But I don't see her for the rest of the day, and I don't see her in the evening. I don't see her the next day either. I figure she and her male friend left the hotel. They got back on their airplane and flew back to the mainland. They flew to a city there somewhere. To a life somewhere. I will never see Sophia again. I am sure of this.

Samantha, I am not telling you about Sophia to hurt your feelings, and I am not questioning my love for you. I do love you. But it's important that we are honest with each other, and I'm trying to be truthful.

It takes me weeks to get over Sophia. Have you ever had a song stuck in your head? Do you know what I mean by that? I have Sophia's image stuck in my head, and I can't get rid of her. When I close my eyes, I can see her angelic face. I can see her tan body. I imagine how she must've smelled, maybe like warm oatmeal and coconut oil. If only I'd come to know her, and if only she'd come to know me. I know we would've hit it off, and maybe we'd have been lovers. Maybe I'd be writing these vows to her rather than to you. I mean, it's sad, in a way, that Sophia and I were never an item and never had a chance to love each other. On the other hand, I have you. I can thank fate for that. You and me against the world.

CHAPTER 4

AS IS

Close your eyes. Do you see what I see? It's our little place: apartment 304 in a tile-roofed three-story stucco apartment building ten miles from the USC campus. We rented it right before we got married and moved in after our honeymoon. It has one small bedroom, a basic bathroom, a tiny kitchen, and a place for a couch and a TV. It's barely big enough for one person, let alone two. But we're both still in college, and neither of us has a job that will pay for more.

We are living off our parents. They've decided to chip in equally to pay for our school and living expenses until we graduate. They like to point out that we're getting a lot more than they received from their parents when they went to college, and we believe them.

Maybe the apartment is small, but we love it. It is our home, and it's nice to be young and in love. Just the fact that we're together makes it all worthwhile and tolerable. We are so in love that we could be living in a cardboard box, and we'd be happy. Our furniture all came from garage sales. It's old and worn. We haven't bought a single new thing for the apartment, and we like it that way. We like the old styles. We like antiques.

On weekends, we go to the antique stores in Southern California, browsing through all the miscellaneous knickknacks and furniture. We haven't got a dime to spend on any of it, but we like looking and dreaming about all the old junk we're going to buy after we graduate, when we both have jobs.

There is one antique store in particular that you especially like, a little place in downtown Orange. It is called Rudy's, and it was named after the proprietor. In this store, Rudy has an old clock you're in love with, a grandfather clock from the early eighteenth century. It is made of brass and inlaid wood, and it is in its original condition. It has charm, and it has character. We have visited Rudy's several times just to look at the clock, just to be sure someone hasn't bought it yet. Someday we'll have money, and you tell me this grandfather clock is the first thing we're going to get. Sure, our apartment is tiny, but there is a perfect spot for the clock in the entry. If we're still living in the apartment, that's where it's going to go. If we've moved, we'll find a place for it.

The clock has come to symbolize something important to us. Buying it and owning it will mean we are getting somewhere with our lives, and when we visit Rudy's, you always say, "It won't be long, Jonathan. It will be ours." Funny, isn't it? How we measure our progress by the things we can afford to buy? But it's true, isn't it?

Several months after we are married, I come up with my plan. I will get a side job and work it in around my classes. I will earn the money we need to buy that darn clock as soon as possible. I don't want to wait until after we graduate. Your birthday is coming up in April, and by hook or by crook, I will have the clock delivered to our place just for you. I will be a provider. I will make you happy. I love you dearly, and your happiness is important to me.

I run an ad in the local paper that says, "Hardworking college student looking for odd jobs. Will do about anything!" Yes, I run the ad, and my phone starts ringing. People want me to work in their yards, paint their houses, move their junk, and clean out their garages. They like hiring me. They want to help out this amiable and hardworking college student, and the next thing you know, all my free time is booked.

You become curious. "What are you working so hard for?" you ask. "What are you saving up for?"

I smile and tell you it's a surprise. I say you'll know what I'm up to soon enough. You have no idea.

Then April comes along, and it will be your birthday on the twenty-eighth. I can't wait to see the look on your face when you find your clock in our apartment. I have the money saved up, and I go to Rudy's. Sure enough, the clock is still there, ticking away the seconds, minutes, and hours. Do you remember Rudy? He's still the same old Rudy. The man is bloated and obese, and he struggles to get around in his store. I tell him I'd like to buy the clock, and he stands up from behind the counter so I can show him precisely which clock I'm interested in. You'd think we were climbing Mount Everest! Each step he takes toward the clock requires a major physical effort, and when we finally reach the clock, he is perspiring something awful. He removes a white handkerchief from his pocket and dabs at the sweat on his forehead. There are several grandfather clocks, and I point out the one I want. "Of course," he says. "This is a good one. I must say, you do have excellent taste."

"It's for my wife," I say.

"She's seen it?"

"Oh yes," I say. "She's had her eye on it for the past couple of years."

"I'll be sorry to see it go," Rudy says. He stuffs his damp handkerchief back in his pocket. He's still trying to catch his breath, and I feel bad for making him walk all that way to the clock. "I got this piece at an estate sale," he says. "The Bertram family. The old man finally died, and the kids didn't want any of his furniture. It's a real find. It's been in their family for generations. It was made in England, then brought to Maine, and then brought to California when the family moved out here. The family was big in buttons. Made buttons. You know, like for shirts. The kids had no interest in making buttons, so they sold the business to an investor in Taiwan."

"Interesting," I say.

"It still works."

"I've noticed it always has the right time."

"A few dings and scratches here and there, but it's in excellent original condition." Rudy then leads me back to the sales counter, where he removes a receipt booklet from below. He then begins to write on the booklet, describing the clock and listing its sales price. "It's nice to see young people interested in antiques. They simply don't make things like they used to. It's sad how people are willing to settle for less."

"We love antiques," I say.

"You say this is for your wife?"

"For her birthday."

"Ah, of course."

"I need it delivered exactly on her birthday. While she's at school. We're both students at USC. Her birthday is on the twenty-eighth. I want her to come home and find it in our apartment. It's a surprise."

"That won't be a problem."

I reach into my pocket and remove the cash I've saved. I place the wad of bills on the counter, and Rudy counts them up to be sure I'm not short. It's all there, and Rudy smiles.

"On the nose?" I ask.

"On the nose," Rudy says. "I just need you to fill in your name, address, and phone number on the receipt. Then sign the bottom, please."

"Okay," I say, and I do as I'm told.

As promised, Rudy has his men deliver the clock right on time. I have them set it in the entry. Then I sit down on the sofa to read and wait for you to come home from class. The clock gongs. The front door opens, and there you are. You see the clock and say, "What the heck?"

"Happy birthday," I say.

"Seriously?"

"I told you I was going to surprise you," I say, grinning from ear to ear.

"I can't believe it."

"Do you like it?"

"I love it. You know that. But it's so expensive."

"It's all paid for."

"That's why you've been working?"

"That's why."

"I don't know what to say."

"Say you love it."

"I do love it."

And I know you do. It makes me feel good to know I've made you happy.

That night, we celebrate your birthday at your parents' house. We have dinner and cake. Your sister, Kate, is there. You took a photo of the clock with your phone when we were back at the apartment, and you show it to everyone. "Look what Jonathan got me," you say.

"An old clock?" your dad says.

"It's an antique," you say.

"It was made in England," I say.

"It looks expensive," your mom says.

"It wasn't cheap," I say.

"Where'd you get the money?" your dad asks.

"Jonathan has been working."

You parents look at each other. Their expressions tell me they're wondering what in the world we're doing buying an expensive antique clock when we can't even pay our rent or general living expenses without their help.

"I think it was a sweet thing to do," Kate says.

"It's a nice present," your mom says.

"Does it work?" your dad asks.

"Like a charm," I say.

The reaction we get from my parents when we tell them about the clock is about the same as the reaction from your parents. None of them say anything directly, but I can tell they all think the purchase is, well, irresponsible. If I am able to work, I ought to be paying for our rent and living expenses, not for an expensive antique clock we don't need. I know this is what they are thinking, but I'm still glad I bought the clock. It was a wise investment. It will hold its value. It's not like I wasted money.

Two weeks after I buy the clock, it stops working. Just like that, the hands stand still, and the pendulum stops swinging. I try winding it, and I try starting the pendulum with my hand, but that doesn't help. "It's probably something simple," I say to you. "I'll call Rudy."

I call Rudy the next day and tell him about the clock, and he says, "You'll need to have it looked at. No telling what's wrong. Could be a number of things."

"Can you look at it?"

"I don't know much about clocks. I can recommend a repairman to you. You can trust him. He won't overcharge you."

"Overcharge me?" I ask.

"His prices are always fair."

I think for a moment. This is not what I expected Rudy to say to me. "Isn't this a warranty issue?" I say.

"Warranty?"

"Yes," I say.

"The clock is an antique. There is no warranty."

"No?"

Rudy laughs and says, "If I warrantied everything I sold here, I'd be out of business in a week."

How does this make me feel? It makes me feel sort of stupid and sort of naive. This is not what I anticipated. I don't want Rudy to think I'm a pushover or some dumb kid who doesn't know what he's doing, so I say, "That's not acceptable."

"Acceptable?" Rudy says.

"I think you should fix it for free."

"Not going to happen, kid."

I hate being called *kid*. I'm frustrated. I spent every last dime I had to buy the stupid clock, and I have no money left for repairing the thing, even if it is my responsibility. And it isn't. Surely there was an implied warranty that the clock would work for longer than two weeks.

After getting nowhere with Rudy, I decide what I'm going to do. I will get an attorney. With an attorney, I'll be letting Rudy know that I mean business. I only know one attorney, and that's Mr. Bates across the street from my parents' house. I've known Mr. Bates ever since I was a boy. He always seemed like a nice guy, and I always felt he liked me. I look him up and call his number. I ask his secretary if I can please speak to him.

Mr. Bates gets on the phone, and he is friendlier than ever. "So what can I do for you?" he asks.

First, I tell Mr. Bates that the matter is between us. I don't want him to tell my parents about what happened. I then tell him about the broken clock and Rudy's refusal to fix it. "Maybe you can call him?"

"And lean on him?"

"Yes," I say.

"Maybe threaten him with a lawsuit?"

"Something like that," I say.

"Give me his number."

Mr. Bates then calls Rudy and asks why he refused to repair the clock for free, and Rudy explains the situation to him. Further, Rudy faxes a copy of the receipt I signed, a receipt that says, "Purchased as is, no warranty of any kind."

Mr. Bates then calls me and asks if I signed the receipt. I say I did, and he asks if I read it. "Not really," I say. "He just asked me to sign it, so I signed it."

"You purchased the clock as is."

"What does that mean?"

"It means what it says. Meaning *as is*. There were no warranties promised. You got exactly what you paid for."

"But it doesn't work," I say.

"Maybe it does, and maybe it doesn't. Legally, it isn't Rudy's problem. I'm afraid you have no case. Your friend Rudy is off the hook."

This is not what I want to hear. Meanwhile, I have to get the clock repaired. What good is a clock that doesn't work? I call the clock repair guy Rudy recommended, and he says to bring the clock into his shop so he can look it over. I then call a friend of mine who owns a pickup truck, and we use the truck to take the clock to the shop.

The clock man is busy, but he says he will get to my clock in a week. And he does. He calls me, and I listen for fifteen minutes as he describes all the problems with our clock. I know nothing about how clocks work, and it is as if the guy is speaking an alien language. I don't understand a word he says. The one thing he says that I do understand is the price for the work he's recommending.

Jesus, I think, *I could buy another damn clock for this price. Is he ripping me off?* I have no way of knowing. I know one thing: I have to get the clock repaired. So I give the guy the green light.

How will I pay for it? I wonder.

I keep working odd jobs. I don't want you to know that I have to pay for the repairs, so I tell you I'm working so we can save up a little cash for a rainy day. You buy my story. So do our parents, and as far as anyone knows, I have convinced good old Rudy to fix the clock for free. It's a lie so convincing that I almost believe it myself.

CHAPTER 5

AFTER ELEVEN

About ten months into the shining bliss of our marriage, I feel cramped. Maybe you feel this way too. I feel I'm losing control of my privacy, and every turn I make in the apartment, every door I open, every place I sit down to rest, there you are. Not that I don't feel joy when I see you, but it would be nice to have some time and space to myself. Perhaps it's because our apartment is so small. It really is small, like a hamster cage.

I learn to love the night. The sun is gone, and the moon and stars are out. The world goes to sleep, and you finally turn off. You are not a night person. Come ten o'clock, you begin to nod off, and by eleven, you are snug in bed. Finally, I have the living area of the apartment to myself.

I cherish this time. I am all alone, and I make a large bowl of popcorn and turn on the TV. We have a big, modern TV. It was a wedding gift from my parents, and we have cable service with God knows how many channels. There's a station for everything under the sun. My favorite is the old-movie channel, and I watch the movies I have recorded after you go to bed. I am an old-movie addict. Ever since I was a kid, I've been hooked on old monster movies, not the ones they make now but the ones with silly plots and childish special effects. There are more of them than one would think. There are the classics, such as *Frankenstein*, *Dracula*, and *The Creature from the Black Lagoon*. There are the semiclassics, such as *The Blob*, *The Thing from Another World*, and *The Tingler*. Who can forget *The Tingler*? Then there are the really lousy ones, such as *Attack of the 50 Foot Woman*. The lousy ones are the best. Childish scripts and terrible special effects make them too good to resist. You hate old movies, and you especially hate old monster movies. That's okay. These are for me.

I turn off the lights. I sit down on the floor with my popcorn and turn on a movie. While you are in bed asleep, I watch the original *Godzilla* for the third time. It is not the Americanized version with Raymond Burr but the subtitled Japanese version that got the whole Godzilla ball rolling. The actual title of the movie is not *Godzilla*. It is called *Gojira,* the name the local Japanese islanders give to the monster. It is a great film. I always thought the Raymond Burr version was the original movie, but it was the second. *Gojira* was released in 1954, and the Raymond Burr version came out two years later. *Gojira* is a real gem. In it, a slew of seagoing vessels are destroyed near Odo Island. Professor Kyohei Yamane; his daughter, Emiko; and marine Hideto Ogata head to the island to investigate. Soon they see a giant monster, called Gojira by the locals, destroying ships and houses on the island.

Emiko meets with a moody scientist friend of hers named Serizawa, and he shows her a project he's been working on. He makes her promise to keep the project a secret. The project involves an invention that he calls an oxygen destroyer, a life-obliterating device that, if placed in the wrong hands, could be used as a horrible weapon of mass destruction. Serizawa is hell-bent on keeping the device out of the reach of politicians and the military. Emiko agrees to keep the secret, but when Gojira threatens Japan, after the army and the navy cannot stop it, Emiko breaks her promise and reveals Serizawa's secret weapon to her lover, Ogata. They then work to convince Serizawa to employ the oxygen destroyer to kill the monster, and Serizawa finally agrees to the plan.

They take the oxygen destroyer to where the monster lives in the ocean. Serizawa and Ogata dive into the water to plant the device. Serizawa then tricks Ogata and stays underwater when Ogata goes back up to the ship. He sacrifices his life to make sure the oxygen destroyer is properly placed and to make sure all his knowledge of the weapon's science is gone, carried to his grave. Once the device is set off, Gojira is finished and destroyed. Water bubbles up from the dying monster's body as it sinks to its death, and the passengers on the ship rejoice. Where had the monster come from? It had been locked safely away beneath the ocean for millions of years but had been set free by recent atomic bomb testing.

You think these movies are dumb. Maybe that's why I like them. Not to irritate you but to have something I can call my own. I tell you about *Them!* You roll your eyes. You don't get it. Enthusiastically, I say, "Then three men and a woman are examining a footprint in the New Mexico desert sand. The wind is blowing, and they are wearing goggles. James Whitmore is a local cop, and James Arness is an FBI agent. Also, there is an older professor and his attractive daughter. The professor says, 'If I'm correct—and the mounting evidence only fortifies my theory—then something incredible has happened in this here desert. None of us will dare risk revealing it, because none of us can risk a nationwide panic.'"

I laugh, and you look at me as if I'm crazy. I continue. "The professor's daughter then wanders off, looking for more footprints, and as she kneels down to look at another one, there is an eerie, high-pitched science-fiction sound. The next thing you know, a gigantic ant appears from out of nowhere and crawls toward the kneeling daughter. She screams and runs away from it. The men come running to see what's happening, and when they see the giant ant, they begin shooting with their pistols. The knowledgeable professor shouts, 'Get the antennae! Get the antennae! He's helpless without them!'

"Whitmore and Arness keep shooting until they hit both of the ant's antennae. Then Whitmore runs to the car and grabs a machine gun. He blasts at the ant with the machine gun until it collapses. The four then walk up to the dead ant's body, looking it over. 'What is it?' Arness asks. When the professor tells him it is an ant, Arness says, 'I don't believe it. It's not possible.'

"Ha, think again! 'No time to lose,' the professor says. 'We must find the colony or nest.'

"Arness blinks and asks, 'You mean there's more of them?'" I laugh out loud. "Oh yeah," I say to you. "There will be plenty of them."

"I can't believe you watch that crap," you say.

"It's good stuff."

"Dumb," you say.

The bad ones are the best. In my experience, the cheaper and more ridiculous a monster movie is, the better it is. Lousy special effects, poor writing, and atrocious acting are the ingredients that make a monster movie great. Forget the slick, realistic multimillion-dollar big-name productions. They're too real to be real. *Alien*, *Jurassic Park*, and *Jaws*? Forget about all of them. Case in point: I watch another movie titled *Squirm*. I've seen it before. It was written and directed by a guy named Jeff Lieberman. As best as I can tell, this was his big-breakout full-length film. It was released in 1976. Jesus, it is really awfully amateurish, which makes it really good. It is one of those films that makes you wonder how in the world they got anyone to finance the project.

The movie starts with a scrolling introduction about the story that says, "Late in the evening of September 29, 1975, a sudden electrical storm struck a rural sea coast area of Georgia. Power lines, felled by high winds, sent hundreds of thousands of volts surging into the muddy ground, cutting off all electricity to the small, secluded town of Fly Creek. During the period that followed the storm, the citizens of Fly Creek experienced what scientists believe to be one of the most bizarre freaks of nature ever recorded." Scientists? It is too funny. As if we were supposed to take this whole silly thing seriously.

The electricity from the downed lines goes into the wet earth and transforms all the earthworms of Fly Creek into manic, flesh-eating monsters. There are tons of the little creatures wriggling and squirming, and of course, there are rules. They don't like the light, for example, so they come out only in the darkness.

They are on the attack during the entire second half of the movie. There is a lot of hysterical screaming, and there are people half out of their minds. There are characters being eaten alive and others who barely escape with their lives. It is a very weird mixture of film footage, sometimes showing actual earthworms and sometimes showing a lot of fake rubber ones. The movie is much more humorous than it is scary or creepy. In the end, the power lines are repaired, and the worms retreat into the soil.

Once the story is over, they roll the credits to let us know all the names of the movie's actors and actresses—none whom I've ever heard of. Then, believe it or not, at the end of the credits, they say, "The characters and events depicted in this film are fictional. They are not intended to represent any real events, or persons, living or dead, and any similarity is purely coincidental." It is great. Whenever I see a film like this, it makes me think of what a troupe of grade school students would do if they had access to cameras and a couple hundred dollars to spend on cheap special effects. It's hard to believe an adult made this film. But it is wonderful. We need more movies like this. In my opinion, the world we live in has become way too slick and too professional.

Meanwhile, you sleep. Maybe you're dreaming about school. Maybe you're dreaming about your older sister, or maybe you're dreaming about finding money under a rock. The old grandfather clock is ticking in the darkness near the front door, and I'm eating popcorn, engrossed in *The Brain That Wouldn't Die*. It makes me feel good. I saw this one when I was a kid, but I've forgotten what happens. It's like seeing it for the first time.

The story is about a doctor-scientist named Bill Cortner. The opening scene is in a hospital operating room, and Bill and his surgeon father are trying to save a dying patient. The patient dies on the operating table, and Bill's father says, "I should've known he was as good as dead when they wheeled him in here." The nurse tells him he did everything he could, and Bill asks if they can now do things his way. Reluctantly, his father agrees. He says, "The corpse is yours. Do what you want to do."

They then run an electrical current directly to the patient's heart, and Bill goes to work on the guy's brain. Soon the patient moves his hand, and the nurse says he has a pulse. "It's unbelievable," the nurse says.

The patient is brought back to life, and the dad says, "I may not approve of your methods, but I'm proud of your results." Then he tempers his enthusiasm by telling Bill how inappropriate it is to experiment on people.

Bill disagrees. He tells his dad he is closer than ever to performing more medical miracles, such as transplantations using a new compound he's created. Oh yeah! Transplantations! A compound! You have to remember that this movie was made in 1962. Transplants were a big thing back then, but they weren't just talking about kidneys. They were talking about all kinds of organs, as well as arms, legs, and heads. Yes, heads!

As Bill is talking to his dad, his girlfriend enters the room and says, "Darling, I'm so proud of you I could kiss you." Little does she know the horrors that await her.

Bill and his girlfriend drive up to their country house for the weekend. Unknown to Bill's girlfriend, this is where Bill has been performing his gruesome experiments on human beings. On the way to the country house, they get into a terrible car accident. Bill is thrown from the car and is not injured. His girlfriend, however, is not so lucky. She is trapped in the car and is beheaded by the windshield glass. Bill runs to the car, reaches into the burning wreckage, and removes his girlfriend's severed head. He then wraps the head up in his jacket and makes a run for the country house. When he arrives at the country house, he takes the head into his laboratory and hooks it up to his mad-scientist apparatus so that the head is sitting in a pan of special fluid—it is alive!

When his girlfriend finally opens her eyes and realizes what Bill has done, she says, "Let me die. Let me die." She does not want to be a living head in a pan. She does not want to be one of Bill's grotesque experiments, but Bill is sure he can transplant her head onto someone else's body, saving her.

Bill leaves the laboratory to search for a body for his girlfriend. Where does he go? To a striptease club, of course. Where else could he find a perfect female body? He wants to attach his girlfriend's head to the neck and shoulders of a modern-day Aphrodite. He finds a stripper, who leads him into her dressing room. She says, "You know a good thing when you see it."

"There was plenty to see," Bills says.

"Where are you from?" the stripper asks.

"Oh, around."

"When you get done looking, then what?"

"I operate," Bill says.

"I get your message," the stripper says. She has no idea what Bill has in mind. She says, "I'm good for you."

"You may be just what I'm looking for," Bills says.

Suddenly, into the dressing room comes some other woman. She is there to change clothes. Unfortunately, she is a witness to Bill's seduction of the stripper, so he must leave and find someone else. There can't be any witnesses. "Come back later," the second girl says. "I'll remember you."

"Yeah," Bill says. "That's what I'm afraid of."

Meanwhile, back at the laboratory, his girlfriend's head shows interest in Bill's monster. The monster is the hideous result of Bill's past unsuccessful experiments with transplants. Bill keeps the monster locked up in a closet in the laboratory, not far from his girlfriend's head. We don't get to see the monster yet. We have to use our imagination to picture what it looks like. But the girlfriend's head talks to it, and it can hear her through the closet door. "You inside the closet," the girlfriend says. "What has he done to you? I know there's someone there. Knock once if you hear me."

The monster knocks once.

"Then I'm not the first," the girlfriend says. "Knock twice if I'm not the first."

The monster knocks twice.

"He should've let me die," the girlfriend says. "I hate him for what he's done to me. If he only knew what it's like being like this. Do you know what it's like?"

The monster knocks.

"Together we could have revenge," the girlfriend says. "You want revenge?"

The monster knocks.

Bill has an assistant, and the assistant is listening to this conversation between the girlfriend and the monster. He is on the other side of the door to the laboratory. He doesn't know what to do. Finally, he decides to enter the laboratory.

"What's locked behind that door?" the girlfriend asks, referring to the closet where the monster is kept.

"Horror," the assistant says. "No normal mind can imagine. Something even more terrible than you. There is a horror beyond yours, and it is in there. Behind that door is the sum total of Dr. Cortner's mistakes."

"He had no right to bring me back to this."

"You should know that before he injected the serum into that, it was but a mass of grafted tissues. Lifeless. Just laying there. Weighted down with its transplants of broken limbs and amputated arms. But with this serum, it began to breathe."

"Impossible."

"Would you have thought possible what he's already done? Take yourself. He's brought you back. You live! Only a few years ago, all transplants were impossible."

The girlfriend then scares the daylights out of the assistant by asserting that she and the monster are now one. "Together we're strong," she says, and the monster beats on the closet door.

The assistant runs out of the laboratory. He bumps into Bill, who has just come home.

"There's something wrong," the assistant says. "Something beyond control in that room."

"There is nothing beyond my control," Bill says. "She's alive, and I'll keep her alive until I find her a body."

The next day, Bill goes on the prowl again for a body. He hops into his convertible and drives. He looks at sexy women walking down the sidewalks. Finally, he comes across a woman he knows named Donna, and she climbs into Bill's car. They pick up one of Donna's friends. Then they drive to a beauty pageant, of all things, and Bill watches the girls in a swimsuit contest. Bill and Donna get to talking about girls with nice bodies, and Donna brings up a girl named Doris. Donna says Doris has the best body she's ever seen, and the wheels start turning in Bill's head. Why not? The best body? He later pays a visit to Doris, and he talks her into coming to his house for drinks.

Meanwhile, all hell breaks loose in the laboratory. When Bill's assistant gets too close to the closet door, the monster, controlled by Bill's girlfriend, reaches through an opening in the door and grabs the assistant. The monster gets a hold of the assistant's arm and rips it right off his body. The assistant then rolls around for a while, smudging blood all over the walls, until he finally drops dead in the laboratory.

Shortly after, Bill arrives with Doris. He has her wait in the living room while he goes to make them cocktails. He goes to the laboratory and finds his dead assistant. Then he makes the cocktails, putting a knockout chemical in Doris's drink. He returns to the living room and gives the glass to Doris, and immediately after drinking the spiked contents, she says she feels funny and then collapses. Bill then carries her unconscious body to the laboratory and places it on an operating table. He is going to cut off her head and perform the transplant.

His girlfriend tries to get the monster to interfere, and Bill puts a piece of tape over her mouth to keep her quiet. It's no use. The monster breaks through the closet door and attacks Bill. We finally get to see the beast. It's hilarious. The monster looks like something a kid created using papier-mâché and skin-colored paint. It's bald and lumpy, with one eye falling out. The monster takes a fatal bite out of Bill's neck, spitting out his flesh and leaving him to die on the floor.

Meanwhile, some chemical has spilled and started a fire, and the laboratory goes up in flames. The monster rescues Doris and carries her out of the burning laboratory while the flames consume Bill and his girlfriend's head. That is the end of the movie.

You sleep through the whole thing. I turn off the TV and put the empty popcorn bowl in the kitchen. I walk through the dark and climb into bed. You wake up as my head hits the pillow. "How was your movie?" you ask.

"It was great," I say.

"I love you."

"I love you too."

CHAPTER 6

GOING PLACES

Finally, we graduate from USC, and we are so different now than we were when we first met. Well, maybe you more than me. I was always a little shy and idealistic, and I always wanted to be a writer. Thus, I focused on journalism. This made sense, but you as an architect? I would never have guessed. But just look at you now! You are sure of yourself and proud of your accomplishments in school. You graduated with highest honors, and you have a job lined up before the ink is even dry on your diploma. Everyone agrees you are going places. Your dad laughs and says, "I remember when the most important thing in your life was the number of likes you got on your Facebook page." I remember those years too.

Do you recall when we first met? Of course you do. It was at the beach. I always liked the salty air and the sound of the waves. The seagulls were always calling, and the foghorns would moan from the distance. I lived almost my entire life in Southern California, and I have many fond memories of the beaches. In high school, my friends and I would go there nearly every weekend in the summer. We'd swim in the water, drink beer, lie in the sun, and play catch with our Frisbees. And we'd try to meet girls. Jesus, girls were everywhere, barely dressed in their swimsuits, with their tan skin glistening in the sunlight.

One night, my friends and I stayed late at the beach and lit a small bonfire in one of the concrete campfire rings. Purely out of chance, you and four of your girlfriends came upon us, and one of my friends invited you guys to sit. At first, you girls hesitated, but then you decided to join us at the fire. You weren't of our kind at the school. What I mean to say is that you were popular kids, and we were not. No, we weren't total losers, but we weren't in your social class. We certainly weren't as popular as you, and never in a million years would any of you have joined us socially at the school. But it was dark, and we were miles from the school. There were no other kids there to judge, so you and your friends sat with us. Looking back now, I realize it was probably because of the beer. We had a whole cooler full of Coors, enough for all of us.

We shared our beer with you and talked. You and your friends drank like fish. I'd never seen anything like it. You were giggling and talking our ears off. We really were having a good time. You had been sitting next to me the entire time. The two of us started talking independently of the rest, and you told me about your boyfriend. The boy's name was Rod Balzer, and I knew who he was—he was the quarterback of the football team. I thought he was a jerk, but I didn't say that to you. Then you said, "I think I'm going to break up with Rod. He doesn't know it yet, but it's time for me to move on. My parents love him, but I've had enough."

I didn't offer an opinion, but I thought you'd be wise to rid yourself of that conceited chimpanzee as soon as humanly possible. I didn't like the guy, and you seemed like such a nice girl. I mean, you really were nice. In fact, you were surprisingly nice. I had always thought you and your kind were too good for me and my friends, yet there you were, talking to me and having a good time.

Anyway, we talked a lot about Rod Balzer, and then you asked me if I wanted to leave the group to walk along the beach. Of course I said yes, and we stood up to stroll barefoot along the shoreline in the moonlight. I enjoyed talking to you, and it was weird how you were treating me like an equal. You didn't talk down to me at all. You told me a story about your cousin Jen, who lived with her dad in Oregon. You said Jen had also been going steady with a boy from the football team. You said that Jen and the boy had sex a few times and that Jen got pregnant last year. You said it was a mess. Jen wanted to get an abortion, but her parents were against that and wouldn't allow it. Instead, Jen went to live with her grandma in Seattle, where she carried the baby to term. She then put the baby up for adoption and returned to school in Oregon.

Jen's parents made her break up with the boy from the football team. "She never will know who raised her child," you said. "She gave birth, and then—*zap!*—the baby was gone. I guess there was really no other alternative other than getting an abortion. But honestly, I think deep down that Jen was just as opposed to an abortion as her parents were. They're very religious, you know. They believe abortions are murder. My family is religious too, but I don't know what they'd do if I got pregnant. Rod and I have been very careful, but you never know. I think Rod would want me to get an abortion, but I'm not sure about my parents. I guess you just don't know for sure until the times comes and a decision has to be made. What would you do? I mean, if you got a girl pregnant. Would you expect her to get an abortion? Or would you encourage her to have the baby?"

I felt like a little kid. Like a dumb little grade school kid. You were asking *me* about getting a girl pregnant. I was so far from having to worry about that happening that the question wasn't even slightly relevant. I was still a virgin. I still thought it was amazing just to kiss a girl, and your willingness to talk about that subject made me feel—what? Uneasy? Hopelessly immature?

I hadn't answered your question, so you asked again, "What would you do?"

I said, "I guess I'd opt for an abortion. I don't think girls our age should be having babies."

You stared at me for a moment, and then you said, "I think I agree with you."

More than anything, I wanted to change the subject, but I couldn't think of anything to say. There were all kinds of subjects I could have brought up, but my mind wasn't operating at full strength. All I could think of was you having sex with Rod Balzer—the bastard! I was out of my league. What a total idiot I was! Then you stopped walking and grasped my arm.

"Let's sit for a while," you said.

"Here?" I asked.

"Sure," you said. "Let's just sit and watch the ocean waves."

I said okay, and the two of us sat on the sand, watching the black waves and listening to them crash one after another under the stars. Suddenly, I felt your warm hand on my knee, and you asked, "Do you want to kiss me?"

Your question took me totally by surprise, and I wasn't sure what I should say. You asked again, and this time, I said, "Yes, that would be nice."

The next thing I knew, your lips were on mine. It wasn't just a quick peck. Do you remember? It was long and passionate, and I remember thinking, *What the hell? What the heck does this girl think she's doing?* But I liked it and did nothing to stop you. It was a wonderful kiss, and I didn't want it to end.

Then you grasped my wrist, brought my hand to your breast, and said, "Feel me, Jonathan. Tell me what you feel."

I said nothing. I had no idea what I was supposed to say. Finally, you stopped kissing me, and I took my hand off your breast.

"It's nice, isn't it?" you asked. "Alone at the beach, in the darkness. I like listening to the waves. They make me think of the future."

"Yes, waves are nice," I said. I wasn't sure what else to say, so I then said nothing.

You stood up, and so did I. We walked along the foamy shore back to our friends, not saying a word. When we got to the fire, one of your friends said to you, "There you are. We were wondering where you went. We've got to leave now. Joanne has to be home by midnight."

You and your girlfriends thanked us for the beer and left. My friends asked me where I had gone with you, and I told them we had just taken a walk. "It was no big deal," I said.

The next Monday at school, I saw you in the hall between our classes. You were standing with a group of friends, talking and laughing. I made eye contact with you, and I smiled. You smiled back nicely. As they say, the rest is history.

Now here we are, college graduates. All grown up, so to speak. I'm going to make a name for myself as a journalist. You will make a name for yourself as an architect. Soon we will be moving out of our tiny apartment, bringing the old grandfather clock along with us. These are exciting times. Our parents want to be part of the excitement, so they get together and plan a dinner for us to celebrate our graduation from college. They decide upon a restaurant in Newport Beach. It's an expensive place, and we have to dress nice. My dad sends me a check for $200 with a note that says, "Buy yourself some decent clothes. See you Saturday." You don't need cash for clothes. Your dad gave you one of his credit cards several years ago. We go to the mall to get prepared for the dinner. We then meet everyone at Reuben's at seven.

We all arrive at the same time. Your parents are there with your sister, and my parents show up alone. They seat us at a big table in a far corner of the restaurant. Our waiter's name is Jason, and he brings us our menus. He takes our drink orders and leaves. Your dad bangs his fist on the table, laughing, and says, "Well, this is something, isn't it?"

"We're so proud of both of you," your mom says.

"Yes," my mom says.

"Look out, world," my dad says. "Here comes Orange County's newest power couple with diplomas in hand."

"The architect and the journalist," your dad says. Then he asks me, "How's the job search coming?"

"It's coming," I say.

"You'll get a job soon."

"Who wouldn't want him on their staff?" my dad says.

"It's a tough job market," I say.

"When the going gets tough, the tough get going," my dad says. He's always liked saying that.

"Winners never quit, and quitters never win," your dad says, adding his own stolen dime-store wisdom to the conversation.

"Took me months to get my first job," my dad says. Then he asks my mom, "Do you remember that?"

"I do," Mom says.

"I've got a question," your dad says. Everyone looks at him, waiting for his question. Then he says to you and me, "Since you're both going to be working, who's going to wear the pants in your family?"

What a strange question, I think. I look at you, and you smile. You're used to your father. The question doesn't seem to surprise you. "We're going to be equals," you say. "We'll both wear the pants."

"Oh really?" your father says.

"Oh really," you say.

"What do you think of that?" your father asks my father.

"I don't know," my dad says.

"Will it work?"

"It might."

"I say this, and I'm speaking from experience. Someone has to be the captain, and someone has to be the first mate. You can't have two captains in charge of the same ship."

"Why not?" you ask.

"What if you disagree on something?"

"Then we'll work it out."

"And what if you can't work it out?"

"We'll have to work it out."

Your dad laughs and looks at my dad. "Dreamers," he says. "What do you think?"

"I don't know," my dad says.

Your dad looks at us and says, "What about when you're looking for a house to buy? You two will be moving out of that tiny apartment soon. And you'll both be working. You'll have money for a larger house payment. You'll spend your weekends with real estate agents, going to open houses, surfing through real estate listings on the internet. So many houses to choose from in so many different neighborhoods. So many options. So many amenities. Which house are you going to buy? Each of you will have your own preferences. And you're going to find that one of you might fall in love with one house while the other falls in love with another. You can't very well live in both houses, can you? One of you will have to bite the bullet and relinquish power to the other. One of you will be the captain. One of you will get your way while the other concedes."

"Maybe we won't buy either house," you say. "Maybe we'll keep looking until we find a house we both like."

"Ah, clever girl," my dad says.

"She is, isn't she?" your dad says.

"It makes sense to me," my mom says.

"Okay then, I'll give you a tougher one. Let's say you have a teenage daughter. Let's say she's a sophomore in high school. Now, I'm speaking from experience. Let's say your daughter comes home from school one day and says, 'Mom and Dad, I want to dye my hair orange and get a nose ring.' One of you has no problem with this, but the other is dead set against it. You talk about it but can't come to an agreement. What's it going to be? Orange hair? Nose ring? You have to make a decision, right? One of you will have to be the captain of the ship, and the other will have to go along. There's no other way. There is no in-between course of action or compromise possible. Orange hair? Nose ring? Which is it going to be? Who will have the final say?"

"Your father has a good point," your mom says to you. "You two are not always going to agree."

"I guess we'll have to cross that bridge when we come to it," you say.

"But you haven't answered my question."

"They've got their whole lives ahead of them," my mom says. "They'll figure it out."

Your mom says, "Of course, if the wife is clever, she'll convince the husband that he's getting his way, whether he is or he isn't."

My mom laughs.

Suddenly, the waiter shows back up at our table with our drinks, and he is ready to take our dinner orders. He has his pencil and notepad in hand, and he starts with your sister. He goes from one of us to the other until he has written everything down.

"Bring us some bread," your dad says. "I'm starving to death. And bring lots of butter."

I am thinking.

Everyone is quiet for a moment. I am thinking about what your dad said about the orange hair and nose ring, and it occurs to me that marriage might be a little like rock 'n' roll music. Do you know what I mean by this? If I ask myself whether I want to wear the pants, as your dad puts it, I come to the conclusion that it isn't really important to me at all. Wear the pants? Who cares? I can enjoy my marriage without having the final say in everything. You hear about irreconcilable differences. You hear about them, but they're not likely to be a factor in our future.

You know I love listening to rock 'n' roll music. It makes me feel good. It makes me drum my fingers and tap my toes, and sometimes I like to try to sing along. But here's the thing: I listen to these songs over and over, and I don't understand 80 percent of the lyrics. I hear what seem to be real words, but I have no idea what the singers are actually singing. When I do understand the words, they seldom make any sense to me. They are cryptic, poetic, and indecipherable. I don't know what they're talking about, yet I love the music. Like I said, the songs make me feel good when I listen to them. I guess I like the feelings they rouse in me, and for me, marriage is a little like this. The content isn't all that important. Never mind the meanings, and never mind the details. I don't really care whether

I'm getting my way, having the final say, or asserting my opinions. I just like the thing as a whole. I like being married, and I like the fact that we are life partners. I like that we met on the beach, went to college together, and are moving on with our lives together as a team. You and me.

CHAPTER 7

IN A HEARTBEAT

Five months after we graduate from college, I get an email from one of my college professors at USC. I can't believe what I'm reading. He has an opportunity for me, and I couldn't have asked for anything better to come my way. Before I tell you anything about it, let me tell you a little about this professor.

His name is Joseph Mack. He is in his early sixties, and I had him for two of my journalism classes. He liked me a lot when I was in school, and I aced his classes with a pair of As.

Most college professors I encountered were not all that inspiring. I mean, they were enthusiastic about their courses but seldom very enthusiastic about their students. Maybe I got lucky with Joseph. Would I call it luck? He thought I was especially talented, and he told me so. "You have a God-given gift," he said to me. "I see you doing great things in the years ahead." He said he loved the papers I wrote, and maybe more importantly, he liked me.

I read his email, and I immediately want to learn more. He has written,

> How are you doing, Jonathan? Have you landed a job yet? I actually hope not. A job opening has come up that I think you would be perfectly suited for. It involves an old friend of mine. The money is good. It's a great opportunity to prove yourself. If you're interested, give me a call at your earliest convenience, and let's talk about it.

Well, yes, I am interested. I am dying to know what this opportunity is, and I call Joseph the same day I get the email. When he answers the phone, he is his usual cheerful self. "I'm so glad you called," he says. "Are you still living in Orange County?"

"Yes," I say.

"That's good. The subject lives in LA."

"The subject?"

"You won't have far to drive."

"Okay," I say.

"The subject is an old friend of mine. He wants to write his autobiography. You know, his memoirs. He's looking for a ghostwriter."

"A ghostwriter?"

"It's a terrific opportunity."

"Who is this friend of yours?" I ask.

"Nicholas Bliss."

"You're kidding," I say.

"I'm dead serious," he says. "Amazing, right?"

"Yes," I say.

"It'll put you on the map."

"But I'll be invisible."

"Only for a short while. And only for this particular book. Publishers will learn who you are."

"I guess so."

"Are you in or out?"

"I don't know."

"I hope you're in. Nick asked me for the name of someone young. He wants someone young and hip. Someone who has his finger on the progressive pulse of today. Someone like you, Jonathan. Can I set up a meeting between the two of you? Are you in or out? What do you say?"

"I'm in," I say. I'd be a fool to turn this down. *Nicholas Bliss? Are you kidding me? Celebrity. Heartthrob. Talk of the town. And I'm fresh out of college.*

I meet with Nick at his home in Beverly Hills. He built this place ten years ago. He purchased four houses, demolished them, and built his house on the land. But it isn't really just a house; it's a mansion! The grounds are breathtaking—rolling green lawns, palm trees, and enough flowers to stock all the florist shops in LA. The house itself is made of stucco with red roof tiles and a hodgepodge of dormers, arches, pillars, and classic architectural details.

I park in the driveway and step up to the massive front doors. I ring the doorbell, and I hear the chimes inside the house playing one of his most popular songs. I wait. Maybe he didn't hear the doorbell, I think, so I press the button again. This time, I can hear him from behind the doors.

"Coming, coming," he says. "Hold your horses." The front door creaks open, and there he is, in the flesh. He's shorter than I thought he would be, but for sure it is him. He is dressed in a navy-blue athletic outfit and white tennis shoes. He reaches to shake my hand. "You must be Jonathan," he says.

"Yes," I say. "And you're obviously Nicholas Bliss."

"Call me Nick."

"Fine," I say.

"Come in, and sit down. Joseph tells me you're just the man I'm looking for."

"Joseph ought to know."

"Yes, yes, he ought to know. Do you know how long I've known Joseph?"

"He didn't say."

"We've known each other since we were kids. We grew up together in Arcadia. When I began thinking about this project, Joseph was the first person to come to mind. Surely he knew where I could find the right person. He knew where I could find what I was looking for. Joseph had nothing but good things to say about you."

"I'm glad to hear that."

"So you just graduated?"

"Yes, five months ago."

"How old are you?"

"I'm twenty-two."

"Perfect."

Nick then asks if I want something to drink. He says he just made a pot of coffee, and I say that sounds good. He then goes to the kitchen to grab us a couple of cups. When he returns, he hands me my coffee, and he sits down, sipping his.

"Joseph said you wanted to write your memoirs," I say.

"Yes," Nick says.

"Sounds interesting."

"Oh yes, it will be interesting."

"Lots of stories?"

"I can tell some good stories. Rock stars all have good stories to tell. They might piss a few people off, but I can tell them."

I laugh.

"But this book is not about stories."

"No?"

"I mean, I will tell a lot of them, and they will entertain my readers. But that is not the point of the book."

"Okay," I say.

"The point? I will get to that. First, let me tell you where I would like this book to start. I want to start at my senior year in high school. Our band was just starting out. There were four of us. I was the only one of us who could carry a tune, so I did the singing. I also wrote most of our songs. I could tell you many stories about the band from those days, and I will. The stories are interesting. But even more important than the band was one of our teenage fans, a girl named Mary Smythe. I'm going to tell you all about Mary because she is important. As you shall see, she is the reason I'm writing this book.

"You'd never know it back then, the importance of this girl with freckles, red hair, and legs like a baby giraffe. She was infatuated with me, and she followed us around wherever we played. She was my first groupie. One thing led to another, and the next thing I knew, I was dating her. I'd take her out for burgers and milkshakes, and we liked going to movies. Sometimes I would come over to her house, and we'd watch TV with her parents. Her parents seemed to like me. They didn't discourage her from seeing more of me.

"We went steady for three years, until finally, we started talking about marriage. It wasn't scary. It seemed right. We loved each other dearly. Meanwhile, the band was getting more and more popular, and we were invited to play all over the place. And we were accumulating fans. It was so exciting. There's nothing in the world quite like having honest-to-God fans who love your music and who love you. I think my songwriting was at its best during those years. I was inspired, happy, and in love with life.

Yes, I definitely wrote my best songs at that time. It was like I couldn't write a bad song if I tried. And my best songs? They were my love songs, fueled by my love for Mary. I couldn't get enough of her, and the music gushed from my heart."

Nick pauses for a moment and then leans forward. "You're married, right?" he asks.

"Yes," I say.

"Then you know what it's like to fall in love?"

"I do."

"There's nothing like it."

"I would agree with that."

"Well, we got engaged. I got down on one knee and proposed to her. When she said yes, I put the ring on her finger, the whole nine yards. No one was surprised. Everyone saw it coming, and everything in my life was now coming together. The band was more popular than ever, and a record company approached us with a recording contract. Jesus, those were great times. Our dream was coming true. It's hard to express just how this sort of good fortune can make a young man feel. I felt invincible, like I could do no wrong. I was superhuman. Maybe even godlike. Then came the night we played up in San Francisco. I would learn that even Nicholas Bliss was fallible."

"What happened?" I ask.

"Cynthia Pound happened."

"Who is Cynthia Pound?"

"A girl. A girl of no importance to me who suddenly became the most important girl in my life."

"I don't understand."

"When we played at a club in San Francisco, Mary stayed home in LA. We were playing on a Saturday night, and her cousin was getting married that day. She was close to her cousin and didn't want to miss the wedding. The wedding was held that day, and the reception was in the afternoon. Mary stayed for the whole thing, and then she decided at the last minute to drive up to San Francisco to see me. She figured if she left at six, she would arrive at the end of our performance. And that's what she did.

"Of course, I had no idea she was coming. When the show was over, the boys and I were going to go back to our hotel room, but then I was approached by Cynthia. She was a fan. I guess you could call her a groupie. It was stupid of me, I know, but I was attracted to this girl, and she was coming on to me. She was gorgeous. I knew better, but I let myself be seduced. Yes, it was wrong, but I figured, *What the hell?* It's not like I was going to marry the dumb girl. I was just having a little fun.

"Cynthia led me out of the club and into the parking lot. She was going to drive us to her apartment. We embraced outside her car and kissed. It was wonderful, and I really did enjoy it. Then I heard Mary's voice. She had just parked her car, and she saw me with Cynthia. 'Nicholas?' she said. 'Is that you?'

"I stopped kissing Cynthia and looked. 'Oh shit,' I think I said. It was something like that. I then said, 'What are you doing here?'

"Mary asked, 'What am I doing here? What are *you* doing?'

"It was horrible. 'Who the hell is she?' Cynthia asked. We were still in each other's arms.

"'I'm his fiancée,' Mary said. 'Who the hell are you?'

"I let go of Cynthia, and I tried to think of something to say. I said, 'It's not what it looks like.'

"Mary just stared at me. At first, she looked more hurt than she did angry. Then she looked angry. I mean, she was really furious. She took off her engagement ring and threw it at me. It hit me in the chest and fell to the pavement. 'We're through,' she said. Then she stormed back to her car, climbed in, and sped away. Just like that.

"We didn't have cell phones back then, so I couldn't call her. She drove back to Southern California that night. When I did get back home, I tried to reach her, but she wouldn't answer her phone. I tried calling her parents, but they were no help. Finally, I went to see her. She wouldn't open her apartment door. She just told me to go away. She said if I didn't leave, she would call the police. We were definitely through."

"Wow," I say.

"I blew it."

"She wasn't very forgiving."

"Not at all."

"And you never did get married."

"Never. Not to anyone. I figured it was either Mary or no one. She was my one true love."

"Surely you've met other women?"

"Lots of them."

"And you've had lots of relationships?"

"You could say that."

"Have you ever talked to Mary since?"

"Not once."

"Any idea where she is?"

"Oh yeah. Three years ago, I hired a private investigator to find her."

"To talk to her?"

"No, just to see what she was doing."

"And?"

"He gave me the complete story. He was very thorough. He said that after she called it quits with me, she went to UCLA to study nursing. She got her degree, and then she landed a job at Cedars-Sinai in Los Angeles. There she met a doctor named Arnold Richards, and she dated him for two years before they got married. They moved into a house in Beverly Hills, and they had three children: two boys and a girl. The boys' names were Thomas and Able, and they named the girl Sarah. Mary quit her job at the hospital to raise the kids, and she did charity work to fill her spare time. Her kids were good kids. I mean, they had their problems now and again, but all in all, they were turning out okay. As best as my private investigator could tell, her husband was a good man as well. No signs of infidelity. No gambling or drug or drinking problems."

"But you never contacted her?"

"What would be the point?"

"I don't know. It seems a shame that you two never got together. At least just as friends."

"She made it clear in that San Francisco parking lot that she never wanted to see me again. She couldn't have made herself any clearer. And I had to respect her wishes. I was the one who messed things up, and I was the one who was obligated to follow the rules. And believe me, she set the rules. There has been no gray area. If she had wanted to talk to me or see me again, she would've done so. But she never made any effort to contact me. Not ever. And she seemed to be happy with her life. Why would I want to disturb her?"

"Do you still love her?"

Nick thinks for a moment. He picks up his cup of coffee, takes a sip, and then sets the cup back on the end table. "Love her?" he says. "I've always loved her. I always will love her. That first flame never goes out. You meet other people, and you love again, and you have new relationships, but that first flame never dies."

"Do you think she'll read this book we're writing?"

"I don't know."

"Do you want her to read it?"

"I do. I mean, that's the whole point, isn't it?"

"The point?"

Then it makes sense to me. The book seems to be Nick's way of saying to Mary, "I've had an amazing and colorful life, but in a heartbeat, I would've traded it all in to have had a life with you. I'm sorry. I'm so sorry. But the truth is that I didn't deserve you. As much as it hurts to say, you did the right thing. Still, I would trade it all."

CHAPTER 8

HOME SWEET HOME

Close your eyes, and imagine more of our future. Days coming and years to come. It is now one year after the autobiography of Nicholas Bliss has hit the shelves, and the book is doing well. When I signed a contract with Nick, unfortunately, I didn't cut myself in for a percentage of the sales. I worked strictly for a lump-sum payment, so I haven't exactly gotten rich on the project. I have, however, established myself as someone who can write a best-selling book. This is no small feat for a writer my age who previously had no more experience to his name than a few published letters to the editor and a four-year college degree. These days, you are proud of me. You say you always knew I had it in me.

We scrimp and save. With the money I earned from Nick's book and the money you're making, we put together what we need for the down payment on a house. We can't wait to move out of our tiny apartment. We aren't able to afford much, but it will be a place we can call our own. Home sweet home.

We find a house in an older section of Anaheim that is within our budget. It is a fixer-upper, which is fine—we can improve the house bit by bit as we earn more money. Since you are putting in twelve-hour days at work, we decide to put me in charge of improving our home. My first task? I need to get a new roof put on the house. The existing roof is in horrible shape, and we want to reroof before the rainy season. I get three prices, all of them beyond our budget. Then a little good fortune comes our way in the form of a glossy flyer someone stuffed into our mailbox.

The flyer has a picture of some clean-cut men working on a roof, and the headline says, "Need a new roof?" It is an advertisement for a roofing company in Santa Ana promising new roofs for 30 percent less than any other legitimate roofer's quote. The flyer says, "Limited-time offer. Many local references. Fully licensed and bonded. Top-quality materials and workmanship with a five-year unconditional warranty."

I call up the company the same day we get the flyer and set up an appointment later that week. The person I am to meet is the owner of the company, a man named Claude Garnet. We meet on a Friday afternoon, and he pulls into our driveway with his new Dodge pickup truck. The name of his company is painted on the door panels: Claude's Roofing. Claude is tall and nicely groomed, and he wears a plaid shirt, jeans, and a clean pair of work boots. In his hand is a clipboard with a notepad and a brochure describing his company, and the first thing he does after we shake hands is hand me the brochure. It is impressive. There are photos of some nice houses Claude has roofed, and there are testimonials from several of his customers. There is also a short paragraph describing Claude's company and how long it has been in business. I look over the brochure for a moment, and then Claude speaks. He has a great voice, like a radio disc jockey.

I am comfortable with Claude. For 30 percent cheaper, I don't know what we'll be getting. Claude explains the type of roof he recommends, and he tells me his workers have been with him for years. He says, "They know what I want, and they're good at what they do." Claude then asks to see the proposals I've received from the other roofers, and I get them for him. I ask if he can really do the work for 30 percent less, and he smiles and says it will be no problem. "I've been a roofer for many years," Claude says. "You wouldn't believe the markup the average roofer hits you with or how many inefficiencies they probably have with their operations. We're a finely tuned machine, and our customers reap the rewards. As do we." I like what Claude is saying, and I have no reason to disbelieve him.

The next week, Claude has a contract ready for me to sign. It is for the price he promised, and everything seems in order. After I sign the contract, Claude tells me he'll need a 50 percent cash deposit in order to get started. He explains that he gets better deals on materials when he pays cash, and this makes sense to me. So we drive to my bank to withdraw the money. I hand Claude the cash, and he stuffs it in his pocket.

"The materials will be delivered in approximately one week," he says. "My workers will show up the next day. It'll take about a week and a half to complete the job, and you won't have to make your final payment until you are completely satisfied."

"That sounds great," I say.

That is the last time I see Claude in person. Oh, I talk to him on the phone several times. I call him after a week. No materials have been delivered after the first week, so I call Claude to ask when they will show up. I'm not trying to bug him. I guess I'm just getting anxious to see the work get done. Then another week goes by, and there are still no materials delivered. I call Claude, and he says his men will be there in the afternoon, and sure enough, they show up. They remove several rolls of black paper from the bed of their pickup truck and set them in the driveway along with some metal flashing.

"Are you guys starting tomorrow?" I ask them, and they say they don't know for sure.

The next evening, I call Claude to find out when they will start, and he says he's sending his demolition crew out the following day. These guys show up as promised, and they spend about four hours tearing a good portion of our roof off. Then they leave. I call Claude again that night. Honestly, I am now getting a little nervous, and I try to be firmer with Claude. I don't want him to think I am a pushover. He says he had to pull the men off to finish another job, but they will be back in three days. Reluctantly, I agree to wait another three days, and Claude sounds appreciative for my patience.

"These things sometimes happen," he says, and those are the last words I hear from him.

After the three days pass and no one shows up, I call him, but this time, his phone is disconnected. The blood rushes from my head. I know this is not good. I don't tell you about it; instead, I tell you that I talked to Claude and that he promised to have his men at our house the next day. Why do I lie to you? I guess I don't want you to worry yet, not until I know for sure what is going on.

The next morning, I drive to Claude's office in Santa Ana, where I find a tow truck driver hooking up to Claude's truck in the parking lot. I ask the driver if the truck broke down, and he just laughs.

"You're the second person to come ask me that," he says. "His landlord asked me the same question five minutes ago."

"His landlord?" I ask.

The guy laughs again and then points toward the building, where a man is unlocking Claude's office door. I approach the man just as he pushes the door open, and I ask him where Claude is. He says, "I wish to hell I knew. That deadbeat owes me three months of back rent, and now it looks like he's made a run for it. See for yourself."

I look through the office window, and sure enough, the place is empty. No desks or chairs. No file cabinets. No pictures on the walls. Just a lot of debris and wires on the floor. The place has been stripped clean.

"Let me guess," the landlord says. "You hired this deadbeat to put a roof on your house?"

"Yes, I did," I say.

The man shakes his head and says, "What a mess. I should've seen it coming. I should've put my foot down."

"He took a cash deposit and tore off half my roof," I say. "What am I supposed to do now?"

"I wish I could help you, friend," the man says. "You probably need to see an attorney."

Telling you about this is awful. The roof project was my domain. You didn't want anything to do with it, and you trusted me to handle the whole thing. Now what am I supposed to say? I say defensively, "You met him too. Didn't he seem trustworthy to you? He had references. And he had that nice brochure. And the price was right."

Two days later, I call an attorney recommended to us by one of your work friends. I set up a meeting with him for the next day, and I go see him at his office in Newport Beach. I tell him briefly over the phone what the problem is, and he tells me to bring Claude's contract with me. Amazing, isn't it? I've only been married a few years, and once again, I'm talking to an attorney. First, there was the uncooperative grandfather clock, and now there is the roof that won't die.

I'll describe the attorney. His name is David P. Swartz. He asks me to call him Dave. His office is on the second floor of a low-rise office building in Fashion Island, and his operations consist of a legal secretary, an assistant, and himself—that's it. He's dressed like an attorney, with the exception of his cowboy boots. I don't know if this is good or bad. Not a lot of people wear cowboy boots in Southern California, and I think it's kind of odd. Maybe it's good, and maybe it's bad. I mean, maybe judges and juries like the boots, or maybe they think they're stupid. Or maybe they don't care one way or the other. I don't know. Anyway, I tell him what happened in detail.

I tell him the whole story, leaving nothing out. While I'm talking, Dave leans back in his chair. I think for a moment that he's going to put his feet up on his desk, but he doesn't. When I am done talking, he asks me, "Did you bring the contract?"

I say I did, and I hand it to him.

"Give me a minute," he says, and he leans forward to read the contract. Suddenly, he stops reading, placing his finger on the payment clause. "Says here you were to pay him in full upon completion of the work. It doesn't say anything about paying an up-front deposit. And it doesn't say anything about having to pay in cash."

Dave stares at me, and I say, "But he asked for the fifty percent cash deposit. He needed it to buy materials."

Dave continues to stare at me, and then he reads the rest of the contract. When he's done reading, he pushes the contract to the center of his desk and leans back in his chair. Again, I think he's going to put his feet on his desk, but he doesn't.

"You got a receipt for the cash payment, right?"

I say no.

Dave says, "What in the world were you thinking? Why didn't you get a receipt?"

"I didn't think I'd need one," I say. "He seemed so honest. He seemed so professional."

"So we have no proof that you gave him this money," Dave says. "And the contract doesn't even call for any down payment. Upon completion, it says. You were supposed to pay him in full upon completion."

"But he asked me for the deposit," I say.

"He'll just deny it, and you'll have no proof he's lying."

"I see what you mean," I say, and now I really feel like an idiot. When I ask Dave what my options are, he says I can either eat the loss or sue Claude. In the case of a lawsuit, he figures I have a fifty-fifty chance. And there will be attorney fees and court costs. And we will have to pay a private investigator to locate Claude. Who knows where he is? Who knows how long it will take to find him or how much it will cost? Plus, since Claude has already torn up our roof, I will need to hire a roofer to finish the job—and not for the 30 percent discount Claude promised but at the full rate.

"Claude is probably broke," Dave says. "So even if you do get a judgment, the odds are that Claude won't pay you a dime. You can't squeeze blood from a turnip."

Just a few months earlier, Claude was able to talk me out of thousands of dollars, and now he's a turnip. The bastard! Now I am caught in an impossible situation. I want to throttle him. Well, maybe not literally, but I do want to confront him to see if he has a conscience, tell him what he's done to me, and make him feel guilty. I don't want him to carry on with his life as though there are no consequences. So while I opt not to sue him, I do hire a private investigator to find him.

The name of this investigator is Charlie Brill. The man is all business, and he doesn't want to hear a speech from me about how Claude wronged me. He just wants facts he can work with, and I give them to him. It doesn't take Charlie long to find Claude. After I pay his fee, he gives me the address of a house in Phoenix, where he says Claude is now living. I picture Claude living in some nice neighborhood, living off the money he conned from trusting customers like me. I want to give this creep a piece of my mind man-to-man. I want to see if he has any conscience at all.

When I tell you my plan to confront Claude, you are immediately against it and tell me I'm wasting my time.

"And what if it gets ugly?" you ask. "What if you wind up getting in a fight? What if he pulls a gun on you? You have no idea what this man is actually like or what he is capable of. You'll just be asking for trouble."

I have a feeling you're right, but I still want to see Claude and speak my mind. "It is personal," I say to you.

It is important to me, so I pack a change of clothes and some toiletries, and against your wishes, I drive to Phoenix. It is a five-hour drive, and the closer I get to Phoenix, the more ready I am to let Claude have it. It will feel good. I will get everything off my chest, and I will come home satisfied that at least I spoke my mind.

When I arrive in Phoenix, I enter the address into my car's GPS. I then follow the instructions, and I arrive at the house at about three thirty in the afternoon. I am surprised. It is a dumpy little neighborhood in the older part of town. The houses are generally run down, and the yards are ugly. When I find Claude's house, I park across the street. I get out of the car, lock the doors, and walk up the oil-stained driveway to the front door, stepping over the children's toys that litter the front yard. I take a deep breath and ring the doorbell.

My heart beats a little faster, and I begin to perspire. *Christ, it must be a hundred degrees.* There is no answer, so I ring the doorbell again. Still no answer. The bastard isn't even home! I go back to my car, and I sit in the driver's seat with the window rolled down. I will wait until Claude arrives.

About a half hour passes, when a car finally pulls into the driveway. It is an old Ford that's missing a taillight and rear bumper, and smoke belches from its rusty exhaust pipe. The driver's door swings open, and a woman steps out. Then the other doors open, and Claude's three children pile out of the car. They are all elementary school age. The doors of the car all slam shut, and the wife and kids make their way to the front door and enter the house. I remain in my car, waiting. I have no bone to pick with Claude's wife or children, and I will wait for Claude. This is between Claude and me.

I wait for more than three hours until a pickup truck pulls into the driveway. Claude is not driving it; instead, he is in the backseat with another passenger. Claude opens his door and steps out of the truck. He looks like a different man. He is a mess. His hair is sweaty and disheveled, and he is wearing dusty work clothes stained with splotches of tar. His hands and face are grimy from laboring all day in the hot Arizona sun. Claude shuts the door, and the pickup backs out of the driveway and speeds off down the street toward its next destination. Claude walks to the front door and enters the house. This is not at all what I expected. I sit in my car for the next fifteen minutes, thinking.

I stare at the house, at the children's toys in the front yard, at the old Ford in the oil-stained driveway, at the weeds, at the rock garden, and at the half-dead cactus plant near the porch. "Damn," I say to myself, and I fire up my car and put it in drive. I then call you and tell you I'm on my way home, and you ask how things went with Claude. I tell you what happened, and you say that it is a big relief and that I made the right decision.

When I arrive home, it is late, and I go to bed.

The next morning, I go through the proposals I received from the other contractors for the roof, and I compare them. They are all about the same price, within a few hundred dollars of each other, and I decide to go with the roofer who was recommended to us by a friend. I call him, and he agrees to meet that afternoon. I tell him I expect a credit for the demolition Claude's guys did, as well as some kind of credit for the materials Claude delivered to our house.

The guy's name is Mike Thomas, and Mike agrees to give me the credit. It only amounts to a few hundred dollars, but I agree to it. I don't think Mike will rip me off. Mike then writes up a contract right there on the spot, and I sign it. Yes, this time, I read it carefully. It requires a 50 percent deposit for materials. Mike says a check will do, and I write him the check.

"We'll finish the demolition tomorrow," he says. "I'll have the materials delivered as soon as possible, and once they're delivered, we'll install the roof. It'll take just a few days, and you'll be good as new."

I say that sounds great, and sure enough, the next day, Mike's workers show up to complete the demolition. It takes them a couple of days. When the demolition is done, Mike calls me to discuss what they've found. They've found termites—not just a few of them but a ton of them, eating away at the roof rafters. "Never seen anything like it," Mike says. "All houses in Southern California have termites, but your house is like Grand Central Station!"

CHAPTER 9

THE IN-LAWS

I will return to the subject of the roof, but first, a memory. I remember the first time I met your parents. I was going to take you to the county fair. It was our first date. Just four days earlier, we had met at the beach, and within those four days, you broke things off with Rod Balzer. Your parents wanted to meet me before I took you out, and I arrived at your house at about four o'clock. Your home was in the nicer part of town, and I felt a little intimidated. Compared to my house, your house was like a castle. Compared to my parents, your parents were rich.

We all sat down in your front room, and your dad took charge of the meeting by saying, "So you want to take Samantha where?"

"To the county fair," I said.

"Sounds like fun," your mom said.

"I guess it sounds okay," your dad said.

"Jonathan has his own car."

"I saw it when he drove up."

"It's ugly but dependable," I said. "You won't have to worry about us breaking down."

"I certainly hope not."

"I just had the car serviced last week. They checked the brakes and changed the oil."

"Yes, yes, but tell us about yourself and your family," your dad said. He didn't seem to be interested in the reliability of my car. "What does your dad do for a living?"

"My dad is an advertising writer," I said.

"Ah, a writer."

"Where does he work?" your mom asked.

"Over in Costa Mesa."

"Which firm?" your dad asked. "Maybe we've heard of it."

"He works at Smith and Parry Associates."

"Never heard of them," your dad said. Then he squinted one eye and said, "Keeps a close eye on you?"

"I suppose so."

"Doesn't care for monkey business?"

"No, sir," I said.

"Good, good. Neither do I."

"What kind of ads does your dad write?" your mother asked.

"All kinds," I said.

"He must be clever."

"He is."

"Writing wasn't one of my favorite subjects," your dad said. "My favorite was auto shop."

"Auto shop?"

"Schools are different now," your mom said.

"I suppose so," your dad said. Then he asked me, "Do you plan to go to college?"

"Yes, I do," I said.

"Which one?"

"I'm not sure yet."

"What are you going to study?"

"I don't know for sure," I said. "A little of everything, I guess."

"I never went to college, and I did okay for myself," your dad said.

"Yes, sir."

"Samantha wants to go to college."

"I do," you said.

"She doesn't know which one or what she wants to study. Everyone wants to go to college these days, but they don't know what for."

"It's so expensive," your mom said.

"Makes you wonder," your dad said. "What exactly do they do with all that money?"

"I don't know," I said.

"Rod got a scholarship," your dad said to you. Then he looked at me and asked, "Do you know Rod Balzer?"

"I know who he is," I said.

"Good kid. Great football player."

"Please, Daddy," you said. You didn't want your dad talking about your ex-boyfriend. Your dad was embarrassing you.

"Just telling it like it is."

"I'm no longer seeing him," you said.

"Terrific quarterback," your dad said, ignoring you. Then he looked at me again. "Do you play any sports?"

"No," I said.

"None at all?"

"I mean, I play with my friends now and again, but I'm not on any school team."

"Your friends play football?"

"Now and then."

"Great sport. I'll tell you what. Rod Balzer has one hell of an arm. Do you go to your school's football games? Have you seen the boy in action? Never seen a high school kid with such an arm. He can really throw the ball."

"So I've heard," I said.

"The kid could be worth millions."

"He could," your mom agreed.

"I guess it will depend on how he does in college. It's very competitive. But I think Rod has what it takes. Rod's a winner. No doubt about that."

I felt like saying, "It's too bad the guy is a total asshole," but instead, I said, "Time will tell."

"Yes, yes," your dad said. "Time will tell."

"Tell us more about your parents. Does your mom work?" your mom asked me, changing the subject.

"She does," I said. "She's a nurse at a walk-in medical clinic."

"That sounds interesting."

"I went to one of those walk-in clinics once," your dad said. "I injured my leg playing tennis. I was playing against a real estate broker named Ed Burroughs. Was trying to shag down one of his lobs, and I twisted my leg. Christ, it hurt like hell. The doctor at the walk-in clinic diagnosed the injury as a hamstring. Then I went to a specialist, and he diagnosed it as a torn ACL. Makes you wonder, doesn't it? All that money they spend on their educations."

"Sometimes they make mistakes," I said.

"They're only human," your mom said.

"Feet of clay," your dad scoffed.

"What time do you want me to have Samantha home?" I asked. I didn't want to talk about doctors.

Your dad looked at you, and then he looked at me. "Have her home by midnight. No later."

"Okay," I said.

"Nothing good ever happens after midnight."

"No, sir."

"That was one thing I liked about Rod," your dad said, praising Rod again. "He always had Samantha home on time. Never late. Not ever. I could always trust Rod. I liked his father too. Great guy. First-rate family. Everyone in town likes the Balzers."

"We'll be home by twelve," I said confidently. "Probably a little earlier."

"That's fine."

"Let us know if you go somewhere other than the fair," your mom said to you.

"I'll let you know," you said.

"And answer your cell phone when we call."

"Okay," you said.

"Is your phone charged up?"

"It is," you said.

Then we left for the fair. It was our first actual date. "I think your dad would rather have Rod taking you out tonight," I said.

"He likes Rod," you replied.

"Do you think he likes me?"

"He'll get used to you."

And he did get used to me. In time. Little did he know back then that I was going to become his son-in-law. Little did he know I was going to need him. Little did he know I would depend on him.

Now back to the roof. Do you remember Mike? He's the roofer I hired to finish our roof job. We are talking about the termites he found.

"What do we need to do?" I ask.

Mike says it's too much for his workers to handle, but he knows a guy who specializes in this sort of work. "That's all he does," Mike says. The

67

guy's name is Jack Arnold. I say I'd like to meet with Jack, and Mike calls him for me.

Jack shows up the next morning, and he climbs up onto the roof to check things out. I hear him say, "Holy shit." Then he comes down off the roof and asks me, "How long have you owned this house?" I tell him when we bought it, and he shakes his head. "I'm surprised someone didn't see this when the house was inspected. You've got more termites in your roof rafters than the state of California has undocumented workers. Jesus, they're everywhere."

At first, I just stare at Jack. Does he say this to everyone, or is it really true? How would I know?

"Climb up here, and I'll show you," Jack says. "You should see for yourself." He then holds the ladder steady, and I climb up to the roof to see what he's talking about.

Sure enough, I can see the little creatures by the hundreds, making a meal of my home. Jack then pokes a screwdriver into several of the rafters to show me the damage they've done. "All these rafters will need to be replaced," he says.

It makes me sick to my stomach. First of all, I don't like bugs. But more than that, I am worried about how much this extra work is going to cost. I am already out thousands more than I planned just to put on the new roof, and now termites?

I ask Jack how much the work is going to cost me, and he says he will do the work for time and materials. "That way, you'll know you're paying for what you get, and I won't have to pad the price to cover my rear end. It's best for all of us. We'll get most of the termites, but you should also fumigate the house when we're done—you know, to catch the stragglers."

"When can you start work?" I ask.

Jack says he can start right away, so I sign a contract with him, and he is off to the races. The next day, his men show up, and for a week, they do their thing, banging and sawing. In the meantime, I arrange for a fumigation company to come out and tent the house when the termite work is done. It is all disturbing, and you and I stay in a nearby hotel for a couple of weeks. The hotel room and meals add even more to the cost. I have a bad feeling that this project is getting out of hand and that I should add up all the costs to see where we stand. But I don't. What's the use? Like it or not, we are in it for keeps, and there is no turning back.

Once the house is fumigated, we return home while Mike proceeds to install the new roof. In the meantime, the publisher who handled Nick Bliss's book has an autobiography project for someone else who requires a ghostwriter. They approach me with the idea, and I jump at it, hoping to get an advance that will cover the roof costs. It sounds too good to be true, and it is.

The man who wants the autobiography read my book about Nick, and he didn't like it. I have no idea why. The publisher tells me the man has opted for a different writer. No project and no advance. Now I will owe Mike thousands of dollars with no means to pay his bill.

"What are we going to do?" you ask, and I say I need to take out a home equity loan.

"People take out home equity loans all the time," I say. "It shouldn't be any problem."

I go to our bank and talk to a loan officer, and he has me fill out a long application. This idiot sits on the application for a week, and when he finally calls me, he says he has bad news. According to their underwriter, I owe too much on my credit cards to qualify. "You can apply at other banks," the loan officer says. "But you'll probably get the same result. They all tend to follow the same rules."

Now I am up a creek. The day after the bank turns down my loan, Mike finishes the roof. He has done a great job, and I don't have a single complaint. Two days after he finishes, he calls to meet with me to settle up and get paid. I am now desperate. Plain and simple, I don't have the money. Maybe this was by my own doing, and maybe not. It doesn't matter. I need the money, and I need it right away.

I sit down with you and explain the predicament again. You are calmer than I expected. Maybe you saw this coming the whole time. I don't know. I tell you I considered borrowing the money from my parents but couldn't bring myself to do it. They are barely getting by as it is. They never have had an abundance of money.

"We'll go to my dad," you say.

"I really don't want to do that," I say.

"We don't have a choice."

"He's going to think I'm a fool."

"He won't think you're a fool. These things happen."

"Well, he won't like it."

"He'll be happy to help us out."

I can think of nothing worse than owing my father-in-law money. For a number of reasons. But it appears I don't have a choice.

I meet with your father, and I explain what happened, telling him about Claude, the deposit money I paid, Claude's house in Phoenix, and the termites and then telling him how much money we need. He gives me a short lecture about being more careful in the future, and then he writes me a check for the full amount. We agree to a repayment plan that you and I can afford. I tell him I'll pay interest on the loan, and he says not to worry about it.

The next day, I pay Mike for the roof. He has no idea how close he came to not getting paid. Two months later, it rains cats and dogs, and we don't have a single leak. We are dry as a bone and in debt up to our ears to your dad.

CHAPTER 10

THE QUESTION MARK MURDERS

M oving a few months forward, you'd think that having just written a best-selling book about Nicholas Bliss, I'd have opportunities to write additional autobiographies and memoirs coming out of the woodwork. But they aren't, and here's what I discover: there are lots of talented writers in the world. I am but a drop in the bucket. Not having my name put on the cover of Nick's book was a big mistake. Only a handful of people even know who I am. I am the ghostwriter. I am the ghost.

Then an idea comes to me: Why not write a novel? I have always liked crime mysteries. So why not sit down and write one? If the mountain won't come to Muhammad, then Muhammad will come to the mountain.

I call the publisher of Nick's book, and I run the idea past him. I tell him I have a great story, which I do. He listens to the story and says he can't promise anything, but he will take a look at the manuscript when I am done with it. The man likes me, and I know he likes my writing. His name is Chet Turner. He says, "I'm not making any promises, but I can put you on the top of the pile." Well, that's good enough for me.

I tell you about my idea for the book, and you're supportive. You encourage me to go ahead with the project.

Step one is to come up with a catchy title, something that will capture the attention of readers. The title is important. A title can make or break a book, in my opinion. I sit down at my computer in the morning with a cup of coffee, and I come up with a list of possible titles. I don't really care for any of them. Then I come up with *The Question Mark Murders*. I like this. I do a search on the internet, and I cannot find a book with this same title. It's a good one, and I decide to use it. I open a file on my computer, and I start writing.

The story opens at a grisly murder scene in Orange County. A young woman's dead body is found in her apartment by a girlfriend. It has been lying on the floor for several days.

The woman's friend is supposed to meet with her on a Saturday. They are going to an art museum up in LA, but when the girlfriend stops by her friend's house to pick her up, there is no answer when she knocks on the apartment door. She figures her friend must've forgotten about going to the museum, and she goes back home to do other things.

She calls her friend later that night, but there is no answer. She calls her the next day, and still, there is no answer. When she calls the third day and no one picks up the phone, she goes to the apartment building and speaks to the landlord. She convinces the man to open her friend's door so she can check on her. That's when she finds the body.

The victim is still in her nightgown, and her throat has been slashed from ear to ear. She is lying on the floor in a pool of her own coagulated blood.

On the floor beside the woman's body is an envelope with a note inside. The note is a poem, brief and to the point. It has been printed out by a computer, but at the bottom of the poem is a handwritten question mark in red ink. The cryptic poem reads as follows:

> Here I am, the first of ten.
> I was once a pretty hen.
> Now I am stiff as a board,
> Head as hollow as a gourd.

The police detective put in charge of the case is Inspector Bill Hanover. The inspector and his team scour the apartment for clues, and they interview all the woman's friends, neighbors, and associates. They discover nothing that suggests a particular suspect or motive. The poem is useless except for the first line's mention of "the first of ten." Will there be nine more victims? Who knows?

The poem and the details of the murder are released to the press, along with a police hotline number. The authorities hope that something in the poem or the killing will hit home with someone, but the leads they receive are all dead ends.

Then, two weeks after the woman is murdered, there is a second killing. This murder involves an elderly woman who is found by her son, also with her throat slashed. She has been tied with rope to a chair, and the crime scene is even bloodier than the first. In the elderly woman's lap is an envelope containing another poem. Again, the poem has been printed out and signed with a red handwritten question mark. The poem reads as follows:

> Here she's sitting, number two.
> A bloody puzzle for you.
> Another trophy for me.
> Who will be my number three?

Detective Hanover reads the poem over and over, and the only thing he gets out of it is that there will likely be another murder. They find no clues at the crime scene. It is just like the first murder. There is nothing to go on. That's when the chief decides to call in the FBI. The chief is convinced the killer is a serial murderer, and the FBI agrees. They immediately assign Special Agent Smith to the case.

Smith is a hotshot thirty-five-year-old agent who has an extensive background in profiling. They hope he can put together a likely description of the killer, something they can release to the press along with the poems. Smith believes the public is still the best resource for solving the case. He believes someone out there will be able to help. He runs down every single lead that comes into the hotline, but the leads are taking him nowhere.

It isn't long before Smith is faced with the third killing. This time, the victim is a homeless alcoholic named Tim Thomas, who was camping recently in a Santa Ana public park. The local police are familiar with Tim, having arrested him several times for his drunken behavior.

Tim has been stabbed three times in the heart with a knife, and his body is discovered by four young boys playing hide-and-seek at the park. The body is found in the bushes, propped up against an oak tree. In the victim's lap is an envelope containing the third poem, also signed with a red question mark. The poem reads as follows:

What do you know about me?
You now know I'm number three.
I wish I could tell you more,
Like who will be number four.

As with the first two killings, there are no significant clues other than the poem. Agent Smith is stumped. There has to be something he is missing, but he can't think of what it is. For days, he goes over the facts and evidence. Over and over. Meanwhile, the press is stirring up the public over the murders. Who will be the next victim? Why can't the authorities nail down even one suspect?

I give you what I have written to get your opinion, and you read the first chapters. You seem to like the story. Of course, you are my wife. What else are you going to say? That it stinks? You seem to believe in me and my abilities, and while murder mysteries aren't really your thing, you say, "I can see how someone who likes this kind of stuff would be interested. And it is well written."

I need to find someone who is into murder mysteries, but I don't know of anyone offhand. I suppose I could have my publisher friend Chet Turner read it and give me his opinion, but I don't want him to read it until I'm done, until the mystery is solved. The whole fun in reading a murder mystery is discovering how it is solved. So I continue to write without any real feedback or guidance. I know I am a good writer. I figure that should be enough.

The fourth victim in the book is a fifty-nine-year-old man named Chester Winthrop. He is a hugely successful real estate developer who made his fortune by turning vacant Southern California land into office buildings and parking lots. The guy is loaded. They estimate his net worth at more than $50 million, and he lives in a waterfront mansion in Newport Beach. His twenty-one-year-old son, Abe, finds his father's body in the house on a Sunday morning, slumped over his desk with two bullet holes in his forehead.

Abe is Chester's only child, and Abe has been living in his dad's house all his life. Abe's mother died six years earlier from cancer, and Chester has been raising Abe on his own. The kid is devastated. He is out of control when Agent Smith arrives at the scene, and it takes a half hour to calm him down. Agent Smith has been called because of the envelope Abe found on his father's desk. Of course, the envelope contains another poem. Signed with a red question mark, the poem says,

No money or lots of money—
It doesn't matter to me.
We've told you there would be more.
Check me off as number four.

"It's like there's no rhyme or reason," Agent Smith says. He is getting frustrated. There are no clues other than the poem and the bullets in Chester's head. Agent Smith checks with Abe and the neighbors, and none of them heard any gunshots. The estimated time of the murder is two in the morning. "The killer must've used a silencer," Agent Smith says. "The window in the front room was wide open. That's how he must've gained entry. Other than that, we know nothing."

Abe isn't about to take this lying down. He is aware the FBI has been working on finding this particular murderer for weeks, and after talking to Agent Smith, he finds out they don't have a single viable suspect. He isn't exactly diplomatic when he tells Agent Smith, "If you morons can't find this killer, I'll hire someone who can. We're going to catch this sick bastard by hook or by crook."

Two days later, Abe meets with Ken Kennedy, Orange County's most renowned private investigator. Mr. Kennedy is well known for solving several local cases that baffled law enforcement authorities.

Abe offers Mr. Kennedy a fee of $1 million if he can prove beyond a reasonable doubt who killed his father. Abe can easily afford the fee since he has inherited the sum of his dad's $50 million estate. The deal he makes with Mr. Kennedy becomes headline news, and the spotlight is now shining on the private eye. In a way, Agent Smith likes this turn of events since it takes the attention away from him and his inability to solve the case. Then along comes murder number five.

The fifth victim is a middle-aged woman named Janet Swanson. She is an interior decorator who is found in her office, beaten and choked to death. Apparently, she was working late the night before. Her assistant finds the body in the morning when she arrives at work, and of course, alongside the body is an envelope containing another poem. "She didn't have an enemy in the world," the assistant keeps telling Agent Smith at the crime scene.

Agent Smith picks up the poem and reads it. Again, it is signed with a red question mark. It says,

> A chair, a table, a vase.
> Just look at my swollen face.
> Yesterday I was alive,
> But now I am number five.

Two days after they find the body of Janet Swanson, Mr. Kennedy calls Agent Smith. He gets right to the point. "I know who your killer is," he says. "If you're interested in catching him, I'll tell you precisely what to do. If you follow my instructions to the letter, not only will you have the proof you need to make an arrest, but you will prevent any more murders from taking place."

Agent Smith is skeptical, but he also knows of Mr. Kennedy's reputation. "What do you think we should do?" he asks.

"Shadow my client. Follow his every move twenty-four hours a day."

"Follow Abe?"

"He is your killer."

"The kid who hired you?" Smith asks. "That makes no sense. Why would the killer hire you?"

"You will see that it makes perfect sense. But there's no time to waste. You must put your men on him. Follow his every move. And your men need to be careful. Abe must have no idea he's being followed."

"I guess we can do that."

"He will try to kill again. You must catch him right before he commits the act."

"Who do you think he's going to kill?" Smith asks.

"I have no way of knowing."

"Then how do you know he's the killer?"

"I know," Mr. Kennedy says. "I'll explain it all to you after you've made your arrest."

As I said, Agent Smith is skeptical. But what choice does he have? He has no other leads to follow. He rounds up a team of agents, and they stake out Abe's house. Wherever Abe goes, the agents follow him. According to Mr. Kennedy, Abe will try to kill again. The men must be careful not to let a murder occur.

Four days later, the men see Abe leaving his house suspiciously at three in the morning. He climbs into his car and backs out of the driveway. He drives, and the men follow him. They drive around Orange County for about a half hour until Abe finally pulls up to an apartment building. He steps out of his car, and as he's walking toward the building, the agents apprehend him. On his person, they find a handgun with a silencer and an envelope. In the envelope is the sixth poem, written about the sixth victim, a male resident in the apartment building. The poem is signed with the telltale red question mark. Later, they check bullets fired from the handgun Abe was carrying with the bullets they found in Chester Winthrop's head, and the ballistics match. They have their man.

"You have to tell me how you knew," Agent Smith says to Mr. Kennedy.

"Nothing fancy," Mr. Kennedy says. "I just followed the evidence."

"But there was no evidence."

"Ah, but there was. The victims spoke to me."

"I don't understand."

"The pattern," Mr. Kennedy says. "It was the pattern."

"But there was no pattern," Smith says. "The victims were all random."

"And that's precisely what led me to suspect Abe."

"I still don't get it."

"According to your own interviews with the people who knew Abe and his father, the father was pretty tough on Abe. Maybe a little too tough. He didn't want his boy to be spoiled by the family wealth, so he made Abe earn his keep. He gave him next to nothing. He wanted his son to learn the value of a dollar, and he wanted him to be self-sufficient. He made Abe get a job to help pay for his college, and when he graduated, he made Abe pay his way for everything. He was allowed to live in the house for free, but he had to contribute his fair share for everything else.

"So here was Abe, living with a man worth fifty million, scraping together nickels and dimes for all he wanted. Abe did not appreciate it. He did not appreciate having to work nine to five at some mundane job just to pay his bills like a common man. In short, he wanted the old man's money, and he wanted it now. And that's when he came up with his plan."

"Plan to do what?" Smith asks.

"His plan to kill his father. With his dad out of the way, he would inherit everything. The fifty million dollars would be his to spend as he saw fit."

"That explains why he might kill his father. But what about all the others?"

"If he had just killed his father, he would have immediately become a suspect. But if he could make it look like his father was murdered by a serial killer, well, no one would suspect him. Thus, the other murders."

"So he was willing to kill ten people to become an heir?"

"Fifty million dollars is a lot of money. People have killed for a lot less."

"It's ingenious, isn't it?" Smith says.

"It was until he got overconfident and made his fatal mistake."

"Which was?"

"Which was hiring me to find the killer."

"But why did he hire you?"

"To make it seem even more likely that he had nothing to do with the murders. If he made himself seem hell-bent on finding the killer, who would suspect him?"

"So he hired you to make it all seem real."

"He didn't think I'd catch on. And to tell you the truth, I nearly didn't. Not until it dawned on me. I asked myself why the killings were all so random. I figured there had to be a reason for it. The murders were almost too random. I've learned over the years that there's always a reason behind murder. People don't just kill for no reason. The reason may be bizarre, or it may be quite calculated and rational, but there is always a reason. Abe was tripped up by his own guile. You might say he was too clever for his own good."

So ends *The Question Mark Murders*. I spend months on this story, writing and rewriting. I neglect my chores. I neglect you, my wife. And now, like a firework shot up into the sky, here comes the moment of truth. *Kaboom!* It will light up the landscape. Readers will love it, and critics will praise it. I am sure of this.

CHAPTER 11

SUZIE STONE

I am proud of *The Question Mark Murders*. I ask you to read the completed manuscript, and you do. You then say you like it. But you also say, "What do I know?"

I forward the file to Chet Turner, hoping he will talk his superiors into publishing the book. I have high hopes.

As promised, Chet reads the story right away. Then I get an email from him that says, "I read your manuscript with interest, but I'm sorry to say it's not quite right for us. This doesn't mean another publisher will feel the same, and I encourage you to submit it elsewhere. Thank you for letting me read your story."

That is it. It is the standard publisher brush-off. I call Chet and try to get more feedback out of him. I can tell I am making him uncomfortable by pressing the issue. It is clear: he just doesn't like it.

For the next six months, I send query letters for the book out to different publishers. I am sure at least one of them will see promise in the story. But all of them send me polite rejection notices just like Chet's. I soon come to the realization that no one is going to publish the book. All those hours I spent writing day and night—for what? A stack of rejection slips?

It is difficult for me to do, but I tell you what a flop the book is one night over dinner. I think you mean well when you say, "Maybe you should get a real writing job. Something that pays. Something that guarantees you a byline. Something everyone can sink their teeth into." By *everyone*, I think you mean you, me, and our families. You are telling me that for the general peace of mind of everyone, including myself, I need to find real employment. I need to be earning a living.

You are straightforward and practical. I always have liked that about you. You never were big on self-pity or chasing unrealistic dreams.

Then, as though it is written right into the script, along comes a phone call from my publishing friend Chet Turner. Maybe he just feels guilty for turning down my book, or maybe he is serious when he says I have a real talent for telling stories about people. "Forget about *The Question Mark Murders.* Your book about Nick Bliss is a work of art. You should be writing about people. You should be writing biographies and autobiographies." Chet then goes on to tell me about a magazine publisher friend of his named Ernest Carroll. Ernest is the publisher of *Orange Life Magazine.* He asks me if I've heard of it, and I tell him yes. Who in Orange County hasn't heard of *Orange Life Magazine?*

Chet tells me there's a job opening at the magazine for a journalist such as myself to write their celebrity bios. Each month, the magazine picks out a local celebrity and does a feature article about the lucky person. People read the bios. People look forward to them. They are probably the most popular feature of the publication.

Chet gives me Ernest's phone number, and I call the man. He is expecting my call. Chet has told him all about me. We set up a time for me to be interviewed in a week. This will give Ernest time to read my book about Nicholas Bliss.

When we finally get together, I am surprised at what I see. I guess with the magazine being what it is, I expect Ernest to look youthful, handsome, and physically fit. Instead, he is short and overweight and has lost most of his hair. His nose is large, and his eyes are too small. He stands up from his desk to shake my hand. I notice his hands are soft and clammy. "You must be Jonathan," he says. "Pull up a chair, and take a seat."

"Thanks," I say, and I pull up a chair.

"Just got done reading your book." There is a copy of Nick's book on his desk. "Fine job you did."

"Thanks," I say.

"Your subject pops right out of the pages."

"Thanks," I say again.

"Has Chet told you much about who we're looking for?"

"He said you need someone to write your monthly bios."

"Yes, yes. We need this person right away. Our previous bio writer quit last month. Took a job with the *Wall Street Journal*. Can't say I blame her for taking the new job, but we were totally unprepared for her departure. We need to replace her now."

"I understand," I say.

"Are you available?"

"I can start yesterday," I say.

"Perfect," Ernest says.

"How much does the job pay?"

"The pay, of course. And all the benefits. We have good benefits. We take good care of our writers." Ernest tells me how much the job pays, and he lists all the company benefits. It is a better deal than I thought it would be. I'm certainly not going to get rich, but the pay isn't bad at all.

"I'll take the job," I say.

"Good, good," Ernest says. "Becky will show you to your desk." Becky is Ernest's administrative assistant. "Task one is to write a bio about Suzie Stone. She is going to be on the cover of our July issue. Becky will give you her phone number, and you'll need to call Suzie to arrange an interview. The sooner the better. July will be here before we know it."

"Yes," I say.

"Have you read the bios in our previous issues?"

"I have," I say.

"Then you know what I'm looking for?"

"Yes," I say. "I know what to do."

"Good, good," Ernest says. "Then hop to it."

I stand up, shake Ernest's clammy hand again, and then leave his office. I find Becky, and she shows me to my desk and gives me Suzie Stone's phone number.

When I call Suzie Stone, I address her as Ms. Stone. She laughs and tells me to call her Suzie. "How old are you?" she asks. Her voice is raspy.

"I'm twenty-five," I say.

"Young."

"I guess so."

"Do you feel qualified to write a bio about a seventy-one-year-old woman?"

Her question takes me aback. Is she questioning my competence? "I'll do my best," I say.

"I'm sure you will," she says. "Do you know where I live?"

"In Newport Beach," I say.

"Get my address from Becky, and meet me here tomorrow morning. Not too early. Ten o'clock would be good."

"Okay," I say.

"You have a nice voice," she says. "Do you look as good as your voice sounds?"

"I wouldn't know," I say.

Suzie laughs. Then she asks, "Are you married?"

"I am," I say.

"Too bad," she says.

This embarrasses me. Is she actually coming on to me? I don't know. I've had little experience with women in their seventies.

"I'll see you tomorrow," I say.

The next morning, I arrive at her house at ten. It takes her a while to answer the door. When the door swings open, I recognize her immediately. She looks like Suzie Stone, except older. "Come in," she says. Her voice is even raspier than it was when we spoke on the phone, probably because it is morning.

She is dressed in a bathrobe and slippers, but her hair is nicely done, and she is wearing makeup. I follow her into her living room, and she tells me to take a seat on her sofa. Then she sits beside me. "Don't be afraid," she says. "I bark, but I don't bite."

I laugh. I don't know why I laugh. I don't really know what she's talking about. Is she going to bark? That would be kind of weird. I open up my notebook and click my pen. "Are you ready?" I ask.

"As ready as I'll ever be. How old did you say you were?"

"Twenty-five," I say.

"So young," she says, looking up at the ceiling and then back at me. "Well, ask your young questions. What do you want to know about me? I'm an open book."

"How long have you lived in Orange County?"

"For around ten years."

"Have you been living in this same house all ten years?"

"I have. I built the house after I divorced my fifth husband. I built the house for myself. I had no plans to get married again."

"You lived up in LA previously?"

"Mostly LA. Mostly Beverly Hills."

"What made you pick Newport Beach?"

Suzie stares at me for a moment. Then she says, "Are these really the questions you want to ask me?"

"Why?" I ask.

"Why don't we just get to the meat?"

"The meat?"

"Your readers aren't going to care why I picked Newport to live in any more than they're going to care about what I eat for dinner every night. You want to entertain your readers? Ask me about my marriages."

"Your marriages?" I act surprised, but she is right. Even I am curious. She has been married and divorced six times. In fact, this is what she's best known for. As for her movies, she's never been in a film that anyone really cares about, and her acting skills are average at best. But her marriages! She has hit the nail on the head. She's a pro. Everyone is going to want to read about her opulent weddings, her six Hollywood husbands, and her six well-publicized divorces.

So we talk about them.

Husband number one was a movie studio executive named Brad Chester. Poor guy. "He was really crazy about me," Suzie says. "I broke the man's heart. When we met, I was eighteen, and he was thirty-six. He was going to make a star out of me. I was beautiful back then. Brad had me take acting lessons from a friend of his at the studio, and a year after we were married, he got me a role in my first movie, *Man without a Name*. Maybe you've seen it. I played the sister of the main character. The main role was played by Cameron Able. The movie was about a man who had amnesia. It wasn't exactly an original idea. It did lousy at the box office, but I didn't care. It was a movie, and I was in it.

"It was during the filming that I got to know Cameron. God, was he handsome! And he was such a nice man, and one thing led to another. I fell in love with him. Poor Brad. The poor sap put me in a movie that eventually destroyed our marriage. After Brad and I were divorced, I began to date Cameron openly. And the next thing I knew, he asked me to marry him, and of course, I said yes. We were so in love. We couldn't get enough of each other."

"Did you ever love Brad?" I ask.

"I thought I did. But I was young. I didn't really know what love was."

"But he loved you."

"I'm sure he did."

"So what happened with Cameron?"

"We were fine for a few years. It was a good marriage as far as marriages go. We bought a nice home in Beverly Hills, and we went to a lot of parties. We were also in a couple movies together, but they were nothing to write home about. If I told you what they were, you probably wouldn't recognize them.

"Then, about the fourth year of the marriage, Cameron began to feel depressed. He was acting in movies, but they were all second-rate films. He wasn't able to land a leading role in anything substantial. He wanted people to take him seriously. This was a great disappointment to him. He had always thought of himself as a very good actor, yet he was going nowhere. At least that's how he saw it. Then he began to drink a lot. The booze was a problem, and he would show up to work drunk. He would get in arguments with directors over petty matters, and then he would come home and get in arguments with me. He began to accuse me of having affairs with other men, which wasn't true. It got bad. It got so bad that I began threatening to leave him. This just made things worse, and finally, I walked out the door. I couldn't take it anymore. I deserved better. I filed for divorce, and six months later, I was free again."

"Then along came husband number three?" I ask.

"Yes," Suzie says.

"And this was Burke Epstein?"

"Good old Burke."

"The screenwriter?"

"Yes," Suzie says.

"How did you meet Burke?"

"We met at a party in Malibu. It wasn't exactly love at first sight. He was such an odd-looking man. He had about as much charisma as a doorknob, but he was so smart. And his intellect intrigued me. People listened when he spoke, and everyone seemed to be impressed by him.

I remember when I first heard him talking, I had no idea what he was talking about. It was something about gestalt theory and modern cinema. But I was hooked. I'd never met anyone quite like him.

"We were in a small group, but he seemed interested only in me. That's how it felt. There was a real connection. Then he said, 'You look like you could use some fresh air. Would you like to join me outside?' I nodded, and he grasped my hand and led me out to the patio overlooking the ocean. I remember exactly what he said. He said, 'Suzie Stone, I think I'm in love with you.' Just like that, right? He really threw me for a loop, but I didn't run off. I agreed to go out with him on a date the following night. And we continued to date, and he continued to fascinate me. He was kind to me. He made me feel smart. No man I ever dated made me feel so intelligent. Then we got married, and let me tell you something about marriage. You think you know the truth about a person, and then you get married. Then you learn. Then your eyes are opened."

"Opened to what?" I ask.

"Opened to the truth," Suzie says. "I didn't see Burke for what he was right away. But I learned. Oh hell, did I ever learn."

"What did you learn?"

"That I married a pervert. At first, it was just us. It was the things he wanted me to do. Weird stuff. You know, kinky stuff. Not my style. I figured, *Fine. I can overlook this.* But then came the girlfriends."

"Girlfriends?"

"The creep had a whole list of girlfriends who would do anything he asked. I found his list. It was buried in his top desk drawer, under a mess of papers. There were phone numbers for all of them. I didn't feel so much hurt as I felt dirty. This filthy little man was my husband! I kissed him. I shared a bed with him. I made a copy of the list, and I gave it to a private detective. My instructions were clear: I wanted enough evidence for a divorce and a fat settlement. Six months later, I was free."

"I never knew any of this," I say.

"Now you know."

"You don't mind if we print it?"

"Not at all. Maybe it will keep other young girls from making the same mistake. Maybe they'll be more careful before they agree to get married.

I was naive. I was dumb. I should've never married the man, God rest his soul. He died, you know. Three years ago."

"I guess this brings us to husband four."

"Randy Williams. The musician."

"When did you marry Randy?"

"About three years after I divorced the pervert."

"And you loved Randy?"

"I truly did. Wonderful man. Straightforward, considerate, and sweet as a Valencia orange. For years, we were good together. He killed himself, you know. Committed suicide. Never understood it. He always seemed so happy and content. Just goes to show that you never know."

"And husband number five?"

"Bart Hanlon."

"Another movie actor."

"Yes," Suzie says.

"What was wrong with him?"

"He cheated on me. I didn't make any effort to make things work. I wasn't a young girl anymore. I figured, *Hell, you want to play around, then do it. But leave me out of it.* He didn't put up much of a fight to keep us together."

"And finally, husband six."

"Ralph Perkins."

"The contractor?"

"Yes, he was a building contractor. He did some work on my house, and I came to like him a lot. Don't ask me why I married him. Deep down, I knew it would never last. He was beer, and I was champagne. But he was obsessed with me, and he wouldn't leave me alone. He was so good to me. He was such a hard worker. And he was a nice-looking man. But after the first year, I asked myself, 'Is this really what you want for the rest of your life?' The answer was no. So I told him I wanted a divorce, and I broke the poor man's heart. But I couldn't bear to live a lie. Like I said, I don't know what the heck got into me when I agreed to marry him."

"What happened to him after the divorce?"

"He married someone else. A nice woman. I think his marriage is going fine."

"Do you ever hear from him?"

"He calls me now and again to see how I'm doing. He says he still loves me."

"I feel kind of sorry for him," I say.

"So do I."

Chapter 12

That's More like It

The Suzie Stone article is a big success, and lots of praise comes my way. Even your parents seem to be pleased at the direction my career is taking. We have a meat loaf dinner at your parents' house and share a copy of the magazine. Your dad reaches over, pats me on the back, and says, "That's more like it." He pats me on the back so hard that I nearly spit my mouthful of meat loaf across the table.

Meanwhile, things are moving along nicely for you at work. You've finally been put in charge of your own project, and your boss, Edwin Taylor, gives you a healthy pay raise to coincide with your increased responsibilities. I am proud of you. You have been given the Chatsworth house. Kaleb Chatsworth is your client, and he is building a new house in Laguna Beach, overlooking the Pacific Ocean. The hilltop lot cost him a fortune. Kaleb has money to burn. He recently sold the controlling interest in his high-tech company for God knows how many millions and is retiring at age thirty-nine. "He'd make a good subject for one of your bios," you say to me. You're probably right.

As the weeks go by, you become more and more consumed with this project, working long days, meeting with Kaleb, going over your drawings, and making revisions upon revisions. What began as an exciting opportunity for you has turned into an obsession. It's all you do and all you talk about. Sometimes you bring home your drawings to show me what you're doing, and you try to explain them to me. It is intriguing, but I don't have any idea what you're talking about half the time. I've never been that good at translating abstract things, such as drawings, into concrete realities. It's not that I'm dumb. It just isn't in my wheelhouse.

While you are working on Kaleb's house, I am working on a bio of Jeffrey Walker, the football quarterback. When he retired from football, he made his home in Huntington Harbor. The guy made a fortune by avoiding tackles and throwing the football, and he's one of those guys people love to love. I don't know that much about him when I start writing his bio, but the more I learn, the more I like the guy. I mean, he has enough money to do whatever he wants, and what is he doing with his life and his money? He is feeding it back into the crazy society that made him rich. He is one of those rare men who amassed a financial fortune and then decided he didn't really have to hoard it all. I've never met anyone like him. All the people I know consider themselves deserving of every nickel and dime they've been able to finagle out of every life circumstance. Oh, they'll give a little here and there to appease their conscience, to prove they're good people, but they seldom go all in. Jeffrey has gone all in. I get worn out just listening to him describe all the charities he's involved in.

Meanwhile, while working on Kaleb's house, you often put in late hours. We don't eat dinner together as often as usual. When we are together, we talk about your work. You are excited about it, and I try to share your enthusiasm. But it's as if you're drifting rapidly into another world. Do you know what I mean by this? I don't think you do. I don't think you can see it. I try to bring you down to earth, and I talk about Jeffery Walker. I tell you what he's been doing for disadvantaged kids in the lower-income neighborhoods of Orange County and what a difference he's been making in their lives, but you aren't listening. I can tell you're not listening. Then you open your mouth to speak, and I'm sure you haven't been listening. You want to talk about roof tiles. Kaleb is insisting that all his roof tiles be imported from Italy. He's been in contact with a supplier who is chomping at the bit to provide the tiles for the house.

"We can't decide," you say.

"Decide what?" I ask.

"Haven't you been paying attention?"

"I think I have."

"Kaleb can't decide if he wants the tiles from Northern Italy or if he wants the Tuscan tiles."

"What's the difference?"

"The Tuscan tiles have redder coloring in them."

"Does Kaleb want that?"

"He's not sure. The tiles need to complement the color of the stucco."

"And what color is the stucco?"

"We haven't decided yet."

"Well, someone is going to have to make up their mind."

"There are also a lot of ceramic tile accents around the windows that need to blend with the stucco color."

"I would go with the Northern Italy tiles," I say, as if I know what I'm talking about. "Red tile roofs in California are a dime a dozen."

"These tiles are hardly a dime a dozen."

"No, I suppose not."

"These are all handmade tiles. They can be up to a hundred years old. They were molded over the artisan's legs."

"Really?"

"Each and every tile."

"I never knew that," I say.

"Of course, there are also the Southern Italian tiles. They haven't been completely ruled out. They're harder to find and a little more expensive."

"What color are they?"

"They have a salmon hue. Kaleb isn't sure if he likes that color. 'Salmon belongs on a dinner plate,' Kaleb says. But like I said, it's going to depend on the color of the stucco and ceramic tile accents."

"It sounds complicated."

"It is," you say. You go back to eating your dinner. I can tell you're now deep in thought, so I try not to disturb you.

It sounds innocent enough, right? Roof tiles, stucco, and ceramic tile accents. There's not much for me to be jealous of. But am I jealous? Maybe *jealous* isn't the right word. What would you call it?

Two days later, Kaleb takes you on a field trip. He picks you up from our home in his big Mercedes, and the two of you drive all over Southern California, looking at big houses. You got the list of houses from the greedy tile supplier. The houses you will be looking at provide examples of the different Italian roof tiles so Kaleb can get an idea in person of what the tiles look like on real homes.

I am disturbed by this field trip. I don't like the idea of my wife driving around with this rich and successful man in his expensive, leather-upholstered German car. Maybe you'll stop for lunch and even dinner like a newlywed couple searching for their first house. I know you're just his architect, but my mind plays tricks on me. And that car! We can barely afford your Toyota. What a letdown it's going to be the next morning when you drive to work in your Corolla after having spent a day in Kaleb's shiny Mercedes. If only you had married a businessman rather than a journalist. I, your husband, only write about people like Kaleb. I will probably never be one of them.

Three days after the field trip, you and Kaleb meet with the roof supplier again. You tell him which houses you liked, and now better informed, the supplier produces photographs of a house up in Santa Clara County. He provided the tile for it, and the house looks perfect.

"That's exactly what I had in mind," Kaleb says. "We need to see this house in person. We need to fly up there pronto."

You agree, and the two of you book a flight to see the house for yourselves. So now you're traveling on a plane together. I don't like it at all, but I don't say anything to you. I keep my lame jealousy to myself. Kaleb picks you up at our house early in the morning for this second field trip. You are dressed very nice, and this bothers me. Are you trying to impress Kaleb? You look attractive, and you smell good. "Have a good time," I say as you leave. As you drive off, I kick at the air. "Fucking roof tiles," I say. "I'd be happy never to hear about roof tiles again."

It isn't the sex. It's the money. I don't think you're physically attracted to Kaleb, but I do think you're intrigued by his money. Maybe even aroused. I've noticed the way you talk about him. You say that he's a perfectionist and demanding and that he's a man who knows what he wants. "That's probably why he was so successful with his business," you say. "He's just that kind of man."

I think to myself, *That kind of man? You mean a man unlike me? Unlike the mediocre man you chose to live the rest of your life with? Unlike the man who wrote a book that no one wants to publish?*

That damn book! How many tries does it take? When will my name on the cover of a manuscript mean something to publishers? When will my name sell books? When will the public say to themselves, "Oh, Jonathan Hart—have you heard? He has a new book out. I can't wait to read it. He's one of my all-time favorite authors! That guy must be worth a fortune!"

I have a dream several days after your plane trip with Kaleb. It is a nightmare that begins while I am driving my car. I am up in the mountains, speeding along a winding road. I am driving a convertible with the top down, and the wind is whipping through my hair. The tires screech as I speed through the turns. To my left is a cliff that falls hundreds of feet down into a valley, but I am not afraid. Faster and faster I go, passing cars and skidding around turns, until I begin to lose control.

I jerk on the steering wheel, but the car is not cooperating. Then the road begins to move under me like a slippery river of dirty black asphalt. Finally, completely out of control, I crash through the guardrail at my left, and I go soaring off the cliff. I am up high in the sky, and it occurs to me that maybe I can fly. *I've flown before. Yes, I remember flying!* I unbuckle my seat belt and jump out of the falling car. The car continues to plummet toward the valley like a falling star, but me? Yes, I am flying! I'm not flapping my arms like a bird; instead, I am doing the breaststroke, as if I'm swimming in water, staying afloat.

For a while, I fly through the sky, enjoying myself, but then I grow bored. I decide to land, and I gradually glide down toward the valley below, toward the tops of the trees. As I look for a place to land, I fly lower and lower until I spy a clearing amid the forest. I hold out my arms and drop toward the clearing, when suddenly, I stop midair. It is as if I am snagged right out of the sky!

I am suspended twenty or so feet above the ground, and right away, I know what happened. I flew into a spiderweb. The strands of the web are thick and sticky, and the more I wriggle to get free, the worse I become entangled in the webbing. It is stuck to my feet, arms, torso, and head. I fight like crazy to get out of it, but it is no use. Finally, I stop wriggling and try to catch my breath.

I look to my right, and I see her approaching: a disgusting, hairy spider about three times my size. She crawls across the webbing like a macabre ballerina across a creaky dance floor, and when she arrives before me, she stops and stares at me. She is hideous and terrifying, and her human mouth is smiling. She has lips and teeth just like a human's. When she finally speaks, a thin line of drool falls from the corner of her mouth and lands on the webbing.

"Welcome," she says. "I've been waiting for you."

"Please untangle me," I say. "Be a good gal, and set me free."

The spider just laughs.

"Please," I say again, but the spider ignores me.

"A fine little feast you'll make for me this evening," she says. "Hold still. This won't hurt a bit." The spider then proceeds to crawl over me, squirting strings of webbing from her spinnerets and wrapping me up, turning me over and over with her creepy, spindly legs. She spins me around until I am enveloped in a cocoon of silk, with only my head poking out at the top. I cannot move. I am wrapped up tight.

"Please," I say again, but the spider continues to ignore me. She drags me across the web and into her lair, where she lays me on her kitchen table. She then crawls on all eight legs into her family room, where she has the TV turned on to a movie. I can't see the TV from where I am, but I can hear the sound and see the spider sitting on her sofa.

"You're a fan of old monster movies, no?" the spider asks, and I say yes, I am.

"It sounds like you're watching *Frankenstein*," I say.

"The original," she says. "The 1931 version with Boris Karloff. Nothing like it. It's one of my favorites. I could watch this movie a hundred times and never grow tired of it."

"No, no, this is all wrong," I say.

"Wrong?" you ask. Yes, it's your voice! You are the spider. I'm certain of that now. You rub your chin with the tip of one of your eight legs and smile. You remove a carton of milk from your refrigerator and pour a glass for yourself. Then you stand there drinking your milk and thinking. Finally, you say, "Okay, so you've figured it out."

"Let me loose," I say.

I look at you. You now have a syringe in your hand, and you set down your milk and step toward me. You are evil. You jab me in the arm with the needle. "One shot of this will liquefy all your internal organs," you say. "By dinnertime, I'll be able to suck them from the top of your head with a straw like a warm milkshake."

"No, no, please!" I cry, but you just laugh. Someone has to help me. Someone! Anyone! I cry again, "No, no, please, no!" You're still laughing.

Then I wake up in bed, yelling, with you shaking my arm. "What the heck are you dreaming about?" you ask.

"Please!" I plead.

You stop shaking me when you see my eyes open. "You were having a bad dream," you say.

"A dream?"

"Yes, a dream."

"Wow," I say. "It seemed so real."

"What was it about?"

"You, I think."

"Me?" you ask, laughing.

"But I can't remember any of it," I say. I am lying, of course. I remember every detail, but the last thing I'm going to tell you is that I just envisioned you as a hairy, man-eating spider.

CHAPTER 13

THIRTY YEARS

"Where did the time go?" my dad says. It is my parents' thirtieth wedding anniversary. Along with my brother, we have taken them out to dinner to celebrate. Lewis has brought along his girlfriend, Shari. Mom and Dad are now in their early fifties, and Lewis is twenty-one. I'm not sure how old Lewis's girlfriend is. We are at Mom and Dad's favorite restaurant, Alberto's, and we have just ordered drinks.

"How does it feel?" you ask my parents.

"To be married thirty years?" my dad asks.

"Yes," you say.

"Jeez," Lewis says. "I can't imagine being married one year, let alone thirty."

"It's been a lot easier than I thought it would be," my dad says, ignoring Lewis.

"Maybe you have the perfect marriage," I say.

"Well, not exactly perfect. But durable."

"What is your secret?" you ask my dad.

My dad gets a serious look on his face and says, "There are many components to a durable marriage. I'm not sure I would say there's a single secret."

"I would agree with that," my mom says.

"My parents say honesty is important," Shari says.

"Yes," my mom says to Shari. "That's a good one. Honesty is important. You have to be able to trust your partner, and there is no trust without honesty."

"Are you guys always honest with each other?"

"We try to be," my dad says.

"And we talk," my mom says.

"Talking is important," my dad says. "The more you talk, the better off you are. You must learn how to talk about everything under the sun."

"And you must learn to be tolerant," my mom says.

"Yes," my dad says.

"Tolerant of what?" Shari asks.

"Of each other," my mom says. "You learn that you're two individuals. You learn to love each other for what you are and try not to make each other what you want each other to be. So many marriages fail because people try so hard to change their partners. I've seen it happen so many times."

"Yes," my dad says. "I agree."

"What do you tolerate with Dad?" Lewis asks Mom. "What does he do that you wish he didn't do?"

"Sports," my mom says.

"Sports?"

"When we were first married, your father had no interest in sports. And neither did I. But now? He watches them all the time. He sits on the couch with his beer and potato chips, glued to the TV for hours."

"I like watching sports," my dad says.

"I know you do."

"What does Mom do that you don't like?" I ask my dad.

"She talks on the phone," Dad says, laughing. "Especially with her mother and sister. For hours on end. They have an opinion on everything. They talk and talk."

"We like to talk."

"I know you do."

"Do you have common interests?" Shari asks my parents.

"Good question," my dad says. Then he looks at my mom and asks, "Do we like any of the same things?"

"We both like eating out."

"Well, I think you like it more than I do," my dad says.

"I don't like having to cook every night."

"And you like being served."

"Yes," my mom says. "I do like being served. I get sick of being the one who does all the serving."

"But restaurants are expensive," my dad says.

"They're worth it."

"That's a matter of opinion."

My mom looks up at the ceiling for a moment and then says, "I know something else we both like to do."

"What?" I ask.

"We both like to watch *American Idol*."

"That's true," my dad says.

"We like to guess who's going to win."

"Although we always root for different contestants."

"That's because you have no ear for music," my mom says.

"Of course I have an ear. You don't know what you're talking about."

"We also watch *Young Sheldon*."

"Yes," my dad says. "That kid cracks me up."

"And we both like walking the dog."

"But not at the same time," my dad says. "You walk too fast. I prefer to take my time."

"I like a brisk walk."

"And I like to take my time. Stop and smell the flowers, I say. You're always in such a rush to get from point A to point B. Hurry, hurry, hurry."

Just then, our waitress arrives with the drinks. She sets the drinks on the table and then takes our dinner orders. Mom orders a filet mignon medium rare, and Dad rolls his eyes. Mom notices and says, "So what's wrong with a filet mignon?"

"You order the same thing every time we go out. Filet mignon. Medium rare. Like a broken record. You'd think that's all they serve."

"I like a filet mignon," my mom says.

"There are other things on the menu."

"Every time I order something other than my steak, I don't like it. Why would I want to spoil my dinner by ordering something I don't like?"

"That's the whole fun of eating at a restaurant," my dad says. "Trying new things. Being adventurous. Being surprised. I like trying new dishes."

"Not me," my mom says to all of us. Then, looking at my dad, she asks, "What are you going to order?"

"I don't know," my dad says. "Maybe the duck."

"The duck?"

"It's right here," my dad says, as if Mom didn't bother to read the selections. He points to the item on his menu by tapping his finger on it.

"Too greasy," my mom says. "And I don't care for sauces. I like my meat plain."

"I think I'll try the salmon," Shari says.

"That looks good to me," Lewis says.

"What's wrong with having salmon?" my dad asks my mom. "Why don't you try the salmon?"

"Too fishy."

"Salmon isn't fishy."

"Of course it is," my mom says. "It's fish, isn't it? How could fish not be fishy?"

Finally, everyone orders his or her dinner, and the waitress walks away. We are all quiet for a moment, and then my dad breaks the silence. He looks around at us and says, "Family."

"Family of what?" I ask.

"Just that," he says. "Just family."

"What does that mean?"

"That's the secret," my dad says. "You asked what the secret was to a successful marriage, and that's the answer. That's the real answer. That's what it all boils down to in the long run. It all comes down to family."

"Meaning?"

"Do you want to have a durable marriage? Do you want a marriage that will last you a lifetime? Then commit! With all your heart, you must dedicate yourself to your family. There's no other answer. Think family. Eat, breathe, and swim in it. And guard it with your life."

"I guess that makes sense," I say.

"I like that advice," you say to my dad, and you place your hand atop mine. Family means a lot to you. I know this. It means a lot to me as well.

Then Shari asks my dad, "What about love?"

"Love?" my dad says.

"You haven't mentioned love."

"Ah, the great four-letter word. The push of a finger that sends the dominoes toppling."

My mom laughs.

"But what about it?" Shari asks. "Isn't love essential for a successful marriage?"

"I guess it's impossible to talk about marriage without talking about love," Dad says. "But as an essential ingredient to a successful marriage? I'm not so sure. Look at us. Sure, once upon a time, we fell in love, and falling in love is wonderful. There's nothing like it in the world. The world suddenly sparkles and shimmers. The sky is bluer than blue. The birds in the trees sing symphonies for you, and the future looks as promising and bright as a burning summer sun.

"But it doesn't last, at least not with the same intensity as it started with. It's kind of a flash in the pan. It's a bolt of lightning. It's a Fourth of July firework. *Boom*—and then it's gone. It burns itself out, and like all things that burn themselves out, it leaves only a trail of warm embers. Nice maybe, but not the same. The thrill runs out of the room. And in the resulting calmness, we wake up. We look around. We survey our surroundings, and we discover what we've done. In the heat of our relentless love, we've made a commitment to live with another human being for the rest of our lives. We've agreed to a contract. We've purchased a license. We've pushed all our chips into the center of the table. We've gone all in.

"Then we examine with clearer vision the person we have chosen, and slowly but surely, we see who they are. We see them flossing food out of their teeth, clipping their thick toenails, cleaning their ears, and stinking up the bathroom. Where there was once a god or a goddess, now there is a human being—a sweating, itching, sour-smelling lump of flesh with arms, legs, a head, and ideas of its own. Then, and only then, do we commence with that activity we refer to as marriage. That's what it's all about. So love? Maybe it is love, and maybe it isn't. If it's still love, it's a very different kind of love."

Dad stops talking, and everyone is quiet. Then Mom says, "It can be very rewarding."

"In its own way," my dad says.

"Thirty years is a long time," my mom says.

"Thirty years," my dad says, now deep in thought. "Did we ever tell you kids how we first met?"

"No," I say.

Lewis shakes his head. He hasn't heard this story either.

"We were in high school."

"We were," my mom says.

My dad looks at my mom and then says, "When we first met, your mom wanted little to do with me. Getting her interested in me took some effort. You should know that I had my sights set on her before we even met. I'd seen her around the school, and she intrigued the heck out of me. Then it was fair to say I grew obsessed with her. You should've seen your mom in high school. God, she was beautiful. I felt drawn toward her like I'd never been before to any other girl. She had long golden hair that cascaded over her shoulders, her skin was like honey, and her eyes were brown like a pair of chocolate candies. And her face was the face of an angel from heaven, always smiling, always beaming, and always showing off her perfect white teeth. Every time she smiled, my heart would do flip-flops inside my chest. I could feel it somersaulting. It drove me crazy that I didn't know her better, and I schemed up ways to bump into her and introduce myself. There had to be some way we could get to know each other! But how? That was the big question.

"We didn't hang out with any of the same kids, and we didn't have classes together. Our lockers weren't even in the same hallways, and she lived way on the other side of town. But I kept my eyes on her. I came to know everything I could about her. I knew where her classes were, and I knew where she ate lunch every day. She always ate near the art buildings, always at the same outdoor table in the shade of a big oak tree. She always sat in the exact same spot. The problem was that her girlfriends were always there with her, and she was never alone. Well, almost never.

"One day, for some reason, her friends didn't show up, and she was eating her lunch by herself. Jesus, I remember how nervous I was. I was scared to death, but I also knew I would probably never have a better chance to introduce myself. Me, her dumb secret lover from afar! I finally mustered up the courage to approach, and walking up to the table, I said, 'Excuse me. May I sit with you?'

"You should've seen the look on her face, as if saying, 'Who the hell are you?' I told her my name, and she said yes, I could sit. 'It's a free country,' she said. 'I guess you can sit wherever you want.'

"She had been reading a book while eating, and I asked her what she was reading. She said it was a book of poems by Emily Dickinson, and

I had no idea who Emily Dickinson was. The truth was that you could have put all I knew about poetry on the head of a pin, and I figured she must have been reading the stupid book for her English class. 'My teacher made us read Edgar Allan Poe,' I said. 'We had to read "The Raven." It was supposed to be such a great poem, but I couldn't make heads or tails of it. I mean, it made sense after the teacher explained it to us, but what the heck? Why would you spend so much time writing something that a darn teacher needs to explain? What are we supposed to do? Call a freaking teacher every time we read a poem? Why do poets make their work so hard to understand? Shouldn't we be able to just read the poems and enjoy them?'

"Well, your mom just shook her head. She said, 'I happen to enjoy reading poetry.' I realized suddenly that your mom was reading this Emily Dickinson book on her own, not because it was a class assignment but because she actually enjoyed reading this stuff. Then she said, 'Poetry is music without the music,' and I thought about this. Her words astonished me. Music without the music? The words were poetic in themselves, right?

"Maybe your mom was a poet, and I asked, 'Do you write poetry?' She said no, that she enjoyed reading poems. She said she wasn't very creative but that she admired people who were. And then, in my adolescently immature mind, I knew what I had to do in order to reach your mother: I would have to write my own poetry!

"Heck, I didn't have the slightest idea what I was doing, but for the next few weeks, I wrote one poem after the other. I wrote poems about nature, about school, about love, and about politics. I wrote poems about everything. And do you know what I did with them? I put each poem into an envelope, and I slipped them one at a time into your mother's locker. I didn't tell her who the poems were from. I didn't sign them. I guess if she knew my handwriting, she would have been able to figure out they were from me, but she didn't know me, only from the time we had lunch together under the oak tree.

"I wrote these poems for weeks, until finally, she caught me. She saw me slipping one of the envelopes into her locker, and just as I turned to walk away, she approached. 'You?' she said. She had the oddest look on her face. She was truly surprised. 'You've been writing all those poems?'

"Well, my face turned bright red. I knew it was red because my cheeks were hot. She caught me! I mean, I guess I knew it would happen eventually, and I wanted it to happen. But I didn't know what she'd say. Would she say she liked the poems, or would she ridicule me? And what did I know about poetry? I don't know if she was just trying to be nice to me, but she told me she loved the poems, and she asked why I was so secretive.

"Then your mom kissed me on the mouth. Can you believe that? She kissed me right on the mouth. It was not a long and sensual kiss but just a nice kiss. Well, I nearly fainted and fell over right then and there. Jesus, she said she liked the poems, and then she kissed me! Listen, I was a senior, and I'd kissed girls before, but it was the first time I'd been kissed by a lovely girl I truly cared about. It was the first time the kiss really meant something.

"Anyway, that's how it all started. That's when we began seeing more of each other. We would eat lunch together, and we began to date. I met her parents and her older sister and her annoying dog. We went to movies, and we went for walks. We went to parties together, and the next thing I knew, we were boyfriend and girlfriend."

Dad finally stops talking, and we all look at him, waiting for more. "And?" I ask.

"And what?" he says.

I ask, "When did you say that you loved each other?" Dad laughs, but I am serious. I want to know.

"Honestly, I don't remember," my dad says. "It just kind of happened. I mean, when we finally said it, we already knew it, so it wasn't a big deal. And now here we are, thirty-some years later, the six of us in this restaurant. What I wouldn't give to go back in time, to be young again. But for better or for worse, that's not the way the world works."

Dad is now in kind of a trance, and we are all quiet. In a way, I feel sorry for him, but in another way, I envy him. Love. I don't think it ever really goes away.

CHAPTER 14

ALL THOSE EGGS

One of the most interesting men I come across while writing bios for *Orange Life Magazine* is Howard Keenan, the basketball player. Everyone has heard of Howard. Even you, Samantha. You don't even like sports, but you know all about Howard. And he interests you. Why is that? He lives a life that is diametrically opposed to everything you stand for, yet he fascinates you. The more I tell you about him, the more you want to hear.

Howard is just five years older than I am. He's played for the Rockets and the Jazz. Now he is playing for the Lakers, and he makes his home in Newport Beach. He is an Orange County darling, and he can't go anywhere without attracting a crowd. Everyone wants to see him up close, and everyone wants his autograph. We decide to conduct my interview with Howard at his home in order to avoid the fans. I am told by his publicist that I have precisely two hours to ask my questions. Howard has a busy schedule, and two hours is all he can spare.

Howard's estate is fenced and gated, and when I arrive, I push a button at the gate. I hear Howard's voice, and I give him my name. The gate opens, and I drive in.

Howard has the front door open, and he is standing on the porch. He is dressed in basketball shorts and a Lakers T-shirt, and he is barefoot. "You must be Jonathan," he says.

"I am," I say.

"Come on in."

"Nice house," I say, walking in through the doorway.

"Thanks," Howard says.

"Did you build it?"

"No, it was built by the CEO of a pharmaceutical company. He lived here for three years and then moved back east. Now I think he's running a building supply company."

"I see," I say.

"Let's sit at the kitchen table. I was in the middle of eating my lunch."

"That's fine with me."

We walk through the house to the kitchen. There is a big wooden table, and Howard tells me to sit. Then he plops into his chair and asks if I am hungry. I tell him no, I already ate. Howard picks up his fork and digs into his large salad.

"Not enough hours in the day," he says.

"No," I agree.

"I meant to eat before you got here, but one thing led to another. I try to eat at noon. What time is it?"

"It's two," I say.

"Ah, two. Tell me—do you like salads?"

"They're okay," I say.

"A little of this, a little of that."

"Yes," I say.

"You wouldn't just want to eat a big bowl of lettuce, would you? Add some diced tomatoes. Add some diced onions. Maybe some mushrooms and maybe some sunflower seeds. I put garbanzo beans in this salad and some shredded parmesan cheese. Then, of course, you have to pick a dressing. I happen to like ranch dressing the best. How about you? Do you like ranch dressing?"

"It's good," I say.

"I make my own dressing. The store-bought stuff doesn't taste quite right. It has a metallic flavor. My ranch recipe includes buttermilk, mayonnaise, sour cream, parsley, chives, lemon juice, garlic, salt, and black pepper. None of those ingredients alone sound very appetizing, but together? You just can't beat homemade ranch dressing."

"Yes," I say.

"But you didn't come here to talk about my salad."

"You're right; I didn't."

"Well then, shoot. Ask me your questions. What do you want to know?"

I open my notepad and click my pen. I know what I want to ask. I've been told what to ask by my boss. I won't be asking Howard about basketball. Enough has been written about Howard's basketball accomplishments to fill a mile-long *Wikipedia* page. My boss wants me to ask Howard about his love life. Specifically, he wants me to ask him about Heather Best, the movie star. Most of our readers are women, and they're going to want to know if Howard and Heather are serious, if they're just dating, or if they're somewhere in between. "See if you can get him to open up," my boss told me.

Rather clumsily, I ask my first question. "So, Howard, our readers want to know. Are you and Heather an item? How serious are you?"

Howard smiles. "I had kind of a feeling that's what this interview would be about."

"Do you object?"

"No," Howard says. "I can tell you about Heather."

"Unless you'd like to talk about something else."

"No, no, no. Heather is fine. I like talking about Heather. I like her a lot. She's not like other women I've been dating. For one thing, she's a celebrity. She knows what it's like to be famous, and she respects my need for privacy. I like that about her. She's also very smart. Did you know she went to Berkeley? She studied mathematics and graduated with honors. Most people just think she's another blonde-haired actress with looks and a nice personality. They don't know the half of it."

"Are you two serious?"

"I guess it depends on what you mean by *serious*."

"The gossip around town is that you're going to ask her to marry you."

"It's just gossip."

"Then it isn't true?"

"I love her too much to marry her."

I am puzzled by this statement, and my face must show my confusion. Howard laughs when he looks at me.

"Did I say something funny?" I ask.

"No. Well, and yes."

"Then you don't plan to marry her?"

"No," Howard says.

"But you do love her?"

"I do. But I love lots of women. I'm not going to pick one out at the exclusion of the rest."

"Okay," I say.

"It's like this," Howard says. "I don't believe in putting all my eggs in one basket." He stuffs another forkful of salad into his mouth.

"What does that mean?" I ask.

"I believe in diversification," he says with his mouth full of salad.

"Diversification?"

"Do you know much about financial investment strategies?"

"Actually, no," I say.

Howard swallows his food and says, "I've made a lot of money playing basketball. One of the first things that comes up when you make a lot of money is figuring out what you're going to do with it all. Of course, you want to spend a lot of it—houses, cars, jewelry, boats, and all that sort of nonsense. But then you need to invest a good chunk of it for your future. I won't be playing ball forever. Ten years ago, I hired a financial adviser named Winston Chalmers. The first thing Winston taught me was to diversify. That meant spreading my money around so that a drop in the value of one investment didn't wipe me out. You don't put all your eggs in one basket. You spread the eggs around, getting the benefits of all different kinds of ventures and assets. Am I making sense to you?"

"Sort of," I say.

"So apply this principle to marriage. What do you come up with?"

"I'm not sure."

"Are you married?"

"Yes," I say. "I am."

"And you, my friend, have put all your eggs in one basket?"

"I guess I have."

"No diversification. Just one wife, for better or for worse."

"That's true."

"You know what people like to call me?"

"What?"

"They call me a playboy."

"I've heard that."

"But this really doesn't describe me. Do you know what the definition of a playboy is?"

"What is it?"

"It's a wealthy and irresponsible man who spends all his time enjoying himself and having many casual sexual relationships with women. True, I am wealthy, and true, I like to enjoy myself. But am I irresponsible? I don't think so. And as to having many casual sexual relationships with women, that really doesn't describe me. Yes, I have relationships with many women, but I wouldn't call them casual. And they're not all sexual. I love women. I respect women. Just because I haven't picked one of them out as my exclusive partner doesn't mean I am consequently either casual or irresponsible. I prefer to think of myself as diversifying, like a wise investor. Do you think all women are the same?"

"No, of course not."

"Each woman has her own strengths and weaknesses."

"True," I say.

"What I get from one woman, I may not be able to get from another. So why not diversify? Where is it written in stone that you can love only one woman? It's a little crazy, isn't it, this whole idea of committing yourself for the rest of your life to one person? There are so many different kinds of women. Some women are sexy, some women are handsome, and some women are not physically attractive at all. Some women are energetic, and some are laid back. Some women are Democrats, and some are Republicans. Some are Independents. Some women are kind and empathetic, and some are downright Machiavellian. Some women are athletic, and some are good in the kitchen. Some women are good in bed, and some make good mothers. Some women are logical, and some are intuitive. Some women love to laugh no matter what, and some take life very, very seriously.

"So which is the best? And why do we even have to pick one over the other? And before you call me a sexist, the same things can be said about men. Why should a woman have to pick one solitary man out of all the possibilities available to her? Marriage is the culprit. Marriage is old hat. Marriage is antiquated. And marriage is debilitating, good for neither husband nor wife. Anyway, that's how I see it; your mileage may vary."

I think to myself, *One day you will meet a woman who will change your mind about all this.* But would he? Maybe he would, but maybe he wouldn't.

When it comes time to write the article, I'm not sure what to do. The problem is this: most of our readers are women, and most of them believe in marriage. That's our demographic. Yet what Howard is expressing goes against everything we all have faith in: the belief that there is a right man for each woman and a right woman for each man. I know you also believe this, Samantha. I believe it too. If I didn't believe it, I would never have asked you to marry me. Writing an article about Howard's unorthodox philosophy of diversification would be like saying his opinions have merit, when we all know he's—what? Misguided? Clueless? Even unhappy? How could anyone truly be happy without devoting himself to the perfect life partner? "You and me, kid," we like to say. "You and me against the world!"

I ask my boss, Ernest, how he wants me to handle this, and he thinks for a moment. Then he says, "There's a way to do this."

"How?" I ask.

"We publish everything he said just as he said it."

"And?"

"Then we pull the plug on it."

"Pull the plug?"

"After you get done telling our readers all about Howard's cockamamie ideas, you close the article by bringing the poor dumb bastard down to earth."

"Saying what?"

"Saying, 'It's obvious to us here at *Orange Life Magazine* that Howard just hasn't met the right girl yet.'"

"That's it?"

"That'll do it."

He's right. That's exactly what I do, and the article is published. We get lots of letters from single women who think they might be a good match for Howard. I guess you could call it fan mail. They are mostly love letters written by women who feel a connection with the man I described in my article. We forward the letters to Howard, but we don't hear a peep from him or from his publicist. I don't even know if he reads the article or any of the letters.

CHAPTER 15

JULIE

I young woman moves in across the street from us around the time the Howard Keenan issue hits the stands. Her name is Julie Stevenson. She is married to a man named Arnie. He is an accountant at a company that makes car parts, and Julie is a housewife. They are trying to have a baby, but so far, no luck. I notice that Julie has a lot of time on her hands, and she spends much of it working outside. She's constantly planting, trimming, and weeding, and their front yard looks like the gardens at Versailles. They're missing only the water fountains.

I am at home often since I am a writer, and it's easier for me to write my bios at home rather than try to write at the office. There are fewer distractions. Plus, I can dress like a slob, and I don't have to shave or comb my hair. But then I notice Julie. I can see her working in the yard from my study window, under the warm sun, out in the fresh air. She is an attractive girl a few years younger than I, and I find myself daydreaming about her. I try not to, but it's no use.

I decide one afternoon to introduce myself. Why not? I don't have anything devious in mind. It's the neighborly thing to do. Of course, I can't go over there looking like a bum, so I put on some nice clothes. I have clipped my fingernails, brushed my teeth, showered, shaved, and combed my hair. I check myself out in the mirror—I am looking pretty good.

Julie is in her front yard, watering the flower beds, when I approach her. She turns, and at first, she is startled when she sees me. Then she relaxes. She smiles, and I smile back at her. "Hi. My name is Jonathan," I say. "I live across the street."

"Yes," Julie says. "I've seen you."

"I thought I would introduce myself."

"My name is Julie," she says.

"I like your yard."

"Thank you," Julie says.

"My wife met your husband last week."

"So I heard. She's an architect, right?"

"She is."

"Arnie is an accountant. And you're the writer?"

"I write for *Orange Life Magazine*."

"We just got an issue in the mail. I didn't read it, but it looked interesting."

"It's different."

"There were a lot of plastic surgery ads."

"That's Orange County."

"I guess so," Julie says, laughing. "Not my thing. I don't understand why people in California are so willing to go under the knife."

"No one is satisfied."

"I guess not."

"Which issue did they send you?" I ask.

"The one with Howard Keenan on the cover. The basketball player."

"Did you read the bio?"

"I didn't. Was it any good?"

"It was interesting. I wrote it. I'm the guy who writes the bios, among other things."

"Do you like writing about celebrities?"

"It's a living."

"You must get to meet some interesting people."

"I do," I say.

"I saw Sylvester Stallone the other day. He was picking up a pizza over at the shopping center. Does he live in Orange County?"

"I think he lives in LA."

"Maybe he was visiting a friend."

"Maybe," I say.

"He's the only celebrity I've seen since we moved here."

"Where did you used to live?"

"New Orleans," Julie says.

"I've been to New Orleans once. But it was a long time ago, with my parents. Before we got married. I was young. I don't even remember why we went there."

We stop talking for a moment while Julie sprays the hose on her blue hydrangeas. Then she asks me, "Do you have the day off?"

"No," I say. "I work mostly out of my home. I'm in the middle of another bio. I was just taking a break. I saw you over here, and I thought I would say hi."

"So it's a workday for you?"

"It is," I say.

"When I met Arnie, I was a dental hygienist. They had me working fifty hours a week. After we got married, he made me quit my job. We're trying to have a baby. Arnie doesn't believe in day care. He wants me to stay home and take care of the kid."

"Is that what you want?" I ask.

"I'm not complaining. I look forward to being a mother. But I didn't think it would take this long to get pregnant."

"It takes as long as it takes," I say. This is kind of a dumb thing to say, but it is what I come up with.

It's hard to believe this innocent little conversation blossoms into the relationship that it does. It is eventually a relationship, isn't it? I don't know what else one can call it. I suspect it's wrong, but I wind up visiting with Julie in her yard every day for the next two weeks. It's a pleasant break from my work, but it's also more than that. With each visit, I find myself more and more attracted to this woman. She looks better each time I see her, and she sounds sweeter each time she talks. She is a good person. She seems to have her head firmly on her shoulders, and she has solid morals. I feel safe with her. I do not have the feeling that the two of us will ever go too far. We like each other, but that's as far as it's going to go.

So how long does it last? A year? Two years? I lose track of time. After our second week of meeting with each other in her front yard, we exchange phone numbers. "Just in case," I say. "You never know. I may need to borrow a cup of sugar, ha ha."

This is a mistake. I don't see it as a mistake right away, but it is a mistake. At first, we call each other occasionally. I think both of us know the in-person meetings are not a good idea. The neighbors might see us together each day and get the wrong idea. But the phone? We can call each other whenever we wish, and no one is the wiser. Fifteen-minute calls turn into half-hour calls. Then half-hour calls turn into hours. It seems we are talking to each other constantly. I love our conversations. They are the best part of my day. We talk about everything. We talk about our childhoods, our experiences in college, our weddings, and our spouses.

I learn all about Arnie. Julie tells me how they met shortly after they graduated from Tulane. They didn't marry until a couple of years after they graduated, and they lived for several years in New Orleans before deciding to move to Orange County. Arnie got a job offer out here that he couldn't refuse. He took the job, and for the first year, things went well. Julie says he seemed happy, and that was when they decided to have a child. Then, out of nowhere, he began to drink. Well, not exactly out of nowhere. She says he always drank, but his drinking never really got out of hand until they moved to Orange County. They put their plans to have a child on hold, but Arnie still doesn't want Julie working, and he continues to drink. Julie then tells me more about Arnie.

I learn that Arnie cries a lot. Julie says he drinks and then cries like a baby. She says he feels that people hate him, and she tries to reassure him that people do like him. But he is convinced otherwise, and the more he drinks, the sadder he gets. Sometimes he talks about suicide. It's hard to picture Arnie crying, let alone talking about suicide. He has always seemed like such a carefree sort. I guess he's a good actor.

Then Julie tells me something else about Arnie. She says that sometimes he gets angry with her, and several times, he has hit her. He's hit her hard enough to cause bruises, but he never hits her where the bruises show. The more I learn about Arnie, the less I like him, but Julie says she isn't going to give up on him. "For better or worse," she says. "That's what I agreed to."

I learn that Arnie isn't the only actor on the stage. That is to say, Julie talks to me about far more than the problems she is having with her husband. She talks to me about her sister. She talks about her two brothers. She talks about her mom, dad, grandfather, cousins, aunts, and uncles. She also talks about her friends and about friends of those friends. Jesus, this woman has a cast of characters that never ends.

I realize something: I am addicted to her life. I can't get enough of it.

I'm sorry about this, Samantha. I shouldn't have let this happen. But I did. Now it gets even worse. Julie and Arnie decide the reason Arnie is unhappy is because they are living in California. They blame the state for their woes, and Arnie looks for employment back in New Orleans. He is offered a job working for a hardware store chain, and he and Julie decide to make the move. I am about to lose my best friend. Julie tells me, "Arnie gave notice last week, and we're moving this month. Things will be better."

"You're moving?" I ask.

"This month."

"Oh wow," I say.

"We found a nice house."

I want to say, "What about us?" But I don't say it. It wouldn't be appropriate. I know that. Instead, I say, "I hope everything works out for you."

"I think it will," she says.

"I'm going to miss you."

"I'll miss you too. But you can still call me."

I know that will never work, but I pretend otherwise. "Yes, I can call you."

That night, I tell you the news while we're eating dinner. You ask me to pass the mashed potatoes. Then you ask, "Did they say why they're moving?"

"They think Arnie will be happier there."

"Maybe he misses his old friends."

"Maybe," I say.

"I hope things work out for them."

"Yes," I say. "So do I."

"New Orleans?" you ask.

"Yes," I say.

"It's so humid there."

"I guess that doesn't bother them."

"And the hurricanes."

"Yes, the hurricanes."

"Funny how people come and go," you say. "We never really got a chance to know them. They moved in, and now they're moving out. We should've had them over for dinner."

"Yes," I say. "That would've been nice."

You have no idea. The sense of loss I'm experiencing isn't even on your radar. When the moving vans pull up to their house a couple of weeks later, you're at work. I go over to say goodbye. I get no time alone with Julie, so I say goodbye to both of them together. Arnie shakes my hand and says, "If you're ever in New Orleans, be sure to look us up."

"I will," I say, but I can't imagine why you and I would ever find a reason to visit New Orleans.

It's you and me again. The two of us. It seems kind of weird, like you're a stranger. Your makeup is in our bathroom. Your hairbrush sits on the counter. Your electric toothbrush is near the sink. Your closet is full of clothes and shoes, and your jewelry box is on the dresser. Who is this person who's been living with me? Have we really been sleeping in the same bed together for all these recent years? I feel as if I'm suffering from some wild kind of amnesia. There is a picture of you on my nightstand, and I pick it up and look at it before going to bed. The picture was taken years ago, before we were married. I set the picture down and climb into bed with you. You are sound asleep, and your body is warm. I can hear you breathing softly, but I am afraid to touch you. You are right next to me, yet I feel as if you're a million miles away.

Why am I going to bed so early? A few minutes earlier, I felt I wanted to be near you, but now I have changed my mind. I climb out of bed, and it wakes you. Half asleep, you ask, "What are you doing?"

"I'm going to watch a movie," I say.

"Oh," you say.

"Go back to sleep."

"You and your movies," you say sleepily. You pull the covers up to your neck.

I go back to the family room and turn on the TV. The sound is low so that it doesn't disturb you. I turn on a movie I recorded the previous week.

It is the original version of *The Wolfman*, starring Lon Chaney Jr., released in 1941. The story line is fairly simple. Lon Chaney plays a young man named Larry Talbot who has been living in America. Upon the death of his brother, he returns to his family castle in Wales to live with his wealthy father, Sir John Talbot, played by Claude Rains. He is going to take over the family estate. Larry meets a beautiful girl named Gwen, and he and Gwen go with Gwen's friend Jenny to a gypsy camp to have their fortunes told. The fortune-teller, Bela, played by Bela Lugosi, is cursed. He turns into a werewolf and chases Jenny through the woods, where he attacks her. Larry sees the attack and comes to Jenny's rescue. He beats the werewolf to death with his silver-handled cane.

When the villagers come to the scene, they find two dead bodies. Jenny is dead, with her throat ripped to shreds, and Bela is dead, beaten about the head by Larry's silver-handled cane. Larry insists he killed a wolf, not a man. Of course, Bela was a wolf, but he turned back into a human after being killed. During their scuffle, Larry was bitten by Bela. The legend is that once one is bitten by a werewolf and lives, he becomes a werewolf himself.

They lay Bela's body in a coffin, and before the coffin is buried, Bela's gypsy mom shows up while no one is around—except Larry, who is hiding around a corner and watching. Bela's mom opens the coffin and speaks to her dead son as Larry listens. She says, "The way you walked was thorny, through no fault of your own. But as the rain enters the soil, the river enters the sea, so tears run to a predestined end. Your suffering is over, Bela, my son. Now you will find peace."

The words get my attention. "Through no fault of your own," I whisper to myself. "Through no fault of your own. Tears running to a predestined end as the rain enters the soil, as the river enters the sea. Through no fault of your own."

Now Larry is a werewolf. With some simple special effects, he turns into the monster and prowls the late-night forest. He comes upon Richardson, the town gravedigger, in the churchyard. He attacks and kills Richardson, and then he runs back to his family castle. When he wakes up the next morning, he is human again. But there are muddy wolf footprints leading up to his window, on the windowsill, and on the floor. Now he knows: he is a werewolf! He is *the* werewolf. He is the one the movie is all about.

"Through no fault of his own." I can't get the words out of my head. Larry the nice and well-intentioned man. Larry the hairy beast. Larry the murderer!

You know, I never intended on striking up an intimate relationship with another woman. It was never in my game plan. I love you, Samantha. I've loved you since we first kissed on the beach that night while our friends were all at the fire. What is it that makes a man's affections wander? What is it that bends and twists his love? What is it that distorts his priorities? It's a curse, isn't it? Do you believe in curses? Do you believe there are forces at work over which we have no control?

I don't know what I believe. I know now that I am ashamed. What I did was wrong. The powerful and painful emotions I'm feeling belong to someone else, not to me. To someone else! To the werewolf! To the wolfman! I keep telling myself, "Through no fault of your own." There are times when, if a man doesn't believe this, he is doomed.

CHAPTER 16

DINNER OUT

Ah, Henry and Amanda Whitman. You know them from work. Well, you know Amanda from work. Henry is her husband. Amanda is one of the new hires at the firm, and you thought it would be fun for the four of us to eat dinner out. Henry is an insurance agent who has an office in Irvine. Henry and Amanda met at UCLA when they were both sophomores. They married as soon as they graduated. We are at Pascal's in Newport Beach, and we've just been seated at our table. You and I are a couple of years older than the Whitmans, but I am a little nervous. I always get nervous when I meet new people.

Amanda is not bad looking. I wouldn't describe her as beautiful, and she could use some professional counseling on making up her face. She is wearing way too much mascara. Henry is a good match for her. He has small eyes, a pointed nose, and a mouthful of teeth that look as if they could devour an entire steer in a single sitting. When he laughs, his teeth glisten—and he laughs a lot. He is one of those kinds of guys. "Ha ha ha, nice to meet you, Jonathan. Ha ha ha, nice to meet you, Samantha. Ha ha ha, I've heard this is a pretty good restaurant. Ha ha ha, but don't hold me to it."

Samantha picked the restaurant. She has always wanted to eat here. Our waiter shows up and introduces himself. He then hands us our menus and takes our drink orders. He walks away, and immediately, Henry starts talking. There is no slowing this guy down. "Do you have any brothers or sisters?" he asks me.

"I have a younger brother," I say.

"No sisters?"

"No," I say.

"I have an older sister. Her name is Natalie."

117

"Henry spoke to her on the phone tonight," Amanda says. "Right before we left for the restaurant."

"She told me our dad told her about the lizard."

"The lizard?" I ask.

"It's a great story," Amanda says.

"Boy, was Natalie pissed," Henry says. "Even after all these years. Funny as hell. God, I laughed."

"What happened?" I ask.

"It was years ago, when we were still kids," Henry says. "My father thought it would be fun to spend the night at O'Neill Park. Mom opted out of the plan, so it was just Dad, my sister, and me. It was only to be for one night, and we'd park our car at a campsite and spend the night there in our sleeping bags. We didn't bring tents. The weather was nice, and we would sleep under the stars.

"I remember there was a picnic table and a barbecue for cooking. We arrived at about noon and set up camp, and then we went for a walk on the trails through the woods. When we returned to camp, Natalie wanted to lie in the sun to work on her tan, and Dad had brought along a book so he could read. I kept myself busy by throwing my knife into an oak tree. I could've done that for hours without getting bored. As I was throwing my knife, I saw a lizard scamper out from behind the tree. It crawled over to a rock and then sat on its belly in the sun. What a stroke of luck! I knew exactly what I wanted to do. I didn't even think twice about it.

"I set down my knife, got down on my knees, and crawled toward the lizard. It didn't move. I reached for it and grabbed it with my fingers. I was careful not to harm it. I needed it to be lively and healthy. I then stood up and carried the lizard over to my sleeping bag, where my jacket was bundled up to be used as a pillow. The jacket had zippered pockets, and I stuffed the lizard into one of them, zipping it up. Then I went back to my knife throwing. 'Don't you ever get tired of that?' Natalie asked.

"I said, 'Tired of what?'

"She said, 'Tired of throwing that stupid knife at that stupid tree.' I just ignored her. She was trying to make me mad. I knew that. Anyway, I would soon get even with her.

"When six o'clock rolled around, dad fired up the barbecue and cooked hamburgers. We had also brought along potato salad and baked beans.

When we were done eating dinner, we played UNO until it got dark, until we could no longer read the cards. 'Time to turn in,' Dad said. Soon it would be time! Time for what? It would be time to carry out my plan. Ah, what a rotten little kid I was, ha ha.

"I crawled into my sleeping bag, resting my head gently on my jacket. Natalie crawled into her sleeping bag, checking it first for bugs with a flashlight. Dad got into his sleeping bag and said good night to us. Then I waited. A half hour later, I whispered to Natalie, 'Are you asleep?'

"She rolled over and said no, she couldn't fall asleep. 'This place is creepy at night,' she said.

"I replied, 'Yeah, I know what you mean.' Then, a half hour later, I whispered to Natalie again, 'Are you asleep?'

"She said, 'How can I fall asleep if you keep asking me if I'm asleep?' I said I was sorry, and I waited another half hour. This time, when I whispered to her, there was no answer. She was asleep. Finally! I sat up, grabbed my jacket, carefully unzipped the pocket, and removed the lizard.

"I got out of my bag and crawled over to Natalie, and with surgical precision, I slipped the wriggling reptile into her sleeping bag. Then I went back to my own bag and waited. I stared at my sister. Nothing happened for about ten minutes. Then, suddenly, in the moonlight, I saw her eyes open wide, and I could not have made my prank go any better if I had written a script.

"Natalie screamed. Oh Christ, did she ever scream. She began kicking her legs and shouting, 'There's something in my sleeping bag!'

"Dad woke up immediately, and he said, 'What the hell?'

"Natalie screamed again, and this time, she scrambled out of the bag and stood up. She started jumping up and down, shouting, 'There's something in my sleeping bag!' Dad told her to calm down, and I started laughing. Natalie was still hysterical as Dad got up and out of his own sleeping bag. He grabbed the flashlight and opened Natalie's bag. 'It was on my leg,' Natalie said. 'I could feel it crawling on me!'

"Well, Dad aimed the flashlight into the sleeping bag as I continued to laugh. Natalie now started to cry. 'Do you see anything?' she asked. 'What is it?'

"Dad then chuckled and said, 'It's just a lizard. A little blue-belly lizard.' He grabbed the bottom of the sleeping bag and lifted it, giving it a good shaking. The little lizard fell out of the bag and hurried away. I think it was more afraid of Natalie than she was of it. I don't think I ever laughed so hard in my entire life, and Natalie was still crying.

"When Dad told Natalie to go back to bed, she said, 'You couldn't get me to climb back into that sleeping bag for a million dollars!'

"Dad told me to be quiet, but I couldn't stop laughing. 'It was probably just looking for a warm place to sleep,' he finally said to Natalie. God, what a great camping trip!

"Natalie spent the rest of the night sleeping in the car with a blanket, with doors locked and windows rolled up. Later, I told Dad that I was the culprit who put the lizard in with Natalie. But I didn't tell Natalie. She was bigger than me back then, and she would've killed me."

"But now she knows," Amanda says.

"I wish I could've seen her face when she found out."

"Henry has always been a practical joker."

"Sounds like it," I say. The story is pretty funny, and I am smiling. In fact, so are you.

"Pull any good ones on your brother?" Henry asks me.

I think for a moment and then say, "I'm sure I did, but none of them come to mind."

Just then, the waiter shows up with our drinks. He sets them on the table and then asks if we're ready to order dinner. We all say yes, and he gets out his notepad and pen.

"Is this price right for the porterhouse steak?" Henry asks. He is holding up his menu.

"Yes, sir," the waiter says.

"Expensive, isn't it?" Henry asks. "I just want to eat it. I don't want to have sex with it."

Amanda laughs.

"I'll have the seafood fettucine," you say.

"Same thing for me," Amanda says.

"I'll try the lobster," I say.

"Hell, I'll get the porterhouse," Henry says. "You only live once."

"Yes, sir," the waiter says.

"And bring me another drink," Henry says. "By the time you make it back, I'll be done with this one."

"Same here," Amanda says.

The waiter looks and you and me, and you say, "We're fine as we are." Then the waiter walks away.

"Not   big drinkers?" Henry asks.

"Not really," I say.

"I come from a long line of drinkers," Henry says.

"You don't say."

"Irish blood. Well, half of it anyway. My mom was Irish. Drank like a fish. My dad used to joke and tell her she had a hollow leg."

"She died last year," Amanda says.

"Cirrhosis," Henry says.

"That's too bad."

"Do you know who W. C. Fields was?"

"Of course," I say.

"He died of a stomach hemorrhage."

"That sounds awful," you say.

"Live by the sword," Henry says. "Have you watched many old Fields movies?"

"I've seen a few."

"Remember this one? He walks into his favorite bar and asks the bartender, 'Say, did I spend a hundred-dollar bill in here last night?'

"The bartender says, 'Yes you did.'

"Fields then says, 'Well, thank God for that. I thought I lost it.'"

"I remember that gag," I say. "Except I think it was a twenty-dollar bill."

"I made adjustments for inflation," Henry says.

"Yes, of course."

"Have you heard the one about the black bartender?"

"I'm not sure I have," I say.

Henry looks around to be sure there are no black people within earshot. Then he says, "There's this black bartender, and a white guy walks into his bar. The white guy steps up, bangs his fist on the counter, and says, 'All right, you nigger, pour me a Crown and water.'

"The black bartender is stunned at first. Then he says, 'Listen, Mac, is that any way to order your drink? How would you like it if I spoke to you like that?'

"The men stare at each other. 'You are black, aren't you?' the white guy asks.

"The bartender says, 'I've got an idea. Why don't you stand here and be the bartender, and I'll order a drink from you? Maybe then you'll understand.'

"The white guy says, 'Fine. Let's do it.'

"The two men then switch places, and the black man bangs his fist on the counter. 'All right, you stupid honky,' he says. 'Bring me a Crown and water. And make it snappy.'

"The white guy smiles and says, 'Sorry, but we don't serve niggers here.'"

Amanda laughs.

You and I just stare at Henry. This is not our kind of joke. Henry smiles and asks, "Don't you get it?"

"We get it," I say.

"But you don't like race jokes?"

"Not really," I say.

"I heard that one from a black friend of mine," Henry says.

I think to myself, *That's a little hard to believe.* Now no one knows what to say.

You promptly change the subject. You say to me, "Henry and Amanda went to UCLA. That's where they met."

"Where did you meet?" Henry asks us.

"At the beach," you say. "We were in high school."

"So young," Amanda says.

"We met at a frat party," Henry says. "Wild party. Lots of people. Lots of alcohol. Jesus, I got pretty drunk that night, but Amanda was even drunker than me. I don't know how we wound up together, but we did."

"I thought Henry was cute."

"You thought everyone was cute," Henry says. "You thought the potted ficus tree by the front door was cute."

"Henry took me home," Amanda says. "I lived in an apartment with a roommate about three blocks away."

"It was a long walk," Henry says. "Amanda had to puke every ten steps. It was hilarious. I'd hold her hair back for her, and she'd barf in the bushes. She had long hair back then."

"It wasn't that bad," Amanda says.

"You were pretty smashed."

"I guess I did have a hair too much to drink. I don't usually get sick like that."

"We made it to her apartment," Henry says. "The roommate was gone, so we had the place to ourselves. I made a pot of coffee for us, and Amanda got to feeling better. She cleaned herself up in the bathroom, and then the two of us sat down on the sofa to watch a little TV together. We were watching *Saturday Night Live*. It wasn't very funny. Then we started to kiss. Then we, you know, started to touch each other. I don't know where she found the energy. I thought she'd be too drunk to do anything, but God, she was a freaking tiger. We ripped off each other's clothes and made love right there on the sofa in front of the TV. And I remember while we were having sex, I thought to myself, *This is my kind of girl!* Yes, I was hooked. I knew we were going to get married."

"Sex is so important to a relationship," Amanda says.

"It is," Henry agrees.

"Isn't it that way with you guys?" Amanda asks us.

"I like sex," you say.

"We drive people crazy," Amanda says.

"Drive them crazy?" you ask.

"You should've been there on our honeymoon. I thought the people in the room next to us were going to kill us. Every several hours, we did it. We gave the bed a workout like it had never seen. And I would scream and yell. I like to make a lot of noise when we're doing it. I can't help it. Sometimes I even sing."

"Sing?"

"Whatever comes to mind. 'She'll Be Comin' Round the Mountain' used to be my favorite. The people in the room next to us pounded on the wall with their fists, trying to quiet us. But we ignored them and carried on."

"It was pretty funny," Henry says.

"Do you make a lot of noise?" Amanda asks you. I can't believe she's actually asking this.

"Not really," you say. You are embarrassed by the question. I can tell you want to change the subject, and so do I. The last thing we want to talk about is our sex life and the details of our comparatively tame lovemaking.

We continue to talk. It becomes clear to me just how different these two people are from us. I feel as if I'm in someone's dream—or, rather, nightmare. Finally, the waiter appears with our dinners. He places the dishes in front of us. He gives you my lobster, and he gives me your fettucine. When he leaves, we switch plates.

Meanwhile, Henry cuts into his porterhouse. "Well," he says, "this is disappointing. I asked for medium rare. This is medium. Wrong shade of pink. Almost no pink at all." Then, to Amanda, he says, "See if you can get the waiter's attention."

Amanda is able to catch the waiter's eye, and he comes to our table. "Ma'am?" he says to Amanda.

"My husband's steak," she says.

"Is there a problem?" he asks Henry.

"This is medium," Henry says. "I specifically asked for medium rare." Henry shows the waiter the bisected steak.

"I'm sorry, sir," the waiter says.

"I want a new one," Henry says.

"A new steak?"

"Cooked medium rare."

"I'll take it back to the chef," the waiter says, and he picks up Henry's plate.

"I'll come with you," Henry says.

"Sir?"

"I'll watch this time."

As Henry and the waiter make their way back to the kitchen, Amanda laughs. She says, "Henry is afraid they're going to spit on his food."

"Oh?" you say.

"They do it, you know. To get even with you for sending back your food."

"Does Henry send his food back often?"

"I guess he does. He likes things done just right. And for what they're charging for that porterhouse, it ought to be done just right, no? I don't think Henry is asking too much."

"My lobster looks good," I say.

While Henry is in the kitchen, watching them cook the new steak and protecting his dinner from a potentially vindictive cook, the rest of us eat. Then you and Amanda talk about one of the projects at your office. As is often the case when you talk about architecture, I have no idea what you're talking about.

Finally, Henry returns from the kitchen with his new steak. He sets down his plate and sits in his chair.

"How'd they take it?" Amanda asks him.

"They were fine."

"Did they agree that your steak was overcooked?"

"The chef didn't say one way or the other. He didn't have a lot of personality."

The waiter appears at our table and asks, "Is everyone else's dinner satisfactory?"

We all nod.

"I'll have another drink," Henry says.

"Same here," Amanda says.

"We're fine," I say.

Henry is now happy. He is chewing on his porterhouse, and the steak juice is glistening on his big white teeth. "Have you heard the one about the pig, cow, and attorney?" he asks. He is laughing before he even tells us the joke.

I can't wait to get the heck away from this couple. I can't wait go home with you and watch TV.

CHAPTER 17

THE WHITEBOARD

Around our seventh year of marriage, I decide I'll no longer be working for *Orange Life Magazine*. I will write another book. I will take another shot at it. I want to be an author—a real author.

Then you give me your gift. Imagine my surprise when you hand it over on our eighth anniversary. It's the size and shape of a cookie sheet, wrapped in shiny silver paper, and it has a gigantic blue bow. I can't imagine what it could be.

"It isn't a big deal," you say. "Just a little something to make your life more manageable."

I begin to unwrap the present and say, "What could it be?" I tear all the silver wrapping paper away and hold it up to look at it. "What the heck is this?" I ask.

"It's a whiteboard," you say.

"A whiteboard?"

"You can hang it in the pantry. I measured it. It will fit on the back of the pantry door."

"What's it for?"

"To help you keep track of your tasks."

"My tasks?"

"Your household action items."

"Ah," I say.

"We can add items when they come up and erase them from the board when they're done."

"Yes, this will be helpful," I say. I pretend to like the idea. I don't want to seem uncooperative.

"I thought you might like it. Now I won't have to keep pestering you about fixing things around the house. No more nagging and no more asking you the same questions over and over. I'll just write each task on the whiteboard, and you'll always have a list you can look at. I got two colors of felt pens. We'll use red for high-priority items, and we'll use the black pen for the not-so-urgent items."

"Good idea," I say.

"Do you like it?" you ask.

"Yes, it will be very helpful."

I don't really like it, but it seems harmless enough. I figure if it makes you happy, then somewhere down the line, it will make me happy.

The first entry soon appears.

I open the pantry one morning to grab a handful of freeze-dried peanuts, and just as I'm about to close the door, I see your handwriting on the whiteboard. It's up at the top, and it says, "Unstick master bedroom door."

Yes, I know the master bedroom door doesn't quite close. I figure this is from the house settling, but up until now, I haven't seen it as much of a problem. So the door doesn't close all the way. There are only the two of us living in the house, and it's not as if anyone else will be spying on us. Up until this moment, it's been fine to just leave the door ajar. But now it's on the whiteboard.

No problem. I'll figure out how to free up the door. I need some advice, so I drive to Home Depot and find someone who can help me. I get the attention of one of the men who works there. I pick one of the older employees, someone who might have some experience. I tell him about the sticky door, and he says, "It's probably because your house is settling."

"That's what I figured," I say.

"How bad is it sticking?"

"It won't close," I say.

"You're going to need to sand it down," the man says.

"With sandpaper?"

"And a sander."

"A sander?"

"We have a variety of power sanders."

The man takes me to the power tool section of the store and helps me pick out an electric sander. He also helps me choose the right sandpaper: a coarse grit to make the door fit and a fine grit to finish off the work.

Then he takes me to the paint section for a paintbrush and some paint for touching up the areas I have sanded. The door is white, so picking the color is easy enough. I take all the stuff to the register and pay for it.

When I get home, I take the sander to the bedroom door. I install the coarse sandpaper and plug in the sander. Then, like a pro, I go to work, sanding down the edge of the door to make it fit. You are at work. You will be pleasantly surprised when you get home and see what I've done. I feel like a good husband. I am doing my duty.

I sand, test the door, sand again, and test the door a second time. I keep doing this until finally, the door closes without sticking. Then I install the fine sandpaper and smooth out the rough edge of the door. It looks nice. Just one problem: there is now sawdust all over the place.

I go get the vacuum cleaner to suck up all the sawdust. Now I have to paint the edge of the door where the wood is raw, and I open my paint can and go to work with the paintbrush. I have painted before, so I know what I'm doing.

When I'm done painting, I take the brush to the kitchen sink and wash off the paint. Then I take the brush, paint can, sander, and sandpaper to the garage and place the items on the workbench. I put away the vacuum cleaner in the hall closet, where I found it. All said and done, between making the trip to Home Depot and doing the actual work, I figure I have put in about three hours. It's not bad, but I would rather have spent this time writing. At least I get to erase the felt-penned item from the whiteboard. It feels good to do this.

The next day, I am writing, and midmorning, I go into the pantry for a handful of peanuts again. Just as I'm about to close the door, I notice the whiteboard. Now there are two items in your handwriting: "Lightbulb out in family room" and "Bedroom clock needs battery."

These tasks seem simple enough. I go to the cabinet in the laundry room, where we keep the lightbulbs and batteries, but we're out of both. Another trip to Home Depot is required, and I get dressed to leave for the store. I purchase a pack of AA batteries and a box of 60-watt lightbulbs, and then I drive back home. I tackle the clock first since the lightbulb change is the more difficult of the two tasks. I take the clock off the wall and flip it over to its back side. Then I open the pack of batteries, and I notice something: I bought AAA batteries by mistake, not the AA batteries

I need. I say a few curse words and then set the clock aside. I will have to go back to the store.

In the meantime, I will change the lightbulb. The bulb that has burned out is in a wall sconce next to the picture window. This light fixture is about twelve feet high, so I will need a ladder to reach it. No problem. We have a ladder, and I go to the garage to get it. The last time I used the ladder was to install Christmas lights last year, and the feet of the ladder are still dirty from having been used in the yard. I don't want to get the dirt on the carpet in the family room, so I take the ladder to the driveway and hose down the feet. The dirt doesn't hose off easily. I need a scrub brush. I look all over the house for one and finally find one hiding in the cabinet under the kitchen sink. Then I return to the driveway, scrub the dirt off the ladder, dry the ladder with a towel, and take it into the house, into the family room. I lean it up against the wall beside the light fixture and climb up to change the lightbulb.

When I am done changing the lightbulb, I put the ladder back in the garage. Then I hop into my car to drive to the store for more batteries. I arrive at the store. They are out of AA batteries, so I will need to go somewhere else. Who ever heard of Home Depot being out of AA batteries? I go to the drugstore, and sure enough, I find the AA batteries. I purchase a pack and return home, where I insert one of the batteries into the wall clock and set the correct time. I hang it back on the wall. By the time I get back to the pantry to erase the tasks from the whiteboard, it is early afternoon. I've burned up another three hours.

Weeks go by, and I am doing more chores and writing less and less. It turns out this whiteboard is one of the worst things to ever creep into my life. I complete the tasks written on the board, and the next day, there are more. I don't actually ever catch you writing on it. The tasks just seem to appear from nowhere, as if some cruel ghost is picking up the felt pens and writing them in your handwriting. No matter how hard I try, I can't keep up, and as each day goes by, the tasks get more and more time-consuming. After starting with lightbulbs, sticky doors, and batteries in clocks, they morph into complicated weeklong projects. I am working in the house and working in the yard. I'm working on the roof and in the garage. The problem is this: because I no longer work for *Orange Life Magazine*, you think I have nothing but free time on my hands, and you seem to think it's your responsibility to fill that free time. You seem to be completely unaware that I am trying to write my book. Remember the book? It's the reason I quit my job at *Orange Life Magazine* in the first place.

In an effort to make you understand how important this book is to me, I tell you what the book is about. I'm hoping for some enthusiasm, and you say it sounds like an interesting idea. But how do I put this? It isn't real to you. It isn't significant. And no one is paying me a dime to write it. Maybe that's the problem.

Because I am technically unemployed and you are who you are, I realize there's probably no way to get rid of the whiteboard. What's going to happen? I don't know. It's a dilemma, to be sure. If I put my foot down and rebel against the whiteboard, I could lose your love and respect. If I don't put my foot down, I'll probably resent you for as long as we're married.

Then I have an idea. A friend of mine at *Orange Life Magazine* was having difficulty with his wife, and they went to see a marriage counselor. The woman worked wonders, and now they are getting along like newlyweds. I ask my friend for the name of this counselor, and he gives me her name and phone number. I ask you to see her with me, and you are surprised. You are not even slightly aware of my frustration. You want to know why we should see a counselor, and I tell you, "Please just come. Do it for me."

The counselor's name is Dr. Powers, and she is older than we are by about a decade. She has all kinds of diplomas and certifications hanging on her walls. She has a bookcase full of psychology books and a big antique desk and leather chair. In front of the desk are two smaller chairs, and you and I sit down in them. Dr. Powers seems friendly enough. She asks, "What can I help you two with today? You were kind of vague over the phone. Was it something about a whiteboard?"

"The whiteboard?" you ask me. This is not what you expected us to talk about.

"That's part of it," I say.

"You don't like the whiteboard?" you ask me.

"It's not that I don't like it," I say. "Well, maybe it is. I don't mean to hurt your feelings, but it's sort of driving me out of my mind."

"But I got it for you."

"I know that," I say. "But it isn't helping."

"What is wrong with it?"

"I guess that's what we're here to find out," Dr. Powers says, and she smiles at you to calm you down.

"If it wasn't for that whiteboard, nothing would ever get done," you say defensively.

"That's not really the issue," I say.

"What is the purpose of the whiteboard?" the doctor asks. She has no idea what the whiteboard is for.

"I got it for Jonathan," you say. "We use it to keep track of all his household chores. He was complaining that I nagged him too much, so I thought the whiteboard would help."

"Is it helping?" the doctor asks me.

"Not really," I say.

"That's the first I've ever heard of this," you say.

"That's why we're here," I say.

"So we're here seeing a counselor? Why didn't you just say something to me?"

"Say what?"

"That you didn't like the whiteboard."

I think for a moment. Then I say, "Because the whiteboard is only a symptom."

"A symptom?"

"Maybe you've been asking too much of Jonathan," the doctor says.

"Too much?" you say. "He doesn't even have a job. Did he tell you he quit his job?"

"You don't work?" the doctor asks me.

"I write," I say.

"Write what exactly?"

"I'm writing a book."

"He doesn't even know if anyone will publish it," you say. "The last book he wrote was never published. He worked on it for a year, and what did he make? He made nothing."

"Is that true?" the doctor asks me.

"It is," I say.

"Do you understand where Samantha is coming from?"

"I do," I say. "But that doesn't mean I should be spending all my time replacing lightbulbs and fixing doors. The book is important to me."

"Ah," the doctor says, rubbing her chin. "I think I'm beginning to understand the problem you two are having. And Jonathan is right. The whiteboard is only a symptom."

"So what is the problem?" you ask.

"You are suffering from a disagreement," the doctor says matter-of-factly.

"And?" you ask.

"Neither of you wears the pants in the household," the doctor says. "You treat each other as equals, and therein lies the heart of the problem. I see this all the time, especially with younger couples. You disagree with each other, and no one is charged with the authority to resolve the disagreement. Am I right? You could vote on it, but the vote would be tied one to one. And a tie vote in such a conflict gets you nowhere. You're both just disagreeing with each other. No, the only solution—and I mean the only solution—is to work out a compromise. Each of you is going to have to cooperate. Of course, this requires some maturity, but it is quite possible. I've seen it work with my other clients. I know it can succeed."

You and I stare at the doctor. Then you say, "Well, I could've told you all this."

"But you didn't," the doctor says.

"She's right," I say to you.

"Fact of life," the doctor says. "Sometimes it takes a third party to point out the obvious."

"What would this compromise look like?" I ask.

"Yes," you say. "Who has to give up what?"

The doctor laughs, and I ask what's so funny. She says, "You're just like all my other clients. They want to know what they have to give up, like it's a negative proposition, like they'll be losing something dear to them. That's not the best way to look at it. Instead, think of what you'll be gaining. Will the glass of water be half full or half empty? You've got to think of it as half full. Do you understand?"

"I think I do," I say.

"And you?" the doctor says to you.

"I understand," you say.

"Very well. Here's what I propose." The doctor outlines her terms for our compromise.

I have to admit she does a pretty good job. I can see how neither of us will be thrilled with its implementation. I will promise to do my fair share of chores, and you will allow me time to work on my book.

"Think of your lives as being half full," the doctor finally says. "Keep telling yourselves that until you believe it."

"And the whiteboard?" I ask.

"What about it?"

"Does it stay or go? You haven't said anything about the whiteboard." This was, after all, the whole point of coming in to see a counselor, getting her opinion, and agreeing to a compromise.

"Samantha," the doctor says, "do you have any preference one way or the other?"

You look at me and say, "The board was a gift to you to begin with. If you don't want it, then get rid of it."

"Seriously?" I ask.

"I'm serious."

"Do I have your blessing?"

"You have my blessing," you say.

"Hallelujah," I say.

That's how I finally get rid of the whiteboard. When we get home, I remove it from the pantry door. I take it to the side of the house and jam it into our trash can along with the rest of our household garbage. I sense this hurts your feelings a little. But that's okay. The truth is that I'll be just fine and dandy if I never see another torturous whiteboard for the rest of my life.

CHAPTER 18

GOOD PEOPLE

They say it's the little things. Yes, it's those little things that make you fall head over heels in love with a person. I remember how it was with us. God, I was crazy about you. I recall being enamored with your hair. Back in high school, you used to weave it into a single thick braid—do you remember those days? It's funny how an innocuous little thing like braided hair can make such an impression, but it made a powerful impression on me. There was something so real about your braided hair. It was so wholesome and so friendly, and it talked without speaking. It said, "Love me, and I will never hurt you. We will love each other."

There were other little things. There was the way you would stare at me and bat your eyelashes. I loved it. I could have watched you bat your eyelashes for hours.

Then there were the stoplights. Do you remember the stoplights? Whenever I was driving and came to a red light, you would lean over and kiss me until the light turned green. It was like a game, and we looked forward to the red lights just so we could kiss.

There was the car radio. You never were satisfied with the song playing, and you would go from station to station until you found something you wanted to listen to. It should've driven me crazy, but I liked it. I liked it because you were doing it. I liked it because it was you. All those little things about you I loved. I'm sure there were many more, but these are the few I remember. They all added up to Samantha, my girlfriend, my girl.

Nowadays it's a little different, and the little things have changed. Several months after we meet with Dr. Powers, you have developed a new little thing. It has to do with the book I'm writing. We might be watching TV, eating dinner, or driving in the car, and you will look at me and ask, "So how's the book coming?"

Why does it bother me so much when you ask this? On its face, the question seems harmless, but it really gets under my skin. I am convinced you're not really interested in the book at all; you're actually just taking a poke at me and my pipe dream. I know this because I know that if you had your way, I would not be writing the book at all. If you had your way, I would be employed somewhere, bringing home a paycheck and pulling my weight.

Well, you finally get your way.

I am eleven months into the book, when I reach the conclusion that this book is a disaster. I stop writing and read all the pages I've written, and I suddenly hate every word of it. I don't like the characters, and I don't like the plot. I don't like the writing style. It is clumsy and stale.

For one month, I brood over this depressing revelation, and finally, I sit down in front of my computer and perform the awful deed: I delete the entire file. It's now gone. There is no way of retrieving it to give it a second reading or rewrite. All that work, and all those hours, vanish into the air like a little puff of smoke from an extinguished candle. Gone.

I don't tell you what I've done. Not right away. I wait for you to ask the question. You will ask. You always do. You and that confounded question! We are on our way out to dinner, and I am driving. You are fiddling with the radio stations, trying to find a song you like, when you ask, "So how's the book coming?" It's time for me to fess up.

"It isn't," I say.

"Are your stuck?"

"I'm beyond stuck."

"Maybe you need to take a break."

"Oh, I've taken a break. A big break."

You look at me. "What's that mean?"

"I'm done with it."

"You've finished?"

"No, I didn't finish it. It was crap. It was no good. I deleted it from my computer."

"You did what?"

"It's gone," I say.

"You're kidding, right?"

"I'm not kidding. I killed it. It lives and breathes no more."

"What was wrong with it?"

"Everything."

"It couldn't have been that bad."

"It was," I assure you.

"Oh," you say, and then you are quiet. You're not sure what to say. This book has been a thorn in your side ever since I started it, but now I think you're sorry to hear I've abandoned it. "What are you going to do?" you ask.

"With my time? I don't know."

"Are you going to start another book?"

"Not a chance."

What am I going to do? Look for a job, I guess. Not right away. I'm too depressed to go knocking on doors. But I will get over it. Then I will look for a job.

Three months after I tell you about the book, I start making phone calls. I've had about all I can take of doing chores and watching daytime TV. I call everyone I know. I even call my old boss, Ernest Carroll, at *Orange Life Magazine* to see if I can get my old job back. He says the gal they hired to replace me is doing a fine job, so they can't exactly fire her to make room for me. He does, however, say he'll make a few calls to his friends.

Two weeks later, Ernest calls me back. "Your timing couldn't have been any better," he says.

"My timing?"

"A friend of mine over at the *Daily Observer* says they're looking for someone experienced in writing bios. It sounds right up your alley, right in your wheelhouse. They're planning to start a new featured weekly column in their Sunday editions. They want to get started right away. The feature is going to be called Good People. It is just what it says it is: a featured weekly article about specific good people in Orange County."

"I'm not sure I understand," I say.

"It's a response to the criticism they've been receiving about all the crap they print. When's the last time you picked up a paper? All they talk about is crime, corruption, scandal, violence, and tragedy. Good People will be different. It will say, 'Hey, there are some good people in this county, and here's a story about one of them.'"

"Interesting."

"You're perfect for the job."

"Who do I need to talk to?" I ask.

"I gave Walter Beasley your name and phone number. Walter is the editor you'll be working with. He's familiar with the work you did for us here, and he said he's very interested in talking to you as soon as possible. He's a good man. I think you'll like him."

I thank Ernest for the lead, and the next day, Walter calls me. He wants to meet in his office. The more I think about this job, the more I like the idea.

I tell you about it, and you are thrilled. You are sure Walter will hire me, given my background in writing bios, and you are right. I meet with Walter, and we talk for about an hour. At the end of our meeting, he offers me the position. I accept, and we shake hands. "Welcome to the *Daily Observer*," he says. "I'll be expecting great things from you."

"I'll do my best," I say.

"Here's your first subject," Walter says. He grabs a file from the table behind his desk and hands it to me. I thumb through the file. There are some photographs and an information sheet with some notes, addresses, and phone numbers. "You're going to like this guy. His name is Miles Hawthorne."

"Okay," I say.

"Good luck."

"Thank you," I say.

I call you on the way home to tell you I was hired. When I get home, I give you a rundown of Miles Hawthorne. According to the notes in the file Walter gave me, Miles is a hero of sorts. In order to understand what Miles did, you first need to know about Susan Jasper.

Susan was a seventy-two-year-old widow who lived in Santa Ana. Susan and her husband, Frank, owned a small market, and they ran the market for their entire working lives. It was a modest business enterprise, but it paid the bills, with a little left over every month for their retirement savings. Frank was an interesting man. He didn't trust banks, so he kept their cash savings hidden in their apartment. When he and Susan turned sixty-five, they sold the market, and then Frank died from a heart attack.

From the sale of the market and from the money they'd put away each month, Susan and Frank had accumulated nearly a quarter of a million dollars in savings. As Frank figured it, along with their Social Security checks, this cash would allow them to retire comfortably. They would by no means be rich, but they would be okay. They had no other assets other than the cash. They rented their apartment, and they didn't even own a car. But they would get along.

When Frank died, Susan wanted to put the cash in a bank. She did not mistrust banks, as Frank had, and she did not feel safe in keeping such a large amount of money in the apartment, so one day she collected all the cash and put it into a brown paper bag. She would take the bus downtown and deposit the cash into a bank savings account.

She climbed aboard the bus with her brown paper bag in one hand and her purse in the other. She took a seat on the bus. In the seat across the aisle was Miles Hawthorne. Now I need to tell you about Miles.

He was a twenty-eight-year-old married man. He was married to a young woman named Cynthia, and they had two small children. Like Susan, Miles did not own a car. He had owned a pickup truck, but the truck had been recently repossessed. He was in a horrible fix financially. He had tried to start his own concrete construction company, but things had not gone well for him.

When the bus stopped downtown at Susan's spot, she got up to leave. Her mind must have been preoccupied with something else. Who knows exactly? She got off the bus, leaving her brown paper bag full of cash behind her on the seat.

Miles noticed the paper bag after Susan got off the bus and the bus was rolling again. At first, he did nothing. Then he wondered, *What did the woman leave behind?* He stood up, grabbed the sack, and took it to his seat. When he looked into the bag, he couldn't believe his eyes. It was filled with bundles of hundreds and twenties.

What was the first thing to go through his mind? It was enough money to rescue him from all his financial problems. It was a windfall. It was a gift. His problems were over! "Finders keepers," he said to himself. He looked around, and no one on the bus was watching him. No one had seen him take the bag. It was wrong, and he knew it was wrong, but he needed the money in the worst way.

When Miles got home, his wife and kids were gone. He dumped the cash onto the floor, and he got down on his knees to count it. He counted nearly a quarter of a million dollars, and he had no idea who the old woman was, where she was, or why she had so much cash. He collected all the cash from the floor and put it back into the bag. He then hid the bag in the hall closet. Would he tell his wife? It might freak her out, he thought. He had to be smart about this. He thought about how he would explain the money he was soon going to be using to pay all his delinquent bills. He could buy a new truck. He could buy new clothes for the kids. There would be money left over to start up a savings account. Finally, he could live like a normal person, and the weight of the world would be off his shoulders. Yes, he would be happy!

Then, later that evening, while he was watching the evening news with Cynthia, the old woman appeared on the TV. She was being interviewed by a reporter and was telling him about her lost money. "It's everything I had in the world," she said. "It took a lifetime to save that money."

The reporter then said to the TV viewers, "Please, if you found this paper bag, call the number on the screen to return it." Well, he said something like that. Miles wasn't sure exactly what was said. His head was spinning. Now he knew who the woman was. Miles was not a bad person. Miles knew the difference between right and wrong. For a few hours, he had faltered, but now he came to his senses. The money was not his. The money belonged to the old woman on the TV. Miles stood up.

"Where are you going?" Cynthia asked.

Miles said, "I'm going to do the right thing." He called the phone number on the TV, and he told the woman who answered that he had the bag of money. He then hung up the phone and said with a sigh, "Easy come, easy go."

Good people.

Miles is a good person. We all struggle with temptation, but good people conquer it. Good people do the right thing eventually. The old woman got her money back, and she offered Miles a $5,000 reward. But Miles wouldn't take it. "You don't need to pay me for being honest," he said. "I just did what was right."

This is a good story. I enjoy writing it, and Walter says he likes it a lot. Are you wondering what happened to Miles and his family? I talk to Miles. "What happened after you returned the money?" I ask.

"They interviewed me on the TV news. I was famous for a few minutes."

"And then?"

"It was on to the next news story."

"I mean, what happened to you?"

"I had to file for bankruptcy."

"I'm sorry."

"We're now living with Cynthia's parents in Placentia. I got a job working as a laborer for a concrete company. It pays just above minimum wage. Cynthia's parents have been very nice about all of this."

"And your future?"

"Who knows? I'd like to take another shot at starting my own company, but my credit is shot, and I have no cash. I don't know. I don't know what I'm going to do."

"And Cynthia?"

"She lined up some housekeeping jobs for a few people. But she can't work full-time. She needs to look after the kids."

"Have you heard anything from Susan Jasper?"

"No," Miles says.

"I talked to her," I say. "She told me to tell you the reward still stands."

"I don't want it."

"Surely you could use it?"

Miles smiles. Then he leans forward and says, "Well, I could use a lot of things."

CHAPTER 19

BOB AND CAROL

Good old Bob and Carol. Do you remember the first night we went out together? You knew Carol from one of your architecture classes, and Bob was her boyfriend. We went on a double date to see a theatrical production put on by the drama department at the school. I don't remember the name of the play, but I do remember laughing a lot. It was a farce, and we all got a big kick out of it. Then we went to Bob's apartment for a few beers afterward, where we wound up playing Scrabble until three in the morning. Those were such good times. I liked being around Bob and Carol. They were a million laughs, and they were madly in love with each other, just like you and me. We had that in common.

That was then. Now we've been married for nine years. Unlike you and me, Bob and Carol held off on marriage until a few years after they graduated from college. Finally, they tied the knot, and we went to their wedding. We stayed friendly with them after the wedding, but we saw less and less of each other as the years went by. Now we've been seeing Bob and Carol only about once a year. You get a call from Carol. You talk to her for a couple long hours, and when you hang up, I ask you, "What was all that about?"

"I'm in shock," you say.

"Over what?"

"They're getting a divorce."

"Bob and Carol?" I ask.

"Yes," you say.

"What the heck happened?"

"I don't even know where to begin."

"Tell me what Carol told you," I say.

"I would never have guessed."

"Guessed what?"

"What an impossible jerk Bob is. Carol told me about his prostitutes. Did you know about Bob's prostitutes? Tell me you didn't know. If you knew, you should've told me."

"I don't know anything about prostitutes," I say, and this is the truth. Bob has never mentioned anything about this to me in all the years I've known him.

"Carol said he has a slew of them."

"A slew?"

"That was her word. Maybe she was exaggerating, but it didn't sound like it."

"Why would he need prostitutes?"

"To satisfy his perversions."

"Perversions?"

"Turns out Bob is kind of a weirdo."

"Like how?"

"Carol said it all started on their honeymoon night. Sure, they'd had sex before, but there was nothing kinky about it. Then, on their honeymoon night, everything changed. Carol said Bob wanted oral sex to get him in the mood, and Carol didn't know what to do. 'He'd never asked for that before,' Carol said. 'At first, I thought he was kidding, and then I realized he was serious. He tried to push my head down toward his lap, and I resisted. There was no way! I had no desire to put his dirty little erection into my mouth.'"

I laugh.

"Bob got mad."

"He got mad?"

"He told her if she truly loved him, she'd go out of her way to prove it."

I laugh again.

"It isn't very funny," you say.

"No, I suppose not."

"And that was only the beginning. It turned out that Bob was a real pervert. He wanted to do all sorts of things with Carol. He kept telling her that if she loved him, she would do what he wanted. Well, she did love him. But she had no intention of doing any of this stuff. She figured if he loved her, he wouldn't ask her to do things she was obviously not comfortable with. So finally, he stopped asking. They went on with their lovemaking like normal people."

"And?" I ask.

"This wasn't enough for Bob. He started going to prostitutes, to women who would do as he asked—as long as they were being paid. It's gross, isn't it? Carol said, 'I had no idea who these women were, where they'd been, or what they'd allowed men to do to them. They could've been teeming with STDs, all of them, the men and the hookers alike. It was disgusting.'"

"How'd she learn about the prostitutes?"

"Bob told her a couple years ago."

"He told her?"

"Carol thinks he was trying to make her jealous. Can you imagine that? What an idiot! All it did was make her refuse to have more sex with him. Carol said they haven't had sex for two years."

"Wow," I say.

"What a nightmare, right?"

"Yes," I say. "So that's why they're getting divorced?"

"That's part of the reason."

"Part of it?"

"There are other problems."

"Such as?"

"Bob's hygiene has been an issue ever since he started working at home. Things were better when Bob had an office. But when he learned he could lower his rates to customers by working out of home, he moved out of the office, as you know. Business has been good, but Bob's hygiene has taken a nosedive. Carol said she can hardly stand to be near him. He doesn't brush his teeth, and his breath smells like a trash pail. Carol can hardly stand to kiss him. He never combs his hair, and he seldom showers. He has body odor, and his clothes all smell like sweat. He doesn't even clip his fingernails or toenails. They are long, sharp, and dirty, and he has a nose hair problem. Carol has asked him over and over to take better care of himself, but he doesn't. He just goes on with his business like it doesn't matter. He cleans up when they go out with others or when they have company. But besides those occasions, he is a slob."

"Weird," I say.

"Isn't it?"

"Has Carol talked to him about it?"

"She brings it up, but he just ignores her."

"That's hard to imagine."

"Isn't it? And that's not all that's been happening. Bob also now is obsessed with sports."

"He took up a sport?"

"No, he watches them on TV."

"Ah," I say. "A lot of men do that."

"But all the time?"

"Well, often," I say.

"It's all Bob does with his free time. He ignores Carol. He ignores his chores. He doesn't help around the house. They don't watch movies together anymore. Or do anything else. He just sits in front of the TV, drinking beer and eating potato chips, watching sports. Any sport will do. He watches football, basketball, baseball, and hockey. And when those sports aren't on, he watches soccer and lacrosse. He even watches poker. Whatever they broadcast on ESPN, he sits and stares at it like a moron, eating chips and drinking his beer. Carol says she feels like she's married to a complete stranger. She said, 'I come into the family room and see Bob on the sofa, and I wonder who this man is. He is not the man I married. He is not the man I fell in love with.'"

"They should see a marriage counselor," I say.

"That's what I told Carol."

"And what did she say?"

"I told her that we saw a counselor and that it was helpful to us."

"And?"

"She said she asked him, but Bob refused to go."

"That doesn't sound like Bob."

"He's not who we think he is."

"No," I say. "Maybe if I talked to him."

"Too late for that. They've already hired an attorney. They'll be signing divorce papers next week."

"Jeez," I say.

I decide I need to talk to Bob. It doesn't sound like I'll be able to do much to rescue their marriage, but I would like to get his side of the story. Every coin has two sides.

I call Bob and ask him to have lunch with me, and we agree to get together a week later. We meet at a café in Newport Beach. I arrive first, and I grab a table for us. Then Bob shows up. He's put on a few pounds since the last time I saw him, but other than that, he looks the same. He seems clean, and his hair is combed. I see no evidence of the nose hair problem Carol complained about. Bob takes a seat at the table and picks up a menu. He reads over the menu and talks at the same time. "I suppose Carol told you guys about the divorce," he says to me.

"She told Samantha," I say.

"She probably got an earful about me."

"She did," I say.

"What did she say?"

"Several things."

Bob says while looking over the menu, "The Reuben sandwich looks good. Or maybe a BLT. What are you going to get?"

"I don't know," I say. "Maybe a bowl of soup."

"I feel more like a sandwich."

"A sandwich sounds good," I say.

"So," Bob says, "what exactly did Carol have to say about me?"

I look at Bob. He is still staring at his menu. I say, "She said you've been seeing prostitutes. Is that true?"

"Christ," Bob scoffs.

"She said your sex life was a problem."

"She's got a big mouth."

"You don't have to talk about this if you don't want to," I say. I say this, but I'm hoping he will talk about it. I want to find out what happened. It's not that I'm nosy; I just want to know what happened to our friends.

"I went to a prostitute once," Bob says.

"Only once?"

"Well, three times. But it was the same prostitute, so it really only counts as once."

"And you told Carol about it?"

"I did," Bob says.

"But why?"

"Why what? Why did I go to a prostitute, or why did I tell Carol about it?"

"Both," I say.

Bob looks me in the eye and asks, "Did Carol tell Samantha that she hates having sex?"

"No," I say.

"Well, she does. The woman is a human icebox."

"That's hard to believe."

"Believe it. Oh, before we were married, we had sex all the time, and she led me to believe she enjoyed it. She led me to believe she was attracted to me physically. And I had no reason to doubt her. She was very convincing. But after we married, everything changed. Not right away, but things did change. I could tell she was about as interested in sex as she was in changing the oil in our car. Having sex was just something she had to do, not something she looked forward to or even enjoyed. You can tell these things. I could tell."

"And?"

"Like a fool, I tried to spice things up. I suggested we try some new things, you know, to see if I could get her aroused. In retrospect, I now realize it was a dumb thing to do. I mean, if she didn't like sex to begin with, why would she want to try anything adventurous? But I didn't give up. I tried, and I tried. And the more often I tried, the bigger a fail it was. I was making a fool of myself, and I was making her even more uncomfortable than she was before. She didn't like it. And me? I was beginning to resent her aversion to me. What was wrong with me? Why was she so turned off by me? Instead of becoming closer to each other after we got married, we were growing further apart. Is any of this making sense to you?"

"Sort of," I say.

"How would you feel?"

"I don't know," I say.

Just then, our waitress shows up at our table to take our orders. I order a bowl of minestrone soup, and Bob asks for a Reuben sandwich. We hand the waitress our menus, and she walks away.

"Eventually, I felt lonely," Bob says.

"Lonely?"

"It's a lousy way to feel when you're married. It should be just the opposite, right? The last thing you should feel when you have a partner is lonely. But that's how I felt. I felt unloved and lonely."

"That's rough," I say.

"Then, one day, I was talking about marriage with one of my clients, and he told me about this escort service he uses. He told me how great the girls are. He told me about one girl in particular named Candy. I laughed at this. I didn't think much of it at first, and then a month later, Carol had to go out of town on business. I got lonely. Oh man, I mean, I was really feeling awful, so I called the escort service to see if Candy was available. She was, and we got together."

"You had sex with her?"

"I sure did."

"Did you enjoy it?"

"I don't know."

"Well, either you did, or you didn't."

"It was not that simple. It was sort of strange. I mean, it felt good to have someone pretend to like me, yet it also felt strange that I was paying for it like so many other men. The woman was an actress, right? She knew all the right things to say and do, yet it was all somehow empty and without meaning. I may as well have been having sex with a blow-up doll. She felt like a woman, she smelled like a woman, and she sounded like a woman, yet she was, for all intents and purposes, just a make-believe experience.

"Like I said earlier, I spent three separate nights with Candy. Then I stopped seeing her. The whole thing bothered me, and then I told Carol about it. I was hoping she would understand what was happening, and I was hoping maybe she'd at least feel some pity for me. But it was just the opposite. She was furious, and she called me a pervert. 'I can't believe I married you,' she said to me."

"I see," I say. I don't really know what to say because now I don't know if I should believe Bob's story or if I should believe Carol's.

"Things went downhill from there."

"How so?"

"We stopped having sex completely."

"Not at all?"

"Not even occasionally. I masturbated in the shower once in a while. That was my sex life."

"Carol told Samantha you've been letting yourself go."

"Letting myself go?"

"Ignoring your hygiene. Dressing like a slob. Watching a lot of sports on TV."

"I guess that's true. I guess I figured if I'm going to be treated like a bum, I may as well be one. I mean, what was the point? Why would I want to go out of my way to be attractive to someone who didn't find me attractive in the first place?"

"But she did once love you."

"She loved me?"

"At one time."

"That's what she told me," Bob says.

"Why would she lie?"

"I don't know. I've never been able to figure it out. Maybe she was confused. Or maybe she doesn't know what love is. Or maybe it's her parents' fault. Or maybe it's in her DNA. Anyway, it's all water under the bridge. The divorce will be final soon. I'll be free of her, and she'll be free of me."

Our waitress suddenly shows up with our food. She places our dishes in front of us and then asks if we want anything else. We both shake our heads, and off she goes. Bob looks down at his Reuben sandwich, and tears well in his eyes.

"Are you okay?" I ask.

"I'll be fine," Bob says.

"I'm sorry if I made you feel bad."

"You didn't do anything."

"I don't know what to say."

"How are you and Samantha getting along?" he asks, changing the subject.

"We're doing good."

"Are you still working at the *Daily Observer*?"

"I am," I say.

"What ever happened to that book you were writing?"

"I stopped."

"You put it on hold?"

"Even worse," I say. "I deleted the entire file. I trashed it. It was crap."

"It's funny, isn't it?" Bob says.

"What's funny?"

"It's funny how we go after things so enthusiastically, only to suddenly trash them and move on to new things."

I think about this for a moment. Then I say, "I guess we learn as we go."

"Do we ever," Bob says.

CHAPTER 20

IT'S A BOY

I couple of years go by. We are strolling through Disneyland in the middle of the summer. They call it the Happiest Place on Earth. It is sunny, hot, and crowded. We are now thirty-two years old, and we've been married for eleven years. It's just you and me, a childless married couple, lost in a busy children's make-believe world of rides, castles, gift shops, restaurants, and costumed characters.

We stand patiently in long and sweaty lines so we can go on the rides. We drink cold yellow lemonade from plastic Mickey Mouse cups and gobble up all the sugary foods we can get our hands on. Hyperactive kids are everywhere, as far as the eye can see, so what the heck are we doing here? We are two young adults, and we should be acting our age. We should be on the sand at the beach, working on our tans; in downtown Orange, browsing the antique stores; or in Laguna Beach, visiting the art galleries, but we've picked Disneyland. Why? We've come here because we are ready. We were drawn to the park like a pair of moths to a lightbulb, fluttering, bouncing, and burning our powdery wings.

I say it first. You are thinking the same thing, but the words leave my lips before they leave yours.

You ask, "What are we doing here?"

"I guess it's about time," I say. You know exactly what I mean.

"Wouldn't it be fun?"

"It would," I agree.

"Boy or a girl?"

"It's going to be a boy."

"You sound so sure of yourself."

"It will be a boy," I say. "I know it will be a boy."

"I have the same feeling."

150

"But if it's a girl, it will be okay," I say.

"Either way."

"But," I say as I take a bite from my churro, "it will be a boy."

"Then we agree?"

"Yes, we agree."

"They say children change your life."

"I've heard that," I say.

"What do you think it means?"

"I don't know."

"Are you ready to have your life changed?"

"I'm ready. How about you?"

"Yes, I'm ready," you say.

We are suddenly on the Matterhorn ride, and our train climbs up to the top of the fake mountain. It is noisy. We can hear people laughing and screaming. You put your hand on my forearm, squeeze it, and ask, "What will we name him?"

"I don't know," I say.

"You must have something in mind."

"Well, I was thinking Taylor."

"Taylor?"

"I always liked that name."

"I don't know any Taylors."

"If he grows up to become a tailor, they could call him Taylor the Tailor."

"That's dumb."

I laugh. "He's not going to be a tailor," I say.

"How about Orville?"

"Orville?"

"That was my great-grandfather's name," you say. "I always liked the sound of that name."

"Too old-fashioned," I say.

"Maybe you're right."

"We should buy one of those books," I say.

"Books?"

"A book of names for children. There are thousands of names to pick from. All kinds of them."

An hour later, we are on the Pirates of the Caribbean ride. We are passing through the town being pillaged by pirates. The pirates are singing a song about drinking rum, and in the dim light, you turn to look at me. "What do you think he'll be like?" you ask.

"He'll be whatever he wants to be," I say.

"But you'll give him guidance."

"And so will you," I say.

"But you'll be his father. Boys listen to their fathers more than they do to their mothers."

"Do they?" I ask.

"Sure they do."

"Don't sell yourself short," I say.

"I think our son is going to do well in school," you say. You are watching the robotic pirates. "He's going to be liked. He's going to be good looking. He's not going to be a bully. He's going to get good grades in his classes, and he's going to be good at sports."

I laugh.

"What's so funny about that?" you ask.

"It's just funny," I say.

"We'll be good parents, won't we?"

"All parents think they'll be good parents."

"Well, tell me this then," you say. "Do you plan on doing something wrong?"

"No, I don't plan on it. But no one is perfect. We're going to make some mistakes."

"Like what?"

"If we knew what they were in advance, we probably wouldn't make them."

"That doesn't make any sense."

"It makes perfect sense," I say.

You think for a moment. Then you say, "Maybe it does make sense, but we'll still be good parents."

"We will," I agree.

Two hours later, we are in one of the gift shops on Main Street. You are going through the stacks of T-shirts. I am watching you. You turn to me and say, "We should get Taylor a T-shirt."

"So we are naming him Taylor?"

"For the time being."

"Sounds good to me."

"Or maybe we should get him a stuffed animal. These Jiminy Crickets are cute." You are now rummaging through the stuffed animals.

"Or Pluto."

"Pluto is good."

"I had a Pluto when I was a kid."

"Do you remember the first time you went to Disneyland?"

"I think my parents took me when I was a toddler," I say. "I've seen pictures. They had me on a leash. Leashes were popular then. But I was too young to actually remember."

"I first went when I was eight."

"You remember it?"

"I do," you say.

"Did your parents get you a stuffed animal?"

"No, but they got me a mouse-ears hat."

"I think I had one of those."

"I lost mine."

"Same here."

"All this stuff to buy," you say. "I wish Taylor was here with us now. I wish I could see his face."

"He'll be a handsome little devil."

"The girls will go crazy for him."

"He'll have a girlfriend."

"What do you think she'll be like?" you ask.

"I have no idea."

"Hopefully she'll be a nice girl."

"Why wouldn't she be?" I ask.

"There are all kinds of girls. Boys are so easily taken advantage of."

"Did you take advantage of me?" I ask.

"Sure I did," you say, and we both laugh.

Seven months later, you're pregnant. You come home from seeing the doctor, and you break the news to me. We go out to dinner to celebrate and then come home to watch some TV.

For the next nine months, we watch your belly grow. We take pictures of you in your new maternity clothes. You get sick to your stomach while driving home from work, and you pull over and puke in the neighbors' bushes. You say, "I hope they didn't see me," and I tell you not to worry about it. There are baby showers, and friends and relatives buy you all sorts of stupid gifts. We go to Lamaze classes. You learn how to breathe. We prepare the nursery. Everything is white because we don't want to have it ready for the wrong sex.

The doctor asks if we want to know the baby's sex, and we tell him we think we already know. "We think it's going to be a boy," I say.

"If you say so," the doctor says.

Our parents keep calling our house to see how you're doing, and during the last month, they call every day. "Did you have the baby yet?" they ask.

We tell them, "No, we'll call you when it happens."

Then they call again the next day and ask the same question.

Then it comes time. The next thing I know, we're in a delivery room. The doctor has his hands between your legs, and the nurse is doing something or other. I'm really not paying attention. Good thing this isn't all up to me. I'm pretty much useless.

Then out comes the baby, along with a bucket of blood and gunk, and the doctor holds the purple creature up in the air. "It's a boy!" he proclaims.

I say, "I told you so."

I call our parents to tell them the good news, and they ask why I didn't call them earlier. Then they say they'll be right there.

Sure enough, they arrive at the hospital, all smiles. I've never seen people smile so much, and everyone wants to hold the baby. Everyone wants to ask you how you feel. Your dad says to me, "I knew she could do it. Was never a doubt in my mind."

When we drive home from the hospital, some of the neighbors come to see the baby, but for the most part, things are quiet that first day home. It's just you, me, and the baby. The three of us. Once there were two, and now there are three. We're no longer just a couple. Now we are a full-fledged family, enjoying the first miraculous day of our upcoming journey. So much anticipation. So much love. We are Jonathan, Samantha, and Taylor Orville Hart—all for one, and one for all!

You tuck Taylor into his crib at about eight at night, and then you go to sleep early. You are exhausted. Me? I'm going to stay awake to watch an old movie. I sit on the sofa and turn on the TV. I'm going to watch the original *The Mummy*, the black-and-white 1932 version starring Boris Karloff. I've seen it before, but it's been years. I press Play, and the movie starts.

Suddenly, it occurs to me that I no longer have to watch these movies alone. I have Taylor, a boy who will appreciate these movies as much as I do. What little boy wouldn't want to watch *The Mummy*? I pause the movie at the opening title and step into the nursery, where I retrieve Taylor from the crib. I bundle him up in his warm blanket and take him to the family room sofa. I prop him up on the sofa pillows so he can watch the TV with me. He is quiet, and he seems to be comfortable. His little eyes are wide open. He is my little pal, my little TV-watching partner.

I press the Play button on the remote, and the movie starts up. I get comfortable on the sofa, and we watch. Have you seen *The Mummy*? Maybe you saw it when you were a little girl.

It is a relatively tame movie as far as monster movies go. But it is entertaining, and Taylor seems interested in it, especially when they show close-ups of Karloff's iconic face. There is something about Karloff's image that intrigues little Taylor. "He was one of a kind," I say. "You should see him in *Frankenstein*." I know he doesn't understand me. I guess I am talking to him the way one talks to a dog. We know dogs don't understand us, but we talk to them anyway.

Taylor and I watch the movie until it's nearly over, and then you appear from the bedroom. You've woken up, and now you are not happy. "What are you two watching?" you ask. "Let me guess. I suppose you're watching one of your awful monster movies."

"*The Mummy*," I say.

"*The Mummy*?"

"The original version."

"You woke the baby up to watch *The Mummy*?"

"He seems to like it," I say.

"What in the world is wrong with you?"

"Nothing is wrong with me," I say. "We're just watching an old movie."

"Watching a horror movie with an impressionable infant? I can't believe you would show such bad judgment."

"Like I said, he seems to like it."

"He shouldn't be exposed to such images."

"The movie isn't that bad."

"It's a horror movie," you say.

"It's barely scary at all. And besides, Taylor likes looking at Boris Karloff's face."

"Honestly," you say. You step to the sofa and pick up Taylor. You hold him protectively against your breast, as if I'd been abusing the little guy. You are about to walk back to the nursery.

"We were just having a little fun," I say.

"Now he's probably going to have bad dreams," you say. "I can't imagine what you were thinking."

"He won't have bad dreams."

"How do you know?"

"He's a little boy. Little boys love this stuff. They eat it up."

"He's an infant."

"Okay, so he's an infant. But he's still a little boy."

"Unbelievable," you say. Then you take Taylor back to his room and place him in his crib. Taylor starts to cry.

I come into the nursery, and you glare at me. "See what you've done? Now he's crying."

"He's probably just hungry."

"You've frightened him."

"He's just worked up a little appetite. I'll go get a bottle for him."

"Poor little thing," you say to Taylor.

I go to the kitchen and prepare a bottle of formula. I heat it up and then test it on my wrist. I then bring it to the nursery and hand it to you. You poke the nipple into Taylor's mouth, and he begins sucking like mad. "See?" I say. "He was just hungry. That's all it was."

You watch Taylor for a moment, and then you look over at me. "You're an idiot," you say. There's no point in arguing about it, so I let the comment slide.

Meanwhile, Taylor finishes off the entire bottle of formula. Then he falls asleep. *Sweet dreams, little man.*

CHAPTER 21

WHAT IS LOVE?

You can't fill an empty bottle with it, you can't wrap it up or put a bow on it, and you certainly can't measure it. It has no weight, yet it can be as heavy as a mountain. It's invisible, yet it can be as plain as the nose on your face. You won't see it coming, yet it can hit you like a ton of bricks. It can knock you out. It can tickle you and make you laugh. It can move you to madness, and it can launch a thousand ships. It provokes you to do the craziest things. It can calm you, agitate you, motivate you, hurt you, and inspire you. No one knows where it comes from, why it is, or where it is going. You can't force it, and you can't ignore it. You can fight it tooth and nail, but odds are that it will be victorious. Sometimes it's logical, and sometimes it makes no sense at all.

I think we all experience it at one time or another. Some of us are much more susceptible to it than others. It makes us yearn, envy, hope, scheme, pity, and hate. Wise men and women will cherish it, and fools will take it for granted.

Me? I don't know if I'm a wise man or a fool—sometimes I'm one, and sometimes I'm the other. Sometimes I wish I'd never heard of it, and sometimes I believe I can't live without it.

Love, the four-letter word. Love, the subject of so many books, poems, and songs. Love, the stuff of dreams. Love, a sweet bouquet of flowers, a flickering candle, a roaring fire, a raindrop in the ocean, a bird in flight, a bloody sunset, a sunrise, and a sparkling star on the horizon, leading the way.

I love you, Samantha. I know this for a fact. There's never been any doubt in my mind. You can call me an idiot, and it doesn't hurt my feelings. Odds are that I have done something stupid. Odds are that I deserve it. You are on a higher level than I am, and I know it. You are on the top of the mountain, and your hair is in the clouds. The birds are below you. I love the way you smell like the sky. I love the sound of your voice. I love the way you are kind to animals and other people's children. I love the way you love Taylor, hold him, feed him, dote on him, dress him, and protect him. There is a wondrous beauty in motherhood. Mother and child. Mother of my son. My wife and true love.

It is my idea to take a two-night trip up to Carmel for our twelfth anniversary. It is my idea to make the trip during the middle of the week so we will be in Carmel on our true anniversary date. It is also my idea to have my mom and dad watch Taylor while we are gone. We drop him off before we leave. My mom says to you, "Don't worry about a thing, honey. I raised two of my own. I know the routine."

We soon are in the car, cruising up the interstate. The radio is playing music low. Our suitcases are in the trunk, and there is a bag of pretzels in my lap. There is a large truck in front of us, trying to make its way around another slow-moving truck. I am probably following the truck too closely, and you say, "What's the hurry?"

"I'm not in a hurry," I say.

"Then why are you so close to that truck? You're making me nervous."

"Sorry," I say.

"How are we doing for gas?"

I look at the gas gauge. "We're half full," I say.

"The sign back there said there's a gas station in ten miles. We should probably stop."

"Already?"

"I need to use a restroom," you say.

"Okay," I say.

"And I need to stretch my legs."

"I could use a cup of coffee," I say.

"Are you getting tired?"

"Not really," I say.

"I can drive if you're getting tired."

"I'm fine," I say.

"I don't mind driving."

"I'm fine," I say again.

"I wonder how Taylor's doing."

"I'm sure he's okay."

"He's not used to being without us. I hope I left your mom enough diapers."

"If you didn't, she can buy some," I say.

You are now looking out the side window. "Do you think Taylor misses us?" you ask.

"He probably doesn't even know we're gone. My mom and dad will keep him busy." I grab a few pretzels and stuff them into my mouth.

"You're still following that truck too close," you say.

"Sorry," I say.

"I don't know why you're in such a hurry."

"I'm not in a hurry," I say.

"I really don't mind driving."

"I'm okay," I say. "Just relax."

We stop talking for a moment. Again, you are looking out the side window. You ask, "Did you show your mom how to hook up the car seat?"

"I did," I say. "But I don't think they'll be driving Taylor anywhere."

"You never know."

"That's true," I say.

"You hear stories."

"Stories?"

"About people hooking up their car seats wrong," you say. "Awful stories. Tragic stories."

"I showed her how to do it," I say. "She knows."

"I'd feel a lot better if they just stayed home."

"Like I said, I don't think they're planning to drive Taylor anywhere."

"The gas station is at the next exit," you say.

"Got it."

"You need to get in the other lane."

"I'm aware of that."

Finally, we pull into the gas station. I stick my credit card into the pump and poke the nozzle into the side of the car while you walk quickly to the restroom. While the car is being filled, I step into the store to get a cup of coffee. I get my coffee and go to the cashier to pay for it. I return to the car. As I put the coffee into the car's cupholder, you show up. You climb into the passenger side while I replace the nozzle on the pump. Then I climb in. "All set?" I ask.

"All set," you say. "Did you get your coffee?"

"I did," I say. "It's right there in the cupholder. How were the restrooms?"

"Disgusting."

"That bad?"

"Really awful. I'll bet they haven't been cleaned for a month."

"Ugh," I say.

"How's your coffee?"

"I don't know," I say. "I haven't tasted it yet."

"Did you fill us up with gas?"

"I did," I say. "We should have enough to make it to Carmel without having to stop at another station. Unless, of course, you need to pee again."

"I should be fine. Do you want any more pretzels?" You hold the bag toward me in case I want it.

"No, thanks," I say.

"We also have some salami."

"I'm good," I say.

"Just let me know if you get hungry."

"I will."

"And let me know if you want me to drive."

"Okay," I say.

I put the car in Drive, step on the gas, and get back on the interstate. We are headed to the Chateau Carmel, the same hotel we stayed at ten years ago. I have a lot of good memories from that visit. I guess by having us go there now, I am trying to re-create those memories. Why not? You and I have been working hard recently, and Taylor has been a huge drain on our time and energy. We deserve a few days to ourselves.

You grab a pillow, put it between your head and the side window, and close your eyes to take a nap. I am glad to see you are relaxed, and I continue to drive and sip my coffee. The radio is still on low. The interstate is filled with cars and trucks. The sun is beginning to drop from the sky, and we'll be arriving at the hotel in just a few hours.

Do you remember our first visit to the chateau? The bed was large, and the room was cozy. The bathtub was big enough for two, so we undressed and climbed into the tub together. It was the first thing we did. We had slippery, soapy fun, washing ourselves, caressing each other's wet skin in the hot water. Then we dried off, climbed into the bed, and made love like two wild animals.

Well, at least it seemed that way. Still out of breath, you called room service and ordered our dinners. Wearing the hotel's terrycloth bathrobes, we sat at the foot of the bed, watching the TV and waiting for our food. We were both famished.

When the food arrived, we signed for it. We laughed and ate and drank champagne, and you said, "Can you imagine living like this every day?"

I said, "We *should* live like this every day. Someday we *will* live like this every day." God, Samantha, how I loved you. You were my world.

After we finally arrive at the hotel, we grab our suitcases and walk to the lobby. It's nice, but it seems different. I can't quite put my finger on the difference. Somehow, it seemed fancier the last time we were here. It was classier and more upscale, but no matter. I step up to the registration desk to get our room key. It is the same room we were in ten years ago. I made sure of that when I made the reservation.

We walk into the room. The sun is setting outside, and the room is dark, so we click on the lights. Cozy? Not exactly. Cramped is more like it. The room seems a lot smaller than it did ten years ago, and the bed does not seem as large. The room smells like disinfectant and old cigarette smoke. "It stinks in here," you say.

"I thought this was a no-smoking room."

"Did you ask for a no-smoking room?"

"I asked for the same room we stayed in before."

"If you want a no-smoking room, you have to ask for a no-smoking room."

"I thought all the rooms were no-smoking rooms."

"Well, someone has been smoking in this one."

"Apparently so," I say.

"At least it's clean."

"It is," I say.

"Open the drapes," you say, and I walk over to the window and open them. It's dark outside, and we can't really see much of anything.

"Do you remember the view?" I ask.

"Not really," you say.

"Me either."

"We should unpack before we get dinner."

"Room service?" I ask.

"I'd rather eat out."

"Okay," I say.

"I feel like something light."

"I'll ask the concierge for a recommendation."

"Hopefully she can suggest something nearby. I'm really tired of being in the car."

"I'll ask."

"And the restaurant should be casual. I don't feel like dressing up."

"Same here," I say. Then I walk into the bathroom and say, "The tub is still here."

"The tub?"

"The bathtub."

"What about it?"

"Don't you remember?" I ask.

"Remember what?" You are now unpacking, and I come out of the bathroom.

"Never mind," I say.

"I'm going to take the top four drawers of the dresser. You can have the bottom two."

"Okay," I say.

"And don't hang up your clothes until I hang up mine. It doesn't look like we have enough hangers."

"Should I call for more?"

"Go ahead."

I get on the phone and call the front desk to ask for more clothes hangers. They tell me they'll send someone right up, and I say thank you.

"Remember," you say, "I'll be getting a call early tomorrow morning."

"A call?"

"I told you about the meeting last night. We're holding the preconstruction meeting for the Randolph house at seven. My assistant will be there, but I promised to be available on the phone."

"Okay," I say.

"Then I have another call scheduled for ten with the plan checker in the Newport Beach building department for the Henderson project."

"No problem," I say.

"The call could take a while."

"Take all the time you need," I say.

We finish unpacking, and I call the concierge. She recommends a restaurant just a few blocks from the hotel, and we walk there. The name of the restaurant is the Corner. The concierge was right. It is casual. But the menu is limited, and you do not see anything you like.

"I don't see anything light," you say.

"You can order a salad," I say.

"I don't feel like a salad."

"I'm going to get the chicken pot pie."

"Too heavy."

"It sounds good to me. I haven't had a good chicken pot pie for years."

"I might get the salmon."

"That sounds good too."

"It says it's encrusted with something. I don't want it encrusted with anything. Just plain salmon. And some steamed vegetables."

"I'm sure they can do that for you."

"Or the pork chop also sounds good. Without the sauce and with some steamed vegetables."

"This place is kind of expensive, isn't it?" I ask, looking at the prices.

"I've seen worse."

"Do you want a glass of wine?" I ask.

"Too many calories. I'd rather get a Diet Coke."

"I'm going to get a beer."

"A beer?"

"Imported. Something special."

"You never drink beer."

"This evening calls for something special," I say. "And they have a great beer selection. Why don't you have a beer with me? For the hell of it."

"Beer makes me feel bloated," you say.

"Or we could order a bottle of champagne."

"Champagne?"

"To celebrate."

"I don't like champagne," you say.

"You drank plenty of champagne on our wedding night," I say, smiling.

"I was young," you say. "I didn't know any better."

I set down my menu. I have made up my mind. "I'm definitely going to get the chicken pot pie," I say. "And a bottle of German beer."

"I guess I'll get the salmon," you say. Then you pick up your cell phone. "Maybe we should call your parents. You know, to see how Taylor's doing."

"I'm sure he's fine."

"I'd feel better if I talked to your mom."

"Then go ahead and call," I say.

My love. My wife. The mother of my child. You have never looked more beautiful. Salmon and steamed vegetables. I should've known.

CHAPTER 22

WHEN IT'S RIGHT

We are now thirty-four, which makes my younger brother, Lewis, thirty. Lewis announced his engagement to a twenty-eight-year-old nurse named Cheryl Mathers nine months ago. Cheryl was working at the hospital in Newport Beach, and Lewis, who is an EMT, met Cheryl in the emergency room. They met over the injured body of a car accident victim Lewis and his partner had wheeled in to be patched up and saved. Lewis told me it was love at first sight. They were up to their elbows in broken bones and blood, and they fell in love.

That is my brother. My dad likes to call him impulsive, but I think there's more to it than that. If so impulsive, he would've gotten engaged years ago to the first young female who caught his attention. But my brother isn't like that. In fact, Lewis waited years before deciding whom he wanted to spend the rest of his life with, and it wasn't until the right one came along that he pulled the trigger. Cheryl was right. "When it's right, it's right," he told me. "All I needed was a second. When our eyes met for the first time, I knew Cheryl and I were going to get married—simple as that."

In a way, I admire Lewis. Not many of us are so sure about the decisions we make. But as I said, that is Lewis. Lewis knew Cheryl for only two short months before asking her to make the lifelong commitment. He asked her to marry him, and she said yes. They surprised all of us with their plans, and they set their wedding date for three months following the engagement. It was crazy. Dad thought they were being way too impulsive, and Mom was worried Cheryl was pregnant. She thought they were in a rush to tie the knot before the baby was born, but it turned out Mom was wrong. It was all about love. Love at first sight, remember?

They've now been happily married for six months. I get a call from Lewis, and he wants me to come over to their house. I haven't talked to him since the wedding, so I'm curious to know what's new in his life.

"What's up?" I ask.

"Nothing is up," Lewis says. "I just thought it would be fun to talk."

"Everything okay?"

"Couldn't be better."

"That's good to hear," I say.

"I have the afternoon off, and Cheryl is at the hospital. Can you come over now?"

"I don't see why not," I say.

When I arrive at Lewis's house, I find him in the driveway, washing his car. He is wearing swim trunks and a T-shirt, and he is drying the hood of the car. "I'm almost done," he says. "I'm glad you came over."

"You said you wanted to talk?"

"There's so much to talk about," Lewis says.

"It's only been six months."

"One can learn a lot in six months."

"I suppose so," I say.

I stand and watch as Lewis finishes drying his car. He then pulls the car into the garage and closes the garage door. We enter the house through the front door, and Lewis has me sit at the kitchen table while he goes to his bedroom to put on a dry T-shirt. He returns to the kitchen.

"Something to drink?" he asks.

"I could go for some coffee," I say.

As Lewis goes to work making the coffee, I notice something. There's a skip in his step. I know what it is right away. My brother seems happy. It's not as if Lewis isn't ordinarily happy—in fact, he's one of the happiest people I know—but now he is extraordinarily happy. He hums while he makes the coffee, and then he asks, "Do you take cream or sugar? I can't remember if you take cream or sugar or if you drink your coffee black."

"Black is fine," I say.

"Black it is."

"Why the good mood?" I ask.

"The good mood?"

"You seem so happy."

"I am happy, brother."

Lewis then goes on to tell me about Cheryl. He wants to tell me everything, and there is much to tell. He sits at the kitchen table with me and talks. He is bursting at the seams. He is enthusiastic. No, he is more than enthusiastic. He is ecstatic. He wants to fill me in on every detail.

"I hardly know where to begin," Lewis says. "I'll start with Cheryl when she was in middle school. She told me she was a kleptomaniac. Mostly shoplifting. She used to steal everything she could get her hands on. It began as just an occasional thing, and then it grew into an obsession. She would steal from everyone, from clothing stores, from gift shops, from supermarkets, from department stores, from drugstores—you name it. At first, the shoplifting went unnoticed, and then her parents began to ask her where she was getting all these things she was bringing home. She told them that friends bought them for her, and for a while, that lie sufficed. Then she got caught stealing a bottle of perfume and then a pair of jeans. Her parents began to catch on to her problem, and finally, they confronted Cheryl. She said she broke down and told them the truth. She knew the stealing was getting out of hand, and she knew she needed help."

"Did she get help?" I ask.

"Her parents took her to a psychiatrist."

"Wasn't that a little extreme?"

"Maybe it was, and maybe it wasn't. But Cheryl liked the doctor. He was a man in his early forties named Chester Rankin. Dr. Rankin was a handsome married man with an eight-year-old daughter and a ten-year-old son. He liked kids, but he especially liked Cheryl. After about three sessions with the doctor, Cheryl began to develop a crush on the man. She listened to every word he said, and she was able to stop her shoplifting habit. But now she had a new problem. She was in love with a forty-year-old psychiatrist.

"A stronger man would've seen this for what it was and nipped it in the bud. But the doctor was flattered by Cheryl's infatuation with him, and instead of resisting her advances, he encouraged her. The next thing the doctor knew, he was having sex with Cheryl on the couch in his office. It was weird, right? The guy was supposed to be helping her. When Cheryl's parents decided that the shoplifting was over and that the sessions with the doctor were no longer necessary, Cheryl's affair with Dr. Rankin came to an abrupt end. But now she had a thirst for older men."

"One obsession replaced the other?" I ask.

"Something like that," Lewis says.

"So what happened?"

"A few years went by. Then she had an affair with a history teacher when she was in high school."

"And?"

"Then she had another affair with a math teacher named Ed Barkley. Ed was in his early fifties and divorced. I don't know if he had any kids. He was crazy about Cheryl, and the two of them got together whenever they could, and Cheryl said the sex was great. Then, suddenly, this affair came to a screeching halt."

"Because?"

"Because Cheryl got pregnant. It was a mess. Cheryl told her parents who the father was, and they were fit to be tied. If it had been a boy her age, maybe they would've been able to understand. But it was a teacher, a man in his early fifties who certainly should've known better. Cheryl's dad wanted to throttle the guy."

"And did he?"

"No, he didn't," Lewis says. "In fact, they decided to keep the whole matter a secret. They didn't want Cheryl's reputation at the school to be sullied. Instead, they had Cheryl get an abortion, and they never did say anything to school officials. They never even called the teacher. They just swept the whole thing under the rug and went on with their lives. And Cheryl's dad said to her, 'I hope you've learned your lesson.'"

"And did she learn?"

"She learned to stay away from men."

"How about boys her age?"

"She stayed away from them too," Lewis says.

"That's too bad."

"That wasn't a problem for Cheryl."

"It wasn't?"

"Around that time, she became friends with a girl at school named Wanda Brickman. Wanda was Cheryl's age and a very attractive girl. Wanda was also a lesbian, and she put the moves on Cheryl."

"So they had an affair?" I ask.

"They did," Lewis says.

"So Cheryl's a lesbian?"

"She's actually bisexual."

"I see," I say.

"She didn't realize it until she met Wanda. She fell head over heels for the girl. They went everywhere together, and Cheryl thought they would be together forever. I guess Wanda was a real knockout. Anyway, that's how Cheryl described her to me. And the sex was great. It was good, clean sex, and there was no chance of getting pregnant. Of course, Cheryl's parents had no idea their relationship was sexual. They just thought the girls were close friends.

"This went on for a couple years, while Cheryl was a sophomore and junior. Then, the summer after their junior year, Wanda broke off the romance. She said she had met another girl and wanted to move on. Needless to say, Cheryl was devastated."

"What'd she do?"

"The two girls stopped seeing each other, and for a year, Cheryl went out with no one. Neither boy nor girl. Eventually, she fell into a bleak and horrible depression. Her grades at school were dropping, and she had no friends. Every day she would just come home and lock herself in her room, and her parents became concerned. She had been so happy when she was friends with Wanda, but now everything had changed. Then she began to talk about suicide, and that was when her parents decided to take Cheryl to a psychiatrist again. They were going to take her to Dr. Rankin, but Cheryl refused to see him, so they found a new doctor, a female. This doctor's name was Madeline Grimes, and she was recommended by the family's physician. Unlike Dr. Rankin, Dr. Grimes specialized in adolescents."

"Was she able to help?"

"At first, no."

"No?" I ask.

"No," Lewis says. "Cheryl saw the doctor once a week for three months, and they weren't making any progress. Then Dr. Grimes recommended that Cheryl take an antidepressant. Cheryl's parents were against this. They didn't feel comfortable giving their daughter drugs, and they had hoped for better results from drug-free therapies. But Dr. Grimes told them if they didn't act fast, the consequences could be serious. The doctor was especially concerned with Cheryl's growing obsession with ending her life. 'At this age, suicide is a very real concern,' Dr. Grimes said. 'If we don't act promptly, you could lose your daughter.' Well, Cheryl's parents then both agreed to try out an antidepressant, and the doctor called the prescription into their pharmacy. He said it would take several weeks for the drug to have an effect. And sure enough, three weeks later, Cheryl began to show signs of improvement."

"So she was cured?"

"She was treated."

"What's the difference?" I ask.

"Dr. Grimes explained that taking away the antidepressant could result in a return to things as they were. In other words, she suggested that Cheryl take the drug continuously to avoid a sudden return to her depressive state."

"Like forever?" I ask.

"Yes, forever."

"That seems like overkill."

"Maybe to us, but not to the doctor. And not to Cheryl and her parents. She still takes antidepressants to this day."

"And they work?"

"She hasn't experienced any serious depressions that I know about. Sure, things sometimes make her unhappy at times but not depressed. Not like she was before."

"I guess that's good."

"It is good."

"So she lived happily ever after?" I ask.

"Well, not quite," Lewis says. "There's more. When Cheryl graduated from high school and went to college, she experienced a whole new kind of problem. She decided to start going out with boys again. She was still bisexual, but I guess Wanda had turned her off to girls. In college, she met a boy named Kaleb Parker. Kaleb was a year older than her and in her English class. She liked Kaleb. He seemed like a nice boy, and when he asked her out, she said yes. The two of them went out often, and eventually, they became an item. You know, as in boyfriend and girlfriend.

"At first, Cheryl didn't see the harm in it. She liked Kaleb a lot and enjoyed being with him. But then things began to change. Kaleb became more and more possessive. And he became extremely jealous. He was also now talking about their future as if they were going to get married, and that was not what Cheryl had in mind. I mean, she liked the boy, and she liked being his girlfriend, but she wasn't in love with him. So she tried to talk to him. She tried to make him understand."

"And did he understand?" I ask.

"He didn't," Lewis says.

"So what'd she do?"

"She did the only thing she could do. She met with him for lunch and broke up with him."

"How'd he take it?"

"He wouldn't accept it. He told Cheryl she didn't really mean what she was saying. He told her she would come around. He told her they were forever. It got bad. He kept calling her to talk, and she wouldn't take his calls. He would come to her dorm room, and she'd refuse to answer the door. When he realized she was really having nothing to do with him, he began to stalk her. He kept his distance so she wouldn't cause a scene, but he was always in the shadows, following her. It was creepy, to say the least, and finally, she became concerned for her safety. She had to get a restraining order to keep him away. After a couple of weeks, he finally stopped stalking her."

"And then?" I ask.

"He disappeared."

"Like how?"

"I don't know," Lewis says. "He just vanished. He must've dropped out of the school. Maybe he dropped out of college completely, or maybe he transferred to a different school. But he was gone. Cheryl still has no idea where he went."

"Weird," I say.

"Isn't it?" Lewis says.

"I feel kind of sorry for the guy."

"He was a pig," Lewis says.

"Yeah, I guess maybe you're right."

"He freaked Cheryl out," Lewis says. "He turned her off to dating completely. For the rest of her time in college, she kept to herself and avoided relationships of any kind. She didn't feel lonely, and she didn't feel depressed. She said she just felt kind of lost. She concentrated on her studies instead, and she graduated."

"Well, that's good."

"I guess so."

"And then she became a nurse?"

"With her school record, she had no problem getting a job. She chose to work in Newport. She went out on a few dates with some doctors, but she kept things at a safe distance. Nothing serious. Besides, all the doctors she was dating already had wives and children. Then, after six years at the hospital, she raised her head one day and saw the man of her dreams."

"Who was?"

"Who was me, dummy."

"Of course," I say, laughing.

"Love at first sight, remember?"

"Yes," I say.

"I didn't know a thing about her, yet I knew everything I needed to know. In an instant, I knew I loved her."

"And she loved you."

"Right," Lewis says.

"And now here you both are."

"Here we are. Everything I know about her I learned after we were married. Funny, isn't it? I really didn't know Cheryl at all before we got married. I mean, I did, and I didn't."

"So where do you stand now?"

"I've never been so happy. Not despite her past life but because of it."

I look down at my empty coffee cup and ask, "Can you pour me another cup of coffee?"

"Sure thing," Lewis says.

"You're a lucky man," I say.

"Luck has little to do with it," Lewis says. He smiles and stands up. Then he refills my cup, and I think maybe he's right. But if not luck, then what?

CHAPTER 23

GOAL!

I never was much one for organized sports. I didn't enjoy playing them as a boy, and I certainly didn't enjoy watching them. It all seemed kind of stupid to me—a bunch of kids kicking, throwing, and running with inflated balls, trying to prove what? Who was better? Who was luckier? Who was tougher? It just wasn't a big deal for me.

Yet now here we are. We have a rough-and-tumble six-year-old son with grass-stained knees and a burning desire to play. Where did he get this desire from? School? Friends? Your sports-fanatic dad? His DNA? I don't know, but there's no denying it: Taylor loves sports.

So I become a sports dad. A soccer dad, a baseball dad, a flag football dad, a basketball dad, and a hockey dad. I'm the one with the flexible schedule, so I am the taxi driver. I take Taylor to all his practices and events, and I buy all his gear and watch all his games. You come now and then, but your job occupies most of your time. For the most part, Taylor's sports are my domain.

Taylor's favorite sport is ice hockey. The rink is a forty-five-minute drive from our house, and it's not a cheap sport. The equipment costs a fortune, and the team fees are astronomical compared to other sports. But Taylor loves it, and you and I decide the price is well worth it. Maybe I'm not a sports nut, but I'm in favor of encouraging Taylor to do well in something, especially something, like ice hockey, that he loves and excels in.

When you're a parent, you discover that your children look up to you. Maybe not when they become teenagers but certainly when they're Taylor's age. He assumes I know everything about everything, and ice hockey is no exception. Sure, he has coaches and other kids to learn from, but I am his dad. He's looking to me for answers, so I order a book on hockey basics from the internet.

The book comes in the mail, and I open the package and thumb through the pages. It tells me everything I need to know in order to come off as an expert to my son. I read about sweep checks, poke checks, wrist shots, snap shots, slap shots, passes, stick-handling techniques, power plays, penalties, and face-offs—the whole ball of wax. By the time I am done reading the book, I am an expert without even having played the game. Heck, I don't even know how to ice-skate without slipping and falling on my butt, and I'm instructing Taylor like a professional.

I take Taylor to the hockey rink every other night so he can practice his skating. It's cold in the rink, so I wear a jacket. They have a snack bar there, and while Taylor is skating, I stuff my face with nachos, big pretzels, and hot dogs. I drink lots of coffee. I talk to some of the other parents whose sons are also learning to play.

One of these parents has a kid on Taylor's team, and we become friendly. This guy is always there. His name is Ryan Haywood, and his son's name is Matt. The kid is good. I mean, he's really good, the best player on Taylor's team. I learn that Ryan works at the post office as a counter clerk. He has a miserable job but a talented son. He has a wife named Della, a beast of a woman who probably weighs more than Ryan and I combined, and she has a big mouth. During the games, one can practically hear this woman shouting from blocks away. Fortunately, she only shows up for the games, so Ryan and I are able to talk in peace while the boys are practicing.

"Did you ever play hockey?" Ryan asks me.

"No," I say.

"What was your sport?"

"I was into baseball," I say. This is sort of a lie. I mean, I played baseball now and again, but I was never on an organized team.

"We're from Canada," Ryan says.

"Oh?" I say.

"Everyone plays hockey up north."

"So I've heard. Where in Canada are you from?"

"Winnipeg."

"Never been there."

"We moved down here right before Matt was born. Got a job with the post office. Agnes works for an escrow company."

"Your son is a good player," I say.

"It's in his blood. Every male in our family played hockey. My brothers still play. I stopped playing when we moved down here and had Matt."

"How long has Matt been playing?"

"We put him on skates when he was three."

"Jeez," I say.

"He takes private lessons here. It's expensive, but it's worth every penny. Matt's instructor used to play for the LA Kings." Ryan tells me the guy's name, but I've never heard of him. Yet I pretend to know who he is.

"Oh yeah," I say. "I think I remember him."

"So your boy likes hockey?"

"He likes it a lot," I say.

"Does he take lessons?"

"Not yet. Maybe I'll look into it."

"Talk to Hank in the hockey office. He'll set things up for you. Hank runs the place."

"I've met him," I say.

"Hank played for the Ducks."

"Did he?"

"For six years. Had to quit because of concussions. He was a pretty good player. One hell of a fighter. You didn't want to trade blows with Hank."

"No kidding," I say. "He seems like such a nice guy. I would never have guessed."

Soon after our conversation, I take Ryan's advice and look into lessons for Taylor at the rink. The pro Ryan recommended is booked, so I sign him up with a young man named Jeff Turnbull. Hank tells me Jeff is an excellent teacher, so I take his word for it. Two nights a week, I bring Taylor down to the rink for his private lessons with Jeff.

Meanwhile, the in-house season is progressing, and Taylor's team is doing well. Unfortunately, this is no thanks to Taylor. Despite all my hard work and the lessons he's been taking, my son has yet to score his first goal. Still, I'm proud of him. He isn't discouraged, and he plays his heart out each and every game. Taylor's team is called the Lightning, and they are in second place. The first-place team is the Predators, and at the end of the season, the two teams play against each other in a championship match. The Lightning have yet to beat the Predators. It's a big game, and everyone shows up to watch.

My parents come to the game, and so do your parents. Everyone is excited to watch Taylor play, especially your dad, and when the kids skate out onto the ice, the people all cheer. It's pretty cute, actually. The boys are wearing so much gear that it's hard to tell one from the other. They wear colored jerseys, helmets, face masks, mouth guards, shoulder pads, elbow pads, hockey pants, shin guards, skates, knit stockings, and big, padded hockey gloves. The boys skate in circles, warming up for the game, taking practice shots at our goalie, when your dad looks over at me.

"This is the one," he says.

"The one what?" I ask.

"The game with Taylor's first goal."

"We'll see," I say.

"Think positive," your dad says.

"Jonathan has been working with him," you say. It sounds as if you're defending me to your dad.

"We know," your dad says.

"And he's been taking lessons," you say.

"Like I said," your dad says, "this is the one. I have faith in the boy."

"We prayed for him last night," your mom says.

"That's right; we did."

"You prayed?"

"Damn right," your dad says.

My dad rolls his eyes when your parents aren't looking. I'm not sure what my mom is thinking. Neither of my parents is used to being around sports people. They are quiet. They just want to watch the game.

It's finally time for the match to begin, and the clock on the electronic scoreboard is set. Some players go to the bench, and others take their positions on the ice. Okay, I'll admit it: I am excited. I want to see how Taylor does, and I hope he'll finally score a goal. The ref takes his place at the center of the rink, and then he drops the puck. The game is on! The kids scramble to get control of the puck.

It doesn't take long for the first goal to be scored. One of the kids on the other team gets the puck and skates right up to our goal. He fakes a shot to the goalie's glove side, and the goalie goes for it. He then shoots to the opposite corner, and sure enough, the puck sails right into the net. The goal immediately appears on the scoreboard, and the parents of the other team yell and applaud. Our goalie pulls the puck out of his net and hands it to the ref.

"Well, that certainly stinks," your dad says.

"It's just one goal," I say.

"This could be a long night," your dad says with a sigh.

"Be patient, dear," your mom says.

"Taylor's turn is coming," you say to your dad optimistically. "He's going to score. I can feel it."

The ref drops the puck again, and the kids are off and running like little wind-up toys. About a minute later, the same kid who scored the first goal for the other team has control of the puck again.

"Get him!" your dad shouts.

"Stop him!" you shout.

"Oh no!"

The kid has scored again. The score is now 2–0, and it hasn't even been two minutes. The parents of the other team are all laughing and giving each other high fives. The bastards!

The coach makes a line change, and the ref drops the puck again. Matt is on the ice now, and his gigantic mother is yelling at him to get the puck. Her voice is loud. It sounds as if she's shouting into a megaphone.

"Put it in the net!" she shouts.

"Come on, son!" Ryan shouts.

"Don't let them intimidate you!"

"You can do it!"

Matt doesn't let the team down. He takes the puck away from one of the other kids and heads toward their goal in a blur. A defenseman tries to stop him, but Matt skates right around the kid. When he arrives in front of the goal, he stops and takes a wicked slap shot. The goalie doesn't have a chance, and the puck sails right over his shoulder. The parents on our team all stand up and cheer.

"That's how it's done," your dad says. "Who the hell is that kid?"

"His name is Matt Haywood," I say. "He's the best player on our team."

"Thank God for Matt."

"Atta boy!" his mom shouts at the top of her lungs. "That's my baby!"

The ref collects the puck, and he drops it again. The boys swat and swing at it until it flies off toward the boards. A tiny kid on the other team gets ahold of the puck, and he skates it up the boards toward our goal. Taylor goes after him, but the kid outskates him and passes to a teammate standing in front of our goal. The kid whacks the puck as hard as he can, and it slides under our goalie's pads and into the net.

"Jesus!" your dad exclaims.

"I thought Taylor had him," your mom says.

"That's three goals already."

"There's still plenty of time," your mom says.

"Come on, Taylor!" you shout with your hands cupped around your mouth. "Show them what you've got! Don't let them push you around!" It's interesting. Every minute that passes, you seem more like your dad.

The game goes on. The teams trade goals back and forth, and the score stays close. Taylor still hasn't scored a goal, but we're not giving up on him. Not yet.

Finally, it is the last two minutes of the game, and the Predators are beating us 8–7. Matt Haywood gets ahold of the puck behind our net, and he skates out to the center of the ice. He whacks the puck into the sideboards, and it bounces right back to him. This confuses the defensemen, and Matt is now on his way to the goal. There is no one between Matt and the goalie, and he makes an amazing move that causes the goalie to slide to the left. The goalie thinks Matt is going to shoot to the left, but instead, Matt swings the puck, taking a wrist shot that flies into the upper right corner of the net. He has scored! The crowd goes crazy, and now it is a tie game.

There is less than a minute left, and the ref drops the puck again. One of our players nabs the puck and tries to skate, but he loses the puck on his way to the other team's goal. No matter. Matt is right there at the ready, and he gets ahold of the puck and skates forward. Taylor is right behind Matt, trying to keep up with him, trying to be useful.

Now there are only forty seconds left. Matt skates around to the side of the goalie and shoots. The puck smacks the goalie in his face mask and bounces onto the ice in front of him. But Taylor is right there! The puck is sitting like a ripe fruit in front of an open net, and the goalie doesn't have a chance. Taylor swings at the puck with his stick, but he misses. Then he swings again, and this time, he connects with the puck. The puck soars into the net, and the people in the bleachers all jump up. Our side cheer like crazy, and the other side moan.

"He did it!" your dad shouts.

"Goal!" you yell.

"We're going to win!"

"Thirty seconds left!"

During the remaining thirty seconds, the other team fails to score a goal, and when the clock winds down to zero, all the boys on our team throw off their gloves and helmets to celebrate after the buzzer sounds.

"He scored the winning goal!" you say.

"My grandson," your dad says.

"My little boy," you say.

It's great. When the celebrating subsides, a young girl wheels out a cart full of trophies: second-place trophies for the Predators and first-place trophies for the boys on our team. One by one, the names of the boys are called, and the trophies are handed out. When Taylor's name is called, there is a burst of applause and cheering from the other kids and their parents. I couldn't have scripted a better end to the season.

You look as if you're going to cry. I've never seen you so happy; you are grinning from ear to ear. "You did it!" you say to me. "I mean, Taylor did it. I mean, you both did it. The winning goal! We won the game!"

As Taylor comes off the ice, you run to congratulate him on the victory, and I suddenly realize something. You gave something up when you fell in love with me all those years ago. You gave up on sports, but now, through Taylor, I have given them back to you. The thrill of the close game. Boys versus boys. Skills versus skills. Bravery and sheer determination. Scrapes, bruises, and blisters—all the things that tough little boys are made of. This is what I'm thinking about as you turn and hug your dad.

"Goddamn!" your dad says.

"What a game," my dad says, finally speaking up.

"So close," my mom says.

"I was beginning to wonder," your dad says.

"There was never a doubt in my mind," you say, looking down at Taylor.

"Did you see my goal?" Taylor asks.

"Of course we saw it," I say.

"It was the game winner."

"It was," I say. "Great job, son."

CHAPTER 24

VEGETABLE SOUP

It is a Thursday. I am in our study, writing about a woman in Anaheim who organizes visits from local professional athletes to the children's hospital in Mission Viejo. It is taking longer than I thought to write this story, and it needs to be completed by first thing in the morning in order to meet the deadline.

You arrive home from work at seven. Taylor is in the family room, watching TV. I hear you come in through the front door, and after taking off your coat, you come to see me. I look at you, and you are not happy. In fact, I can tell you are quite angry, but I'm not sure why.

"What's up?" I ask.

"What are you doing?" you ask.

"Writing," I say. "What does it look like?"

"While Taylor watches TV?"

"I guess so."

"I thought I told you this morning that Taylor has his science homework due tomorrow."

"Yes, I remember that."

"Well?"

"Well what?" I ask.

"Is it done?"

"I don't know," I say.

"I told you I was going to be home late tonight and that you needed to be sure Taylor worked on his homework."

"I'm on deadline," I say.

"So is your son."

"Maybe he already finished the homework."

"I asked him," you say. "He hasn't even started."

181

"Well, maybe you can get him going."

"It looks like I'll have to."

"Sorry about that," I say. "But I really need to get this piece done by tonight."

You glare at me. I can tell that Taylor's homework isn't the only thing you have on your female mind. "I see the tree still isn't planted," you say.

"No," I say. "You're right." The jacaranda you bought for the front yard still hasn't been planted. It is sitting in its crate on the front lawn.

"Have you been watering it?"

"I thought you were watering it."

"No, I haven't been watering it," you say. "It's going to die before you even get it into the ground. Another couple hundred dollars down the drain."

"It's not going to die."

"When are you going to plant it?"

"I can do it tomorrow."

"Always tomorrow," you say, and you storm out of the room.

I go back to work on my story, assuming you are getting Taylor started on his homework. Then you reappear in the doorway.

"Where are the pork chops?" you ask.

"Pork chops?"

"I told you to pick up pork chops for dinner."

"I didn't have time. I was going to text you to ask you to stop at the store on the way home, but I guess I forgot."

"What am I supposed to make for dinner?"

"I don't know."

"I was looking forward to pork chops."

"Sorry," I say.

You leave and go back to the kitchen. Then you return again. "Just thought I'd tell you we're also out of milk."

"I'll pick up some milk tomorrow," I say.

You say nothing. You stare me down for a moment, and then you leave.

Back to my writing. I get about twenty uninterrupted minutes to work on my story before you show up again in the doorway. "Dinner is ready," you say.

"Okay," I say.

"Are you coming or not?"

"I'm coming." I stand up and follow you to the kitchen table, and you serve dinner. Taylor is not there yet, and you yell up the stairs for him.

"Coming!" he shouts.

"This whole family would fall apart if it wasn't for me," you say, shaking your head.

"What's this?" I ask, looking at the bowl in front of me.

"Soup."

"Just soup for dinner?"

"It's all we have. I told you to go to the store."

Taylor shows up and sits down. "What's this?" he asks.

"It's soup," you say. "Your father forgot to go to the grocery store."

"I don't like soup."

"You'll eat it, and you'll like it," you say.

"Eat your soup," I say.

"Your dad promised to go to the store tomorrow. We'll have pork chops tomorrow night."

"How's your homework coming?" I ask Taylor.

"It sucks," Taylor says.

"Did you guys make it to hockey practice this afternoon?" you ask. "Wasn't there a practice after school?"

"There was," I say.

"I don't like that coach," Taylor says.

"What's wrong with him?"

"Too many drills. We never get to scrimmage."

"The drills are important," you say.

"By the way, there's a tournament next weekend," I say.

"That's the first I've heard of any tournament," you say. "It'd be nice if you told me these things."

"I'm telling you now."

"Are you going to be there?" Taylor asks you.

"I'll try," you say. "I might have to work. Things have been very busy at the office."

"You always have to work," Taylor says.

You are looking at your soup. "I wish I didn't *have* to work," you say.

"What's that supposed to mean?" I ask.

"Nothing," you say.

"It meant something."

"It meant nothing. Forget I even said it."

"I thought you liked your job," I say.

"I like it fine. But I don't like being responsible for everything."

"Responsible for everything?"

"It's too much, Jonathan."

"You're not responsible for everything."

"How blind you are," you say.

"Blind?"

"You always just think of yourself. You never think of me. You never stop to think about how I feel about having to work so many hours."

"That isn't even true," I say.

"Can I be excused?" Taylor asks.

"You didn't finish your soup."

"I don't like soup."

"There's nothing wrong with soup."

"It's gross," Taylor says.

"Gross?"

"Too many vegetables. They're gross."

"It's supposed to have vegetables," you say. "That's why they call it vegetable soup."

"But I don't like it."

"I don't like it either," I say.

"Can I make myself a peanut butter sandwich?" Taylor asks.

"Be my guest," you say.

"Can I eat it in my room?"

"You don't want to eat with us?" you ask.

"I need to work on my homework. I can eat while I work on my homework."

"Fine," you say.

Taylor goes to the pantry and gets what he needs to make his sandwich. As he puts it together on the kitchen counter, you look at me and say, "This is all your fault."

"My fault?"

"I told you to get the pork chops."

"We're back to the pork chops again?"

"Do you think I like eating vegetable soup for dinner? All you had to do was text me. I could've stopped at the store."

"I said I was sorry."

Taylor now has the refrigerator door open, and he says, "We're all out of milk?"

"Yes, we are," you say.

"How am I supposed to eat a peanut butter sandwich without milk? How am I going to wash it down?"

"Have a glass of orange juice."

"That's gross."

"Or water," I say.

"That's even grosser."

You glare at me. Taylor closes the refrigerator door and leaves the kitchen. We listen to him walk up the stairs, and we wait until we hear his bedroom door close before we continue talking.

"I don't understand why you're so mad," I say.

"You frustrate me."

"Frustrate you?" I ask.

"I feel like I married a ten-year-old."

"Oh, come on."

"I'm serious, Jonathan. It's so infuriating."

"I think you need to calm down."

"I'd like to calm down. Don't you think I'd like to calm down? Do you think I like being angry?"

"I don't know," I say.

"Do you think I spend all day at the office thinking about how fun it will be to come home and be angry? Do you think that's what I look forward to?"

"Probably not," I say.

"Probably not? What the heck is wrong with you? Do you ever think of me? Listen, nothing would've made me happier than to come home from work tonight and find Taylor doing his homework. I don't ask for that much. And were a few pork chops too much to ask for? I don't want to eat vegetable soup for dinner. Are you kidding? Why would I want to eat vegetable soup for dinner?

"And the jacaranda tree. That stupid tree has been sitting on the front lawn for nearly a week now. Is it really asking too much to have you dig a simple hole and plant it? Don't I do all the rest of the yardwork? Don't I trim the hedges and weed the flower beds? Don't I do more than my fair share around here? You've had all week to finish your article. It's not like the deadline is a surprise to you. Why are you spending so much time on it anyway? Those cheapskates hardly pay you anything."

"Aha!" I say. "So now we get to the heart of the matter."

"The heart of the matter?"

"Your contention that I don't make enough money."

"I didn't bring that up."

"But you just did," I say.

"Well, why don't you make more money? How long have you worked there now? You make as much as a convenience store clerk. When's the last time you asked for a raise?"

"They'd never give it to me."

"And why not?"

"Just because."

"Just because? I suppose you're going to say you're lucky to have the job."

"I am lucky."

"You're telling me that you can't do better? It's not like you haven't had other opportunities."

"Like what?"

"Like my dad," you say.

"Your dad?"

"He offered you a job at the dealership. He would've made you a salesman."

"What do I know about selling cars?"

"Dad would've taught you. He would've shown you the ropes. His salesmen make twice what you make, and they work half the hours. Would that be so bad?"

"Seriously? Now you want me to be a car salesman?"

"It was good enough for my dad. That's how he got his start, and look at him now."

I push my vegetable soup away from me. "Sometimes I wonder if you even know who I am," I say.

"Maybe I wonder the same thing," you say. You drop your spoon into your soup bowl, disgusted. "When was the last time we bought a new car? When was the last time I bought any new clothes? When was the last time we went to Hawaii? It was on our honeymoon, and we didn't even pay for it. Our parents paid for it. Everyone goes to Hawaii except us."

"Hawaii is expensive," I say.

You stand up and start taking the dirty dishes into the kitchen. "I've had enough of this," you say. You turn on the faucet and start rinsing off the dishes.

"And what's that supposed to mean?"

"It means what it means."

"That you've had enough of me?"

"I've had enough of everything," you say.

"I suppose you wish you'd never married me."

"Did I say that?"

"That's what you're implying," I say.

"It figures you would say something like that rather than seek a solution to the problem."

"And what are you doing about anything? Always bitching and moaning. Complaining about me. When did you ever try to put yourself in my shoes? How do you think I feel?"

"Oh, your life is so hard," you say.

"That's not what I said."

"Then what are you saying? That you want a divorce? Is that what you're saying?"

"Who said anything about divorce? It sounds like *you* want the divorce. Maybe that's what this is all about. All this dissatisfaction. All this crazy complaining."

"So now I'm crazy?" you ask.

"Christ, I didn't say you were crazy."

"Sure you did. You just said it."

"You're twisting my words."

"Your words don't need twisting," you say. "It's obvious what you meant to say."

"I'm done," I say.

I stand up and leave the kitchen, going back to the study to resume work on my article. I can hear you angrily banging around the dishes as you load them into the dishwasher. Then, suddenly, it is quiet. The whole house is quiet. I look at what I've written, but I can't concentrate.

I stare at my computer monitor and ask myself the same questions I always ask when we fight like this. Was this a brief glimpse of the truth? Do we actually dislike each other? Or was it just the inevitable case of two people in love getting on each other's nerves? Which was it?

I'm never sure how to answer these questions. We will make up tonight or tomorrow. We will get along fine the next day and the next and the next—until we do it again, until the pot boils over, until we forget our love and throw around another batch of hurtful words. But until then, we will get along fine. Still, I can't help but wonder if one of these times, we're going to go too far. It happens, right? Married couples get divorced all the time, and I'll bet half of them don't even know what hit them. They blame the kid's science homework, and they blame the unplanted jacaranda tree. They blame the vegetable soup.

CHAPTER 25

THE MOURNING DOVE

Taylor is growing up fast. He's shooting up like a weed. He is ten years old, and we are at the local sporting goods store to buy him a new hockey stick. We are meandering around the place, looking at all the crazy things they sell. This place has everything. When we come across the wrist rockets, I tell Taylor, "I used to have one of those when I was your age. Have you ever seen a wrist rocket? Do any of your friends own one?" Taylor shakes his head, and I explain how the contraption works. "It's a slingshot, son, except there is a stabilizing arm that rests on your wrist, giving the device enough power to shoot a marble through a brick wall."

"Awesome," Taylor says.

"It is," I say. I was exaggerating about the marble and the brick wall, of course. But wrist rockets are powerful.

"Can I get one?" Taylor asks.

"I don't know."

"Please, Dad," Taylor whines.

"I suppose we can get one. Are you responsible enough? Will you be careful with it?"

"I promise," Taylor says. He makes the promise so fast that I know he hasn't even thought about it. He just wants his own wrist rocket, and he wants it now.

I laugh.

Oh hell, why not? I think. How can I deprive him of one of the greatest projectile-hurling inventions ever to come down the pike? I grab a wrist rocket from the display shelf, and we proceed to the hockey equipment aisle, where we pick out Taylor's new hockey stick. We then go to the front of the store, and the cashier rings up our sale.

On the way home, Taylor sits in the passenger seat of my car, examining his new acquisition, and I drive us home, happily daydreaming about my childhood and my own wrist rocket.

My dad bought me my wrist rocket when I was in sixth grade. He gave it to me with the proviso that I would not shoot at other kids with it. Or shoot at people's pets. Or shoot out windows. "You can really do serious damage with this thing," he said. "If you do something stupid, I'll take it away."

I promised not to misuse it, and then Dad showed me how it worked. We set up a row of empty pop bottles in the backyard, against the fence, and we took turns blasting away at them. It was fantastic! I got better and better with practice. I spent hours shooting at junk in the backyard after school and on weekends. Seriously, I loved that darn thing. It gave me a feeling of power, probably a lot like the feeling one has when he's armed with a gun.

Not long after Dad gave me the wrist rocket, I got into an altercation with a boy named Brad Curtain. I didn't like this kid. He was one of those idiots who always claimed to be better than me at everything. To prove his point, one day he challenged me to a game of H-O-R-S-E. His dad had installed a basketball hoop and backboard onto their house, over their garage doors, so we played in his driveway. We played for nearly an hour, and so far, we were even. He would win, and then I would win, over and over. Finally, Brad said, "Let's play for the championship."

"The championship of what?" I asked.

"Proving who's the best."

Like an idiot, I agreed to this. It would be our final game. It was awful. I couldn't make a basket to save my life, so Brad won as the other kids watching cheered for him. I can't even put into words how infuriating it was. God, how I hated that kid. I hated his face, and I hated his voice. I hated his bragging. I stormed away and went home, where I went to my bedroom, grabbed my wrist rocket, and carried it to the front yard. I wanted to hurt Brad, and I wanted to make him cry. I picked up a stone and put it in the wrist rocket, and I looked for Brad. He was now across the street, talking to the same kids who had watched our match and cheered for him. I took aim and fired the pebble at Brad, and so help me Christ, it hit him square in the face, just below his stupid eye.

Brad reached up with both hands and cried out in pain. He then looked at the red blood in his hands. The pebble had torn his skin, and the blood was dripping from the wound. The other kids ran away while Brad ran home bleeding and crying. I felt a sudden lump in my throat. He knew I had done something terribly wrong. When he got home, Brad told his parents what I had done, and they immediately came over to our house to complain to my mom and dad.

"He could've put Brad's eye out!" Brad's mom said to my dad. Jesus, the woman must've said this ten times. It was quite a scene, and needless to say, Dad took my wrist rocket away from me and hid it so I couldn't find it. I was grounded for a week, and Dad told me how disappointed he was in me. I felt bad, not because I had injured Brad but because I had let my father down. Also because I had lost my wrist rocket.

That night, I heard Mom tell my dad that the wrist rocket was an inappropriate toy for any boy, and I heard Dad say she was probably right. Dad never did give my wrist rocket back to me, and in time, I forgot about it—that was, until I was a freshman in high school.

One weekend, I got a flat tire on my bike. It was no big deal. I knew how to fix it. All I needed was a new inner tube, a screwdriver, and a crescent wrench. I had the inner tube since we kept spares on hand in the garage, and I found a screwdriver on top of my dad's workbench. But I couldn't find a crescent wrench, and Dad wasn't around to ask where one was, so I went through the workbench drawers, looking for the wrench. Lo and behold, in the back of one of the drawers, I found my old wrist rocket where Dad had hidden it from me.

Ha! It was great. It was like finding money! I removed the wrist rocket from the drawer and took it to the backyard. Surely my dad wouldn't care if I played with it now. It had been such a long time since I'd shot Brad Curtain and since Dad had taken it away from me.

I got some old cans out of the trash and set them up against the fence for target practice. I shot at them using pebbles out of the rock bed around our barbecue, and it didn't take me long to get the hang of it. So far so good, but as I was setting the cans back up, a robin flew down from our roof and landed on the top of the fence. I raised my wrist rocket and took aim.

"Birds are just sewer rats with wings," Dad had said. Not to blame my dad, but he did say that. Things like that stick in a boy's memory bank. One well-aimed shot and one less beady-eyed rat with wings. One less filthy robin!

I shot at the bird, but unfortunately, it immediately took to flight. The pebble sailed over the top of the fence, bounced off a tree trunk in the neighbors' backyard, and—*crash!*—smashed right into the neighbors' kitchen window. "Oh shit!" I said. This was a problem.

These were not nice neighbors, not the sort of people who would laugh at a kid's lack of judgment. They were a pair of kooks named Mr. and Mrs. Apple, and they didn't like children. Not at all. They were always at odds with the young people in the neighborhood. So what did the Apples do? Well, Mrs. Apple was in the kitchen when the rock smashed through her window, and she freaked out. The first thing she did was call the police, and twenty minutes later, the cops were at our front door. Between the time I broke the window and the time the cops showed up, I stashed the wrist rocket back where I'd found it in my father's workbench drawer.

Mom was the one who answered the ringing doorbell. She was in her sewing room when they came, and the cops explained the situation to her. She then came to get me. I was in the garage, working on my flat tire, pretending I had been there all the time. Then Dad showed up. He had been in the family room, watching a football game.

"What the hell are the police doing here?" he asked, and Mom filled him in. Dad just looked at me. He gave me the sort of look that says, "I can see right through you, so don't bother telling me one of your lies."

I decided to be honest and tell my dad about finding the wrist rocket and shooting at the robin. I had to be honest. I didn't have a choice. I told Dad exactly what had happened, and he then got a strange look on his face, as if he didn't know whether to laugh or to beat the snot of me. He then grabbed me by my shirtsleeve and dragged me out of the garage and to the Apples' front door.

All said and done, Dad explained what had happened to the police and to the Apples. I was right there with him when he told them about the wrist rocket and the robin. He made me apologize, and he said he would pay to repair the broken window.

"We thought we were being attacked," Mrs. Apple said. God, what a kook. Attacked by whom? Indians? Communists? Maybe revolutionaries? Who knew what was going through that hysterical woman's mind?

When we came home, Dad took the wrist rocket out of his workbench drawer, and he hid it again. I have no idea where he put it, and I've never seen it since.

Maybe you're now asking, after all this trouble I had with my own wrist rocket, why I bought one for Taylor. It's a fair question, and I don't have a good answer. Maybe I had faith in Taylor, and maybe I thought he would be smarter than I was.

When you see the wrist rocket, you are furious with me. "Nothing good comes from handing over a weapon to a child," you say. "What were you even thinking?"

I don't tell you about my experiences as a boy, but I say, "I had a wrist rocket when I was Taylor's age. Maybe you're overreacting."

"Overreacting?"

"Just a little, don't you think?"

"I think it's a bad idea."

I would've been wise to listen to you, but we come to a compromise: we keep the wrist rocket, but the weapon will remain in my possession, and Taylor will be allowed to use it only under my supervision. Taylor is disappointed, but he'll take what he can get. So will I.

The weeks pass, and Taylor and I play with his wrist rocket in the backyard, sometimes after school and sometimes on the weekends. We set up bottles and cans against the fence, just as I did when I was a kid, and we blast away at them. We don't leave a mess. We always clean up after ourselves when we're done, and I put away the wrist rocket, as promised. Taylor never tries to find out where I keep it. He's a good kid, and he plays by the rules.

You become more and more comfortable with this, and when you see us using the wrist rocket in the backyard, you shake your head and smile as if to say, "Boys will be boys." You even come out once to join us, and Taylor shows you how to use the wrist rocket. At first, you miss wildly, but after a few shots, you hit the cans, and you pretend to enjoy yourself.

Then comes the day.

It is after school, and Taylor and I are home while you're at work. Taylor wants to play with his wrist rocket, and I could use a break from my writing, so I take the weapon out of hiding and meet Taylor in the backyard. He has already set up some Coke cans in a row against the fence.

"Me first," I say.

"Go ahead," Taylor says.

"Second can from the left," I say, and I load the weapon and take aim. I hit the can square on.

"My turn," Taylor says.

"Call your can," I say.

"Third from the right," he says, and he shoots, hitting the can and knocking it backward. "First on the left," he says, and he hits that one too.

Then Taylor looks up into our mulberry tree. He has spotted a bird, a gray-and-white mourning dove. It is perched on a branch, watching us. It's just sitting there minding its own business.

"Do you think I can hit it?" Taylor asks.

"Probably," I say.

Taylor takes aim, and I watch. I know I should probably stop him, but I do nothing. I am curious, and I want to see the outcome of this boy-versus-bird confrontation. Taylor pulls the leather pouch back as far as he can, and then—*snap!*—he releases it, and the pebble jets through the air. The bird's head jerks back, and it then tumbles off the branch, falling to the lawn.

"Jesus!" I say. "You actually got it!"

"Right in the head!" Taylor exclaims.

"What a shot!"

"Look at it!"

"Is it dead?"

We both step toward the bird as it lies still on the lawn, and then it moves. It is horrible to watch. It is flapping one wing and moving in circles. It flaps, then it holds still, and then it flaps again. It is probably wondering what the hell happened to it.

"I hit its eye!" Taylor says, horrified about what he has done. He is bending over and looking at the injured bird.

"Oh wow," I say.

"It knocked its eye right into its brain."

"Poor bird," I say.

"What are we going to do with it?"

The bird is still flapping one wing. "We ought to put it out of its misery," I say.

"How?"

"Twist its head off."

"Do *what*?" Taylor asks.

"You can hold its body with one hand and twist off the head with the other. Birds are fragile. Its head ought to twist right off."

"I'm not doing that," Taylor says. He sounds as if he's going to cry.

"Fine," I say, and I bend over and pick up the bird. It is in my hands, still warm, struggling to get free. It's awful. I'm really feeling bad now, but without even thinking about it, I kill the injured bird. I'm left with its body in one hand and its head in the other. "I guess I'll throw it away," I say.

"Where are you going to put it?"

"In the trash can," I say.

"In the trash?"

"Do you have a better idea?"

"No," Taylor says.

I carry the bird remains to the trash can at the side of the house and drop the bird into the can with the rest of our household garbage. Taylor is not with me. He is still in the backyard, holding on to his wrist rocket. When I return to the backyard, Taylor hands me the wrist rocket and says, "Here. You keep it." I look at Taylor. He is obviously upset. Children his age do not hide their emotions well, and Taylor is no exception.

A couple of months later, you ask me about the wrist rocket because you've noticed Taylor isn't playing with it. I don't give you the satisfaction of learning you were right. I just say that Taylor lost interest. And me? I'm still Jonathan Hart, loving husband and father to a ten-year-old boy. And yes, men are idiots. I've heard you say this, but I now come to the illuminating conclusion that you are right.

CHAPTER 26

A DAYDREAM

My car registration is about to expire, and I am at the DMV. I could've renewed it by mail a month ago, but I put it off. I'm a forty-four-year-old man who still puts things off. After all these years of experience, you'd think I'd be more on top of my life, but no. I'm still a hopeless procrastinator.

I've taken a number, and I'm now sitting in an uncomfortable plastic chair, waiting for the magic digits to appear on the overhead screen. It's like a scene from Orwell's *1984*, except it is real, and it is now. We are all just cases and numbers.

The walls are all painted beige, and there are brown water stains on the ceiling. I listen to the mind-numbing murmur of dehumanized DMV voices, the claps of staplers, and the steady hum of fluorescent lights and electronic office equipment. I smell the annoying body odor of the man sitting to my right and the strong perfume of the elderly woman to my left. There is dandruff on the shoulders of the man sitting in front of me—his hair looks as if it hasn't been washed for weeks.

My mind begins to wander, and I fall headfirst into one of my daydreams. I close my eyes, and I can hear the voices. I am no longer in the DMV. I am in a publisher's office, sitting in a big, comfortable leather chair. The publisher's name is Clyde Baker, and he speaks authoritatively and ambitiously.

"So how does it feel?" he asks me.

"How does what feel?" I ask.

"Success, fame, money."

"It feels good."

"Better than just good, right?"

"Yes, much better," I say.

"Success and all its trappings are difficult for some people to handle at first."

"I'm not having much difficulty," I say. "I feel like this was meant to be."

"That's good," Clyde says. "That's very good. You know, when I first read your manuscript last year, I said to myself, 'Clyde, this is a winner. This book is going to sell truckloads of copies.'"

"And you were right."

"Heck yes, I was right. I'm seldom wrong. Let me tell you something. You don't last long in this business if you don't have a nose for this kind of thing."

"I'm glad you had your nose."

Clyde laughs and says, "I liked your title right off the bat: *The Question Mark Murders*. Did you think of that title on your own?"

"I did," I say.

"Genius," Clyde says.

"It's intriguing, isn't it? It sort of gets one's curiosity juices flowing. I happen to think that a title can make or break a book."

"Maybe so, and maybe not. But there's no doubt about the fact that the title is important. But so is the book. Tell me—is it really true? Did you write this book when you were in your twenties?"

"I did," I say.

"Remarkable."

"I couldn't find anyone interested in publishing it."

"Even more remarkable."

"Until I heard from you. Your call came out of the blue. I really wasn't expecting it."

"Funny how things work out, isn't it?"

"It is," I say.

"There I was," Clyde says, looking up at the ceiling for a moment. Then he looks at me and says, "It was on a Saturday afternoon. I was sniffing around the office for another best seller, when lo and behold, your manuscript had been sitting there all along, gathering dust on Everette Wooley's desk. Do you remember Everette?"

"Actually, no," I say.

"No?"

"I sent out query letters and manuscripts to a lot of publishers and agents, and I don't remember all their names. In fact, I don't think I remember any of them. I just remember spending an awful lot of money on postage and then getting tons of rejection notices."

"Did Everette actually reject your work?"

"I don't remember."

"I don't think he did. When I found your manuscript on his desk, it had a yellow Post-it note attached to your title page that read, 'Maybe.' Like me, he saw something in your work. You were in his maybe pile."

"And yet it sat there for all those years?"

"The publishing business is funny."

"I guess so."

"I didn't even know your manuscript existed until after Everette died. I found it and read it, and look at us now," Clyde says, grinning. "Now it's selling like hotcakes. We can barely keep up with the orders."

"I guess it's a good thing he died."

"A good thing?"

"You know, in a way."

"Yes, I guess so. Although his wife probably wouldn't share our enthusiasm."

"No, of course not."

"I have to ask you. I don't mean to pry, but I have to know. What are you spending your money on? All newly successful authors are different. What's the first thing you did? Some authors just pay off their credit cards. Some buy a new car. Some purchase a new house, and some go on long vacations. I'm always curious to know about the first shiny thing they can't resist. What was it with you? Maybe you bought your wife some nice jewelry?"

"Actually, I didn't buy anything."

"Nothing?"

"I give the money to my wife. She has a better head for finances than I do."

"Well then, what did she buy?"

I think for a moment, and then I say, "She bought her happiness."

"Her happiness?"

"Yes," I say. "Whoever said that money can't buy happiness never had any."

Clyde laughs. "Well, if that isn't ever the truth!" he says.

"I've never seen Samantha happier."

"I'm glad to hear that."

"It seems that it's not so much what you buy, but it's knowing what you can afford. It's knowing that the struggle is over. It's knowing you're no longer competing with everyone else in the world for the low-hanging fruit."

"So true," Clyde says.

"And do you know what else? Before the book was published, I would never have admitted that our marriage needed saving, but I can say quite honestly that *The Question Mark Murders* rescued our marriage. Samantha now seems so pleased that she married me. She loves me, and she respects me. And she no longer believes I'm wasting my time. She used to shake her head and complain about my crazy dreams about writing books, but now she's all in. 'What's your next book going to be about?' she asks me. Can you imagine that? She actually cares."

"She has faith in you."

"She does," I say.

"And her parents? How about them? Are they finally glad that she married you?"

"They are," I say. "They came right out and said it. Well, in so many words. Her dad said, 'Jonathan, I used to wonder about this writing thing, if it would ever pay off. But you have done it, kid. You've turned your dream into a reality. Who would ever have thought?'"

"Let me guess," Clyde says. "When you first got married, her parents had you pegged as a loser?"

"Something like that," I say. "Her dad wanted me to work at his car dealership. He wanted me to sell cars."

Clyde laughs. "You've got to be kidding."

"I kid you not."

Clyde smiles. Then he leans back and puts his hands behind his head. "You know, I heard that you quit your job at the *Daily Observer*," he says.

"I did," I say.

"No more Good People?"

"No, no more Good People. Samantha wants me to concentrate on writing my next novel. You should see her. She now goes out of her way to encourage me to write. She takes care of everything else in our lives so that I can concentrate on my writing. I'm the goose that lays the golden eggs. And I like being the pampered goose. I like the way she now treats me, and I like the way she sees me."

"What are you writing now?"

"Now?" I ask. "Well, I was going to keep it secret until I was sure I was really onto something. I haven't told anyone about my next novel, not even Samantha. But I guess it won't hurt to let the cat out of the bag. I'm almost done with the outline, and I think I like it. In fact, I like it a lot."

"And?" Clyde says.

"It's the story of two thirty-five-year-old identical twins," I say. "Their names are Richard and Carl Paulson. They live in Southern California. Richard lives in a Beverly Hills mansion, and Carl lives in a tiny tract house in Pasadena. Richard married an oil heiress, and he inherited her fortune when she recently passed away. Carl, however, never did get married. Carl has been working as a software engineer for a large computer company, and he has an idea for a start-up company. It is something high tech. Something entrepreneurial. I haven't yet decided what his idea is precisely. But it has something to do with computers, and it's Carl's big chance to become rich like his brother."

"Do the brothers get along?"

"They have a complicated relationship. They are brothers, and they love each other. But they are also very competitive, and Carl has always resented Richard's wealth."

"So he starts this business?"

"He does, but it doesn't go as planned. He works night and day, but within a year, he doesn't find himself getting rich. Instead, he is just deep in debt, with a mountain of unpaid bills and a long list of angry customers. Lawsuits start flying. People are demanding their money. Carl is in way over his head, and he finally does something he swore he would never do. He goes to Richard and asks if he can borrow the funds he needs to bail himself out."

"And what does Richard say?"

"He tells Carl that he loves him and would like to help, but he won't loan him the money. He says it would ruin their relationship. He says he made a promise to himself never to loan money to either family or friends. He says, 'Our relationship is too important to me to jeopardize this way.'"

"And what does Carl say?"

"He promises Richard that their relationship will not be harmed, and he assures Richard he will pay the money back. But Richard holds his ground. Carl then goes to an attorney to see if there's anything he can do to put off his creditors and appease the angry customers, and the attorney tells him his only recourse is to file bankruptcy. This is not what Carl wants to hear, but it is the truth. And Carl knows the attorney is right. He is a failure. It's very upsetting. He's made a total mess of his life, and by filing for bankruptcy, he's going to leave everyone holding the bag for his mistakes. They will curse him and look down upon him as scum. As a snake in the grass. As a liar and a thief. It is too much for him to bear, and he doesn't know what to do. Then a rage begins to boil inside him, consuming him. His brother! That no-good bastard could easily have bailed him out, but no! And then a plan is born."

"A plan?" Clyde asks.

"It's an ingenious plan. It's an evil plan. It's the sort of plan only a truly desperate man could come up with. He invites Richard to come to his house in Pasadena for dinner. He says he wants to show there are no hard feelings about Richard's refusal to loan him money. Richard likes this idea, and he tells Carl he's glad he understands. He agrees to come to Carl's house, having no idea what Carl actually intends to do. And what does Carl have planned? It isn't a dinner. It is cold-blooded murder!"

"Ah," Clyde says.

"When Richard arrives at Carl's house for dinner, Carl pours Richard a scotch and water. It's Richard's favorite drink. But Carl has spiked the drink with a lethal dose of barbiturates, and Richard downs the drink, suspecting nothing. In a matter of minutes, Richard is sound asleep on Carl's sofa, and then he is dead. Carl then carries out the second part of his plan. He removes all of Richard's clothes and dresses Richard in his clothes. He puts on Richard's clothes and looks at himself in a mirror. 'Hello, Richard Paulson,' he says. 'So nice to meet you. Sorry to hear about your brother, ha ha.' Then he calls the police to report the death.

Pretending to be distraught and pretending to be Richard, Carl tells them he came to Carl's house for dinner and found his brother dead on the sofa. 'It looks like suicide,' he says. 'My brother was having a lot of serious problems.'"

"So Carl kills Richard and takes his place?"

"Exactly."

"Does he get away with it?"

"He does, and he doesn't."

"Meaning?"

"Richard's body is buried, and everyone now thinks Carl is Richard, and he lives in his brother's mansion, wears his brother's clothes, drives his brother's cars, and spends his brother's money. Everything is going according to plan, until one day, the police show up on his doorstep. It is a detective named Frank Hill, and he has a warrant for Richard's arrest. The charge is murder, but it's not for the murder of Richard. The charge is for the murder of Richard's heiress wife. Apparently, Frank Hill has been trying to prove that Richard murdered his wife for her money, but until now, he didn't have enough evidence. But they now have the proof. Carl is up a creek."

"So they arrest Carl, thinking he is Richard?"

"Exactly."

"And Carl is now charged with murdering Richard's wife?"

"But he can't say that he is actually Carl, because it would be an automatic admission that he killed Richard."

Clyde thinks for a moment and then says, "So he's going to be convicted of murder either way?"

"Either way."

"Genius," Clyde says, and he laughs.

"The name of the book is *Murder Either Way*."

"I love it," Clyde says.

Yes, he loves it. But now back to reality, where there are no best-selling books. There is no Clyde, and I am not a famous author. There is no Carl Paulson, Richard Paulson, or detective named Frank Hill. I am still seated at the DMV, and my chair is still uncomfortable. The man on my right still has body odor, and the elderly woman to my left still smells like a vat of cheap perfume. The guy in front of me still has dandruff on his shoulders. I am waiting for my number to appear on the overhead screen.

Finally, the number appears, and I am instructed to go to window twelve. I stand up and walk to the window, where a middle-aged woman is busy stapling papers together.

"Hi," I say.

The woman sets her stapled papers aside. "Your paperwork?" she says. She is like a dystopian robot. In fact, if I didn't know better, I'd say she is a dystopian robot.

"Here you go," I say, and I set my papers on the counter.

The woman takes them, looks them over, and then begins typing on her computer keypad. "Do you have your smog certificate?" she asks.

"Smog what?" I say.

"Where's your smog certificate?"

"I don't have one," I say.

"You can't register this vehicle without a current smog certificate."

"I can't?"

"No," the woman says. She has stopped typing and is now looking at me.

"I had no idea," I say.

"It says it right here on your notice," she says. She taps the notice that I handed to her with her finger. "Didn't you read the notice?"

"I thought I did."

"Get your smog certificate, and then bring all the required paperwork back. Once we have the smog certificate, then we'll renew your registration."

Then and only then.

I now wish I were rich. I wish I were successful. If I were, you would be taking care of this nonsense because you would handle all the details. You are good at details. I could concentrate on my writing, and you would take care of me, admire me, love me, and respect me.

CHAPTER 27

CAPTAIN JACK'S

I've been working for the *Daily Observer* for more than sixteen years if you can believe it. It's an awful long time to be glued to the same job, but I still enjoy what I do, writing about the quote-unquote good people of Orange County. I get the names for my subjects from my boss, Walter Beasley, who has a talent for finding interesting and compelling characters for me to write about. Two of my recent favorites are Zachary and Linda Winchester of Anaheim Hills, a couple who are about to celebrate their sixtieth wedding anniversary. Their enduring marriage is their claim to fame, and Walter wants me to write an article delving into the secrets of their marital success.

Zachary and Linda are the same age. They are both seventy-eight, and they married when they were eighteen. My idea is to interview them separately in order to get a more illuminating and multifaceted perspective of their relationship. The Winchesters agree to this, and Zachary will be first to answer my questions. I ask Zachary where he wants to meet, and he picks a restaurant near his office. He is still working, even at his age. "When you stop working, you stop living," he tells me.

We are to meet at noon at the restaurant, and when I show up, Zachary is there to greet me. But it turns out we are going elsewhere. Zachary has no intention of eating at the restaurant. He tells me to climb into his car, and he drives us a half mile away to a little place called Captain Jack's.

Are you familiar with Captain Jack's? Of course not. Captain Jack's is a strip club. The odds of you ever going to a strip club are about a million to one. Come to think of it, the odds are about the same for me. I have never been attracted to this sort of thing. Not that I'm a prude, and it's not like I haven't enjoyed seeing a naked woman or two in men's magazines or in the movies. But in person? Naked strangers in the flesh? It's always seemed sort of bizarre to me and a little too desperate. But so be it. This is where Zachary wants to have lunch with me and talk about his sixty-year marriage.

Captain Jack's is located in the industrial part of Anaheim, nestled between a steel-fabrication company and a factory that makes concrete architectural treatments. There are no windows. There is just a single door, and when we push the door open, we have to walk down a dismal little hallway until we finally get to the interior of the building, a big room with a center stage, rows of chairs, a bar, and a grouping of round tables and chairs farther away from the stage. There is also an area toward the back with leather-upholstered overstuffed chairs and sofas, a place for the girls to give customers lap dances. There is loud music, and the entire place is dark. It takes a moment for my eyes to adjust after I first walk in from the bright outdoors.

"We'll sit here," Zachary says.

"Okay," I say. We take a seat at one of the tables, and Zachary laughs.

"You've never been to one of these places before, have you?"

"No," I say.

"I've been coming here for seventeen years," Zachary says. "Ever since they first opened their doors. Are you a little nervous?"

"Maybe," I say.

"Just relax. Nothing to be nervous about. Just relax, and take it all in."

"Okay," I say.

"The girl on the stage is Sandra."

"You know her name?"

"I know everyone in this place," Zachary says.

I look toward the stage, and I see Sandra dancing naked with a brass pole. She is sliding up and down, and the men seated in the front row of chairs are watching her every move. She has long blonde hair. I don't know why, but I notice her hair. It is exceptionally thick and shiny.

"Mesmerizing, isn't she?" Zachary asks.

"She is," I say.

"Hard to believe she's in her thirties. Wait until she gets off that pole."

I laugh nervously while Zachary gets the attention of a waitress who is walking by. The waitress comes to our table with her notepad in hand. "Here for lunch?" she asks.

"Of course," Zachary says.

"Need menus?"

"No need, darling," Zachary says. "Bring the usual for my friend and me."

"The usual?" I say.

"What does your friend want to drink?"

"A Coke would be fine," I say.

"I'll have an iced tea," Zachary says.

"Two burgers, a Coke, and an iced tea," the waitress says, and Zachary nods and smiles. The waitress then walks away toward the kitchen.

"The burger is the only edible thing they serve here," Zachary says to me.

"A burger sounds fine," I say.

"It comes with fries."

"Sounds good," I say.

"The fries are only average. They're kind of soggy, and they're too salty. But like I said, the burgers are pretty darn good."

"I'm not that picky," I say.

I look toward the stage again, and Sandra is off the pole. She is bending and twisting her body for the men in the chairs, and they seem to be having a good time staring at her. It's bizarre, and it actually embarrasses me a little. Sandra smiles while she performs for the men. She smiles while twisting, bending over, and stretching. Oddly enough, she seems to enjoy what she's doing.

"Zachary!" a woman's voice exclaims. I turn to see a young woman standing at our table and smiling at Zachary. She is dressed in a robe, and she is wearing a lot of makeup.

The woman and Zachary obviously know each other. "I want you to meet Cindy," Zachary says to me. "Cindy, this is Jonathan."

"Hi, Jonathan," Cindy says.

"Hello," I say.

"Can you sit with us?" Zachary asks.

"Just for a minute," Cindy says. "I'm onstage next. Right after Sandra."

Zachary pushes a chair from the table with his foot, and Cindy sits in the chair. "Something to drink?" Zachary asks her.

"No, thanks," she says.

"Cindy is a good one," Zachary says to me with a wink. "You're going to like her."

"I'm sure I will," I say. What else would I say? I am trying to be polite. It is hard for me to fathom any woman actually liking working in a place like this, but hey, as they say, different strokes for different folks. Who am I to say?

"I'll bet you can't guess what Cindy does for a living," Zachary says. "I mean, when she isn't working here."

"A waitress?"

"Nope."

"An actress?"

"You're ice cold."

"What then?" I ask.

"Cindy is a schoolteacher. She teaches fourth grade."

"I have this summer off," she says.

"Interesting," I say. And it is interesting. In fact, it's sort of unbelievable.

"Can you imagine if the school ever found out she was working here?"

"I'd be fired for sure. Our principal would freak. Jesus, he would throw a fit."

"I can imagine," I say.

Zachary laughs. "See Sandra up there?" he asks me.

"Yes," I say.

"She's a housewife. Has two kids. Does this on the side. Her husband knows all about it, but he doesn't care. He likes the extra money."

"The money is good," Cindy says.

"It must be," I say.

Suddenly, our waitress appears, and she sets our lunches down on the table. "Anything else?" she asks.

"I think we're good," Zachary says.

The waitress walks away. Then the music stops, and Cindy stands. "I'm up," she says. "It was nice to meet you," she says to me.

"Likewise," I say.

"Break a leg," Zachary says.

Cindy walks toward the stage, steps up onto the platform, and removes her robe.

"She's a looker, right?" Zachary asks me.

"She's very attractive," I say.

"Wait until you see her dance."

I watch as Cindy starts her routine on the brass pole. "Can I ask you a question?" I ask.

"Sure," Zachary says.

"Does your wife know that you come to this place?"

"Linda?" Zachary says, and he laughs. "You've got to be kidding, right?"

"I was just curious."

"If Linda knew I came here, she'd chop off my head and mount it on a pole."

"So she doesn't know?"

"She has no idea."

"I was wondering about that."

Zachary takes a bite from his burger and then talks with his mouth full. "How long have you been married?"

"A long time," I say.

"The secret to a successful marriage is one's secrets. If you're smart, you'll learn this before it's too late. Every husband needs a secret that he keeps from his wife. Every man needs to hold on to something all his own, and I mean all his own. A man needs to be a man. Some men drink whiskey on the sly. Some men smoke cigars and cigarettes when they're away from the house. Some men have affairs. Some men play golf for money. Some men gamble on the horses. Some men look at pornography on their computers late at night. Some men just flirt with girls at the office. Me? I have Captain Jack's."

"And you're sure Linda doesn't know?"

"She has no idea."

"So what am I supposed to write about?" I ask.

"What do you mean?"

"If I mention Captain Jack's in my story, Linda is sure to read about it."

"That does pose a problem," Zachary says. He watches Cindy dance while he talks to me. "Make something up," he finally says.

"Make something up?"

"You can say the secret to a successful marriage is honesty. Yes, you can quote me on that. Honesty about everything under the sun. No secrets ever." Zachary is still chewing on his hamburger and staring at Cindy. He then says, "Watch this. Watch what she does with her legs."

The next day, I meet with Linda. We meet at their house in Anaheim Hills while Zachary is at work. Linda makes a pot of coffee and offers me a cup. We sit at their kitchen table, and I realize something. I like Linda. She seems like a nice person.

"This is good coffee," I say.

"Thanks," Linda says.

"I enjoyed meeting with Zachary yesterday."

"He took you out to lunch?"

"He did," I say.

"Did he have anything interesting to say?"

"He told me the secret to a successful marriage was honesty," I say, lying. I feel funny about lying on Zachary's behalf. As I said, I like this woman. She seems nice, and I feel she deserves better.

"He took you to Captain Jack's, didn't he?" Linda says.

"Captain Jack's?" I ask. I pretend not to know what she's talking about.

"You don't have to lie to me."

I stare at Linda for a moment, and she finally smiles. She thinks this is funny. "You know about Captain Jack's?" I ask.

Linda laughs and says, "I've known about that place for years."

"Zachary said you didn't know anything about it."

"Zachary doesn't think I know. That's why he goes there. He thinks it's a big secret."

"Doesn't that bother you?" I ask.

"Bother me?"

"I'd think it would bother you. I mean, if you're like most women, you wouldn't exactly be thrilled to know your husband spends so much of his time at a strip club."

"It's harmless."

"I see," I say.

"Do you?" Linda asks.

"Well, maybe I don't."

"Listen," Linda says. "He just likes to look at the merchandise. He likes to think he's still young. He likes to pretend he's still virile. But seriously, the man is seventy-eight years old. He couldn't rise to the occasion if his life depended on it. Do you get what I mean? He doesn't even have his own teeth."

"So you let him go there?"

"I do," Linda says.

"And he doesn't know that you know about it?"

"He doesn't have a clue."

"Wow," I say.

When it comes time to write the article about Zachary and Linda, I am a little confused. Do I write the truth, or do I go with Zachary's honesty angle? The couple were honest with me, but does that give me the right to reveal their secrets? I decide what to do.

The article appears in the paper on Sunday, and you read it, as you always read my articles. We are at the kitchen table, eating breakfast and drinking coffee. When you are done with the article, you set the paper down beside your plate. "That's a sweet story," you say.

"They're a nice couple," I say.

CHAPTER 28

DAYTIME TV

I'm as sick as a dog. It's a Tuesday morning, and I've come down with either the flu or a bad cold. My sinuses are clogged, and my head is pounding something awful. I feel dizzy and disoriented, and I keep getting chills. There's no way I can concentrate on my work, so I put on a pair of sweatpants, an old T-shirt, and a pair of warm socks. I stretch out on the sofa in the family room with a blanket and a pillow.

You bring me a cup of coffee and say, "Maybe this will make you feel better." Then you and Taylor leave the house. You will drop Taylor off at school and go to work while I watch TV and feel sorry for myself.

I tune in a rerun of the original *Star Trek* series. I've seen all of these shows two or three times each, but I still like watching them. The episode I now watch is titled "Arena." The *Enterprise* responds to a call from an Earth outpost on the planet Cestus 3, and when they beam down to the planet, they discover that the outpost has been destroyed. In the rubble, they find a survivor suffering from shock, radiation burns, and internal injuries. Kirk tells Bones to keep the poor guy alive so they can find out what happened to the outpost. Then Spock gets another life reading on his tricorder. He says, "Not warm-blooded, Captain. Living creatures but not human."

Suddenly, bombs start falling out of the sky, and one of the landing party is disintegrated. Then another. Kirk calls the *Enterprise* and tells them to beam them back up, but the *Enterprise* is also under attack and unable to help. But who is attacking them? And why?

Kirk and his men dig up a grenade launcher and aim it at the aliens up on a hill. After one big grenade blast, the aliens stop bombing them. They also stop attacking the *Enterprise*. Their ship beams up their survivors, and they make a run for it. The *Enterprise* beams Kirk and his remaining men back aboard, and then they take off in pursuit of the fleeing alien space vessel. Still, Kirk has no idea why the aliens attacked the Earth outpost. They question the survivor they saved while he's in Bones's sick bay, but he has no idea why they were assaulted. The act of aggression is a mystery.

Kirk decides the only logical course of action is to hunt down the alien ship and destroy it before it returns to its home base. Kirk believes that if the aliens' attack goes unpunished, they will be back for more. Spock, the perpetual voice of reason, questions Kirk's logic, but Kirk does not agree with him. Then, as the *Enterprise* and the alien vessel whiz past an uncharted solar system in the area, the *Enterprise* is scanned by someone in the mysterious solar system. Who is scanning them? And why? No one has any idea what is going on. Spock says, "It would appear someone is curious about us."

Then it happens: both the alien ship and the *Enterprise* are forced to come to a screeching halt. They are both dead in space, going nowhere, powerless and disabled. Spock says they are being held by a force from the solar system they passed. Then, on the big screen, there are brilliant colors, and a voice says, "We are the Metrons. You are one of two crafts who have come into our space on a mission of violence. This is not permissible. We have analyzed you and learned that your violent tendencies are inherent. So be it. We will control them."

It turns out the Metrons are a highly advanced civilization inhabiting one of the planets in the solar system. They say, "We will resolve your conflict in a way most suited to your limited mentalities." The Metrons then tell Kirk they will send him to one of their planets to settle the dispute between the *Enterprise* and the aliens. The aliens are referred to as Gorns.

Per the plan, Kirk and the captain of the Gorn ship will be set loose on the planet to do battle between each other mano a mano to determine a winner. The winner will be allowed to leave the area unharmed and with ship intact, and the loser will be destroyed "in the interest of peace."

Next thing he knows, Kirk is down on the planet, and so is the Gorn. The Gorn is a big reptilian creature with green skin, silvery bug eyes, and jagged crocodile teeth. God, I love monsters, and the Gorn is a monster!

The Metrons tell Kirk and the Gorn that there are resources on the planet sufficient to make lethal weapons. Thus, the contest begins. At first, Kirk tries out a little hand-to-hand combat, but the Gorn is too strong for him. Then Kirk runs into the rocky hills and picks up a boulder. He hurls the boulder at the Gorn, but the boulder just bounces off the creature. It's going to take more than a measly boulder to slay this beast!

He finds a larger boulder, and he rolls it off a cliff. It lands on the Gorn, but still, it's no use. The ugly, hissing creature seems indestructible. Then—yes!—Kirk finds a diamond deposit, some sulfur, some coal, some potassium nitrate, and a hollow stick, and he puts together a small cannon that will shoot one of the diamonds at the Gorn. "Basic chemistry," Spock says to Bones. Kirk, the hero, aims his cannon at the deadly creature, and *bang!* He wins the battle! The creature is incapacitated.

Kirk then grabs the creature's makeshift dagger and holds it to his ugly green throat. He is about to kill it, but then he says, "No, maybe you thought you were protecting yourself." Good old Kirk. He spares the Gorn's life.

Kirk looks up to the sky and says, "No, I won't kill him. You'll have to get your entertainment somewhere else."

Then a Metron shows up out of nowhere, and he says he's impressed with Kirk's demonstration of mercy. The contest is over. Thanks to Kirk, the Gorns are consequently free to leave. The *Enterprise* is also free to leave, and everyone lives happily ever after.

I know it's corny, but I like it. I like stories that involve describing the good side of human beings. We aren't so bad. Despite what some people might have you believe, there is hope for humanity. Of course, you can thank good old gunpowder. Without the gunpowder and his makeshift cannon, Kirk would've been toast. Interesting, isn't it? The last words of the episode are "Take us back to where we're supposed to be, Mr. Sulu. Warp factor one."

I smile, and then I feel bad again. This cold, flu, or whatever it is really has me feeling awful. I change channels on the TV. I stop at *Let's Make a Deal*. This is what I need to be watching, something really stupid. I am giving in to my sickness. My eyes are growing heavy. The show is just starting, and I am falling asleep.

I slide into a dream. I am in the audience, jumping up and down. I am dressed like a Gorn, making a fool of myself. *Pick me*, I think. *Oh please, pick me.*

The host of the show is Abraham Lincoln. That's right; it's Honest Abe, complete with his stovepipe hat and iconic beard. Abe welcomes everyone to the show, and then he calls on a woman named Denise, who is dressed like a slice of pizza. "Hello, Denise," he says. "Tell us about yourself. Where are you from, and what do you do?"

"I'm from Simi Valley," Denise says. "I'm a health coach."

"A health coach?" Abe asks.

"I help people stay healthy and feel healthy."

"Okay," Abe says. "Give us one piece of commonsense advice we can do every day to stay healthy and feel healthy."

"Well," Denise says, "don't eat sugar, exercise, and ease up on the wine."

"Ah," Abe says. "So no more milkshakes with tequila for a while."

"Ha ha!" Denise laughs.

"Let's get started, shall we?"

"I'm ready, Abe."

"I'm holding in my hand a golden envelope. In the envelope is either five dollars or five hundred dollars. I can give the contents of the envelope to you, or you can pick what's behind curtain number two."

"Oh my," Denise says.

"Which is it, dear?"

"Oh, I just don't know," Denise says, and she begins jumping up and down. The audience are telling her to take the envelope, but Denise doesn't listen to them. "I'll take the curtain!" she finally exclaims.

"You're sure about that?"

"Yes, I'm sure."

"Let's see what you passed up for what's behind the curtain, shall we?" Abe opens the envelope, and inside is the $500.

"Oh dear!" Denise says.

"You're passing up five hundred dollars for what's behind the curtain. Shall we see what you've won?"

Tiffany, the model, is standing beside the curtain, smiling. She waves her arm toward the curtain, and Denise jumps up and down again.

"Yes, yes, open the curtain!" Denise exclaims.

"Tiffany, open up the curtain. Let's see what Denise has won. What's behind curtain number two?"

The curtain opens. There is a great big hammock, and lying in the hammock is a big stuffed hippopotamus.

"Aw, it's a hippo in a hammock!" Abe says.

"Oh no," Denise says.

"Sorry, Denise, but you've been zonked. But thanks for playing. You can take a seat now."

"Thank you, Abe," Denise says.

Denise runs back to her seat empty-handed. Her husband, who is dressed like a bottle of catsup, puts his arm around her to console her.

"Let's bring up our next contestant, shall we?" Abe says. He shades his eyes with his hand and looks out over the studio audience. "Jonathan Hart? Are you out there, Jonathan? Come on down, and play."

I stand up. I can't believe my name has been called! I run to the stage, and I'm out of breath when I get there. "I'm Jonathan," I say, gasping for air. "I'm ready to win!"

Abe laughs. "First, tell us something about yourself, Jonathan. What do you do?"

"I'm a writer, Abe."

"A writer?"

"I write for the *Daily Observer*."

"Aha," Abe says.

"I write about good people."

"Well, good for you. So what brings you here? Why do you want to play *Let's Make a Deal*?"

"More than anything, I'd like to win a car, Abe. I really need a new car. My old hunk-of-junk Toyota has over a hundred thousand miles on it."

"Okay, okay, but this costume you're wearing. What are you supposed to be?"

"I'm a Gorn," I say.

"From *Star Trek*?"

"Yes," I say.

"I remember that episode," Abe says. "Good episode. Making gunpowder? Who would've thought, right? But back to the business at hand. Are you ready?"

"I'm ready, sir," I say.

"First, let's see what you can win. Tiffany, show us what's behind curtain number three."

"It's a new car, Abe!" Tiffany says. "You can hit the road in this Mazda CX-3 featuring a six-speed automatic transmission, a fuel-efficient four-liter engine, Bluetooth audio capability, and keyless illuminated entry system! It can all be yours!"

"Wow!" I exclaim.

"You can buy this car for two thousand dollars," Abe says. "And I'll show you how."

"How?" I ask. I'm really getting excited now, and I'm jumping up and down again.

Tiffany brings out a game board with a matrix of dollar-shaped rectangles. Abe points to the board and says, "On this board, we have fifteen cards. These are your cash cards. You will be picking cards one by one. Each card is worth either two hundred or four hundred dollars. Two of the cards say, 'Zonk.' If you pick a zonk, the game is over. But if you're able to accumulate at least two thousand dollars without picking a zonk, the car is yours. Best of luck to you, Jonathan. Start picking!"

"Jeez," I say.

"Which card do you pick?"

I think for a moment and then say, "Let's go with lucky number seven."

"Seven it is. Tiffany, turn number seven." The card is worth $400.

"Eleven next," I say, and this card is worth $200. "Six," I then say, and this card is also worth $200.

"Do you want to keep going?" Abe asks. "Or do you want to keep the cash? Right now, you can go home with eight hundred dollars in your pocket. Which is it? Keep playing or keep the money?"

"I'll keep playing, Abe," I say. "Turn over number four."

Tiffany turns the card.

"Ah, another four hundred dollars!"

"I'll keep going," I say.

"Are you sure?"

"I want the car, Abe."

"Okay, which next?"

"Number nine," I say. Tiffany turns over the card, and I hear the audience moan. It is a zonk. I have lost the game. No car. No money. No nothing.

"Tough luck," Abe says.

"Story of my life," I say.

"At least you still have your wife and son."

"I do," I say.

"And your job and your house."

"And my old Toyota," I say.

"That's more than a lot of people have."

"But I wanted the new Mazda," I say. "I really wanted that darn car."

"You know what they say," Abe says. "People in hell want ice water."

The audience laugh and applaud, and the show cuts to a commercial. They are selling laundry detergent, when I wake up.

Weird. Abe Lincoln? Where the heck did that come from? I haven't thought about Abe for years.

I reach for a tissue from the Kleenex box on the coffee table, and I blow my nose. Then I grab the TV remote and change the channel. My head is still pounding, and blowing my nose does nothing to relieve the pressure in my sinuses. In fact, if anything, it just makes me feel worse. The TV is now tuned to a soap opera, and I watch.

As best as I can tell, Clara and Nick love each other. They are in bed. Sheets and blankets cover their nude bodies. They have just made love, and they are talking. They seem concerned about a man named Nate. Apparently, Nate is Clara's husband, and he is unaware of the love affair between Clara and Nick. But as best as Clara can tell, Nate has a mistress named Arlene, who is married to Nick's brother. Nick's brother is a doctor at the local hospital. He is a good man, but he has the hots for one of the nurses, a lovely young thing named Ashley. Ashley's father is a big wheel in town, and he donated an entire wing to the hospital. He is married to Margaret, and besides Ashley, they have three other children: Jeff, Thomas, and Della. Jeff is happily married to a woman named Sandra, but Sandra is actually in love with Jeff's cousin, who happens to be Clara's half-sister. The cousin's name is Lauren, and she owns a cosmetics company that employs models to show off their products. One of the models is named April, and she is the girlfriend of Thomas, Jeff and Della's brother. But they don't know that Thomas was adopted when Margaret thought she couldn't have any more children, and Thomas's actual parents have just arrived in town to tell Thomas who his real parents are.

When Clara tells Nick about this, he says, "We're so lucky to be who we are," and Clara agrees.

Lucky?

I blow my nose again. I toss the soiled tissue onto the coffee table beside the Kleenex box. My headache is now worse than ever. It feels as if someone has jabbed a rusty knife into my eye, and I'll be glad when you get home. I love you. I need you. It is you who keeps me grounded, and I know it. If I know anything at all, that's what I know.

CHAPTER 29

MOM AND DAD

I get a call from Dad. Lewis gets the same call. Dad and Mom want Lewis and me to come to their house for a family meeting. Dad says they have something important to tell us, but he doesn't say what it is. He says the news is big and that it's the kind of thing that needs to be told to us in person. I try to get more information out of him over the phone, but Dad refuses to say any more. "Just show up," he says. "Your brother will be there. Your mom and I have something we need to tell both of you, and the sooner we tell you the better."

I call Lewis after I talk to Dad. I ask him if he has any idea what is going on, but Lewis knows no more than I do. We are both in the dark. Of course, we can speculate. I think Mom and Dad are moving to Tennessee. They've been talking for years about making this move, packing up all their things, and leaving the great state of California. They have friends who moved to Tennessee eight years ago, and they've visited them twice. When they got home from the trips, they showed us pictures. They couldn't say enough good things about the place, how friendly the people are, how cheap the gas is, how green it is, how much better the quality of life can be, and how awfully crowded and expensive California has become. "One of these days, we're going to pull up our stakes and move," my dad said. "We're going to pack everything up and get the hell out of here."

So is this the news they now want to share with Lewis and me? Have they finally decided to call a moving company and make a run for it?

"It could be," I say to Lewis.

"It would be a huge change," he says.

"It would," I agree.

"But that's not necessarily what they want to tell us. It could be something completely different."

"Like what?" I ask.

"I almost hate to say it."

"Just say it," I say.

"It could be their health."

"Their health?"

"Maybe one of them is ill."

I think about this for a moment and say, "I didn't even think of that."

"What if one of them has cancer?"

"Jesus, Lewis," I say.

"It happens. People get cancer all the time."

"I guess," I say. "It would be horrible news. But it would explain why they want to tell us in person."

"Or maybe it's not cancer. Maybe it's something like Alzheimer's."

"I haven't noticed either of them acting any differently."

"Maybe they just found out," Lewis says. "Maybe it's in the early stages."

Cancer? Alzheimer's? Christ, I am really feeling bad now. I don't mean *bad* as in sad. I mean *bad* as in unpleasantly shocked. This is the kind of thing that happens to other families, not ours.

"It must be something else," I say. "I'm still betting it's Tennessee. Or maybe some other state. Dad's been wanting to move for years. And where Dad goes, Mom goes."

It turns out that neither of us is right. We show up at my parents' house for the meeting, and we all sit in the living room. The sun is setting outside, and Mom clicks on the lights so we can see. "We've been trying to figure out the best way to tell you this," my father says.

"We don't want to upset either of you," Mom says.

"But these things happen," Dad says.

Mom nods in agreement and says, "We've made our final decision, so don't try to change our minds."

"Change your minds about what?" I ask.

"We're parting ways," Dad says.

"Parting ways? What does that even mean?" I ask.

"It means we're getting a divorce," Mom says.

"A divorce?" Lewis says. "You mean the two of you are splitting up?"

"Yes," Dad says.

"Oh hell," Lewis says.

"You're pulling our legs, right?" I ask.

"We're not pulling anyone's leg," Dad says. "The paperwork is nearly complete. We'll be at our attorney's office to sign the papers later this week."

Lewis and I are both in shock. Neither of us would've guessed in a million years. Our parents? Getting a divorce?

Lewis says, "But why?"

"Why?" Dad asks.

"It's a fair question, isn't it?"

"Of course it is," Mom says.

"We no longer love each other," Dad says. "It's really no more complicated than that."

"You don't love each other?" Lewis asks.

"It happens," Dad says.

"It doesn't mean we don't love you," Mom says.

"This is between your mom and me. It has nothing to do with either of you."

"Jesus," Lewis says.

"Since when did you stop loving each other?" I ask.

"It didn't happen overnight," Dad says. "It happened gradually, but it did happen. We still love you and your wives, and we will love our grandchildren. But I'm afraid our love for each other did not stand up to the test of time. It's not that we don't like each other. We like each other fine, and we are still friends. But love? I'm afraid that train left the station long ago. It's long gone. It has been gone for years. We have only been fooling ourselves, telling each other that we were still in love. No, we are not in love. We have just been two people living in the same house together, pretending we're forever lovers, pretending the candle is still burning. But the candle has been snuffed for whatever reason, and there's no use in all this silly pretending. We've been living a lie, and this isn't good for either of us. It turns out you can fall out of love just as easily as you can fall into it."

"I don't know what to say," I say.

"Me neither," Lewis says.

During the months that follow, I try to get used to the idea of my parents being divorced. I'm not a child. I know these things happen, and I know it isn't fair for me to expect my parents to stay together if they're not in love. But knowing all this doesn't make the situation any easier to swallow. There's something in every child's psyche that tells him his parents are going to stay married forever, true love means something, and true love does not wilt and die.

It's awful to watch. My mom and dad split up all their possessions. They are civil about it: "You take this, and I'll take that." They put the house up for sale, the house that Lewis and I were raised in. It will be purchased by a new family, and slowly but surely, all our family memories will be replaced with the queer new memories of total strangers, their strange children, their strange dogs, and their strange cats. The mail will be addressed to the new occupants. There'll be new holidays and new birthday parties, cakes, and presents. There will be all-new furniture, photos, and paintings. The rain will fall on someone else's roof, and the sun will no longer shine on our backyard. The neighbors will talk about our family for a while, and then they will forget us. "Oh yeah," they will say someday. "I remember when the Harts lived in that house. I wonder where they're living now."

Dad moves into an apartment in Costa Mesa, closer to his job. Mom moves into a town house in Tustin, near to hers. I visit both of them, but somehow, it just doesn't seem real. It seems as if the situation is only temporary, as if they'll eventually come to their senses. They seem much happier, but how can they be? But they are.

I talk to you about this, and you tell me I just need to learn to accept things the way they are; there's nothing I can do about it.

"Do you think it will ever happen to us?" I ask.

You say, "Not if we don't let it." But I wonder. I think my mom and dad probably used to say the same thing to each other.

Then comes Thanksgiving. Usually, we all celebrate the holiday at either Lewis's house or ours. All the families get together. We've been doing this for as far back as I can remember. But now the holiday changes to accommodate the divorce: Dad will go to Lewis's house, and Mom will come to ours. I don't like it, but there's nothing I can do about it.

To make things even worse, Mom shows up to our house with a date, and Dad shows up to Lewis's with a young girl on his arm, a girl young enough to be his daughter. When Mom arrives at our house, she introduces her new partner to us. "Thanks so much for inviting me," the guy says, smiling like an idiot. Mom must've told him we wanted him to come. I am cordial, and I play along.

"Any friend of Mom's," I say.

"This is Randy," Mom says to me. "Randy, this is my son, Jonathan."

"Nice to meet you," I say.

"Nice to meet you too," Randy replies.

"Come on in," I say.

My mom and her date come into the house, and you come from the kitchen to greet them. Mom introduces Randy to you, and you're polite and welcoming. You then go back to the kitchen, and Mom, Randy, and I sit down in the living room.

"Randy is a doctor," Mom says.

"Oh?" I say.

"He's an orthopedic surgeon."

"Well, that sounds interesting."

"Your mom tells me you write for the *Daily Observer*," Randy says to me.

"I do," I say.

"You write the Good People articles."

"Guilty as charged."

"I read your articles every Sunday."

"Do you?"

"It's very nice work," Randy says.

"Thanks," I say.

"We're proud of Jonathan," Mom says.

"You should be," Randy says.

"You should write an article about Randy," Mom says to me. "He's a good person. He does a lot of free work down in Mexico."

"It's only four days out of the month," Randy says.

"Four days is four days."

"You work for free?" I ask Randy.

"I help out at their hospitals." Randy acts as if his contribution is smaller than it actually is.

"They love him down there."

"I think they appreciate me. I do whatever I can to help. Those poor people have nothing."

"We don't realize how good we have it here in America," Mom says.

"That's for sure," Randy says.

I don't want to like Randy. I want to think of something demeaning to say about Randy's charitable work, but I can't think of anything.

"Your mom tells me that Samantha is an architect," Randy says.

"She is," I say.

"What kind of buildings does she design?"

"She works for a firm called Able and Associates. They do all sorts of work. They design custom homes, shopping centers, medical buildings, and offices, and they've done a couple schools."

"Sounds interesting."

"It keeps her busy."

My mom glares at me for a moment while Randy is not looking at her. She is not pleased with the answers I'm giving to her date. I am being polite, but I'm not going out of my way to be especially friendly.

"Randy's ex-wife is an architect too," Mom says.

"You don't say," I say.

"She's retired now," Randy says.

"Are you divorced?" I ask.

"Three years ago," Randy says.

"Did you have any children?" I ask.

"We have a boy and a girl. They're adults now, like you and your brother. The boy is a financial adviser, and the girl is an interior decorator. She gets her design aptitude from her mother. I couldn't design my way out of a paper bag."

"Any grandchildren?" I ask.

"None yet, but I have my fingers crossed."

"We have a twelve-year-old kid. You'll meet him. His name is Taylor, and he'll be joining us for dinner."

"I look forward to meeting him."

"On the way over here, Randy told me that Thanksgiving is his favorite holiday," Mom says.

"Is that so?"

"I like Thanksgiving," Randy says.

"Who do you usually eat with?"

"I usually eat at my daughter's house. Everyone will be there this year, including my ex-wife. My daughter fixes a turducken every year."

"A what?"

"A turducken."

"I don't think Jonathan knows what that is," my mom says, laughing.

"What is it?" I ask.

"It's a deboned chicken placed inside a deboned duck placed inside a turkey."

"Never heard of it."

"It's a New Orleans dish. My daughter's husband is from New Orleans."

"Interesting," I say.

I can't help it. I want to know what secrets this man is keeping. Why did he really get divorced? What could his ex-wife tell me? Sure, he's coming across as a nice guy, but don't all these freaks come across as nice guys? Did he abuse his wife? Was he mean to her? Did he knock her around? Does he have a horrible temper? Is he the jealous and possessive type? Or maybe he's an alcoholic, a drug addict, a gambler, or some kind of pervert. Does he spend every night glued to his computer, looking at pornography? Or maybe he gets his kicks by hooking up with prostitutes. Or maybe he's dishonest. Is he falsifying medical bills to insurance companies? Is he on the verge of being found out and thrown in jail? Or losing his medical license? Or filing for bankruptcy? Who knows? I don't know anything about this guy, and most likely, neither does my mom. What kind of monster did she invite into our home? That is the question.

The next day, I call Lewis. I ask him how things went with dad and his girlfriend, and he tells me the girl's name is Janet, and she's thirty-two—if she was being honest about her age. Lewis says she looks more like she's forty going on fifty.

"She's an artist at the agency. You know the type. I guess she and Dad have had kind of a thing going on for years."

"You mean an affair?"

"I'm not sure they had an affair."

"But you suspect it?"

"It's possible. I have no idea what Dad sees in her."

"She bothered you?"

"She was annoying. The way she hangs on Dad's arm and laughs at all his stupid jokes."

"Unlike Mom."

"Mom has class. If they sold girlfriends at Walmart, Dad could've bought Janet there. In a box. Made in China. The artist model—four dollars and ninety-nine cents, batteries not included."

I laugh. "It doesn't sound like your Thanksgiving went any better than ours," I say.

"What was Mom's date like?"

"He tried to be nice."

"Mom told me he is a doctor."

"An orthopedic surgeon."

"Gawd," Lewis scoffs.

"What's wrong?"

"I can't believe she'd go after a doctor."

"It's all so weird, isn't it?" I say.

And it is weird, seeing our parents with new partners. Seeing whom they picked. I liked the way it was. I liked it when it was just Mom and Dad. I realize people get divorced all the time, but I'm not sure I'll ever get over the strangeness of it all. Not ever.

CHAPTER 30

BULLIES

Shortly after Taylor turns fourteen, he faces a problem at school with a kid named Chris Hamner. I don't know anything about Chris, except for what Taylor has told us. He tells us about the boy only after we question him relentlessly. He doesn't want to talk about Chris, and he especially doesn't want us getting involved in his problems. We're just his stupid parents, and we won't understand.

But we notice something is wrong. It is clear Taylor doesn't want to go to school. He comes up with every lame excuse imaginable to stay home. His head hurts, his stomach aches, he is too tired, or he is having growing pains in his leg—you name it. Getting him off to school becomes a major undertaking every morning. He is also quieter than usual. He is not his happy-go-lucky self. We figure at first that it's just teenage moodiness, but then it is obviously something more. I recognize the reluctance to go to school from my own childhood. So we sit down with Taylor to get to the bottom of the matter, and finally, he comes clean. He is being bullied, and the culprit is Chris Hamner.

I have a father-son talk with Taylor, and I tell him I know a thing or two about bullies. I tell him that bullies are just insecure people who deal with their insecurities by picking on people they figure won't fight back. "Somehow," I say, "Chris has you pegged as someone who won't hit back, as someone who will stand there and take his abuse. If you want to get him to stop bullying you, you will need to stand up to him."

"Stand up to him?" Taylor asks.

"You need to fight back," I say.

"You mean hit him?"

"I mean do whatever it takes."

"But Mom told me fighting was wrong."

"It is wrong," I say. "But sometimes it can't be avoided. I'm telling you this man-to-man. Sometimes you just have to clench your fists and stand up for yourself."

"And if I lose the fight?"

"He'll still back off."

"Are you sure about that?" Taylor asks. For the time being, he doesn't seem to have a lot of confidence in my advice.

"Bullies don't like to pick on kids who fight back," I say. "If you hold your ground, he'll leave you alone and find someone else to harass."

"I don't know," Taylor says, shaking his head.

"I know I'm right about this," I say. "I know what I'm talking about. I was picked on by a few bullies in my time. I fought back, and they left me alone. They learned not to mess with Jonathan Hart."

This is true. I remember one bully in particular, a kid named Scott Burns. We were in the seventh grade. I tell Taylor about this kid and how he made my life miserable. It was awful. I don't know why this kid picked me out as a target, but it was as if one day he suddenly discovered me. We had physical education class together, and it never failed: no matter what we were doing or which sport we were playing, he would ridicule me in front of his friends. He'd say I played like a girl. He'd say I was a mama's boy. He'd call me gay. Not that I had anything against homosexuals. But I wasn't gay, and I didn't like being called that. His friends would all laugh and join in on the abuse, but Scott was always the one who got things started. He was the instigator. The rest of them were following along, having fun at my expense. But why me? Why did Scott single me out? I was miserable.

I tell Taylor how I came to dread PE class. I'd come home every day after school with a knot in my stomach. I would daydream about standing up to Scott and letting him have it. I would beat up the pillow in my bedroom, pretending it was Scott. I spent a lot of my time in my room back then, hiding out from the world.

My dad was the first to notice the change in my behavior. Like Taylor, I was no longer a happy-go-lucky kid, and like Taylor, I tried to stay home from school as often as possible, pretending I was sick. One morning, when I told Mom my stomach hurt, Dad came into my room to talk to me. He asked me what was wrong. He said he wouldn't leave my room until I told him what was going on, and I broke down and told him about Scott and the PE class. I thought he was going to get mad at me, but instead of getting mad, he spoke calmly and sincerely.

"You need to put your foot down," my dad said.

"Put my foot down on what?" I asked.

"You need to stand up for yourself, son. I know it seems impossible, but you need to fight back."

"Against Scott Burns?"

"Yes," Dad said.

"He'd kill me."

But he didn't kill me. It took all the courage I could muster, but I finally stood up, following my father's advice, and faced this bully. We were playing basketball, and Scott had called me gay for the last time. I stepped up to Scott, and with all my might, I threw a punch right into his ugly nose. I could feel his nose collapse under the force of the blow, and there was blood. A slight stream of red blood trickled from one of his nostrils and into his mouth. I just stared at him. He must've seen the fire in my eyes, because he failed to fight back. Or maybe he was just in shock. Or maybe I was too pathetic to waste any punches on, but he wiped the blood away from his nose and didn't kill me.

One of his friends said, "Hit him back," but he didn't.

Scott just shook his head and said, "If I beat the little faggot up, I'll just get in trouble. He isn't worth it. Come on. Let's finish our game."

That was that. It was the last time Scott harassed me. We didn't become friends—far from it. But finally, he left me alone.

I tell Taylor about this experience with Scott Burns, and he listens. To tell you the truth, I'm not sure what he's going to do. He is hard to read.

I tell you about my father-son talk with Taylor and the advice I gave him about standing up for himself, and you are furious. "I can't believe you would encourage Taylor to get into a fight," you say. This surprises me. It shouldn't, but it does.

"He needs to stand up for himself," I say.

"He can stand up for himself without fighting."

"You say that because you were never a boy."

"I say that because I'm right."

"You want your son to just lie there and take it?"

"That's not what I said," you say.

"Then what are you saying?"

"I just don't want Taylor fighting." You are adamant about this, and the more we argue about it, the more entrenched in your opinion you get.

Two days later, we get a call from the school. It is the principal, and he has Taylor in his office. It turns out Taylor took my fatherly advice to heart and stood up to Chris Hamner. But he didn't just stand up to him. He beat the heck out of the kid. Chris now has a black eye and a split lip that requires three stitches. Chris's mom picks him up from school and takes him to the hospital to be treated. Chris's mom is furious. She wants to know what kind of school allows this kind of violence against her son to take place. "Where were your teachers?" she asks the principal. "Why wasn't someone there to stop this assault?"

Assault?

That's what the principal is calling it. Suddenly, Taylor is the bully, and Chris is the victim. Can you believe it? The principal wants us to come to the school immediately. You are busy at work, so I make the trip to see the principal. I'll admit it: I am proud of the boy.

As I take a seat in the principal's office, Taylor waits on the bench outside. The principal and I are alone together. He wants to talk to me privately.

"I told you over the phone what happened," he says.

"You did," I say.

"We have a problem."

"Do we?" I ask.

"Chris Hamner's parents are very upset."

"Upset at Taylor?"

"You should see what Taylor did to their child. He really worked the boy over. I don't know what to do. Chris's parents want me to expel your son."

"Expel him?"

"They don't feel comfortable having Taylor remain in the same school with Chris."

"Did you ever stop to think that Taylor may have had a good reason for doing what he did?"

The principal stares at me. It's like talking to a wall. "Listen, we've never had any difficulty with Taylor before," he says. "But I'll tell you what troubles me, Mr. Hart. I talked to Taylor, and he said you encouraged him to fight with Chris."

"I told him to stand up for himself."

"For what reason?" the principal asks.

"Chris was bullying my son," I say.

"I find that hard to believe, Mr. Hart. Chris is one of our better students. We've had no complaints about him bullying anyone."

"I can only tell you what Taylor told me."

"Did he tell you Chris hurt him or struck him?"

"Well, no," I say.

"Did he threaten to hurt him? Did he say he was going to do him bodily harm?"

"I don't know," I say.

"Yet you felt it was appropriate to encourage your son to fight the boy?"

"Like I said, I told him to stand up for himself."

"We don't tolerate violence between any of our students for any reason."

I sigh.

The principal continues to lecture me. "We teach our students to use their words, not their fists. Can you imagine if these kids got into a fistfight every time they had a disagreement? This place would be completely out of control. And we depend on our parents to back us up. A parent who encourages his child to fight makes it impossible for us to do our job."

"Right," I say. I say it as in, "Right—where were you when my son was being bullied?"

The principal begins fiddling with a pencil. He is thinking about something, and then he says, "That still leaves me with a decision to make."

"A decision?"

"What to do with your son. I'm not going to expel him. This is the first time we've had a problem with him. But fighting is a serious offense, so I have to do something."

So what does this idiot do? He suspends Taylor for three days and tells me I have to pay the Hamners' doctor bill for sewing up their kid's lip. He also wants Taylor to write an essay about how fighting is wrong. Further, the principal decides it would be a good idea to have the boys meet in his office and apologize to each other. To bury the hatchet and call a truce. To put an end to their hostilities. I wonder if this buffoon was ever a kid.

I can tell you this: all said and done, Chris stops bullying Taylor, and it has nothing to do with them shaking hands or apologizing to each other. Remember Captain Kirk and the Gorn? It took gunpowder and a diamond projectile to make peace between the adversaries. It took violence to end the violence. In Chris and Taylor's case, it took a black eye and a split lip.

I point this out to you about six months after Taylor's fight. You are appalled. "You still think you did the right thing?" you ask.

"I think I did," I say.

"You'd make an interesting doctor."

"What's that supposed to mean?" I ask.

"A patient comes to you with a pain in his toe, and you amputate his leg and say, 'See? No more pain in the toe. Aren't you glad we cut off your leg?'"

"I hardly think that's an appropriate analogy."

"No?"

"I don't understand why you don't get it," I say.

"Oh, I get it."

"Then why aren't you agreeing with me?"

"Because what you did was wrong," you say. "It's wrong to encourage your child to fight. A boy can stand up for himself without resorting to violence. There are other ways to deal with disagreements. Intelligent ways. Peaceful ways. Fighting solves nothing. Fighting only makes things worse. The principal knew what he was talking about."

Bah, the principal. The Gorn captain would've killed him for sure, and the *Enterprise* and all its crew members would've been destroyed. That's the reality of it. I know this like I know that two plus two equals four, like I know the sun will rise in the east.

CHAPTER 31

THREE STORIES

I hit my stride in my late forties. They like to say that bad things come in threes. Do you believe this? Listen, I have three stories to tell you.

Story number one is the egg incident. I'm talking about our neighbors Jim and June Crawford, who live across the street. They are in their late thirties and have no children. A fine-looking pair they are, and they are as happy as little lovebirds. Am I envious? Maybe I am. It doesn't seem fair to me that a couple their age should be off the hook, having no kids to raise or worry about. They are carefree, happy, tan, and physically fit, and they call each other sweetie, darling, and honey. It all comes to a head for me two days after my forty-eighth birthday, when Jim buys himself a brand-new sports car.

Two bucket seats are all he needs because he doesn't have any kids to lug around. It's just Jim and June, the lovebirds, roaring down the road together as if there's no tomorrow. Gawd! Maybe it would be tolerable if it were a domestic vehicle, but it isn't just any sports car; it's a brand-new red Lamborghini. It isn't fair. It's the car I have always fantasized about owning, my dream car, and only God knows how fast it goes.

Every time Jim hops into the car and starts up its overpowered Italian engine, it gives me a huge stomachache. It should be me in that car with my leather driving gloves, my foot on the gas, and my hands on the wheel.

That car!

Jim always keeps it parked in his driveway, probably so everyone can see that he owns it. Every morning, when I step out of my house to go to work, there it is. And there I am, stepping into my beige hunk-of-junk Toyota with its cracked windshield and coffee-stained seats.

Our bedroom window looks out across the front yard and street at the Crawfords' house and driveway. Every night, when I go to bed, I look out the window, and I can see the sleeping Lamborghini. Christ, there is no escaping it. Then, one night, it becomes too much for me. It is three in the morning, and I can't fall asleep. I swear to God I can hear the Lamborghini laughing and then saying something to me in Italian. Then it laughs again cruelly, and it speaks again. Then it laughs, ha ha ha. I decide enough is enough.

Without waking you, I climb out of our bed. I put on my bathrobe and slippers and go downstairs to open the refrigerator door. I remove a carton of large AA eggs and then walk to the front door, step out of the house, and walk across the street. After opening up the carton, I proceed to smash the eggs one by one onto the car. I smear them and rub them on the windshield, roof, hood, door panels, and fenders. About halfway through, I trip over a pot of succulents, but that isn't going to slow me down. Nothing will stop me!

When I'm done with the entire carton, I stand back to admire my work. What a mess! Jim will go out of his mind for sure!

Then, out of nowhere, I hear a voice, and I turn to look. It is Jim's voice. He says, "Jonathan, is that you?" The porch light clicks on, and there he is, standing in front of the open door in his pajama bottoms.

My first inclination is to turn and run, but it would be pointless. Obviously, he has already recognized me. And where would I run to? To my house? No, I am screwed. "Yes, it's me," I say.

"What are you doing out here?" Jim asks.

"I heard a noise," I say. "It woke me up. I thought I heard some kids laughing, so I put on my robe and came outside. The kids were gone, but they left this empty egg carton in the street. Then I looked around, and I noticed your car. Looks like they really did a number on it."

Jim steps up to the Lamborghini to get a closer look. "Darn," he says. "What a mess! Looks like they didn't miss a spot."

"No kidding," I say. "They were very thorough."

"I guess I'll wash it tomorrow morning."

Now I suddenly want to be helpful and say, "You don't want to let the eggs dry on your paint. It will be murder to get dried eggs off, even with vinegar. You'll be scrubbing all day."

"What do you suggest?" Jim asks.

"You need to clean your car now while the eggs are still wet. They'll come right off."

"Jesus," Jim says. "You're probably right."

"Get a pail and some soapy water," I say. "I'll help you out. It won't take us long."

Jim opens the garage door and gets a pail, some dishwashing soap, and a couple of rags. He squirts the soap into the pail and fills it with water. He turns on the outside floodlights so we can see what we're doing. He then hoses off the car as best as he can, and the two of us go to work on it. "I sure appreciate this," Jim says.

"It's no problem," I say.

So how do I feel? I feel like a total idiot. It is three in the morning, the neighbors are all sleeping, and I am helping Jim wash his car in my bathrobe and slippers.

Several months after the Lamborghini incident, you send me to the market to pick up a couple of steaks for dinner. You have everything else you need. You just need the steaks, so I hop into my Toyota and drive to the grocery store. So begins story number two.

In the meat section, I find two perfect porterhouse steaks. I have the butcher wrap them up and stick the price on them, and I then walk toward the checkout lanes to make my purchase. Suddenly, it hits me: I left my wallet at home on my desk. I removed the wallet from my pocket to access my credit cards because I was making an internet purchase of a box of trash compactor bags, bags that were only available on the internet. After making the purchase, I left my wallet on my desk, and when you asked me to go to the store, I forgot all about it. Now I am on my way to the checkout lanes, when I remember. *Dang it!* I am going to have to leave the steaks with the butcher, drive all the way home, get my wallet, and then drive all the way back to the store.

Am I just being lazy? Maybe I am. Rather than going all the way back home to get my wallet, I decide to shoplift the steaks. I stuff the steaks under my jacket and make my way straight to the exit. I am sure no one has seen me, but as I step out of the store, I hear a man shout, "You there! Stop!"

I turn around and see the store manager running toward me. "Are you talking to me?" I ask.

"What have you got in your jacket?" he asks.

"Nothing," I say, but that doesn't slow him down. The next thing I know, he is standing right in front of me, reaching for my jacket, trying to pull it open. "What the hell?" I say. That doesn't stop him, and he finally has a hold of my jacket and pulls on it. Out tumble the steaks, which land on the sidewalk.

"Aha!" the manager exclaims. He picks up the steaks with one hand and grabs me by the sleeve with the other. He pulls me back into the store and says, "Not on my watch, buster."

I ask where he's taking me, and he says to just follow him. I don't have much of a choice since he is holding on to my jacket, and he takes me to the back of the store and through the employee-only doors, to his little office. He tells me to sit down, and I do. Then he picks up the phone and calls the police.

"Do we really need to get the police involved?" I ask.

"I've had it with you people," he says. "You all think you can waltz in here and grab anything you want. But not on my watch. I'm going to make an example of you."

I plead with the man to call off the cops, and I explain to him that I simply left my wallet at home. "I would've paid for the steaks the next time I came here," I say.

He smirks and says, "Sure you would've—who do you think you're kidding?"

The cops arrive and lead me out of the store in handcuffs. It is humiliating. They put me in the back of their cop car and drive me to the station, where I am booked for shoplifting. I call you, and you come to get me. They let me go on my own recognizance, and as we sit in your car on the way to the grocery store to pick up my car, you say, "What in the world is wrong with you?"

I don't have a good answer.

Now for story number three. Just weeks after the porterhouse steak incident comes the baseball game. I'm talking about the softball game at the park. Every year, the *Daily Observer* holds a summer picnic for the employees, and every year, you and I attend. But this year is different. Each year, all the younger employees get together to play a game of baseball, but

I have never taken part until now. I say to you, "I'm going to play with them. It looks like fun. I haven't played baseball for years."

"Are you sure?" you ask.

"Why not?" I say.

"You're almost fifty years old. You're not exactly an athlete, and those kids are all young and healthy."

"What's wrong with my health?" I ask.

"Nothing's wrong with your health, but you're not a kid anymore. You're forty-eight years old."

"I'm perfectly capable of playing baseball," I say. Then I laugh. "It's not like I'm an old man."

"You might hurt yourself," you say.

"Doing what?" I ask.

"I don't know."

"Don't worry about me."

I join in and grab one of the mitts. I'm told to play in the outfield, which is fine with me. I stand out there, banging my fist into the mitt, waiting for a ball to come my way. It brings back some good memories. I mean, I never was a huge baseball player, but I do like to play, and there is not much to being an outfielder. All I have to do is catch the stupid ball and throw it back into the infield. I wait.

Finally, a hit comes my way, and I run to the ball, catch it, and heave it like a pro. The hitter is thrown out at second base, and I smile.

"Nice throw," one of the kids says, and I nod.

I can do this! I'm playing baseball!

When it comes time for our team to bat, they put me fifth in the order. I sit on the sidelines and watch the kids swing at the pitches. Some of them get base hits, and some strike out. When it is my turn, I grab a bat and step up to the plate.

"Come on, grandpa!" one of the kids yells.

"Hit it out of the park!" another shouts.

Everyone laughs.

I'll show them. The first pitch is a ball, and I let it sail past me. The second pitch is a strike, but I fail to swing. "Come on," I say to myself under my breath. "You can do it. Let's hit this next one right down the pitcher's throat!"

The pitch comes. It is coming right over the plate, and I close my eyes and swing at the ball with all my might. I miss, and the catcher yells, "Strike!"

I suddenly notice something. There is a sharp pain in my groin. "Ouch!" I say, and I drop the bat.

"Are you okay?" the catcher asks.

The pain hasn't gone away. "I don't know," I say.

"Grandpa hurt himself," the catcher says to my teammates on the sidelines.

"I'm okay," I say.

I pick up the bat I dropped, but the pain does not go away. I try to ready myself for another pitch, but I can't get in a comfortable position.

"Maybe you should have someone take your place," the catcher says.

"Maybe you're right," I say.

"What's wrong?" one of my teammates asks me.

"I think I pulled a muscle," I say.

One of my teammates comes out to the plate and takes the bat from my hands. "You'd better sit down," he says.

"I'll be fine," I say.

"You don't look so fine."

There is more pain, and then I say, "Maybe you're right. Have someone take my place."

You haven't been watching any of this. You've been talking to my boss's wife, and I approach the two of you, limping. You notice my limp and ask, "What did you do?"

"I don't know," I say.

"Did you get hit by a ball?"

"No, I think I pulled a muscle."

"Pulled a muscle?"

"Swinging at a pitch."

"What did I tell you?" you say.

"It was a freak accident. It could've happened to anyone."

"You never listen to me. Are you going to be okay?"

"I'll be fine."

You then look at my boss's wife and say, "I told him not to play."

Well, it isn't a pulled muscle. I limp around for three days before I finally go to the doctor to have the injury examined. It turns out I tore my stomach lining when I swung for that pitch, and now I have a hernia. "A little old to be playing baseball?" the doctor asks.

"I guess so," I say.

"We'll schedule you for surgery."

"Surgery?"

"We'll put in a piece of mesh. It's a simple operation. Done all the time."

Three days later, I'm recovering from the surgery, coming out of my anesthetic. The nurse offers me a plastic cup of apple juice. "Don't cough," she says.

"Don't cough?"

"It'll hurt."

"Okay," I say.

"Your wife is here to take you home. Are you feeling okay?"

"I feel fine," I say. Then I cough, and it feels as if someone has just gored me in the groin with a red-hot fireplace poker. "Jesus!" I exclaim.

"I said not to cough."

"I'll remember that," I say.

You then show up, and the nurse leaves. You help me get dressed. "Does it hurt?" you ask as you tie my shoes.

"Only when I cough."

"They want me to take you home now."

"Good," I say. "I can't wait to get out of this place."

"The car is right outside," you say.

As we drive home, I know what you're thinking. You're thinking that if I had only listened to you at the picnic, I wouldn't be here. We wouldn't be doing this. You would be at work rather than wasting half a day tending to your invalid husband, who is now deathly afraid of coughing.

Then I cough again. "Son of a bitch!" I shout.

"We have some cough drops at home," you say.

"Sounds good." My groin is throbbing, and my eyes are watering. That last cough really hurt like hell.

Here's what I am thinking. This is the thing. We are never going to see you swing a bat, throw a ball, or get a hernia operation. We are never going to see you be arrested and booked for shoplifting porterhouse steaks from the local grocery store, and we are never going to see you wash eggs from the neighbor's car in the middle of the night. I turn and look at you when we come to a stoplight. "How do you do it?" I ask.

"How do I do what?"

"You know what I mean," I say.

But do you?

CHAPTER 32

WAGES OF LOVE

I am about to turn fifty. The Earth has circled the sun nearly fifty times since I was born. I stare at myself in the mirror, and I look like a fifty-year-old man. There are wrinkles where my skin used to be smooth. There is gray in my hair, and my hair is thinner. Also, my eyes don't sparkle like they used to, and my teeth are yellower. I've noticed recently that my eyebrows are getting bushier, and I trim them every week. I also find myself trimming the hairs growing in my ears and nostrils. With the proper grooming, I can make myself look a little younger, but I am no longer young.

It is a time of reflection. I look back on the fifty years I have lived, and I ask myself, "What have I done? What have I accomplished?" I realize these questions are normal for someone my age, and I am not unique. We all look back and question our lives at one time or another. We all look back and compare what we've done with what we expected to do when we were young.

But what have I accomplished? I'm a writer, a father, and a husband. That's about it. Yes, I'm a decent husband, and I have been an okay father. As a writer, I guess I have been successful in a mediocre sort of way. I am being paid, and people like to read what I've written. But what about the big dreams of my youth? Where did they go? When I ghostwrote the autobiography of Nicholas Bliss in my twenties, I thought I was on the doorstep of something big. Something substantial. Little did I know I'd one day turn fifty and find myself chained to a desk, writing twenty years' worth of inconsequential feel-good articles for the *Daily Observer*.

Wow.

We have a party for my fiftieth birthday. Mom and Dad are there, and so are Lewis and Cheryl and their daughter. Your parents also come, and so do your sister and her husband. And Taylor is there. You bought a red velvet cake at the grocery store, and there are gifts to open. It's nice, and I'm glad everyone showed up.

You all sing "Happy Birthday" to me, and I make a wish and blow out the candles on the cake. I then open the presents and thank everyone for his or her thoughtfulness. It's one gift after another. A new shirt. A nice pen for my office. A frame for a photograph. A paperweight. Tickets to a hockey game.

The hockey tickets are from Taylor, of course, one for each of us to a Ducks game in Anaheim. It's a father-son thing, and we'll surely have a good time eating peanuts, drinking Cokes, and yelling at the refs.

Then there's the book. The book is from you.

"It's Milton Blackstone's latest," you say.

"I can see that," I say.

"It's supposed to be very good."

"I've heard about it."

"It's been on the *New York Times* best-seller list for the past three months," you say. "Everyone is reading it."

"I've heard of it too," your dad says.

"He's such a good writer," you say.

True, I like to read, and yes, Blackstone is a good writer, but the gift is like a bullet to my heart. How do I explain this? The last thing I need is a reminder that there are writers who are more successful than I am. Plus, Blackstone isn't even forty, and already he's had three best sellers. They call him a genius, and his books are sold worldwide.

"I'll be sure to read this," I say.

"I'd like to read it when you're done," you say.

I wonder where Milton Blackstone lives. He probably lives in a mansion somewhere, on some large estate with a long, winding driveway. He probably has gardeners who tend to the grounds, and he probably owns his own red Lamborghini. No doubt about it, and I fantasize about sneaking up his winding driveway with a carton of eggs in the middle of the night. I won't be helping him clean up the mess.

It's envy, and I know it. But I can't help how I feel. I know you mean well by giving me the book, but I want to cram it into our trash can and never look at it again. No, I don't want to read it. I should be writing best sellers, not reading them. I've been letting my life pass me by, and now I'm fifty years old with little to show for my time. Who am I? What have I become? Even more importantly, who should I be?

After everyone goes home and you go to sleep, I stay up late at night, watching old movies on TV, but I'm not following them. The dialogue goes in one ear and out the other, and the scenes all melt into each other like fuzzy images in a thickened fog. I am not tired. I am brimming with energy. I want to write! I go to my study, turn on my computer, and open a new file. Then I stare at the blank page and think.

The next morning, you are in the kitchen, making coffee and breakfast. The TV is on, and the window is open. I step into the kitchen, and you are totally unaware. Then you notice me and say, "Good morning, Jonathan. You're up so early. I didn't even hear you get out of bed. How'd you sleep?"

"I didn't," I say.

"You've been up all night?"

"I have," I say.

"What on earth for?"

"I've been writing."

"Writing?"

"Chapter one of my new novel."

"You're writing a novel? I didn't know that."

"I just started."

"I see," you say. You are not concerned. You don't take it seriously. I might as well have said I am plotting to overthrow the government or make an atomic bomb.

"I'm serious," I say.

"Do you want your eggs scrambled or fried?"

"Scrambled," I say. "And you should know that I'm quitting my job at the paper."

This gets your attention. "Don't be silly," you say. "That job is your bread and butter."

"I'm tired of eating bread and butter."

Well, my idea goes over like a lead balloon. We talk about it, and you try to talk me out of it. I'm at a loss. I can't understand why you are so adamant about my having a steady job. The job doesn't even pay that much, and you make plenty for us to live on. How do I get it through your head that this is something I must do?

I guess I'm proud of myself. I don't give in, and later that day, I call Walter and give him my formal resignation. I agree to stay on until they can find someone to replace me. Walter understands. In fact, I think he's surprised I kept with it for as long as I did. He knows what it's like to be a writer. He is a writer. In a way, I think he envies me for having the courage to pursue my dream, and he wishes me luck. "Anything I can do to help, I'm here for you," he says.

You are not thrilled about it, but you go along with my plan. You say you want me to be happy. "I think you should write a story about a dog," you say, putting in your two cents. "You know, a book about the world seen through a dog's eyes. Everyone likes stories about dogs." Then you pose the question: "What *is* this great book of yours going to be about?"

It's not about dogs. I tell you about the book. It will be the story of a fifty-year-old man named Charles Taggert. The truth is that I've been thinking about this story on and off for years, and I have it all mapped out in my head. The title of the book will be *Wages of Love*.

Charles is a bookkeeper for a construction company in Southern California. He has a wife, Dorothy, and two children, and they live in a modest house in Mission Viejo. His daughter's name is Pamela, and his son's name is Mike, and they are both enrolled at the community college. Dorothy is a housewife, but she makes some money on the side as a seamstress. There is nothing spectacular about this little family, and for the most part, they are happy and content with their middle-class lives. Everything is fine—that is, until the owner of Charles's company, Ted Colton, hires a young administrative assistant by the name of Veronica Black.

Veronica is a lovely young woman in her late twenties, and she has a wonderful personality to match her good looks. She's one of those people who makes everyone feel like a best friend. She is warm and friendly and always has a smile on her youthful face. The first thing Charles notices about her is her hair: thick, shiny, and raven black. And those eyes! Big, round, and burnt-sienna brown. And her mouth! And her nose! And her cheeks, chin, and ears! She is probably the most beautiful young thing

Charles has ever seen, and he finds himself staring at her whenever she is in his vicinity.

Veronica is a hard worker. She doesn't waste valuable work time by spending a lot of time talking to the other employees. She always has her head in her work, and Charles likes this about her. Unlike many other girls her age, she is not frivolous. Charles tells himself there is nothing worse than an attractive girl who uses her good looks to skate through life on a free pass, and Veronica Black is not one of those. She's the real deal.

But how to get to know her? That is the question for Charles. He must get to know the girl, but he can't figure out a way to make their paths cross. She is always busy working for Ted Colton and the job superintendents, and Charles is always busy crunching numbers for the company. Every day, like a machine, he adds, subtracts, multiplies, divides, and categorizes. Eight hours a day, and sometimes ten or twelve, he does whatever it takes to keep the company in good financial order, watching expenses, maximizing profits, and minimizing taxes. Yes, just like a machine. No one knows the real Charles—his depth, his deepest dreams, the vastness of his soul. Not even his wife, Dorothy. Especially not his children.

A man's family should make him whole, Charles thinks. *But what have I become?* He is a drone who goes to work each morning and comes home from work each day. He is a man who has eggs and bacon for breakfast with one cup of coffee and the morning news on the kitchen TV. Every day is the same: Kiss the wife, and thank her for the food. Say goodbye to the kids, and tell them to do well in school. Start the car, and drive through traffic. Say good morning to everyone at work, and sit down in front of the computer. Wrap things up at about five, and drive through traffic again.

His evenings are all the same too, day after day, month after month: Eat dinner, put on some comfortable clothes, and sit on the sofa with Dorothy. Watch TV. At eleven, it's time to brush his teeth, climb into bed, and dream. Even his dreams are boring.

But now there is Veronica! He can't stop thinking about the girl. Her raven hair and dark brown eyes. That voice. Sweet and melodic but all business. No gossip. No whining. Not a mean or angry word in her vocabulary. Charles has never actually talked to Veronica, but he imagines her.

Then comes the day Charles has been waiting for. Ted Colton is applying for a line of credit with their bank, and he needs an accurate inventory of all the company's assets. He assigns this task to Charles and Veronica, and they must work together as a team. It is the best news Charles has had in years. He will be working side by side with the girl, and they will get to know each other—and maybe they will become friends!

At home on the morning of the day Charles is supposed to have his first meeting with Veronica, he hops out of bed before the alarm goes off. He is electric with anticipation, and he can't wait to get to the office.

"What are you doing up so early?" Dorothy asks.

"I don't know," Charles says. "I just have a feeling today's going to be a good day."

"I'll be downstairs soon," Dorothy says.

"I'll make breakfast," Charles says.

"You'll make breakfast?"

"You heard me."

Sleepily, Dorothy says, "We're out of bacon, but there's some ham in the meat drawer."

"Got it," Charles says, and he puts on his bathrobe and slippers to go downstairs.

Charles outdoes himself. He cooks up a breakfast good enough for kings, making scrambled eggs, ham, toast, and hash browns, with coffee, milk, and a pitcher of orange juice. He turns on the kitchen TV to the morning news, and sure enough, his family shows up one by one to eat. First is Dorothy, and she is bewildered but happy. Then there is Pamela, and then there is Mike.

"This is wonderful," Dorothy says. "I like this. You should do this more often."

"Since when does Dad make breakfast?" Pamela asks.

"Hell must've frozen over," Mike says.

"What has gotten into you?" Dorothy asks Charles.

"Don't look a gift horse in the mouth," Charles says as he pours himself a glass of orange juice.

"The eggs are a little soft," Dorothy says.

"I like them this way," Mike says.

"So do I," Pamela says.

After eating breakfast with his family, Charles goes upstairs to shower, shave, brush his teeth, and dress. He splashes on some cologne. Dorothy bought it for him last Christmas, and it's the first time he's used it. He is careful when he picks out his clothes: the blue-and-green plaid shirt and khaki slacks. He has always looked good in blue and green. He looks at himself in the full-length mirror, adjusting the collar of his shirt and picking a couple of pieces of lint from his shoulder. Then he hums "Here Comes the Sun" as he makes his way back downstairs.

Dorothy is there, rinsing off the dishes and putting them in the dishwasher. "Why such a good mood?" she asks.

"I love you," Charles says.

"I love you too," Dorothy says, and then she sniffs. "Are you wearing cologne?"

"I am," Charles says.

"I thought you told me you didn't like cologne."

"I changed my mind."

"It smells good on you."

"I'll see you tonight," Charles says, and he's out the door and driving to work before she can say, "Rumpelstiltskin."

He turns the radio to a music station and sings along with the songs all the way to work.

The meeting with Veronica goes great. They put a plan together to list and value all the company assets, and they divide up the work. It is Charles's idea for them to meet every morning until the work is done, and Veronica agrees.

One thing leads to another, and as Charles gets friendlier with Veronica, he suggests they have lunch together. Veronica sees no harm in this, and she agrees. They take Charles's car to a small café about ten minutes from the office, where they order lunch and talk.

Veronica tells Charles about her best friend, Amy, who is going to quit her job soon. She tells Charles about the trouble she's had with her car and its transmission. Then she tells him about her cat. The cat's name is Andy, and he likes clawing at Veronica's chairs, but Veronica thinks it would be cruel to have the cat declawed.

Charles listens in awe. *I'm getting to know her*, he thinks. *She's comfortable with me, and she likes me. Yes, she likes me!*

Weeks go by, and the asset-valuation project has been long since completed, but Charles continues to talk to Veronica every chance he gets. They go out to lunch several more times, and Charles brings her flowers on her birthday. She is surprised. Charles knows the date of her birthday, just as he knows the date of everyone's birthday, since he does the payroll. When he hands Veronica the flowers, she says, "Oh, Charles, how thoughtful, but you shouldn't have."

"They're for you," he says.

"They're nice."

"You've brought so much recent joy to my life I thought I'd return the favor."

Has he gone too far? What is too far? He is in love with Veronica, and he knows it. When it comes to Veronica, there is no such thing as too far.

Meanwhile, his home life is the same. Maybe worse. He is losing interest in his dreary existence and in his annoying wife. He is losing interest in his children and their self-centeredness and immaturity. Every night, he eats dinner with his family, and then he watches TV in the family room with Dorothy. But he isn't paying attention to the TV, and he certainly isn't thinking about Dorothy. He is thinking only of Veronica, wondering what she's doing, wondering where she is at the moment, and wondering if Andy is clawing at her chairs. Does she plan to get her car's transmission fixed? Will her friend Amy ever move on and find a new job?

Charles grows more and more obsessed with Veronica. He won't leave her alone. He is under the impression that she likes all the attention and that she loves him too. He becomes less and less rational, until finally, Veronica is forced to take action. Somehow, she has to get Charles to leave her alone. She is convinced he won't listen to her, so she goes to their boss. She meets with Ted Colton and explains the situation, asking Ted to please talk to Charles and set him straight. "He'll listen to you," she says. "And he'll do what you say."

Ted agrees to talk to Charles, and they meet the next day.

"I need to talk to you," Ted says to Charles.

"What about?" Charles asks. He has no idea why Ted has called him in for a meeting.

"It's about Veronica."

"Veronica?"

"She has asked me to talk to you."

"About what?" Charles asks.

"You need to leave her alone."

"Leave her alone?"

"She's an attractive young woman," Ted says. "I can see why you like her. But how can I put this? She doesn't feel the same way about you as you feel about her. And you're making her very uncomfortable."

"Uncomfortable? She told you this?"

"She did," Ted says.

It's like being hit in the side of the head with a baseball bat. Suddenly, Charles is hurt and embarrassed. Veronica might as well have slapped him in the face in front of everyone. How could Charles have misjudged her so badly? It is horrible. Charles maintains his composure with Ted, but after he leaves Ted's office, he goes to a stall in the men's room and cries his eyes out. He's made a total fool of himself. He's a fifty-year-old doddering, deluded fool!

Charles finally stops crying and dries his eyes. He leaves the men's room and goes to his office. He turns off his computer and grabs his jacket to leave early. He goes to his car and drives home. When he arrives, the house is silent and empty. The kids are at school, and Dorothy is running errands. Charles goes into the bedroom, opens the nightstand drawer, and removes a revolver he keeps there for protection.

He sits on the edge of the bed, and he begins to cry again as he presses the end of the gun against the side of his head. He thinks of Veronica. Dear, sweet Veronica! Then he pulls the trigger, and the pain goes away. Charles is dead.

When I'm done telling you this story, you stare at me.

"Well?" I ask. "What do you think? Do you like it?"

"Do I like it?"

"Yes," I say. "Is it a good story?"

"I don't like it at all," you say.

"It's a tragedy," I say.

"A tragedy?"

"Yes," I say.

"I guess I don't get it."

And you *don't* get it. Well, that's fine. I'm going to write the book anyway. A book about a dog? No, I don't think so. Not a chance.

CHAPTER 33

MY DOG STORY

Death is an odd thing, isn't it? I don't mean for the people who die. Their hearts just cease to beat, and we don't know what happens to them after that. They leave us, but death is queer for the rest of us, for the survivors. How many people close to you have died? For me, it is now one. My father. He passes away at the age of eighty-one.

I get the news while I'm working on the fourth chapter of my book. It's a Saturday morning; the sunlight is spilling in through my open window, and there is a nice breeze. It is spring, and the birds outside are singing a symphony. Then the phone rings, and I have no idea who it is. I wait for you to answer it, and you do. I can hear you talking, but I can't make out what you're saying. When you're done, you come into my office. I ask who called, and you put your hand on my cheek and say, "Your father is gone."

"What do you mean he's gone?" I ask.

"I mean he's gone, Jonathan. That was Janet on the phone. We need to go over there."

I don't want to believe it. "That can't be," I say. "I just talked to him yesterday."

"He died this morning. Janet said she went to her aerobics class, and when she returned to the apartment, she found him on the floor in their bedroom. She doesn't know what happened. She said your dad was fine when she left."

I quietly say, "Jesus Christ." I don't have much else to say. What am I supposed to say?

"We need to go over there," you say.

"Of course," I say, and I stand up.

We leave the house and drive to my dad's apartment, which is about twenty minutes away. When we get there, I park in one of the guest spaces. The medical examiner is already there since Janet called the police to report the death. Dad's body is in the bedroom, but I don't go in to see him. I don't want my last memory of him to be of his lifeless corpse sprawled on the carpet.

The medical examiner is a young woman who looks more like an attractive corporate junior executive than a coroner. You and I sit with Mom on the living room sofa, and the woman sits on a chair across from us.

"Did your dad have heart problems?" she asks me. I say no, and then she asks, "Did he have any other medical issues?"

I tell the woman that my dad was as fit as a fiddle, and he was. Janet agrees with this. There was nothing wrong with him, and I tell her my dad's death is a total surprise. The woman says she's sorry for being so nosy, but she asks more questions. Then the doorbell rings, and the woman stands up to answer the door, telling us to stay on the sofa.

Two young men with a gurney have arrived to haul the body away. They wheel the squeaky gurney into the bedroom, and as they load him up, I can hear them talking. They are trying to figure out how to negotiate the sharp corner between the bedroom and the living room. Then I hear them trying to get past the bend, bumping the gurney into the wall, and one of them suddenly exclaims, "Goddamn it!"

They had to tilt the gurney to get through the sharp corner, and Dad's body slid off and landed on the floor. I wince and look at you. You have your eyes closed.

Janet starts to cry. "I can't wait until they get him the hell out of here," she says. "This is so unbearable."

What a strange morning. But here's the even stranger thing about the whole morbid scene: I don't cry. I don't shed a single tear, and although I am in shock, I am completely in control of my emotions. The two men are hauling away the body of my dear dad, and I feel nothing.

The emotion doesn't catch up with me later in the day, the next day, or the day after that. I never do cry, not once. Not ever.

This surprises me because I was close to my dad. I talked to him often on the phone, and I visited him every other week. He meant the world to me, but when he dies, I don't feel much of anything. Sure, I am a little sad, but I am not overwhelmed with grief or anger. *People get old and die*, I tell myself. *That's what they do.* Crying because my father has died would be like crying because the sky is blue.

Now I'll tell you what happens during the months that follow. We have a Boston terrier named Butch, a great little dog who, at the age of seven, begins to have serious health issues. First, I notice his eyes are gray and cloudy, so I take him to the vet. It turns out he has a bad case of cataracts. I ask the vet what we can do about it, and he refers me to an animal eye doctor. I take Butch to visit this doctor, and the guy says they can perform surgery to remove the cataracts, but the odds are fifty-fifty. When I ask what this means, he says Butch has a 50 percent chance of being cured and a 50 percent chance of going completely blind. When I ask how Butch would be without the surgery, the doctor says Butch would eventually go blind anyway. Worst case, the poor dog is going to go blind either way; therefore, we opt for the surgery.

Thousands of dollars later, Butch's eyes are clear. For a few months, the operation seems to have been a success. Slowly but surely, however, his eyesight gets worse and worse until he goes completely blind, and on top of that, he now develops glaucoma. He keeps rubbing his eyes with his paws. It is awful. We are told to give him eye drops four times a day to control the eye pressure, and then we are finally told there is a new option to consider, which is to surgically remove Butch's eyes and suture the empty sockets.

"What the hell?" I say to you. "First, his eyes are a little cloudy, and now they want to cut them out of his head and sew up the sockets?"

Meanwhile, as Butch is dealing with these eye issues, he is also refusing to eat. He nibbles at his food but not much. We try out some new brands of dog food, but he has no appetite. He's lost weight rapidly, and his ribs are now showing. I take him to the vet again, and for several hundred dollars, the vet does an MRI. It turns out Butch has a tumor the size of an apricot in his stomach. From the MRI, the vet can't tell if the tumor is malignant or benign, but we are told we need to either put Butch to sleep or remove the tumor. It is killing him, and the vet gives him two months to live.

We decide to go for the surgery, and several thousand more dollars later, the tumor is removed. The vet tells us it was cancerous and malignant, and it's all over his intestines. They say we can now try chemotherapy, and he refers us to an animal oncologist. This new doctor says he believes he can keep Butch alive a little longer, but there are no guarantees. We hand the oncologist our credit card and hope for the best.

The chemotherapy does keep Butch alive longer but not much. Less than a year after we start the chemotherapy, the cancer turns into a large malignant mass consuming Butch's entire abdomen. He is now in a lot of pain and as blind as a bat, and we decide it's finally time to end Butch's life. You find a woman who will come out to our home to euthanize our pet, and we call the woman up.

This woman comes to our house on a Saturday afternoon to put Butch to sleep. It is one of the worst days of my life. Christ, I cry my eyes out. I retreat to my den during the procedure. I cannot watch. The sorrow is excruciating, and when the task is done, I come out of my den to pay the lady. Butch is now in a wicker basket, on his side. It looks as if he's sleeping, but he is dead. I stroke his body, and he is still warm. I start sobbing even more. I can't control myself.

I later wonder about this. Was I crying over losing Butch, or was it a latent response to my dad's passing? Had I been holding in all this grief? It seems a little odd that I could be so upset over a dead dog after having shown so little emotion over my own father.

Now I can't help but wonder how I'd feel if you died. Would I fall apart? Would I cry my eyes out? Would I fall into a deep depression, or would I be stoic? What would I do with myself? How would I measure up? What kind of example would I set for Taylor? How long would it take me to file a claim against your life insurance policy? Would people go out of their way to be kind to me, or would they be angry with me and say you would've been better off marrying someone else?

Don't be mad at me. We all fantasize about our loved ones dying at one time or another. It isn't an evil thought. It's only natural to wonder what would happen. I can tell you this: if you were to die tomorrow, I would lose the most important person in my life. I don't say this to make you feel good; I say it because it's true. In my opinion, when it works out, there is nothing like the love and the bond between a husband and a wife. That's how it should be. That's how it is, and that's how it shall always be.

A couple of months after Butch dies, I write the final chapter of *Wages of Love*. It is fitting that I'm thinking about death. It is on my mind. I don't have any second thoughts about the ending. It is as it should be. Sometimes the best way to describe something is by pulling the rug out from under it and letting it topple to the floor.

CHAPTER 34

SCISSORS

There's nothing quite like wrapping up a book. It has taken more than a year for me to write *Wages of Love,* and now I have a finished manuscript in hand. I read it all the way through and make some minor corrections here and there. I then read it a second time, and I like the way it turned out. In my opinion, it's the best thing I've written to date.

Now comes the hard part: getting it published. Before I start sending out queries to publishers and literary agents, I send a copy to Walter at the *Daily Observer.* He said he would help me out, and I have always valued his opinions and advice. He tells me he's excited to read it, and one week later, he calls me. He has read the entire book, and I can't wait to hear what he has to say.

"I loved it," he says.

"Did you?" I ask.

"I did, but you'll never get it published."

"Oh?" I say.

"Not a chance."

"Why do you say that?" I ask. I'm not sure if Walter is serious or if he's just pulling my leg.

"Maybe years ago but not today."

"Not today?"

"Don't get me wrong. You've written a great book, and people should read it. But they won't. It's too real. And being so real, it's too depressing."

"It's supposed to be a tragedy."

"It hits too close to home. Tragedies these days only work if the reader doesn't identify with the main character in the story. People want to read about someone else's misfortunes, but they don't want you holding up a mirror."

"But I only wrote about one man."

"You wrote about all of us," Walter says.

I will always remember those words. They don't mean much to me when he says them, but later, I get the news from one of the reporters I know at the *Daily Observer*. His name is Clarence Woodrow, and he calls me three weeks after my conversation with Walter. Clarence tells me that Walter just committed suicide. The news hits me like a ton of bricks.

"When did this happen?" I ask, and Clarence tells me they just found the body. Walter's wrists were cut, and he was found in his bathtub. There was no suicide note. Apparently, he had been in the tub for several days, and his ex-wife found him in the bloody bathwater. She had been trying to call him to talk about their son, but he wasn't answering the phone. Then she called him at work, and they said he'd been absent. No one knew where he was. She had a key and let herself into Walter's house. It was awful. Clarence says everyone at the paper is in shock. He also says they are holding a memorial service in two days if I want to come.

Did my book have anything to do with this? It's hard for me to believe Walter would take his life just because he read a book. But maybe it was the book. Maybe it pushed him over the edge. In all the years I knew him, Walter never let on that he was particularly unhappy. I mean, I knew he wasn't thrilled about his divorce. In fact, I knew it bothered him a great deal. We talked about it a couple of times, and he told me it was one of the great regrets of his life.

I tell you about Walter, and you say, "He must have been a very unhappy man."

"The book is history."

"What book?" you ask.

"The book I just wrote. I'm through with it. I'm not going to look for a publisher."

"After all that work?"

"It's history," I say, and I mean it. Maybe I'm overreacting, but maybe I'm not. But I don't want anything to do with it, not ever. I go to my office, and just like that, I delete the entire file from my computer. Then I start to cry. "Fuck!" I exclaim. "Fuck all of this!"

You show up in the doorway, and you look deeply concerned. I know you care about me, and I know you realize how significant this is. I know you want to make me feel better, but there's nothing you can do. I should've used my head years ago. Writing is for the birds. I should be selling cars for your father. "You're just upset," you say.

"You think so?" I ask.

"You'll feel better."

"I don't see how."

"You'll feel better. I promise you."

I know you love me, and I know you mean well. That's why you sit down with me the next day and say, "I think you need help, Jonathan. I hate to see you like this. It hurts me to see you in such pain. I want you to see a psychologist. I think you need professional help. Sweetheart, listen to me. This is beyond my skills as a wife. I have a friend at work whose husband went to a psychologist, and I can get the name of the doctor. She said the man did wonders with her husband, and I'm sure she'll share his name with me. I won't say anything about you to her. I'll just get the name."

I look at you. I hate myself for getting you involved with this. But I do need help. I know this. "Go ahead and get me the name," I say.

The doctor's name is Laurence Ball, and I meet with him a week later. His place of business is in an office building, on the second floor, between a civil engineer's office and an insurance agency. I have made an afternoon appointment, and I show up ten minutes early. There is a reception area but no receptionist, just a sofa, a couple of chairs, and a coffee table covered with magazines. On the wall is a sign that says, "Take a seat, and someone will be with you soon." So I sit and wait. I pick up a *National Geographic* and look at the pictures. Sure enough, when it's time for my appointment, the door opens, and the doctor appears to greet me.

"You must be Jonathan," the doctor says.

"I am," I say.

"I am Dr. Ball. Won't you please come in?"

"Sure," I say. I stand up and walk toward the doctor. I follow him down a short hall to his office, and after we enter the room, he closes the door.

"Please take a seat," he says.

"Which chair?" I ask. There are several chairs to choose from.

"Take your pick."

"I guess this is as good as any," I say, and I pick the chair closest to the man's desk. I sit and look around at the office. There are no diplomas or certificates on the walls. There are no bookcases, and there are no oil paintings or photographs. But there are a lot of children's drawings on big sheets of paper thumbtacked to the drywall. I look at them.

"My grandchildren," the doctor says.

"I see," I say.

"Lights of my life."

"How many do you have?" I ask.

"Three," the doctor says. "Two girls and a boy. They are my daughter's children." The doctor then grabs a pen and gets poised to make notes on a notepad. "So tell me," he says. "What can I do for you?"

"My wife said I needed help."

"Ah, your wife."

"And I guess I agreed with her."

"What seems to be the problem?"

"That's a good question," I say. "I thought about it on the way over here. I wondered what I was going to tell you. What I've come up with is very simple. I don't think I'm a complicated person. My problem is that I'm unhappy."

"Unhappy with what?"

"My life," I say.

"Have you always been unhappy?"

"I don't know," I say. "I suppose not."

"So this is a recent feeling?"

"Yes, I guess."

"Was there something that triggered this unhappiness?"

"I think it was the book."

"A book you read?"

"No, a book I wrote."

"Ah," the doctor says. "That's right. You are a writer. What is the book about?"

"It's about a married family man who falls in love with a young girl at work. He falls in love with her, and he comes forward with his feelings. The girl shuns him, and she goes to their boss to get the man to leave her alone. The man is hurt and humiliated, and he can't live with the rejection. So he kills himself."

"I see," the doctor says.

"I titled it *Wages of Love.*"

"Not exactly a happy subject."

"No," I say.

"I've always believed that when writers write, they write about themselves."

"That's probably true," I say.

"Tell me—did you happen to fall in love with a younger girl at work?"

"No," I say.

"But the girl—she definitely represents something in your life."

"Such as?" I'm not sure what the doctor is driving at. I never really thought of Charles's girl as being anything other than a girl.

"Perhaps she represents a more meaningful life. A life filled with love, hope, beauty, and promise. An interesting life. An engaging life. The kind of life a man deserves. Tell me about your day-to-day life before you started writing this book. Tell me about your work, your wife, your son, and your social life. What has it been like to be Jonathan Hart?"

I think about this before I answer. Then I say, "I remember when Samantha and I first got married. It was so exciting. Opportunity was at our fingertips. It was the first day of our journey, and we had no idea what to expect. And the world seemed so huge. Every day was an adventure into the unknown, and every minute was an exhilarating thrill. There was so much to do, so much to see, so much to experience, and so much to learn. And our love for each other was the magic that held it all together, the fuel in our spaceship, the navigational charts that would guide us through the stars and planets of the universe. We were going where no man and woman had gone before.

"'Will you take this man to be your husband?'

"'I do,' Samantha said.

"'And will you take this woman to be your lawfully wedded wife?'

"'I do, I do, I do,' I said. We were so in love. There was a ton of champagne, hors d'oeuvres, and music, and then we boarded our plane to Hawaii. We went to luaus, and we swam in the warm ocean, and we made love for hours on end. That's what I remember. It now seems like such a long time ago, but I remember it clearly."

"And then?" the doctor asks.

"Then? It was great at first. We were going places. We were getting somewhere. The newness of the journey was still like a fast-beating heart. *Thump, thump, thump.* Samantha got a job. *Thump, thump, thump.* I wrote a book. *Thump, thump, thump.* Then we bought two cars, and we bought a house. And the sun was whizzing through the sky every day, sunrise to sunset, and then another sunrise to bloody sunset. Then Samantha got pregnant, and we brought a soul into the world and named him Taylor. It was a miracle. He was ours—all ours! And then? Well, then it began to happen—slowly at first, insidiously, almost imperceptibly, but as real as real gets. The routine."

"The routine?" the doctor asks.

"Change the baby's diapers, mop and vacuum the floors, clean the dishes, wash the laundry, gas up the cars, mow the lawn, pull the weeds, trim the hedge, replace the burned-out lightbulbs, go to the grocery store, watch a little TV, maybe read a book or a magazine, do a little clothes shopping, buy a Christmas tree, decorate it, take down the decorations and store them in the attic, celebrate a birthday, buy new tires for the car, take out the trash on Wednesdays, bring in the mail, pay the bills, balance the checkbook, cook dinner, talk to the neighbors, go to a movie, go out to dinner, stroll through the mall, and take Taylor to the pediatrician when he coughs. You get the idea, right? This is what our lives became. There were no new lives or civilizations to discover. No, we were not explorers. We were doing our duties: 'Yes, sir. No, sir. What should we do next, sir?' Custodians. Janitors. Drones. Worker bees. Do you know what the life span is of the average bee? A worker bee lives two to six months—the blink of an eye. Here today and gone tomorrow. Just like us, they come and go, and they do their jobs."

"Do you love your wife?" the doctor asks.

"Yes, of course," I say.

"So that hasn't changed?"

"Well, I wouldn't say it hasn't changed. I do love Samantha, but I wouldn't say I feel the same way I did when we first got married."

"Did you think you'd feel the same after all these years?" the doctor asks.

"I guess I did."

The doctor writes down some notes on his notepad, and then he looks up at me. "I'm going to share something with you that it took me sixty-eight years to learn. I am sixty-eight years old. I have been married for forty-five years. I have three children and three grandkids. I think I know what I'm talking about, so listen. I'm going to reveal the secret of love to you. The secret of happiness. The secret of life. You won't find this in a textbook, in a college class, on a TV show, or in a Hollywood movie. The secret is maintenance."

"Maintenance?"

"Pure and simple."

"Maintenance of what?"

"The maintenance of everything."

"What does that even mean?" I ask.

"The routine you talk about, all the mundane things you do in your life, is what life is all about. Life is not just about falling in love. Life is about being in love. You have it. You take care of it. You feed it, lubricate it, service it, water it, trim it, nurture it, and buy it a present every now and again. You maintain it. And why? Because you have something amazing that no one else in the world has: your life. Your wife, your children, your humanity, and your existence. The sooner you come to terms with this the better. Am I making any sense to you?"

"Kind of," I say.

"I'm going to give you a homework assignment," the doctor says.

"Okay," I say.

"I want you to do something. I want you to go out and buy a small gift for your wife. Nothing expensive but something thoughtful. Something out of the blue. Maybe something that will make her life a little easier. No reason for it other than to make her smile. Then wrap it up and give it to her. Just say, 'This is for you.' Can you do that?"

"I can," I say.

"Very good. I'll see you in a week."

"That's it?" I ask.

"Yes, that's it for now."

We agree on our next appointment date, and I leave the doctor's office. I get into my car and drive home. When I get home, you aren't there. I walk around the house with my homework assignment in mind. What can I get for you? What will make your life a little easier? I walk around the family room and then around the kitchen. Then it hits me: a pair of scissors! You're always complaining that our scissors are no good. They're cheap. "They don't make them like they used to," you always say. "When I was a little girl, scissors used to last a lifetime."

I get in my car, drive to the local hobby and craft store, and ask a clerk if they have *good* scissors for sale. I tell her I need them for my wife. The woman leads me to the aisle where they sell them, and she grabs a pair of metal scissors off a hook and hands them to me. "These are our best," she says. "They cut like a dream, and they'll last your wife for years."

"Perfect," I say.

"They're not cheap."

"Money is no object," I say.

"Can I help you with anything else?"

"No, that'll do it. Thanks," I say, and I take the shiny scissors to the cashier. Then I bring them home and wrap them with some wrapping paper I find in the hall closet. I set the gift on the kitchen counter and wait for you to come home.

When you find the gift in the kitchen, you ask me who it's for.

"It's for you," I say.

"For me?"

"It's just a little something," I say.

"What's the occasion?"

"There is no occasion. Just open it."

You open it. "Scissors?" you ask. You seem a little bewildered, but you are smiling.

"You're always complaining about our scissors. These are the best scissors money can buy."

"How much were they?"

"Never mind that," I say.

I meet with Dr. Ball a week later, and the first thing he asks me is whether or not I completed my homework assignment. I tell him I did, and he says, "So tell me. What did you get her?"

"A pair of scissors," I say.

"Scissors?"

"She's always complaining about our cheap scissors. I got an expensive pair. The best they had."

"Ah, I see."

"She seemed surprised."

"I'll bet she was."

"Should I have gotten her something else?"

"No, no, scissors are fine."

"You said to get her something that would make her life easier."

"I did say that."

"She would never have bought them for herself."

"How did this make you feel?"

"I felt a little silly at first."

"And then?"

"I felt good," I say.

I wonder. What if Walter had bought his wife a pair of scissors while they were still married? For no reason. Just to make her life a little easier. We think of gestures like this as inconsequential, but they mean everything, don't they? I mean, in the long run. Maybe Walter would still have been married today, and maybe he wouldn't have felt compelled to take his life.

"In the long run, all the little things we do for each other add up," Dr. Ball tells me, and I have no reason to doubt his words.

CHAPTER 35

THE FAMILY GAME

Taylor is now a senior in high school, and you are still working your tail off at Able and Associates. I am writing a new book, a book that is nothing like *Wages of Love*. I've learned my lesson. The title of this new novel is *The Family Game*, and it pokes fun at modern twenty-first-century family life. It is lighthearted and entertaining, and the characters are cheerful, optimistic, and happy. The book was actually Dr. Ball's idea. He said, "Write for the pleasure of it, Jonathan, and then let your life imitate your art." I liked his advice, and I am having a lot of fun writing this book. Life is good, and our marriage is as solid as a rock. Our family life is giving me pages of good material for my novel.

Take Taylor and his most recent girlfriend. Taylor has had girlfriends before but none quite like this one. We are not sure what to make of her. Neither you nor I had even an inkling that Taylor would fall for this kind of girl, as she is so different from him. Taylor has always been a pretty normal kid, with normal interests, a normal IQ, and a normal outlook on life. Hockey is still his sport of choice. After school and on weekends, he does nothing but play hockey. He's on three different teams, and it's good for him. It keeps him out of trouble, and it keeps him in good physical condition. So where is he headed with his life? Who knows? A forward for a minor-league hockey team? The guy who drives the Zamboni? Your guess is as good as mine.

We have been letting Taylor find his own way. We haven't been steering him toward one life ambition or the other. But maybe we should've been providing more guidance. Maybe it has been a mistake to think a teenager is capable of choosing the right path for himself on his own. We certainly scratch our heads when he brings home his latest girlfriend.

It's your idea to invite her to Taylor's eighteenth birthday party. It is the first time we meet her in person. Your mom and dad are there, along with my mom, my brother and his family, and your sister and her husband. The girl's name is Jennifer Mayfield. She is a good-looking girl. She isn't wearing any makeup. She looks kind of like a hippie or a gypsy, dressed in a sleeveless yellow top and a full-length purple paisley skirt. Her hair is long and brown, braided down the middle of her back, and she has two of the largest silver hoop earrings I have ever seen. Gypsy? Hippie? Take your pick. She could pass as either.

"We've been wanting to meet you," you say.

"I'm glad you invited me," Jennifer says. "I've been wanting to meet you too."

"I love your skirt," you say.

"Oh, thank you."

"Taylor says you're now a junior."

"Yes, ma'am," Jennifer says politely. "We met in our art class."

"Taylor says you're a great artist."

"I don't know about that," Jennifer says. "But I do like art. It's my favorite subject. I also like English. I like to read at night before I go to bed. I especially like the old classics."

"There are a lot of good books to read," I say.

"Taylor's dad is a writer," you say.

"I know," Jennifer says, looking at me. "Taylor told me. He said you've written a few books."

"I actually haven't written much to speak of," I say.

"You've written plenty," you say.

"What's your favorite classic?" I ask Jennifer.

"My favorite?" she asks. "There are so many of them. Lately, I've been reading *Zen and the Art of Motorcycle Maintenance*. I like it a lot."

"Interesting choice."

"I don't like the way the guy treats his son, but his thoughts on quality are intriguing."

"Yes," I say.

"I also liked *Don Quixote*."

"That's another good one," I say.

"I liked his little friend."

"Sancho Panza?"

"Yes," Jennifer says.

"I keep telling Jonathan he should write a book about a dog," you say. "People love books about dogs."

"Or cats," your mother says.

"I'd rather read about a dog than a cat," your father says. "Don't care much for cats."

"I have a cat," Jennifer says.

"Do you?"

"His name is Picasso."

"That's a good name," I say.

"He paints. He paints with his paws, and he's very good at it. I dip his paws in the paint and let him have at it. I turned one of his paintings in for my art class and said it was mine. I got an A on it."

Everyone laughs.

We all like this girl. She seems down to earth, and she has a sense of humor. These are both good traits, but as the afternoon goes on, I begin to wonder just how in the world Taylor became involved with such a girl. I ask Jennifer if she's been to any of Taylor's hockey games, and she grimaces and says, "I'm working on him."

"Working on him?" I ask.

"I'm against competition," she says.

"She doesn't like me playing hockey," Taylor says.

"Hockey is a great sport," your dad says. "And there's nothing wrong with a little competition. Competition is what has made this country great."

"Taylor's been playing hockey since he was a little kid," I say. "The games are a lot of fun."

"And he's pretty good at it," my brother says.

"Do you all remember when he scored his first goal?" my mom asks. "It was the game-winning goal."

"That was pretty cool," I say.

"Have any of you read James Kraft?" Jennifer asks.

"James who?" your dad asks.

"James Kraft," Jennifer says. "He's a sociologist and a writer. He's written several books about sports."

"Never heard of him," your dad says.

"Kraft says sports are both the source and a reflection of almost all of the difficulties we have in the world today. Think about it. We are all taking sides. We are fighting one another for victories. We are obsessed with becoming winners at the expense of our opponents. War. Politics. Discord. Violence. They can all be traced back to sports. It's always us versus them. You versus me. Him versus her. Who has the most points? Who gets to raise the trophy over his head? Who takes over the throne and lays down the law?"

"I like sports," your dad says. I can tell by the way he says this that he thinks Kraft must be an idiot.

"We need to find more constructive ways to entertain ourselves," Jennifer says, ignoring your dad. "We need to seek harmony and cooperation rather than competition. And we need to seek love. They say love conquers all, and they are right. It is the answer to everything. Love and friendship. People need to learn how to get along with each other. Abraham Lincoln said it best when he said, 'I destroy my enemies when I make them my friends.'"

"I like that quote," my mom says.

"So do I," your mom says.

"Bah," your father scoffs. "This was coming from the president who presided over one of the bloodiest wars in our country's history."

I laugh.

But Jennifer doesn't laugh. She isn't perturbed, but she is committed to her opinion. Meanwhile, Taylor is quiet. I can't tell if he's amused or just confused. I'm having a hard time seeing Taylor hanging up his ice skates, no matter how crazy he is about this girl. But stranger things in the world have happened.

And it does happen. Just three months after becoming friends with Jennifer, Taylor tells me he's done playing hockey. He tells me while we're on our way to the rink. He says, "This is my last game."

"Your last game for what?" I ask.

"My last hockey game."

"I don't get it," I say.

"I don't want to play anymore. It all seems so pointless. I guess I'm tired of it."

"Are you serious?" I ask.

"I am," Taylor says.

"What are you going to do with your time?"

Taylor thinks for a moment, and then he says, "I'm going to be an artist."

"An artist?"

"Jennifer says I have talent," Taylor says.

"You mean like a painter?"

"Something like that."

I'm not sure what to say. He's gone from hockey to art with one single girlfriend. I tell Taylor not to make any rash decisions, but he tells me his mind is made up. He tells his coaches the news, and he tells his teammates.

How do I feel about this? To tell you the truth, it saddens me. I have enjoyed going to Taylor's games. It's true that when I was his age, I didn't participate much in sports, but I think I missed out. All kids should play a sport, and through Taylor, I have been an athlete vicariously, as an adult, as a cheerleader, and as a hockey dad. I've gotten a big kick out of it, and I've scored goals even though I can't skate to save my life.

You are equally disappointed when Taylor tells you the news, and you ask him what he's going to do with his time. Taylor tells you the same thing he told me. "I'm going to be an artist," he says.

"Since when are you so interested in art?" you ask.

"Jennifer says I have talent."

"Jennifer?" you say.

"She has an art studio at her house. We're going to work together."

"An art studio?"

"In the garage. Her parents let her use half the garage for her art projects."

For the next three months, we see little of Taylor. He is always over at Jennifer's house, in her parents' garage, presumably painting. It's Taylor, Jennifer, and Picasso, the painting cat.

Your dad tells you that you should put your foot down and put an end to this insanity, and you and I talk about it. We decide to let Taylor do what he wants. We figure if we interfere, he's just going to resent us. Besides, he's a senior in high school, and he'll be on his own soon anyway.

He's been staying out of trouble, and he's still doing well in school. What right do we have to complain?

Then it happens: Jennifer meets another boy, and she begins spending time with him instead of Taylor. The boy is in college and is three years older than Jennifer. He is a philosophy major. Taylor begins spending more time at home with us while Jennifer goes out with this new and interesting boy, and the next thing we know, Jennifer breaks up with our son. Is Taylor devastated? It's hard to tell. He mopes around the house a little, and he seems a bit lost at first. But this only lasts about three weeks before he brings home a new girl for us to meet. He knows this girl from school, and her name is Chloe Lake. One could've knocked us over with a feather. This girl is nothing at all like Jennifer. Not even close.

Chloe is a rock 'n' roll girl. You know the type. She has short blue hair, a nose ring, multiple ear piercings, and a tattoo on her forearm of a Chinese dragon. She is as skinny as a heroin addict, and she's dressed like a ghoul in a low-budget zombie movie. You actually gasp when you meet this girl, and maybe I do too. She is the last thing we expected.

It turns out Chloe is the singer for a rock 'n' roll band called the Plague. She doesn't play a musical instrument or write any of the songs; she just sings. Taylor says that she is ultratalented and that the band is becoming popular.

When she comes to our house, we all sit down for dinner. Taylor warned you ahead of time that she's a vegan, so you serve a vegan vegetable lasagna dish you found on the internet. It tastes like it came out of the garbage disposal, but Chloe seems to like it. Taylor also likes it. At least he says he does.

"So you're a singer?" I say to Chloe.

"I am," she says.

"Taylor says the name of your band is the Plague."

"It is."

"Who came up with that name?"

"Needle did. He writes all our lyrics. He has a way with words. He's a genius."

"Needle?" I ask.

"He founded the band."

"I see. And how old is Needle?"

"He's twenty-four."

"So he graduated from high school six years ago?"

"Well, he didn't actually graduate."

"No?" I say.

"He's a friend of my older brother's."

"So that's how you met?"

"Yes," Chloe says.

"You should hear Chloe sing," Taylor says.

"I'd like that," I say.

"Do you plan on graduating from your high school?" you ask Chloe.

"I might. But the band does take a lot of my time. My parents want me to graduate. But I don't know. If the band is successful, what good is a diploma? I'll be making plenty of money without one."

"Might just be a good thing to have," I say.

"Maybe. Maybe not."

"Chloe says they might have a recording contract soon," Taylor says.

"Oh really?" I say, looking at Chloe.

"According to Needle," she says, "some big shot from Los Angeles has been following us."

"One hit, and they'll be rolling in money," Taylor says.

"What are you going to do with all this money you make?" I ask Chloe. The question isn't posed seriously, but it gets a serious answer.

"I'm going to buy a house in Laurel Canyon."

"Laurel Canyon?"

"It's in LA."

"I know where it is," I say.

"Then I'm going to buy a new Tesla. Maybe two or three of them so I can drive one while the others are charging."

"That's smart," I say.

"Then I'm going to clean up the oceans."

"Clean up the oceans?"

"I'm going to declare a war on plastics. Do you have any idea how much plastic waste we dump into our oceans each day? Soon plastic waste will outweigh all marine life."

"That's true," Taylor says.

"Scary," I say.

I will say this about Chloe: she has a plan, and one has to admire a kid her age who has a plan. But what are the odds? I mean, what is the chance she'll rise to rock 'n' roll stardom and buy her two or three Teslas and her house in Laurel Canyon? What are the odds she'll clean any of the plastic waste from the oceans? About a million to one. Odds are that ten years from now, she'll be working as a bank teller at some Wells Fargo bank branch office or processing claims for State Farm insurance.

One has to have a sense of humor. If a person can't learn to laugh, he or she is screwed. Life goes on. Around and around we go, up and down, in and out, falling in and out of love, achieving goals and falling short.

I finish writing *The Family Game* when I am fifty-two. Taylor is in college, and he no longer has a steady girlfriend. He tells me he's "playing the field." Which young woman will he fall permanently in love with? I haven't got the slightest idea.

In the meantime, I send out query letters for my new book to prospective agents and publishers, and then I wait for them to respond.

Chapter 36

For Worse

I haven't said much so far about your sister, Kate. You talk to her about once a month on the phone, but you don't tell me much about her life. There just isn't much news to share. Then Kate pays us a visit. She shows up without her husband, Brock, and her eyes are red and swollen from crying. You put on a pot of coffee, and the three of us sit down in the living room, where Kate tells us the whole story—the whole long, bloody, and depressing tale of woe. We listen to her.

You are in shock. "I had no idea," you say.

In a nutshell, it goes like this. It turns out Brock is a compulsive gambler. You and I knew nothing about this. Prior to Kate's visit, we both had Brock figured for an ordinary guy. We figured he went to work each morning as a financial adviser and came home each night for dinner with Kate. They watched TV. Sometimes he'd read before going to sleep. He played golf on the weekends with his pals, and he mowed the lawn and trimmed the shrubs on Sundays. He got his hair cut every two weeks. He kept his face shaved and his fingernails clipped. He drove a silver Lexus, and he liked to do crossword puzzles. He is now sixty-two years old. Kate is sixty.

"Our life was so good," Kate says. "Now I don't know what to do. I thought Brock was happy. I thought he was content and stable. I feel like I've been blindsided."

"When did you first notice something was wrong?" you ask.

Kate looks up at the ceiling to think. Then she looks at us and says, "It was the credit cards. Two years ago."

"The credit cards?"

"I went grocery shopping and tried to pay for the groceries with a credit card. But the charge was declined. It was the first time I've ever had a charge declined. I tried another card, but it was also declined."

"Why were they declined?"

"We were over the limit. This was so unusual for Brock. He's always been in charge of our finances, and he always paid the cards off in full each month. I had to pay for the groceries with a check, and when I got home, I asked Brock about it. He acted like there was nothing wrong, and he said he'd take care of it. 'Maybe they just haven't received this month's payment,' he said. 'The mail can be slow. I'll give them a call.'"

"And?"

"Well, a couple days later, I tried to use the cards again, and again, the cards were declined. And again, I had to write a check. When I got home, I told Brock, and I told him he needed to put some money in my checking account to cover the check I wrote. And when I asked him about the credit cards, he said, 'I don't know what their problem is. I pay them every month.'"

"But he wasn't paying them?"

"No, he was gambling—and losing. And to make things even worse, he failed to put money into my checking account to cover the checks I was having to write. He said he did, but he didn't. I began bouncing checks."

"That's illegal," I say.

"I know," Kate says.

"So what did you do?"

"Brock gave me the cash to cover the bounced checks. He said he just forgot to make the deposit into my checking account. 'It won't happen again,' he said, and I believed him. Why shouldn't I have believed him? He'd always done such a good job with our finances. He was good at it."

"And then?"

"Well, that was just the tip of the iceberg."

"You bounced more checks?"

"Yes, I bounced more checks. The credit cards were still being declined. I asked Brock what the heck was going on, and he pretended to be as surprised as I was. 'I've been very busy with work lately,' he said. 'I'll try to pay closer attention.' I had to cover the bad checks again. It was very embarrassing."

"I can imagine," you say.

"I couldn't figure out what was wrong. We were making plenty of money to pay our bills, with a good chunk left over each month to put toward our retirement. There shouldn't have been any problem. Then I did something I'd never done before. I always got the mail when I came home from work each day, but I never opened the bills. I just put them on Brock's desk in the study, unopened. It was his domain. The bills were his business. But now I opened them—I guess because I was curious."

"And?"

"The bills were almost all past due. The credit cards were charged to their limits. And there were bills for things I knew nothing about. There were several personal loans Brock had taken out in both of our names without my knowledge. It was like a bad dream. I had no idea what was happening. I confronted Brock, and I asked him about it."

"And what did he say?"

"He told me he'd made a bad stock investment on margin for our retirement and that he was having difficulty in covering his losses."

"And was he telling the truth?"

"I thought he was. He wasn't a liar. He had always been honest with me. 'I thought I could make us a little extra money,' he said. 'It seemed like a sound investment, but I was taken by surprise. I learned my lesson, believe me. I'm going to stick with less risky investments.'"

"But he was lying to you?" you ask.

"Right to my face. There never was any such stock investment. But I was naive, and I believed him. He said, 'Things will sort themselves out soon, and we'll be back to normal.' Why wouldn't I have believed him? He'd always done such a good job of handling our money. And he was an investment adviser, right? I mean, if you can't trust an investment adviser with your money, who can you trust?"

"Good point," I say.

"Well, for a while, things got back to normal. The credit cards worked, and I was no longer bouncing checks. Then, one day, we got a letter from the IRS. It came certified mail, and I had to sign for it. I opened the letter. It was a demand for money, for tens of thousands of dollars. The letter said if we didn't pay the amount due within thirty days, they were going to file a tax lien and levy our accounts. I couldn't believe this. Brock had always paid our taxes on time."

"What did you do?" you ask.

"I showed Brock the letter when he came home from work, and he told me it must've been a mistake. 'The IRS makes mistakes sometimes. I'll call them and clear it up. There's no way we owe them this much money.' Again, I believed Brock's lie. Yes, I was concerned, but I believed him. Then the thirty days passed, and the IRS took all the money out of our checking accounts. Until our next paychecks, we were completely without money. 'Just use the credit cards,' Brock told me. I did this, and again, the credit cards were declined.

"Now, I'm not much one for snooping, but I had to find out what was going on. I went through the desk in the study, looking through Brock's papers. I looked through every drawer in the desk, but I found nothing that explained our cash shortage. I then found an old cell phone bill, and I looked at all the calls Brock made. It's funny how the mind works. I was looking for the phone number of a girlfriend. I was thinking, *He's spending all our money on a woman! He's buying her expensive gifts! He's giving her cash! He's paying her rent!* But I didn't find any suspicious phone numbers."

"So where was the money going?" I ask.

"I still didn't know."

"What did you do?" you ask.

"I did what I had to do. I confronted Brock. I sat him down on the living room sofa, and I told him we needed to talk. I said, 'You need to be honest with me. I need to know where our money is going, and you need to tell me the truth. Is it another woman? If it is, you need to tell me. Something is going on, and I have a right to know what it is.' It's funny, isn't it? I still thought it had to be another woman. The idea that Brock had a gambling problem never even crossed my mind. It would've been so unlike him."

"What did he say?" you ask.

"He just sat there staring at me. At first, he didn't say anything. Then I put my hand on his shoulder and said, 'Sweetheart, you have to tell me.'"

"And he told you?"

"He did."

"What did he say?"

"He told me he'd been gambling. He said he was still gambling and that he couldn't seem to stop. He said he'd been betting on sports through an offshore betting website on the internet. 'I think I have a problem,' he said. I couldn't believe my ears! I guess I was relieved that it wasn't another woman, but I was horrified to be married to a man with a gambling problem. I'd heard such awful stories about compulsive gamblers going bankrupt and going to jail.

"Well, we continued to talk, and Brock cried like a baby. I hadn't seen him cry like this since his mom passed away. But these were not tears of sadness. They were tears of fear, hopelessness, and humiliation. I suddenly felt so sorry for him. I knew he never wanted things to turn out like this, and I knew he was embarrassed. I knew this was the last thing in the world he ever wanted to tell me."

"What did you say?" you ask.

"I told him we'd get him help."

"Help from whom?"

"I didn't know, but I immediately looked into it. My goal was to help Brock, not to make him feel worse. I'd heard of Gamblers Anonymous, and I went to their site on the internet. They had a twenty-question quiz designed to determine if you were a gambling addict, and I had Brock take the quiz. It was a real eye-opener. I had no idea of the extent of Brock's problem. They asked questions like 'Have you ever felt remorse after gambling?' and 'Does gambling make you careless of the welfare of yourself or your family?' and 'Have you ever considered or done an illegal act to finance your gambling?' You get the general idea. Well, poor Brock answered yes to nearly every question on the quiz. My God! All these years I'd lived with him, I'd had no idea I was married to an addict."

"Did Gamblers Anonymous work for Brock?"

"At first, it seemed to."

"At first?"

"They have twelve steps, the same sort of steps followed in Alcoholics Anonymous. Brock completed each step like a trooper. He seemed to take the program seriously. And as he worked the steps, I learned just how serious his addiction was. It turned out that despite all our years of hard work and efforts to save money, we now had nothing. Brock had squandered our entire retirement in betting on sports. He had spent all our savings. He had loaned against our annuities. He had cashed in all our stocks. He had taken out several loans at ridiculously high interest rates. There wasn't an angle he hadn't pursued to feed his addiction, and now we not only were broke but also were deep in debt."

"Good Lord," you say.

"It made me sick to my stomach."

"I'll bet," I say.

"This was about a year ago," Kate says. "We didn't tell anyone about our situation. As he's a financial adviser, we had to keep things quiet. We also had to file bankruptcy. We lost everything except for the cars and the house. But Brock was clever, and no one knew what had happened. The bankruptcy was virtually invisible, and from the outside looking in, it just seemed like we were going about our lives, business as usual. Unless, of course, you ran our credit reports. They were a disaster. Our bankruptcy attorney told Brock to stick with Gamblers Anonymous. 'I've had other clients in similar situations,' our attorney said. 'Gamblers Anonymous saved their hides. Most of them are doing well now. It took most of them years to get back on their feet, but they did it. Just keep in mind that they didn't do it alone. And they stuck with the program.'"

"And was he sticking with the program?" you ask.

"I thought he was," Kate says.

"But he wasn't?"

"He may have at first. Honestly, I think he had the best of intentions. I don't think he ever really wanted to be a gambler, just like an obese person doesn't really want to be obese. But all the time he was going to meetings and supposedly working on his twelve steps, he was still gambling. Not as much as before but enough to keep the flame alive. Then it got worse. Since he had no money to gamble with and since he needed to keep it secret from me, he began using funds from his clients' investment accounts. He was using their money for his bets. It was totally illegal, but that's what he was doing. Over and over. And now he wasn't just a gambler; he was a thief! He was stealing money from people who trusted him with their life savings, and the more often he did it, the easier it became to do. This went on for a year."

"Jeez," I say.

"Then something triggered the police to investigate him. He says he doesn't know what it was, but a detective was assigned to probe his business affairs. They brought Brock into the station and interrogated him. He lied to them, of course. He was lying to everyone. He didn't tell me about the interrogation. He kept everything to himself, and he pretended like nothing was wrong. And I still thought he had quit gambling. What a fool I was! He was gambling more than ever! Then, finally, it happened."

"What happened?" you ask.

"It was this morning."

"What happened this morning?"

"The police came to our house. The detective and two uniformed officers. They rang the doorbell, and I answered it. When I saw who was at the door, I didn't even think of Brock. I had no idea why they were there. I thought maybe it had something to do with a neighbor. But then they asked to see Brock. I asked them what they wanted with him, and the detective said, 'Your husband will know.' Then Brock appeared from behind me, and the detective said, 'You're under arrest, sir. You need to come with us.'"

"They arrested him?" you ask.

"They did. Read him his rights and put him in handcuffs. The whole nine yards."

"Wow," I say.

"He's now at the Orange County Jail. They haven't set his bail yet."

"Are you going to bail him out?"

"I will if I can. I don't even know if we have enough money. There's only a couple thousand in our checking account. Do you think that'll be enough?"

"I have no idea," I say.

"What am I going to do?" Kate says, and she begins crying. She is sobbing. The poor woman is really upset. You put a hand on her shoulder, and it calms her down.

"We'll help if we can," I say.

"I don't think I should get you involved."

"You're family," I say. "And Brock is family."

"That's very nice of you, and I appreciate it," Kate says. "But who knows what Brock has actually done? It could be worse than any of us realize."

The three of us are quiet for a moment. Then Kate says, "Thirty-two years ago, we took our vows. We both said, 'I do,' for better or for worse. That's what we agreed to. But if I'd known then what I know now, what would I have said? I don't know. I just don't know. And what am I going to do? What in the world am I going to do?"

You and I stare at Kate, not saying anything. Neither of us knows what to say. Finally, you pick up Kate's coffee cup and say, "I'll get you some more coffee."

CHAPTER 37

BIG PLANS

It takes a couple of years, but I finally find a publisher for *The Family Game*. The book is released when I'm fifty-four, and it is a success. It isn't exactly a *New York Times* best seller, but it does quite well, and I am making money off it. And so is my publisher. I'm now getting letters from readers, mostly from women who like what I've written and want to get to know me. They ask me questions. They want me to write them back. It's great, and I can see how people get addicted to fame. Sure, I'm not exactly famous, but I am getting a taste of what it would be like. I have fans!

Meanwhile, there is Taylor. I can't believe how much he has changed since I wrote and published my book. He's now a senior in college, and he's going to graduate in just a few months. Remember those girls he dated when he was in high school? The hippie? The rock 'n' roll singer? Even though it's only been a few years, it seems as if eons have passed. Now he's engaged to a girl named Julia Silverstone. You call her a go-getter. You like her a lot, and you think she's perfect for Taylor. "The two of them are going places," you tell me. "We're going to be proud of both of them. Just you wait and see."

Taylor met Julia in college. They were in several business classes together. That's right: Taylor is a business major. Who would've guessed? I've never had much of a head for business, and I know little about the classes the kids are taking. But I guess they talk about business-type things all the time, and they never get tired of it. They have big plans. They're going to be rich, and then they're going to retire when they're in their forties to travel all over the planet. "There's so much to see," Julia says. "There's so much to experience."

It's funny, isn't it? Taylor and Julia are going to make a fortune. They are going to retire in their forties, and they're going to spend hundreds of thousands of dollars traveling all over the globe, seeing all the sights. When I was Taylor's age, my lofty goal was figuring out a way to buy you that broken-down grandfather clock. Then I had to get the stupid thing repaired.

We have Taylor and Julia over for dinner on your fifty-fifth birthday. I do the cooking. I make meat loaf, green beans, and mashed potatoes. I also bought a birthday cake from the grocery store. It is late winter, and it is rainy and cold outside. We are eating in our dining room.

"I'll be glad when spring is here," I say.

"I like the winter," you say.

"I've had enough of it."

"I like the winter too," Julia says. "It's invigorating. It makes me feel productive."

"It makes me feel cold," I say.

"That's because you don't dress right," you say. "Look at you. Shorts and a T-shirt? You dress like it's the middle of July."

I laugh.

"So you two are almost done with school," you say to Taylor and Julia. "It must feel good."

"It does," Julia says.

"Time to get the show on the road," Taylor says. "Julia's already had two job offers."

"No kidding?" I say.

"They're not exactly what I'm looking for," Julia says.

"How about you?" I ask Taylor.

"I've been looking too," Taylor says. "I haven't decided which way I want to go yet: management or marketing. I'm not sure which will have the biggest payoff."

"Do you think you might both work for the same company?" I ask.

"No, no," Julia says.

"We're going to work for different companies," Taylor says. "We need to keep our personal lives separate from our business lives."

"Romance and business don't mix," Julia says.

"I see," I say.

"That makes sense to me," you say.

"Have you decided on a date for the wedding yet?" I ask. The kids are engaged, but they still haven't announced a date for the ceremony.

"When we both are working, we'll announce an actual date," Taylor says.

"We want to get our feet on the ground before we marry," Julia says. "It just makes more sense. We both want to be employed and earning money."

"Where we're working and how much money we're making will determine where we decide to live," Taylor says. "And we need to decide where we're going to live before we get married."

"Are you going to stay in Orange County?" you ask.

"Maybe," Taylor says.

"Maybe LA," Julia says. "There's lots of opportunities in Los Angeles."

"Or New York," Taylor says.

"New York?" you say.

"It's a big world," I say. You throw me a look. You don't want me encouraging the kids to move out of the area.

"I think you'll find what you're looking for in Orange County," you say.

"We'll see," Taylor says.

We finish eating dinner, and I bring out the cake. You make a wish and blow out the candles. The kids leave, and we watch a little TV together. It's a weird feeling. Our son is growing up, and soon he'll be living—where? Orange County? Los Angeles? New York?

"It doesn't sound like we'll be having grandchildren anytime soon," you say.

"You never know," I say.

"It won't be long before they get married."

"Are you looking forward to it?" I ask.

"I am," you say.

"They have big plans."

"They do," you say.

"How do you feel?"

"I suddenly feel so old," you say.

"Same here."

Age is a weird thing. It isn't just the physical changes you go through. True, the body gets stiffer. There are aches and pains. Your energy level wanes, and your memory gets worse. You are sharp mentally, and you have a lifetime of experiences to draw from. You are wiser. But you can't remember where you left your reading glasses half the time, and you have trouble recalling names. "Who was that guy?" you ask. "Dammit, his name is on the tip of my tongue."

You fall asleep on the couch at about ten thirty while we're in the middle of watching a rerun of *Law and Order*. I wake you up, and you say you need to go to bed.

"Are you coming with me?" you ask.

"I'm not tired," I say.

"I'm beat."

"I think I'll watch a movie."

"Keep the volume down," you say.

"I will," I say, and you leave for the bedroom. I grab the remote, and I go to the list of movies I've recorded. I've been into old 1940s movies most recently, mostly black-and-white film noir. I haven't watched a monster movie for quite some time. I guess I've lost interest in them. But is that really the reason I've stopped watching my monsters? Maybe it is something altogether different. Maybe I am tired of the lie.

What lie? I'm talking about the lie that monsters can be vanquished, appeased, or avoided. The lie that fire-breathing dragons can be slain. We all start our lives fresh and full of starry-eyed hope. We see the world as a great and vast opportunity, and we leap from the starting line as soon as the gun is fired. Yes, I had dreams when I was Taylor's age. True, my dreams were different from his and different from Julia's, but they were no less real. What did I dream about? I dreamed about becoming a respected journalist or author, becoming a good husband and father, and doing something meaningful with my life. I had no reason to doubt the outcome of my efforts. I was young, full of life, and brimming with brilliant ideas, ideals, and aspirations, and I had you. We were going to conquer the world together.

Do you remember those years? They were so real. They were as real as a newborn baby. Do you remember the conversations we used to have? I remember telling you there was no way I would ever turn out like my dad. It wasn't that I didn't love him, and to an extent, I respected him. But he sold out. He laid down his sword. The monster had its way with him early on, sucking the life right out of him. My dad the writer. Do you know what he wanted to write about when he was Taylor's age? He told me. He said he wanted to write the next great American novel. That was his dream: to pen something insightful, powerful, and significant and take his place on the short list of great American authors. To be someone. But what did he do? He took a job with an advertising agency and wrote copy that would convince the public to buy filtered cigarettes, washing machines, antidepressants, automobiles, deodorants, toothbrushes, and toilet-bowl cleaners. Then he died.

The monsters will eventually win. We defeat them in the movies, but in real life, they endure. Dreams morph into realities, and childhoods morph into adulthoods. Flesh is burned, hair is charred, eyes are poked, and hot blood is spilled by the gallons. Our hearts finally cease to pound, and the monsters live on, energized by our demise. On and on, from one generation of misguided warriors to the next.

I chuckle.

What's so funny? It's all funny, isn't it? It's funny how we sweat and toil, how we give it our best shot and aim for the stars. It's funny how sure of ourselves we are. Listen, if you don't have a sense of humor, you're going to be sorely let down. When we approach the ends of our lives, we look back on the years and sigh. Some of us are disappointed. Some of us make excuses. Some of us blame ourselves, but few of us can say we were a genuine success. I say go ahead and laugh. We're all in the same boat, and it's all the same joke with the same predictable punch line.

CHAPTER 38

HOORAY FOR THE UNICORNS

Your sister and her husband have a difficult couple of years. No doubt about it. Brock is sentenced to two years in a minimum-security prison for gambling away his clients' money. For those two years, Kate has to get by on her own. Among other things, this means moving into a less expensive house since Brock is no longer working, and Kate has to get by on her income only. She sells their big house in Newport Beach and finds a new place in Costa Mesa. I know your dad helps her out with the down payment for the new house. Brock went through all their savings with his gambling, and he took out second and third mortgages on their house, leaving no equity for Kate to work with. "It's a good thing we decided not to have kids," Kate tells us. "Can you imagine how difficult this could've been? Having to explain things to them. Moving them to new schools. Keeping them fed and clothed. I can't even imagine."

Before all the turmoil, I didn't know your sister that well. I mean, we talked, and you and I invited her and Brock over to our house on occasion. But I never really knew her. I knew she is a real estate agent, and she likes to collect all things unicorn. It is an odd hobby. She has stuffed unicorns, toy unicorns, unicorn plates, unicorn glass figurines, unicorn needlepoints, unicorn coffee mugs, unicorn wineglasses, and even a pair of unicorn salt and pepper shakers. Unicorns are all over the house, and now I wonder if they actually symbolize something. What is the deal with all the unicorns? Whenever I used to think of these unicorns, I'd feel kind of sorry for Kate, a grown woman with all her stupid unicorns and a husband sentenced by a judge to two years in prison.

When Brock is released, Kate is waiting for him. Kate and her menagerie of unicorns. You and I now wonder if their marriage will survive. Did prison change Brock? Will Kate have changed? Will she be bitter or loving? Will she be happy to have Brock home, or will she be angry? What if I had done something similar? Would you have stayed with me, or would you have told me to pack my things and take a hike? I don't know, and neither do you. One never knows until something like this actually happens to him or her.

As it turns out, Kate welcomes Brock home. She takes him in with open arms. She is glad to have him back, and their love endures. I have to tell you the truth. I always looked at your sister and Brock as kind of a joke—two shallow people only ankle deep in life, living in their big house in Newport Beach, going on their vacations to Hawaii, driving in Brock's Lexus, bragging about their retirement portfolios, and going out to eat at expensive restaurants. That was their life. Two peas in a pod. Yet when the crap hit the fan, they made it all work, and they are now showing the rest of us what love is.

"I admire your sister," I say to you. We are taking a walk through the neighborhood.

"You admire Kate?"

"I do," I say.

"What's to admire?"

"A lot," I say. "I like her. I even like her unicorns."

"Her unicorns?" you ask, laughing.

"She's a special person."

"What makes you say that?"

"The way she's treated Brock," I say.

"Oh, Brock," you scoff.

"You don't approve?"

"You could say she's special. You could also say she's foolish."

"Foolish?"

"For taking him back in after everything he did. Jesus, Jonathan, what a sad excuse for a husband. It was like he was trying to get rid of her."

"I don't think he was doing that."

"Well, what do you think he was doing?"

"It was the gambling. He was out of control. I don't think he meant anyone harm. He just lost control."

"I guess that's one way of looking at it."

"How do you look at it?"

"I don't know."

"The older I get, the more I realize how little control we have over our lives," I say. "We're shaped, pummeled, molded, bent over backward, and tossed about by forces that are completely beyond our control. Our hands may be on the wheel, but the act of steering is an illusion. We may have navigational charts, we may have maps of the continents, and we may have our maritime rules and regulations, but we are ships lost at sea. We only think we know where we're going.

"Look at all these houses. We walk past the same houses every weekend, and we make assumptions. We assume we know what goes on under their roofs and behind their draped windows. But do we really know anything? The people who live in these houses are as helpless as we are. There's a white house with brown trim. The windows are clean, and the lawn is mowed. There are flowers in the flower beds, and there is a big mulberry tree by the street. Everything seems to be in working order. The doorbell rings when you press it, and the front door opens when you unlock the dead bolt and twist the knob. The sprinklers go off every morning at six, and the mailman delivers the mail each afternoon. But inside? What is going on inside?"

"What's your point?" you ask.

"The forces," I say.

"Forces?"

"Think about it. Who lives in this house? Maybe an alcoholic and his wife. Do you have any idea how many alcoholics there are in the world? This alcoholic is named Harry, and his wife's name is Eve. Harry is addicted. Some say he was born that way, and some say it was his upbringing. Some say his wife drove him to drink, but he drinks day and night. He can't stop himself, and slowly but surely, the booze is killing him. He is having trouble at work, and his boss is thinking of firing him. He is having trouble with Eve, and the two of them argue. He is full of resentments, and he is jealous and self-destructive. He has even thought of killing himself. It's a good thing they don't keep a gun in their house. He remembers what life used to be like when he had goals and ideals, when he was going places, when he got married to the girl of his dreams. 'Do you take Eve to be your lawfully wedded wife?'

"He said, 'I do, I do.' And then? Along came the forces."

"What forces?"

"The forces that shape us. The forces that mold us into the creatures we are. The forces that cause us to live as we do. Let's say Harry isn't an alcoholic at all. Maybe he's addicted to pornography. He can't help it. He has a burning desire to look at photos and videos of naked women. He needs to watch them posing suggestively. He needs to see them having sex with themselves or with partners. It is an incontrovertible need. He can't help himself. Or maybe it's even worse. Maybe he's into child pornography. Or rapes. Or bestiality. Who knows what this poor soul craves? And he can't seem to get enough. Night after night, he stares at his computer screen, fulfilling the force, gobbling up images, touching himself, masturbating, while his wife is in the other room—doing what? Watching TV? Putting away the dishes? Sleeping?"

"Ick," you say, making a face.

"It happens."

"I guess it does."

"Or maybe it's not Harry. Maybe it's Eve. Maybe the woman has an eating disorder. She could be obese, or she could be anorexic. Who knows? She is out of control. She stays at home because she's embarrassed, and she doesn't want anyone to see her. Or maybe she's a nymphomaniac. Or maybe she's clinically depressed. Or maybe she has a compulsion to steal everything she can get her hands on, or maybe she's a hoarder. Have you ever seen those shows on TV about hoarders? Everything looks fine on the outside, but step into the house, and you can't believe your eyes. And you ask yourself, 'How do people live like that? What is wrong with them? Why don't they just change?'

"It's not as easy as it looks. We are victims, Samantha. We are all victims of one kind or another, aren't we? We are bumbling, imperfect, tarnished, warped, and freakish in our own ways, living out our lives in our little white-and-brown houses with our mowed lawns, mulberry trees, and colorful flower beds."

"And all of this has what to do with Kate?"

"It has everything to do with her. Kate and her unicorns. Kate and Brock. The two of them, living in their little Costa Mesa house, eating at their kitchen table, vacuuming the floors, washing the cars, changing the burned-out lightbulbs, and sleeping in their bed at night."

"I don't get it."

"You said Kate was foolish."

"Did I?" you ask.

"Yes, you did."

"Maybe she is."

"Or maybe she's a lot wiser than you think. Maybe she's put her dreams in perspective."

"What does that even mean?"

"It means I can relate to her."

"You aren't making any sense."

"No?" I ask.

But maybe I've hit the nail on the head. I think as we walk. We are now past the white house with brown trim. We pass a yellow house and then a blue house, and I wonder. What did I sign up for when we got married? Whom did I fall in love with, and whom have I been living with? When I was younger, I had dreams. We all have dreams, don't we? I wanted to do something significant with my life, something that would mean a lot. I think I could have achieved this goal if encouraged to do so, if there was someone behind me who believed in me. I know now that the adage is true: no man is an island. We all need to be loved, admired, and emboldened by those who care about us. We need to be spurred on and lifted up toward the sun. Inspiration doesn't just come from within. It never did, and it never will.

Now about you. I'm going to be completely honest. I'm not trying to hurt your feelings, complain, or make excuses for myself. But you have been a problem for me. I love you, Samantha. I will always love you, no matter what you do. But that doesn't make you immune to the forces that make you into the person you are, and it doesn't mean I'm getting what I need. You are you. That's for certain, and let's be honest: you like reading my books about as much as you like going to the grocery store or filling your car with gas. They don't mean that much to you, and if anything, they leave you perplexed. You aren't impressed, inspired, or even entertained. "Why don't you write about a dog?" you say. "Everyone likes to read about dogs. It could be a best seller." Do you have any idea how this makes me feel? When you tell me to write a book about a dog, it only shows me that you don't understand me at all.

Yet I love you, and I've never given up on us. And you don't give up on me. I know if you had your way, I would write a book about a dog, something you could share with your friends, something you could be proud of. Maybe it would be a best seller, and maybe you could brag to others about me, your best-selling-author husband, who knows how to write a darn good book. I guess the truth is that I disappoint you as much as you disappoint me. Funny, isn't it? We survive all the disappointment because our dreams live on. It's as if we live in two different universes: the real universe and a die-hard fantasy. Two worlds at one time, side by side, the prison sentence and a house full of unicorns.

I say, "Hooray for the unicorns!" They keep us going in a world fraught with pitfalls and shortcomings. And who knows? One of these days, you might read one of my books from cover to cover and say to me, "Wow, Jonathan, this is really something. You are so talented. I'm so glad you wrote this, and I'm so proud of you. Forget about the dog book. I obviously didn't know what I was talking about."

Unicorns. We all collect them. We keep them, think of them, hold them, and treasure them. It's when we liquidate our collections that our lives lose their meaning.

CHAPTER 39

ALL THE GANGLIA

A h, the inscrutable future! Who really knows with any certainty what the years ahead have in store for us? There are many paths and roads. There are many choices to make, many directions to go, and many varied consequences. Pick a card, any card. Up, down, right, left, over, and under. Your guess is as good as mine, yet we still have the audacity to make promises.

We are about to get married. I am twenty-one years old, and so are you. We are writing our own vows. I'm a moderately talented writer, and I should be good at this. As I told you before, I am not a fortune-teller. I have no crystal ball, and I don't own a deck of tarot cards. Regardless, I have tried to imagine the future. I have tried to imagine our future. You and me. Husband and wife. Mother and father. Son and daughter. It's a weird thing to do by any stretch of the imagination, but it's all I have to go on. Clues here and there. Some evidence. A lot of conjecture and outright guessing, and there you have it: Mr. and Mrs. Jonathan Hart. Here we are, and off we go!

Some people say that promises are made to be broken. I don't happen to agree. Promises are made to be kept. One of the most important things a man and woman can do in their lives is to make promises to each other and keep them. Promises are the glue that holds the world together. We should be careful what we promise, why we promise, and how we promise. So yes, I have gone out of my way to be careful about what I will say on our wedding day. I don't think any commitment I make during my entire life will be as important as the commitment I make to you when I slip your wedding band on your finger. It's a commitment of love, and love is all-important. It's a lifetime commitment, and what could be more profound?

I believe in the institution of marriage. Even as a young boy, I always pictured myself getting married one day. Being free from commitment never really held any attraction for me, and I suppose in that way, I was sure to find you. And I did find you, on that beach, on that summer night. Remember the ocean waves? You said they sounded like the future, and you were right. I didn't realize it then, but it was destiny that brought us together, the hand of God, the natural order of things. There is nothing quite like first falling in love, discovering each other, learning about each other, and yearning for each other. For months, you were all I could think about. I was lucky! You felt the same about me. We were made for each other.

You know, I've never really considered myself a lucky person. Good things never fall into my lap. I have never been naturally popular, good at sports, exceptionally intelligent, remarkably handsome, rich, or extraordinarily charismatic. But I found you. You were the first truly wonderful thing to happen to my life. Your hair. Your eyes. Your mouth. Your laughter and your smile. You made me feel ten feet tall, and you made the sky bluer than blue. The birds in the sunlit trees sang along with us. We were at one with the universe, the spectacular, golden, diamond-studded universe. I'm the luckiest man in the world.

Now we're about to be married. It's a little scary. It shouldn't be, but it is. It isn't exactly comforting to know that close to half of all marriages end in divorce. I'm pretty sure all those broken relationships begin with the same starry-eyed optimism and enthusiasm we have. So how do we keep our ship afloat? How do we keep it from capsizing and sinking to the bottom of the sea? How do we survive the wicked storms, the waves, the rough waters, and the voracious leviathans? How do we make our marriage work?

I observe. I see, and I listen. I watch an old episode of *Star Trek*, and it sends shivers up and down my spine. The title of the episode is "Spock's Brain." Have you ever seen this one? Do you remember what happens? The episode starts as the *Enterprise* comes across a mysterious space vessel. It has ion propulsion and an interior atmosphere of conventional oxygen and nitrogen. There is one humanoid life-form aboard, and this life-form beams itself to the *Enterprise*'s bridge. The life-form turns out to be a beautiful young woman dressed in a purple miniskirt and knee-high purple boots. Kirk introduces himself as the captain of the *Enterprise*, and the woman smiles. She then presses several buttons on a curious device on her wrist, and everyone on the *Enterprise* falls to the floor, unconscious. When they regain consciousness, they look around. Everything is normal on the bridge, except for one thing: Spock is missing. Bones suddenly calls Kirk and tells him to come to the sick bay right away. When Kirk arrives at the sick bay, Spock is lying asleep on one of the beds with a bandage on his head.

"What happened?" Kirk says.

"I don't know," Bones says.

"You've got him on complete life support. Was he dead?"

"Worse than dead," Bones says. "His brain is gone! It's been removed surgically. It's the greatest technical job I've ever seen. Every nerve ending in the brain must've been neatly sealed. Nothing ripped, nothing torn. No bleeding. It's a medical miracle."

"If his brain is missing, then he's dying," Kirk says.

"No," Bones says. "His body lives. Autonomic functions continue. But there is no mind."

"That girl," Kirk says.

Everyone in the sick bay looks at each other.

"Aye," Scotty says.

Obviously, the girl in the purple miniskirt has made off with Spock's brain. But why? "We'll have to take him with us," Kirk says.

"Take him where?" Bones asks.

"In search of his brain, Doctor."

"Where are you going to look?" Bones asks. "In this whole galaxy, how are you going to find it? And even if you do find it, I can't restore it. I don't have the medical technique."

Of course, this isn't going to hold Kirk back. No challenge is too great for the intrepid captain of the *Enterprise*. He goes back to the bridge and instructs his helmsman to follow the mysterious spaceship's ion trail. According to Bones, they have twenty-four hours to find Spock's brain and put it back in his head before he dies.

Following the ion trail, they come to a solar system. There are three possible planets in the system that the ship could have come from, and on a hunch, Kirk picks a planet. They beam down to the planet's surface. The place is inhabited by giant cavemen dressed in hides and carrying clubs for weapons. A group of these cavemen attack Kirk and the landing party, but the clubs they wield are no match for the party's phaser pistols. One of the cavemen is stunned, while the others run away. When the caveman regains his wits, Kirk tries to talk to him. Remarkably, the caveman speaks English.

It turns out the cavemen aren't the only humans living on the planet, but there are no cavewomen. The women on the planet live in an underground city, away from the cavemen. It is a bizarre underground society of beautiful young women.

Kirk has Bones beam down to the planet's surface with the brainless Spock, and they enter the underground city of women to search for Spock's brain. They soon discover that the underground women are controlled by a ruling computer—and the computer is being powered by Spock's brain! Apparently, the computer needs a living brain to function, and the old brain that used to run the city needed to be replaced with a new one. Spock's brain was stolen and installed as its replacement.

Well, one thing leads to another, and Kirk and his team find the room where Spock's brain is kept. They find the girl with the purple miniskirt there, and they interrogate her. They discover that she acquired the knowledge to remove and transplant Spock's brain by using a teacher, a clear plastic helmet. By putting the teacher on one's head, a person is given the amazing knowledge of the ancients. It is obvious what they must now do: Bones must wear the magic helmet and then put Spock's brain back into his head.

Indeed, this is what he does. With Spock's body lying on a table, the doctor goes to work. The doctor suddenly has the knowledge. "Of course," he says. "A child could do it! A child could do it!"

However, there is a slight problem: the knowledge the doctor has gained begins to leave him in the middle of the operation. It is a classic scene. One moment, the doctor is busy at work, restoring the brain in Spock's head. Scotty says, "I've never seen anything like it. He's operating at warp speed!" Then, the next moment, Bones forgets what the teacher taught him. He is losing the knowledge! He begins to panic. "Captain," Scotty says, "he's forgetting!"

"All the ganglia," the doctor says with a look of horror on his face. He is breaking out in a sweat. "The nerves! There are a million of them! What am I supposed to do? It's like trying to thread a needle with a sledgehammer! What am I supposed to do? I can't remember!"

This is the scene I remember. The panic and confusion. The dread. All the ganglia and all the nerves! It is precisely how I now feel about writing the vows for our marriage, like Bones losing his knowledge in the middle of the operation. All the variables. All the possibilities. How can I possibly cover every situation we will face in the years ahead? To say we'll love each other is insufficient. Bah! Millions of people love each other, and millions of them get divorced. It seems the only thing one can say for certain about the future is that it is uncertain.

I have tried to envision our future. I have done my best, but who really knows? Will we adore each other forever, or will we fall out of love over time? Will we lose interest in each other or get on each other's nerves and simply annoy each other? I can't tell you how many times I've seen older married people bickering and wondered, *Did these two people really once love each other?* Surely you know what I'm talking about.

And why should love last forever? What lasts forever? Circumstances change, feelings change, and loyalties change. Assuming love will last forever is a little like assuming the weather will never change. It will not always be summer, and it will not always be winter. There are progressions, cycles, and deteriorations. Flowers bloom and then die, and new flowers bloom. Then they will wilt and die. Yes, I love you now. But will I love you forever? Who's to say?

Thinking about this makes my head ache. Then I think even further. They say you only hurt the one you love. Is this true? I have to ask. How will I hurt you, and how will you hurt me? When two people love each other, care about each other, and depend on each other, it is inevitable they will eventually hurt each other. You can count on it as sure as you can count on the sun rising and falling each day. I won't want to hurt you, but I will. I can just about promise it, and you will hurt me. You might not appreciate me. You might cause me to be jealous. You might ignore my feelings, or you might discount my accomplishments. I don't know what you will do exactly, but you will do it. You won't do it intentionally, but it will be done. We'll both do it. We won't be able to help ourselves—because we are human beings and because we love each other.

All the nerve cells! All the ganglia! All those confounded synapses! It's overwhelming, isn't it? Do you feel the same way I do? Or maybe you're comfortable with it. Maybe it doesn't bother you the way it bothers me. Maybe I'm just making a federal case out of a misdemeanor. Maybe I'm trying to do too much. Maybe what I need is conviction. I have always lacked conviction. I realize that about myself, but I have always attributed it to being smart. I'm no genius, but I'm certainly smart enough to see all the variables in a given equation. Too many! Too many ways to go and too many solutions that aren't really solutions at all.

I've always felt that people, as a rule, are uncommonly biased, shortsighted, and dead set in their ways. They're firm of opinion, and they know right from wrong. There is the right way to do something and the wrong way. I guess my problem is that I've never been able to tell one from the other. I hate to say it, but maybe I need to be dumber.

Wouldn't that be an odd thing to wish for—to be dumber? To say, "My way or the highway"? But the truth is that people who have this attitude also have a talent for getting things done in the world. Your mother and father are like this, and I'll bet they stay married forever, even after they die. They'll go to heaven as husband and wife, and they'll live out eternity like the good mister and missus that they are. Your dad will wear the pants in the house and kill the spiders, and your mom will wear her apron and wash the dishes every night after dinner. Your dad will work and earn money, and your mom will manage the household budget. Your dad will mow the lawn every weekend, and your mom will dust and vacuum all the floors. That will be their personalized paradise up in heaven, wherever that may be. Not an inkling of discontent. No gnawing longings.

Do you remember me telling you about Alex Hardy? He was my childhood friend, the one with whom I got in trouble with the cop for lighting firecrackers in front of old Mrs. Bartlett's house. Remember how Alex got even with the woman for calling the police by creating a concoction of raw eggs, rubber-cement glue, wood varnish, house paint, and Drano and smearing the goo all over the front seat of her Mercedes? I had promised my dad I would never lie to him, yet when he asked me about Alex and the concoction, I pretended to know nothing. I decided it was more important to protect Alex than it was to tell the truth to my father, but now I wonder. In fact, I wondered then: Was I doing the right thing? Did Alex really have any right to vandalize old Mrs. Bartlett's Mercedes? In truth, he had done something terribly wrong, and now I was a party to it. I was led by my convictions, and I was wrong. I see that now.

On the other hand, was it really fair of my dad to expect me to rat on my best friend? Maybe my lie was my dad's fault, not mine. It's confusing. Maybe there is no right answer. We try to make sense of the world, but maybe it is like trying to thread a needle with a sledgehammer.

In the *Star Trek* episode I was telling you about, Bones is able to successfully complete the operation, and Spock's brain is put back in his head. But that is TV, not real life. In TV shows, dilemmas are resolved. We like it that way, but in real life, dilemmas are nagging, awkward, bewildering, and often unsolvable. And that, Samantha, is a fact of life.

CHAPTER 40

THE DAY

It has taken me a while. Maybe I got a little carried away, but can you blame me? It's not as if I'm going to get a second chance at this. At least I hope not.

Finally, it is the day. I am on my way to the church with my mom and dad. My dad is driving, and Mom is sitting quietly in the backseat, watching the scenery pass. It's early afternoon, and the traffic is light. Am I nervous? You bet I am. I'm not having any second thoughts, but my mind is racing a million miles per hour. I have the vows I wrote on a folded piece of paper tucked in my pocket. Soon I will be reading these vows to you, and you will read yours to me. We will say, "I do," and that will be that. We will be husband and wife, Mr. and Mrs. Jonathan Hart.

Tom is my best man. He is probably already at the church, waiting for us to show up. I've known Tom since high school. In fact, he was one of the kids at the beach on the night we first met. It was his older brother who bought us the beer. I've always liked Tom, and I liked that he had a brother who could buy us beer. We were good friends all through high school, and we kept in touch after we both moved on to college.

Indeed, Tom is already at the church when we show up, and he is all smiles. "Today's the day," he says to me.

"It is," I say.

"Are you ready?"

"I guess I am."

"Everything's on schedule?"

"As far as I know."

"You must be nervous," Tom says.

"You have no idea."

"Did you finish writing your vows?"

"Of course," I say.

"When did you finish?"

"Late last night," I say. "I didn't go to bed until three in the morning."

"That's cutting it close."

"I wanted to say the right things."

"And will you?"

"Will I what?" I ask.

"Will you say the right things?"

"I hope so."

Tom laughs and says, "You'll do fine."

"Take it all in," I say. "You're next."

"Me?" Tom says. He laughs again. "My wedding day is a long way off."

"A long way off? You don't plan on asking Amanda soon?" Amanda is Tom's girlfriend.

"Maybe someday."

"How long have you two been going together now?"

"Over three years."

"Heck, you're practically married already."

"There's a big difference between having a girlfriend and having a wife."

Chuck joins us. He is one of the ushers. I met Chuck in college, and we have become good friends over the past year. Like me, he is a journalism major. "Big day today," Chuck says.

"It is," I say.

"Are you ready?"

"I'm as ready as I'll ever be."

"Did you finish writing your vows?"

"I just got done telling Tom that I finished them late last night. At three in the morning."

"Samantha hasn't read them?"

"No," I say.

"You're going to surprise her?"

"I guess I am."

"Good luck with that," Chuck says, and he laughs.

The three of us stand there staring at each other. Finally, Tom says, "I heard a good one."

"A good what?" I ask.

"A good joke. It's a wedding joke."

"Let's hear it," Chuck says.

Against my better judgment, I say, "Yeah, let's hear it. A joke would be good."

"Okay," Tom says. "It goes like this. There was this guy who was about to marry his longtime girlfriend. The girlfriend had a younger sister. She was eighteen years old and a knockout. The guy loved his girlfriend, but he couldn't ignore the sister. She often went braless, and she wore short dresses. He'd pretend not to notice her, but she was hard to ignore.

"The wedding was a family affair. His girlfriend put her little sister in charge of the wedding invitations, and a couple months before the wedding, the sister called the guy and asked him to come over to their house to check the invitations. It sounded innocent enough, so he went to the house. No one else appeared to be home, and the little sister came on to him. She told him she had feelings for him, and she said that more than anything, she wanted to make love to him. 'One last fling before you marry my sister,' she said with a smile.

"Well, the guy was floored. This was completely unexpected. So what did he do? The blood rushed from his head, and he beelined it to the front door. He went out the door, and he ran toward his car. Suddenly, he heard laughter, and he turned to look. There in the front yard was his future family. His relieved future father-in-law was standing there with the others, with a smile as big as Texas. 'Congratulations,' he said. 'You passed our test. We couldn't have asked for a better man to marry our daughter.'"

Tom smiles at us and then says, "Do you know what the moral of the story is?"

"What is it?" Chuck asks.

"Always keep your condoms in your car," Tom says.

"Ho ho!" Chuck laughs.

"Jesus," I say. I am smiling. I know Tom means well. He is only trying to calm me down, and yes, I am still nervous. I'll be standing in front of all those people soon, and I suddenly feel as if I have to puke.

"Hang in there, Jonathan," Tom says.

Everything suddenly turns to a blur, and about twenty minutes later, I am standing at the altar. You are standing in front of me. You are beautiful.

Seriously, I have never seen you look so wonderful. The next thing I know, I am removing my written vows from my pocket. I didn't have time to memorize them, so I read them from the paper. I can hear myself talking. At first, my hands are trembling, but then I settle down.

This is it!

Everyone in the audience is quiet. The only sound in the room is the sound of my voice. My vows to you. "Samantha," I say, "I love you."

As for the rest of the vows, if you can't figure out what I go on to say, then you haven't been paying attention.

It will work out. It will all work out. I am looking forward to our life together. By hook or by crook, we will make this a successful journey. We'll be in love. We'll be frustrated. We'll be happy, angry, jealous, disappointed, and hurt. We will fight a thousand armies, and we will make good friends with an equal number of allies. We'll be pulled apart and drawn together.

Then, one day, when we're old and nearing the end of our lives, we'll sit at the dining room table, eating dinner and recalling the day we got married. You'll bring up my vows and ask me if I remember what I said.

"Of course I do," I'll say.

"One question."

"Yes?" I'll ask.

"I've always wanted to ask you something."

"What is it?"

"What are ganglia?"

I'll laugh. I won't be sure if you're serious or if you're just pulling my leg, so I'll ignore you and say, "Can you pass the mashed potatoes? And the gravy while you're at it? I skipped lunch today. I can't believe how hungry I am."

CPSIA information can be obtained
at www.ICGtesting.com
Printed in the USA
LVHW111355090421
683998LV00035B/509